# Carson of Venus

## Volume One

# Carson of Venus

VOLUME ONE

THE FIRST ADVENTURE

## Pirates of Venus

THE SECOND ADVENTURE

## Lost on Venus

Edgar Rice Burroughs

LEONAUR

*Carson of Venus Volume One:*
*Pirates of Venus and Lost on Venus*
by Edgar Rice Burroughs

FIRST EDITION

Published by Leonaur Ltd



ISBN (10 digit): 1-84677-114-5 (hardcover)
ISBN (13 digit): 978-1-84677-114-9 (hardcover)

ISBN (10 digit): 1-84677-113-7 (softcover)
ISBN (13 digit): 978-1-84677-113-2 (softcover)

**http://www.leonaur.com**

**Publisher's Notes**

In the interests of authenticity, the spellings, grammar and place names used by the author have been retained.

The views expressed in this book are not necessarily those of the publisher.

# Contents

## The First Adventure



## The Second Adventure

The First Adventure

# Pirates of Venus

# CHAPTER 1

# Carson Napier

*If a female figure in a white shroud enters your bedchamber at midnight on the thirteenth day of this month, answer this letter otherwise, do not.*

Having read this far in the letter, I was about to consign it to the wastebasket, where all my crank letters go; but for some reason I read on, "If she speaks to you, please remember her words and repeat them to me when you write." I might have read on to the end; but at this juncture the telephone bell rang, and I dropped the letter into one of the baskets on my desk. It chanced to be the "out" basket; and had events followed their ordinary course, this would have been the last of the letter and the incident in so far as I was concerned, for from the "out" basket the letter went to the files.

It was Jason Gridley on the telephone. He seemed excited and asked me to come to his laboratory at once. As Jason is seldom excited about anything, I hastened to accede to his request and satisfy my curiosity. Jumping into my roadster, I soon covered the few blocks that separate us, to learn that Jason had good grounds for excitement He had just received a radio message from the inner world, from Pellucidar.

On the eve of the departure of the great dirigible, O-220, from the earth's core, following the successful termination of that historic expedition, Jason had determined to remain and search for von Horst, the only missing member of the party; but Tarzan, David Innes, and Captain Zuppner had persuaded him of the folly of such an undertaking, inasmuch as David had promised to dispatch an expedition of his own native Pellucidarian warriors to locate the young German lieutenant if he still lived and it were possible to discover any clue to his whereabouts.

Notwithstanding this, and though he had returned to the outer world with the ship, Jason had always been harassed by a sense of responsibility for the fate of von Horst, a young man who had been most popular with all the members of the expedition; and had insisted time and time again that he regretted having left Pellucidar until he had exhausted every means within his power of rescuing von Horst or learned definitely that he was dead.

Jason waved me to a chair and offered me a cigarette. "I've just had a message from Abner Perry," he announced, "the first for months."

"It must have been interesting," I commented, "to excite you."

"It was," he admitted. "A rumour has reached Sari that von Horst has been found."

Now as this pertains to a subject entirely foreign to the present volume, I might mention that I have alluded to it only for the purpose of explaining two facts which, while not vital, have some slight bearing on the remarkable sequence of events which followed. First, it caused me to forget the letter I just mentioned, and, second, it fixed the date in my mind—the tenth.

My principal reason for mentioning the first fact is to stress the thought that the matter of the letter, so quickly and absolutely forgotten, had no opportunity to impress itself upon my mind and therefore could not, at least objectively, influence my consideration of ensuing events. The letter was gone from my mind within five minutes of its reading as completely as though it had never been received.

The next three days were exceedingly busy ones for me, and when I retired on the night of the thirteenth my mind was so filled with the annoying details of a real estate transaction that was going wrong, that it was some time before I could sleep. I can truthfully affirm that my last thoughts were of trust deeds, receivers in equity, and deficiency judgments.

What awoke me, I do not know. I sat up with a start just in time to see a female figure, swathed in what appeared to be a white winding sheet, enter my room through the door. You will note that I say door rather than doorway, for such was the fact; the door was closed. It was a clear, moonlit night; the various homely objects in my room were plainly discernible, especially the ghostly figure now hovering near the foot of my bed.

I am not subject to hallucinations, I had never seen a ghost, I had never wished to, and I was totally ignorant of the ethics governing such a situation. Even had the lady not been so obviously supernatural, I should yet have been at a loss as to how to receive her at this hour in the intimacy of my bedchamber, for no strange lady had ever before invaded its privacy, and I am of Puritan stock.

"It is midnight of the thirteenth," she said, in a low, musical voice.

"So it is," I agreed, and then I recalled the letter that I had received on the tenth.

"He left Guadalupe today," she continued; "he will wait in Guaymas for your letter."

That was all. She crossed the room and passed out of it, not through the window which was quite convenient, but through the solid wall. I sat there for a full minute, staring at the spot where I had last seen her and endeavouring to convince myself that I was dreaming, but I was not dreaming; I was wide awake. In fact I was so wide awake that it was fully an hour before I had successfully wooed Morpheus, as the Victorian writers so neatly expressed it, ignoring the fact that his sex must have made it rather embarrassing for gentlemen writers.

I reached my office a little earlier than usual the following morning, and it is needless to say that the first thing that I did was to search for that letter which I had received on the tenth. I could recall neither the name of the writer nor the point of origin of the letter, but my secretary recalled the latter, the letter having been sufficiently out of the ordinary to attract his attention.

"It was from somewhere in Mexico," he said, and as letters of this nature are filed by states and countries, there was now no difficulty in locating it.

You may rest assured that this time I read the letter carefully. It was dated the third and post marked Guaymas. Guaymas is a seaport in Sonora, on the Gulf of California.

Here is the letter:

> *My dear Sir:*
>
> Being engaged in a venture of great scientific importance, I find it necessary to solicit the assistance (not financial) of some one psychologically harmonious, who is at the same time of sufficient intelligence and culture to appreciate the vast possibilities of my project.
>
> Why I have addressed you I shall be glad to explain in the happy event that a personal interview seems desirable. This can only be ascertained by a test which I shall now explain.
>
> If a female figure in a white shroud enters your bedchamber at midnight on the thirteenth day of this month, answer this

letter; otherwise, do not. If she speaks to you, please remember her words and repeat them to me when you write.

Assuring you of my appreciation of your earnest consideration of this letter, which I realize is rather unusual, and begging that you hold its contents in strictest confidence until future events shall have warranted its publication, I am, Sir,

Very respectfully yours,
*Carson Napier*

"It looks to me like another nut," commented Rothmund.

"So it did to me on the tenth," I agreed; "but today is the fourteenth, and now it looks like another story."

"What has the fourteenth got to do with it?" he demanded.

"Yesterday was the thirteenth," I reminded him.

"You don't mean to tell me—" he started, sceptically.

"That is just what I do mean to tell you," I interrupted. "The lady came, I saw, she conquered."

Ralph looked worried. "Don't forget what your nurse told you after your last operation," he reminded me.

"Which nurse? I had nine, and no two of them told me the same things."

"Jerry. She said that narcotics often affected a patient's mind for months afterward." His tone was solicitous.

"Well, at least Jerry admitted that I had a mind, which some of the others didn't. Anyway, it didn't affect my eyesight; I saw what I saw. Please take a letter to Mr. Napier." A few days later I received a telegram from Napier dated Guaymas. *Letter received + thanks + shall call on you tomorrow*, it read.

"He must be flying," I commented.

"Or coming in a white shroud," suggested Ralph. "I think I'll phone Captain Hodson to send a squad car around here; sometimes these nuts are dangerous." He was still sceptical.

I must admit that we both awaited the arrival of Carson Napier with equal interest. I think Ralph expected to see a wild-eyed maniac. I could not visualize the man at all.

About eleven o'clock the following morning Ralph came into my study. "Mr. Napier is here," he said.

"Does his hair grow straight out from his scalp, and do the whites of his eyes show all around the irises?" I inquired, smiling.

"No," replied Ralph, returning the smile; "he is a very fine looking man, but," he added, "I still think he's a nut."

"Ask him to come in," and a moment later Ralph ushered in an exceptionally handsome man whom I judged to be somewhere between twenty-five and thirty years old, though he might have been even younger.

He came forward with extended hand as I rose to greet him, a smile lighting his face; and after the usual exchange of banalities he came directly to the point of his visit.

"To get the whole picture clearly before you,"We commenced, "I shall have to tell you something about myself. My father was a British army officer, my mother an American girl from Virginia. I was born in India while my father was stationed there, and brought up under the tutorage of an old Hindu who was much attached to my father and mother. This Chand Kabi was something of a mystic, and he taught me many things that are not in the curriculums of schools for boys under ten. Among them was telepathy, which he had cultivated to such a degree that he could converse with one in psychological harmony with himself quite as easily at great distances as when face to face. Not only that, but he could project mental images to great distances, so that the recipient of his thought waves could see what Chand Kabi was seeing, or whatever else Chand Kabi wished him to see. These things he taught me."

"And it was thus you caused me to see my midnight visitor on the thirteenth?" I inquired.

He nodded. "That test was necessary in order to ascertain if we were in psychological harmony. Your letter, quoting the exact words that I had caused the apparition to appear to speak, convinced me that I had at last found the person for whom I have been searching for some time.

"But to get on with my story. I hope I am not boring you, but I feel that it is absolutely necessary that you should have full knowledge of my antecedents and background in order that you may decide whether I am worthy of your confidence and assistance or not." I assured him that I was far from being bored, and he proceeded.

"I was not quite eleven when my father died and my mother brought me to America. We went to Virginia first and lived there for three years with my mother's grandfather, Judge John Carson, with whose name and reputation you are doubtless familiar, as who is not?

"After the grand old man died, mother and I came to California, where I attended public schools and later entered a small college at Claremont, which is noted for its high scholastic standing and the superior personnel of both its faculty and student body.

"Shortly after my graduation the third and greatest tragedy of my life occurred—my mother died. I was absolutely stunned by this blow. Life seemed to hold no further interest for me. I did not care to live, yet I would not take my own life. As an alternative I embarked upon a life of recklessness. With a certain goal in mind, I learned to fly. I changed my name and became a stunt man in pictures.

"I did not have to work. Through my mother I had inherited a considerable fortune from my great-grandfather, John Carson; so great a fortune that only a spendthrift could squander the income. I mention this only because the venture I am undertaking requires considerable capital, and I wish you to know that I am amply able to finance it without help.

"Not only did life in Hollywood bore me, but here in Southern California were too many reminders of the loved one I had lost. I determined to travel, and I did. I flew all over the world. In Germany I became interested in rocket cars and financed several. Here my idea was born. There was nothing original about it except that I intended to carry it to a definite conclusion. I would travel by rocket to another planet.

"My studies had convinced me that of all the planets Mars alone offered presumptive evidence of habitability for creatures similar to ourselves. I was at the same time convinced that if I succeeded in reaching Mars the probability of my being able to return to earth was remote. Feeling that I must have some reason for embarking upon such a venture, other than selfishness, I determined to seek out some one with whom I could communicate in the event that I succeeded. Subsequently it occurred to me that this might also afford the means for launching a second expedition, equipped to make the return journey, for I had no doubt but that there would be many adventurous spirits ready to undertake such an excursion once I had proved it feasible.

"For over a year I have been engaged in the construction of a gigantic rocket on Guadalupe Island, off the west coast of Lower California. The Mexican government has given me every assistance, and today everything is complete to the last detail. I am ready to start at any moment."

As he ceased speaking, he suddenly faded from view. The chair in which he had been sitting was empty. There was no one in the room but myself. I was stunned, almost terrified. I recalled what Rothmund had said about the effect of the narcotics upon my mentality. I also recalled that insane people seldom realize that they are insane. Was

I insane? Cold sweat broke out upon my forehead and the backs of my hands. I reached toward the buzzer to summon Ralph. There is no question but that Ralph is sane. If he had seen Carson Napier and shown him into my study—what a relief that would be!

But before my finger touched the button Ralph entered the room. There was a puzzled expression on his face. "Mr. Napier is back again," he said, and then he added, "I didn't know he had left. I just heard him talking to you."

I breathed a sigh of relief as I wiped the perspiration from my face and hands; if I was crazy, so was Ralph. "Bring him in," I said, "and this time you stay here."

When Napier entered there was a questioning look in his eyes. "Do you fully grasp the situation as far as I have explained it?" he asked, as though he had not been out of the room at all.

"Yes, but—" I started.

"Wait, please," he requested. "I know what you are going to say, but let me apologize first and explain. I have not been here before. That was my final test. If you are confident that you saw me and talked to me and can recall what I said to you as I sat outside in my car, then you and I can communicate just as freely and easily when I am on Mars."

"But," interjected Rothmund, "you were here. Didn't I shake hands with you when you came in, and talk to you?"

"You thought you did," replied Napier.

"Who's loony now?" I inquired inelegantly, but to this day Rothmund insists that we played a trick on him.

"How do you know he's here now, then?" he asked.

"I don't," I admitted.

"I am, this time," laughed Napier. "Let's see; how far had I gotten?"

"You were saying that you were all ready to start, had your rocket set up on Gaudalupe Island," I reminded him.

"Right! I see you got it all. Now, as briefly as possible, I'll outline what I hope you will find it possible to do for me. I have come to you for several reasons, the more important of which are your interest in Mars, your profession (the results of my experiment must be recorded by an experienced writer), and your reputation for integrity—I have taken the liberty of investigating you most thoroughly. I wish you to record and publish the messages you receive from me and to administer my estate during my absence."

"I shall be glad to do the former, but I hesitate to accept the responsibility of the latter assignment," I demurred.

"I have already arranged a trust that will give you ample protection," he replied in a manner that precluded further argument. I saw that he was a young man who brooked no obstacles; in fact I think he never admitted the existence of an obstacle. "As for your remuneration," he continued, "you may name your own figure."

I waved a deprecatory hand. "It will be a pleasure," I assured him.

"It may take a great deal of your time," interjected Ralph, "and your time is valuable."

"Precisely," agreed Napier. "Mr. Rothmund and I will, with your permission, arrange the financial details later."

"That suits me perfectly," I said, for I detest business and everything connected with it.

"Now, to get back to the more important and far more interesting phases of our discussion; what is your reaction to the plan as a whole?"

"Mars is a long way from earth," I suggested; "Venus is nine or ten million miles closer, and a million miles are a million miles."

"Yes, and I would prefer going to Venus," he replied. "Enveloped in clouds, its surface forever invisible to man, it presents a mystery that intrigues the imagination; but recent astronomical research suggests conditions there inimical to the support of any such life as we know on earth. It has been thought by some that, held in the grip of the Sun since the era of her pristine fluidity, she always presents the same face to him, as does the Moon to earth. If such is the case, the extreme heat of one hemisphere and the extreme cold of the other would preclude life.

"Even if the suggestion of Sir James Jeans is borne out by fact, each of her days and nights is several times as long as ours on earth, these long nights having a temperature of thirteen degrees below zero, Fahrenheit, and the long days a correspondingly high temperature."

"Yet even so, life might have adapted itself to such conditions," I contended; "man exists in equatorial heat and arctic cold."

"But not without oxygen," said Napier. "St. John has estimated that the amount of oxygen above the cloud envelope that surrounds Venus is less than one tenth of one per cent of the terrestrial amount. After all, we have to bow to the superior judgment of such men as Sir James Jeans, who says, 'The evidence, for what it is worth, goes to suggest that Venus, the only planet in the solar system outside Mars and the earth on which life could possibly exist, possesses no vegetation and no oxygen for higher forms of life to breathe,' which definitely limits my planetary exploration to Mars."

We discussed his plans during the remainder of the day and well into the night, and early the following morning he left for Guadalupe Island in his Sikorsky amphibian. I have not seen him since, at least in person, yet, through the marvellous medium of telepathy, I have communicated with him continually and seen him amid strange, unearthly surroundings that have been graphically photographed upon the retina of my mind's eye. Thus I am the medium through which the remarkable adventures of Carson Napier are being recorded on earth; but I am only that, like a typewriter or a Dictaphone—the story that follows is his.

## CHAPTER 2

# Off for Mars

As I set my ship down in the sheltered cove along the shore of desolate Gaudalupe a trifle over four hours after I left Tarzana, the little Mexican steamer I had chartered to transport my men, materials, and supplies from the mainland rode peacefully at anchor in the tiny harbour, while on the shore, waiting to welcome me, were grouped the labourers, mechanics, and assistants who had worked with such whole-hearted loyalty for long months in preparation for this day. Towering head and shoulders above the others loomed Jimmy Welsh, the only American among them.

I taxied in close to shore and moored the ship to a buoy, while the men launched a dory and rowed out to get me. I had been absent less than a week, most of which had been spent in Guaymas awaiting the expected letter from Tarzana, but so exuberantly did they greet me, one might have thought me a long-lost brother returned from the dead, so dreary and desolate and isolated is Guadalupe to those who must remain upon her lonely shores for even a brief interval between contacts with the mainland.

Perhaps the warmth of their greeting may have been enhanced by a desire to conceal their true feelings. We had been together constantly for months, warm friendships had sprung up between us, and tonight we were to separate with little likelihood that they and I should ever meet again. This was to be my last day on earth; after today I should be as dead to them as though three feet of earth covered my inanimate corpse.

It is possible that my own sentiments collared my interpretation of theirs, for I am frank to confess that I had been apprehending this last moment as the most difficult of the whole adventure. I have come in contact with the peoples of many countries, but I recall none with more lovable qualities than Mexicans who have not been contaminated by too close contact with the intolerance and commercialism of Americans. And then there was Jimmy Welsh. It was going to be like parting with a brother when I said goodbye to him. For months he had been begging to go with me; and I knew that he would continue to beg up to the last minute, but I could not risk a single life unnecessarily.

We all piled into the trucks that we had used to transport supplies and materials from the shore to the camp, which lay inland a few miles, and bumped over our makeshift road to the little table-land where the giant torpedo lay upon its mile long track.

"Everything is ready," said Jimmy. "We polished off the last details this morning. Every roller on the track has been inspected by at least a dozen men, we towed the old crate back and forth over the full length of the track three times with the truck, and then repacked all the rollers with grease. Three of us have checked over every item of equipment and supplies individually; we've done about everything but fire the rockets; and now we're ready to go—you are going to take me along, aren't you, Car?"

I shook my head. "Please don't, Jimmy," I begged; "I have a perfect right to gamble with my own life, but not with yours; so forget it. But I am going to do something for you," I added, "just as a token of my appreciation of the help you've given me and all that sort of rot. I'm going to give you my ship to remember me by."

He was grateful, of course, but still he could not hide his disappointment in not being allowed to accompany me, which was evidenced by an invidious comparison he drew between the ceiling of the Sikorsky and that of the old crate, as he had affectionately dubbed the great torpedo like rocket that was to bear me out into space in a few hours.

"A thirty-five million mile ceiling," he mourned dolefully; "think of it! Mars for a ceiling!"

"And may I hit the ceiling!" I exclaimed, fervently.

The laying of the track upon which the torpedo was to take off had been the subject of a year of calculation and consultation. The day of departure had been planned far ahead and the exact point at which Mars would rise above the eastern horizon on that night calculated, as well as the time; then it was necessary to make allowances for the rotation of the earth and the attraction of the nearer heavenly bodies. The track was then laid in accordance with these calculations. It was constructed with a very slight drop in the first three quarters of a mile and then rose gradually at an angle of two and one half degrees from horizontal.

A speed of four and one half miles per second at the take-off would be sufficient to neutralize gravity; to overcome it, I must attain a speed of 6.93 miles per second. To allow a sufficient factor of safety I had powered the torpedo to attain a speed of seven miles per second at the end of the runway, which I purposed stepping up to ten miles per second while passing through the earth's atmosphere. What my speed would be through space was problematical, but I based all my calculations on the theory that it would not deviate much from the speed at which I left the earth's atmosphere, until I came within the influence of the gravitational pull of Mars.

The exact instant at which to make the start had also caused me considerable anxiety. I had calculated it again and again, but there were so many factors to be taken into consideration that I had found it expedient to have my figures checked and rechecked by a well-known physicist and an equally prominent astronomer. Their deductions tallied perfectly with mine—the torpedo must start upon its journey toward Mars some time before the red planet rose above the eastern horizon. The trajectory would be along a constantly flattening arc, influenced considerably at first by the earth's gravitational pull, which would decrease inversely as the square of the distance attained. As the torpedo left the earth's surface on a curved tangent, its departure must be so nicely timed that when it eventually escaped the pull of the earth its nose would be directed toward Mars.

On paper, these figures appeared most convincing; but, as the moment approached for my departure, I must confess to a sudden realization that they were based wholly upon theory, and I was struck with the utter folly of my mad venture.

For a moment I was aghast. The enormous torpedo, with its sixty tons, lying there at the end of its mile long track, loomed above me, the semblance of a gargantuan coffin—my coffin, in which I was presently to be dashed to earth, or to the bottom of the Pacific, or cast out into space to wander there to the end of time. I was afraid. I admit it, but it was not so much the fear of death as the effect of the sudden realization of the stupendousness of the cosmic forces against which I had pitted my puny powers that temporarily unnerved me.

Then Jimmy spoke to me. "Let's have a last look at things inside the old crate before you shove off," he suggested, and my nervousness and my apprehensions vanished beneath the spell of his quiet tones and his matter-of-fact manner. I was myself again.

Together we inspected the cabin, where are located the controls, a wide and comfortable berth, a table, a chair, writing materials, and a well-stocked bookshelf. Behind the cabin is a small galley and just behind the galley a storeroom containing canned and dehydrated foods sufficient to last me a year. Back of this is a small battery room containing storage batteries for lighting, heating, and cooking, a dynamo, and a gas engine. The extreme stern compartment is filled with rockets and the intricate mechanical device by which they are fed to the firing chambers by means of the controls in the cabin. Forward of the main cabin is a large compartment in which are located the water and oxygen tanks, as well as a quantity of odds and ends necessary either to my safety or comfort.

Everything, it is needless to say, is fastened securely against the sudden and terrific stress that must accompany the take-off. Once out in space, I anticipate no sense of motion, but the start is going to be rather jarring. To absorb, as much as possible, the shock of the take-off, the rocket consists of two torpedoes, a smaller torpedo within a larger one, the former considerably shorter than the latter and consisting of several sections, each one comprising one of the compartments I have described. Between the inner and outer shells and between each two compartments is installed a system of ingenious hydraulic shock absorbers designed to more or less gradually overcome the inertia of the inner torpedo during the take-off. I trust that it functions properly.

In addition to these precautions against disaster at the start, the chair in which I shall sit before the controls is not only heavily overstuffed but is secured to a track or framework that is equipped with shock absorbers. Furthermore, there are means whereby I may strap myself securely into the chair before taking off.

I have neglected nothing essential to my safety, upon which depends the success of my project.

Following our final inspection of the interior, Jimmy and I clambered to the top of the torpedo for a last inspection of the parachutes, which I hope will sufficiently retard the speed of the rocket after it enters the atmosphere of Mars to permit me to bail out with my own parachute in time to make a safe landing. The main parachutes are in a series of compartments running the full length of the top of the torpedo. To explain them more clearly, I may say that they are a continuous series of batteries of parachutes, each battery consisting of a number of parachutes of increasing diameter from the uppermost, which is the smallest. Each battery is in an individual compartment, and each compartment is covered by a separate hatch that can be opened at the will of the operator by controls in the cabin. Each parachute is anchored to the torpedo by a separate cable. I expect about one half of them to be torn loose while checking the speed of the torpedo sufficiently to permit the others to hold and further retard it to a point where I may safely open the doors and jump with my own parachute and oxygen tank.

The moment for departure was approaching. Jimmy and I had descended to the ground and the most difficult ordeal now faced me—that of saying goodbye to these loyal friends and co-workers. We did not say much, we were too filled with emotion, and there was not a dry eye among us. Without exception none of the Mexican labourers could understand why the nose of the torpedo was not pointed straight up in the air if my intended destination were Marte. Nothing could convince them that I would not shoot out a short distance and make a graceful nose dive into the Pacific—that is, if I started at all, which many of them doubted.

There was a handclasp all around, and then I mounted the ladder leaning against the side of the torpedo and entered it. As I closed the door of the outer shell, I saw my friends piling into the trucks and pulling away, for I had given orders that no one should be within a mile of the rocket when I took off, fearing, as I did, the effect upon them of the terrific explosion that must accompany the take-off. Securing the outer door with its great vault like bolts, I closed the inner door and fastened it; then I took my seat before the controls and buckled the straps that held me to the chair.

I glanced at my watch. It lacked nine minutes of the zero hour. In nine minutes I should be on my way out into the great void, or in nine minutes I should be dead. If all did not go well, the disaster would follow within a fraction of a split second after I touched the first firing control.

Seven minutes! My throat felt dry and parched; I wanted a drink of water, but there was no time.

Four minutes! Thirty-five million miles are a lot of miles, yet I planned on spanning them in between forty and forty-five days.

Two minutes! I inspected the oxygen gauge and opened the valve a trifle wider.

One minute! I thought of my mother and wondered if she were way out there somewhere waiting for me.

Thirty seconds! My hand was on the control. Fifteen seconds Ten, five, four, three, two—one!

I turned the pointer! There was a muffled roar. The torpedo leaped forward. I was off!

I knew that the take-off was a success. I glanced through the port at my side at the instant that the torpedo started, but so terrific was its initial speed that I saw only a confused blur as the landscape rushed past. I was thrilled and delighted by the ease and perfection with which the take-off had been accomplished, and I must admit that I was not a little surprised by the almost negligible effects that were noticeable in the cabin. I had had the sensation as of a giant hand pressing me suddenly back against the upholstery of my chair but that had passed almost at once, and now there was no sensation different from that which one might experience sitting in an easy chair in a comfortable drawing-room on terra firma.

There was no sensation of motion after the first few seconds that were required to pass through the earth's atmosphere, and now that I had done all that lay within my power to do. I could only leave the rest to momentum, gravitation, and fate. Releasing the straps that held me to the chair, I moved about the cabin to look through the various ports, of which there were several in the sides, keel, and top of the torpedo Space was a black void dotted with countless points of light. The earth I could not see, for it lay directly astern; far ahead was Mars. All seemed well. I switched on the electric lights, and seating myself at the table, made the first entries in the log; then I checked over various computations of time and distances.

My calculations suggested that in about three hours from the take-off the torpedo would be moving almost directly toward Mars; and from time to time I took observations through the wide-angle telescopic periscope that is mounted flush with the upper surface of the torpedo's shell, but the results were not entirely reassuring. In two hours Mars was dead ahead—the arc of the trajectory was not flattening as it should. I became apprehensive. What was wrong? Where had our careful computations erred?

I left the periscope and gazed down through the main keel port. Below and ahead was the Moon, a gorgeous spectacle as viewed through the clear void of space from a distance some seventy-two thousand miles less than I had ever seen it before and with no earthly atmosphere to reduce visibility. Tycho, Plato, and Copernicus stood out in bold relief upon the brazen disc of the great satellite, deepening by contrast the shadows of Mare Serenitatis and Mare Tranquilitatis. The rugged peaks of the Apennine and the Altai lay revealed as distinctly as I had ever seen them through the largest telescope. I was thrilled, but I was distinctly worried, too.

Three hours later I was less than fifty-nine thousand miles from the Moon; where its aspect had been gorgeous before, it now beggared description, but my apprehension had cause to increase in proportion; I might say, as the square of its increasing gorgeousness. Through the periscope I had watched the arc of my trajectory pass through the plane of Mars and drop below it. I knew quite definitely then that I could never reach my goal. I tried not to think of the fate that lay ahead of me; but, instead, sought to discover the error that had wrought this disaster.

For an hour I checked over various calculations, but could discover nothing that might shed light on the cause of my predicament; then I switched off the lights and looked down through the keel port to have a closer view of the Moon. It was not there! Stepping to the port side of the cabin, I looked through one of the heavy circular glasses out into the void of space. For an instant I was horror stricken; apparently just off the port bow loomed an enormous world. It was the Moon, less than twenty-three thousand miles away, and I was hurtling toward it at the rate of thirty-six thousand miles an hour!

I leaped to the periscope, and in the next few seconds I accomplished some lightning mental calculating that must constitute an all-time record. I watched the deflection of our course in the direction of the Moon, following it across the lens of the periscope, I computed the distance to the Moon and the speed of the torpedo, and I came to the conclusion that I had better than a fighting chance of missing the great orb. I had little fear of anything but a direct hit, since our speed was so great that the attraction of the Moon could not hold us if we missed her even by a matter of feet; but it was quite evident that it had affected our flight, and with this realization came the answer to the question that had been puzzling me.

To my mind flashed the printer's story of the first perfect book. It had been said that no book had ever before been published containing not a single error. A great publishing house undertook to publish such a book. The galley proofs were read and reread by a dozen different experts, the page proofs received the same careful scrutiny. At last the masterpiece was ready for the press—errorless! It was printed and bound and sent out to the public, and then it was discovered that the title had been misspelled on the title page. With all our careful calculation, with all our checking and rechecking, we had overlooked the obvious; we had not taken the Moon into consideration at all.

Explain it if you can; I cannot. It was just one of those things, as people say when a good team loses to a poor one; it was a break, and a bad one. How bad it was I did not even try to conjecture at the time; I just sat at the periscope watching the Moon racing toward us. As we neared it, it presented the most gorgeous spectacle that I have ever witnessed. Each mountain peak and crater stood out in vivid detail. Even the great height of summits over twenty-five thousand feet appeared distinguishable to me, though imagination must have played a major part in the illusion, since I was looking down upon them from above.

Suddenly I realized that the great sphere was passing rapidly from the field of the periscope, and I breathed a sigh of relief—we were not going to score a clean hit, we were going to pass by.

I returned then to the porthole. The Moon lay just ahead and a little to the left. It was no longer a great sphere; it was a world that filled my whole range of vision. Against its black horizon I saw titanic peaks; below me huge craters yawned. I stood with God on high and looked down upon a dead world.

Our transit of the Moon required a little less than four minutes; I timed it carefully that I might check our speed. How close we came I may only guess; perhaps five thousand feet above the tallest peaks, but it was close enough. The pull of the Moon's gravitation had definitely altered our course, but owing to our speed we had eluded her clutches. Now we were racing away from her, but to what?

The nearest star, Alpha Centauri, is twenty-five and a half million million miles from earth. Write that on your typewriter—25,500,000,000,000 miles. But why trifle with short distances like this? There was little likelihood that I should visit Alpha Centauri with all the wide range of space at my command and many more interesting places to go. I knew that I had ample room in which to wander, since science has calculated the diameter of space to be eighty-four thousand million light years, which, when one reflects that light travels at the rate of one hundred eighty-six thousand miles a second, should satisfy the wanderlust of the most inveterate roamer.

However, I was not greatly concerned with any of these distances, as I had food and water for only a year, during which time the torpedo might travel slightly more than three hundred fifteen million miles. Even if it reached our near neighbour, Alpha Centauri, I should not then be greatly interested in the event, as I should have been dead for over eighty thousand years. Such is the immensity of the universe!

During the next twenty-four hours the course of the torpedo nearly paralleled the Moon's orbit around the earth. Not only had the pull of the Moon deflected its course, but now it seemed evident that the earth had seized us and that we were doomed to race through eternity around her, a tiny, second satellite. But I did not wish to be a moon, certainly not an insignificant moon that in all probability might not be picked up by even the largest telescope.

The next month was the most trying of my life. It seems the height of egotism even to mention my life in the face of the stupendous cosmic forces that engulfed it; but it was the only life I had and I was fond of it, and the more imminent seemed the moment when it should be snuffed out, the better I liked it.

At the end of the second day it was quite apparent that we had eluded the grip of the earth. I cannot say that I was elated at the discovery. My plan to visit Mars was ruined. I should have been glad to return to earth. If I could have landed safely on Mars, I certainly could have landed safely on earth. But there was another reason why I should have been glad to have returned to earth, a reason that loomed, large and terrible, ahead—the Sun. We were heading straight for the Sun now. Once in the grip of that mighty power, nothing could affect our destiny; we were doomed. For three months I must await the inevitable end, before plunging into that fiery furnace. Furnace is an inadequate word by which to suggest the Sun's heat, which is reputedly from thirty to sixty million degrees at the centre, a fact which should not have concerned me greatly, since I did not anticipate reaching the centre.

The days dragged on, or, I should say, the long night—there were no days, other than the record that I kept of the passing hours. I read a great deal. I made no entries in the log. Why write something that was presently to be plunged into the Sun and consumed? I experimented in the galley, attempting fancy cooking. I ate a great deal; it helped to pass the time away, and I enjoyed my meals.

On the thirtieth day I was scanning space ahead when I saw a gorgeous, shimmering crescent far to the right of our course; but I must confess that I was not greatly interested in sights of any sort. In sixty days I should be in the Sun. Long before that, however, the increasing heat would have destroyed me. The end was approaching rapidly.

CHAPTER 3

# Rushing Toward Venus

The psychological effects of an experience such as that through which I had been passing must be considerable, and even though they could be neither weighed nor measured, I was yet conscious of changes that had taken place in me because of them. For thirty days I had been racing alone through space toward absolute annihilation, toward an end that would probably not leave a single nucleus of the atoms that compose me an electron to carry on with, I had experienced the ultimate in solitude, and the result had been to deaden my sensibilities; doubtless a wise provision of nature.

Even the realization that the splendid crescent, looming enormously off the starboard bow of the torpedo, was Venus failed to excite me greatly. What if I were to approach Venus more closely than any other human being of all time! It meant nothing. Were I to see God, himself, even that would mean nothing. It became apparent that the value of what we see is measurable only by the size of our prospective audience. Whatever I saw, who might never have an audience, was without value.

Nevertheless, more to pass away the time than because I was particularly interested in the subject, I began to make some rough calculations. These indicated that I was about eight hundred sixty-five thousand miles from the orbit of Venus and that I should cross it in about twenty-four hours. I could not, however, compute my present distance from the planet accurately. I only knew that it appeared very close. When I say close, I mean relatively. The earth was some twenty-five million miles away, the Sun about sixty-eight million, so that an object as large as Venus, at a distance of one or two million miles, appeared close.

As Venus travels in her orbit at the rate of nearly twenty-two miles per second, or over one million six hundred thousand miles in a terrestrial day, it appeared evident to me that she would cross my path some time within the next twenty-four hours.

It occurred to me that, passing closely, as was unavoidable, she might deflect the course of the torpedo and save me from the Sun; but I knew this to be a vain hope. Undoubtedly, the path of the torpedo would be bent, but the Sun would not relinquish his prey. With these thoughts, my apathy returned, and I lost interest in Venus.

Selecting a book, I lay down on my bed to read. The interior of the cabin was brightly illuminated. I am extravagant with electricity. I have the means of generating it for eleven more months; but I shall not need it after a few weeks, so why should I be parsimonious?

I read for a few hours, but as reading in bed always makes me sleepy, I eventually succumbed. When I awoke, I lay for a few minutes in luxurious ease. I might be racing toward extinction at the rate of thirty-six thousand miles an hour, but I, myself, was unhurried. I recalled the beautiful spectacle that Venus had presented when I had last observed her and decided to have another look at her. Stretching languorously, I arose and stepped to one of the starboard portholes.

The picture framed by the casing of that circular opening was gorgeous beyond description. Apparently less than half as far away as before, and twice as large, loomed the mass of Venus outlined by an aureole of light where the Sun, behind her, illuminated her cloudy envelope and lighted to burning brilliance a thin crescent along the edge nearest me.

I looked at my watch. Twelve hours had passed since I first discovered the planet, and now, at last, I became excited. Venus was apparently half as far away as it had been twelve hours ago, and I knew that the torpedo had covered half the distance that had separated us from her orbit at that time. A collision was possible, it even seemed within the range of probability that I should be dashed to the surface of this inhospitable, lifeless world.

Well, what of it? Am I not already doomed? What difference can it make to me if the end comes a few weeks sooner than I had anticipated? Yet I was excited. I cannot say that I felt fear. I have no fear of death—that left me when my mother died; but now that the great adventure loomed so close I was overwhelmed by contemplation of it and the great wonder that it induced. What would follow?

The long hours dragged on. It seemed incredible to me, accustomed though I am to thinking in units of terrific speed, that the torpedo and Venus were racing toward the same point in her orbit at such inconceivable velocities, the one at the rate of thirty-six thousand miles per hour, the other at over sixty-seven thousand.

It was now becoming difficult to view the planet through the side port, as she moved steadily closer and closer to our path. I went to the periscope—she was gliding majestically within its range. I knew that at that moment the torpedo was less than thirty-six thousand miles, less than an hour, from the path of the planet's orbit, and there could be no doubt now but that she had already seized us in her grasp. We were destined to make a deaf hit. Even under the circumstances I could not restrain a smile at the thought of the marksmanship that this fact revealed. I had aimed at Mars and was about to hit Venus; unquestionably the all-time cosmic record for poor shots.

Even though I did not shrink from death, even though the world's best astronomers have assured us that Venus must be unfitted to support human life, that where her surface is not unutterably hot it is unutterably cold, even though she be oxygenless, as they aver, yet the urge to live that is born with each of us compelled me to make the same preparations to land that I should have had I successfully reached my original goal, Mars.

Slipping into a fleece-lined suit of coveralls, I donned goggles and a fleece-lined helmet; then I adjusted the oxygen tank that was designed to hang in front of me, lest it foul the parachute, and which can be automatically jettisoned in the event that I reach an atmosphere that will support life, for it would be an awkward and dangerous appendage to be cumbered with while landing. Finally, I adjusted my chute.

I glanced at my watch. If my calculations have been correct, we should strike in about fifteen minutes. Once more I returned to the periscope.

The sight that met my eyes was awe inspiring. We were plunging toward a billowing mass of black clouds. It was like chaos on the dawn of creation. The gravitation of the planet had seized us. The floor of the cabin was no longer beneath me—I was standing on the forward bulkhead now; but this condition I had anticipated when I designed the torpedo. We were diving nose on toward the planet. In space there had been neither up nor down, but now there was a very definite down.

From where I stood I could reach the controls, and beside me was the door in the side of the torpedo. I released three batteries of parachutes and opened the door in the wall of the inner torpedo. There was a noticeable jar, as though the parachutes had opened and temporarily checked the speed of the torpedo. This must mean that I had entered an atmosphere of some description and that there was not a second to waste.

With a single movement of a lever I loosed the remaining parachutes; then I turned to the outer door. Its bolts were controlled by a large wheel set in the centre of the door and were geared to open quickly and with ease. I adjusted the mouthpiece of the oxygen line across my lips and quickly spun the wheel.

Simultaneously the door flew open and the air pressure within the torpedo shot me out into space. My right hand grasped the rip cord of my chute; but I waited. I looked about for the torpedo. It was racing almost parallel with me, all its parachutes distended above it. Just an instant's glimpse I had of it, and then it dove into the cloud mass and was lost to view; but what a weirdly magnificent spectacle it had presented in that brief instant!

Safe now from any danger of fouling with the torpedo, I jerked the rip cord of my parachute just as the clouds swallowed me. Through my fleece-lined suit I felt the bitter cold; like a dash of ice water the cold clouds slapped me in the face; then, to my relief, the chute opened, and I fell more slowly.

Down, down, down I dropped. I could not even guess the duration, nor the distance. It was very dark and very wet, like sinking into the depths of the ocean without feeling the pressure of the water. My thoughts during those long moments were such as to baffle description. Perhaps the oxygen made me a little drunk; I do not know. I felt exhilarated and intensely eager to solve the great mystery beneath me. The thought that I was about to die did not concern me so much as what I might see before I died. I was about to land on Venus—the first human being in all the world to see the face of the veiled planet.

Suddenly I emerged into a cloudless space; but far below me were what appeared in the darkness to be more clouds, recalling to my mind the often advanced theory of the two cloud envelopes of Venus. As I descended, the temperature rose gradually, but it was still cold.

As I entered the second cloud bank, there was a very noticeable rise in temperature the farther I fell. I shut off the oxygen supply and tried breathing through my nose. By inhaling deeply I discovered that I could take in sufficient oxygen to support life, and an astronomical theory was shattered. Hope flared within me like a beacon on a fog-hid landing field.

As I floated gently downward, I presently became aware of a faint luminosity far below. What could it be? There were many obvious reasons why it could not be sunlight; sunlight would not come from below, and, furthermore, it was night on this hemisphere of the planet. Naturally many weird conjectures raced through my mind. I wondered if this could be the light from an incandescent world, but immediately discarded that explanation as erroneous, knowing that the heat from an incandescent world would long since have consumed me. Then it occurred to me that it might be refracted light from that portion of the cloud envelope illuminated by the Sun, yet if such were the case, it seemed obvious that the clouds about me should be luminous, which they were not.

There seemed only one practical solution. It was the solution that an earth man would naturally arrive at. Being what I am, a highly civilized creature from a world already far advanced by science and invention, I attributed the source of this light to these twin forces of superior intelligence. I could only account for that faint glow by attributing it to the reflection upon the under side of the cloud mass of artificial light produced by intelligent creatures upon the surface of this world toward which I was slowly settling.

I wondered what these beings would be like, and if my excitement grew as I anticipated the wonders that were soon to be revealed to my eyes, I believe that it was a pardonable excitement, under the circumstances. Upon the threshold of such an adventure who would not have been moved to excitement by contemplation of the experiences awaiting him?

Now I removed the mouthpiece of the oxygen tube entirely and found that I could breathe easily. The light beneath me was increasing gradually. About me I thought I saw vague, dark shapes among the cloud masses. Shadows, perhaps, but of what? I detached the oxygen tank and let it fall. I distinctly heard it strike something an instant after I had released it. Then a shadow loomed darkly beneath me, and an instant later my feet struck something that gave beneath them.

I dropped into a mass of foliage and grasped wildly for support. A moment later I began to fall more rapidly and guessed what had happened; the parachute had been uptilted by contact with the foliage. I clutched at leaves and branches, fruitlessly, and then I was brought to a sudden stop; evidently the chute had fouled something. I hoped that it would hold until I found a secure resting place.

As I groped about in the dark, my hand finally located a sturdy branch, and a moment later I was astride it, my back to the bole of a large tree—another theory gone the ignoble path of countless predecessors; it was evident that there was vegetation on Venus. At least there was one tree; I could vouch for that, as I was sitting in it, and doubtless the black shadows I had passed were other, taller trees.

Having found secure lodgement, I divested myself of my parachute after salvaging some of its ropes and the straps from the harness, which I thought I might find helpful in descending the tree. Starting at the top of a tree, in darkness and among clouds, one may not be positive what the tree is like nearer the ground. I also removed my goggles. Then I commenced to descend. The girth of the tree was enormous, but the branches grew sufficiently close together to permit me to find safe footing.

I did not know how far I had fallen through the second cloud stratum before I lodged in the tree nor how far I had descended the tree, but all together it must have been close to two thousand feet; yet I was still in the clouds. Could the entire atmosphere of Venus be forever fog laden? I hoped not, for it was a dreary prospect.

The light from below had increased a little as I descended, but not much; it was still dark about me. I continued to descend. It was tiresome work and not without danger, this climbing down an unfamiliar tree in a fog, at night, toward an unknown world. But I could not remain where I was, and there was nothing above to entice me upward; so I continued to descend.

What a strange trick fate had played me. I had wanted to visit Venus, but had discarded the idea when assured by my astronomer friends that the planet could not support either animal or vegetable life. I had started for Mars, and now, fully ten days before I had hoped to reach the red planet, I was on Venus, breathing perfectly good air among the branches of a tree that evidently dwarfed the giant Sequoias.

The illumination was increasing rapidly now the clouds were thinning; through breaks I caught glimpses far below, glimpses of what appeared to be an endless vista of foliage, softly moonlit—but Venus had no moon. In that, insofar as the seeming moonlight was concerned, I could fully concur with the astronomers. This illumination came from no moon, unless Venus's satellite lay beneath her inner envelope of clouds, which was preposterous.

A moment later I emerged entirely from the cloud bank, but though I searched in all directions, I saw nothing but foliage, above, around, below me, yet I could see far down into that abyss of leaves. In the soft light I could not determine the colour of the foliage, but I was sure that it was not green; it was some light, delicate shade of another colour.

I had descended another thousand feet since I had emerged from the clouds, and I was pretty well exhausted (the month of inactivity and overeating had softened me), when I saw just below me what appeared to be a causeway leading from the tree I was descending to another adjacent. I also discovered that from just below where I clung the limbs had been cut away from the tree to a point below the causeway. Here were two startling and unequivocal evidences of the presence of intelligent beings. Venus was inhabited! But by what? What strange, arboreal creatures built causeways high among these giant trees? Were they a species of monkey-man? Were they of a high or low order of intelligence? How would they receive me?

At this juncture in my vain speculations I was startled by a noise above me. Something was moving in the branches overhead. The sound was coming nearer, and it seemed to me that it was being made by something of considerable size and weight, but perhaps, I realized, that conjecture was the child of my imagination. However, I felt most uncomfortable. I was unarmed. I have never carried weapons. My friends had urged a perfect arsenal upon me before I embarked upon my adventure, but I had argued that if I arrived on Mars unarmed it would be prima facie evidence of my friendly intentions, and even if my reception were warlike, I should be no worse off, since I could not hope, single-handed, to conquer a world, no matter how well armed I were.

Suddenly, above me, to the crashing of some heavy body through the foliage were added hideous screams and snarls; and in the terrifying dissonance I recognized the presence of more than a single creature. Was I being pursued by all the fearsome denizens of this Venusian forest!

Perhaps my nerves were slightly unstrung and who may blame them if they were, after what I had passed through so recently and during the long, preceding months They were not entirely shattered, however, and I could still appreciate the fact that night noises often multiply themselves in a most disconcerting way. I have heard coyotes yapping and screaming around my camp on Arizona nights when, but for the actual knowledge that there were but one or two of them, I could have sworn that there were a hundred, had I trusted only to my sense of hearing.

But in this instance I was quite positive that the voices of more than a single beast were mingling to produce the horrid din that, together with the sound of their passage, was definitely and unquestionably drawing rapidly nearer me. Of course I did not know that the owners of those awesome voices were pursuing me, though a still, small voice within seemed to be assuring me that such was the fact.

I wished that I might reach the causeway below me (I should feel better standing squarely on two feet), but it was too far to drop and there were no more friendly branches to give me support; then I thought of the ropes I had salvaged from the abandoned parachute. Quickly uncoiling them from about my waist, I looped one of them over the branch upon which I sat, grasped both strands firmly in my hands, and prepared to swing from my porch. Suddenly the screams and snarling growls ceased; and then, close above me now, I heard the noise of something descending toward me and saw the branches shaking to its weight.

Lowering my body from the branch, I swung downward and slid the fifteen or more feet to the causeway, and as I alighted the silence of the great forest was again shattered by a hideous scream just above my head. Looking up quickly, I saw a creature launching itself toward me and just beyond it a snarling face of utter hideousness. I caught but the briefest glimpse of it—just enough to see that it was a face, with eyes and a mouth—then it was withdrawn amidst the foliage.

Perhaps I only sensed that hideous vision subconsciously at the time, for the whole scene was but a flash upon the retina of my eye, and the other beast was in mid-air above me at the instant; but it remained indelibly impressed upon my memory, and I was to recall it upon a later day under circumstances so harrowing that the mind of mortal earth man may scarce conceive them.

As I leaped back to avoid the creature springing upon me, I still clung to one strand of the rope down which I had lowered myself to the causeway. My grasp upon the rope was unconscious and purely mechanical; it was in my hand, and my fist was clenched; and as I leaped away, I dragged the rope with me. A fortuitous circumstance, no doubt, but a most fortunate one.

The creature missed me, alighting on all fours a few feet from me, and there it crouched, apparently slightly bewildered, and, fortunately for me, it did not immediately charge, giving me the opportunity to collect my wits and back slowly away, at the same time mechanically coiling the rope in my right hand. The little, simple things one does in moments of stress or excitement often seem entirely beyond reason and incapable of explanation; but I have thought that they may be dictated by a subconscious mind reacting to the urge of self-preservation. Possibly they are not always well directed and may as often fail to be of service as not, but then it may be possible that subconscious minds are no less fallible than the objective mind, which is wrong far more often than it is right. I cannot but seek for some explanation of the urge that caused me to retain that rope, since, all unknown to me, it was to be the slender thread upon which my life was to hang.

Silence had again descended upon the weird scene. Since the final scream of the hideous creature that had retreated into the foliage after this thing had leaped for me, there had been no sound. The creature that crouched facing me seemed slightly bewildered. I am positive now that it had not been pursuing me, but that it itself had been the object of pursuit by the other beast that had retreated.

In the dim half-light of the Venusian night I saw confronting me a creature that might be conjured only in the half-delirium of some horrid nightmare. It was about as large as a full-grown puma, and stood upon four hand like feet that suggested that it might be almost wholly arboreal. The front legs were much longer than the hind, suggesting, in this respect, the hyena; but here the similarity ceased, for the creature's furry pelt was striped longitudinally with alternate bands of red and yellow, and its hideous head bore no resemblance to any earthly animal. No external ears were visible, and in the low forehead was a single large, round eye at the end of a thick antenna about four inches long. The jaws were powerful and armed with long, sharp fangs, while from either side of the neck projected a powerful chela. Never have I seen a creature so fearsomely armed for offence as was this nameless beast of another world. With those powerful crablike pincers it could easily have held an opponent far stronger than a man and dragged it to those terrible jaws.

For a time it eyed me with that single, terrifying eye that moved to and fro at the end of its antenna, and all the time its chelae were waving slowly, opening and closing. In that brief moment of delay I looked about me, and the first thing that I discovered was that I stood directly in front of an opening cut in the bole of the tree; an opening about three feet wide and over six feet high. But the most remarkable thing about it was that it was closed by a door; not a solid door, but one suggesting a massive wooden grill.

As I stood contemplating it and wondering what to do, I thought that I saw something moving behind it. Then a voice spoke to me out of the darkness beyond the door. It sounded like a human voice, though it spoke in a language that I could not understand. The tones were peremptory. I could almost imagine that it said, "Who are you, and what do you want here in the middle of the night?"

"I am a stranger," I said. "I come in peace and friendship."

Of course I knew that whatever it was behind that door, it could not understand me; but I hoped that my tone would assure it of my peaceful designs. There was a moment's silence and then I heard other voices. Evidently the situation was being discussed; then I saw that the creature facing me upon the causeway was creeping toward me, and I turned my attention from the doorway to the beast.

I had no weapons, nothing but a length of futile rope; but I knew that I must do something. I could not stand there supinely and let the creature seize and devour me without striking a blow in my own defence. I uncoiled a portion of the rope and, more in despair than with any hope that I could accomplish anything of a defensive nature, flicked the end of it in the face of the advancing beast. You have seen a boy snap a wet towel at a companion; perhaps you have been flicked in that way, and if you have, you know that it hurts.

Of course I did not expect to overcome my adversary by any such means as this; to be truthful, I did not know what I did expect to accomplish Perhaps I just felt that I must do something, and this was the only thing that occurred to me. The result merely demonstrated the efficiency of that single eye and the quickness of the chelae. I snapped that rope as a ringmaster snaps a whip; but though the rope end travelled with great speed and the act must have been unexpected, the creature caught the rope in one of its chelae before it reached its face. Then it hung on and sought to drag me toward those frightful jaws.

I learned many a trick of roping from a cowboy friend of my motion picture days, and one of these I now put into use in an endeavour to entangle the crablike chelae Suddenly giving the rope sufficient slack, I threw a half hitch around the chela that gripped it, immediately following it with a second, whereupon the creature commenced to pull desperately away. I think it was motivated solely by an instinctive urge to pull toward its jaws anything that was held in its chelae; but for how long it would continue to pull away before it decided to change its tactics and charge me, I could not even guess; and so I acted upon a sudden inspiration and hurriedly made fast the end of the rope that I held to one of the stout posts that supported the handrail of the causeway; then, of a sudden, the thing charged me, roaring furiously.

I turned and ran, hoping that I could get out of the reach of those terrible chelae before the creature was stopped by the rope; and this I but barely managed to do. I breathed a sigh of relief as I saw the great body flipped completely over on its back as the rope tautened, but the hideous scream of rage that followed left me cold. Nor was my relief of any great duration, for as soon as the creature had scrambled to its feet, it seized the rope in its other chela and severed it as neatly as one might with a pair of monstrous tinner's snips; and then it was after me again, but this time it did not creep.

It seemed evident that my stay upon Venus was to be brief, when suddenly the door in the tree swung open and three men leaped to the causeway just behind the charging terror that was swiftly driving down upon me. The leading man hurled a short, heavy spear that sank deep into the back of my infuriated pursuer. Instantly the creature stopped in its tracks and wheeled about to face these new and more dangerous tormentors; and as he did so two more spears, hurled by the companions of the first man, drove into his chest, and with a last frightful scream, the thing dropped in its tracks, dead.

Then the leading man came toward me. In the subdued light of the forest he appeared no different from an earth man. He held the point of a straight, sharp sword pointed at my vitals. Close behind him were the other two men, each with a drawn sword.

The first man spoke to me in a stern, commanding voice, but I shook my head to indicate that I could not understand; then he pressed the point of his weapon against my coveralls opposite the pit of my stomach, and jabbed. I backed away. He advanced and jabbed at me again, and again I backed along the causeway. Now the other two men advanced and the three of them fell to examining me, meanwhile talking among themselves.

I could see them better now. They were about my own height and in every detail of their visible anatomy they appeared identical with terrestrial human beings, nor was a great deal left to my imagination—the men were almost naked. They wore loincloths and little else other than the belts that supported the scabbards of their swords. Their skins appeared to be much darker than mine, but not so dark as a negro's, and their faces were smooth and handsome.

Several times one or another of them addressed me and I always replied, but neither understood what the other said. Finally, after a lengthy discussion, one of them re-entered the opening in the tree and a moment later I saw the interior of a chamber, just within the doorway, illuminated; then one of the two remaining men motioned me forward and pointed toward the doorway.

Understanding that he wished me to enter, I stepped forward, and, as I passed them, they kept their sword points against my body—they were taking no chances with me. The other man awaited me in the centre of a large room hewn from the interior of the great tree. Beyond him were other doorways leading from this room, doubtless into other apartments. There were chairs and a table in the room; the walls were carved and painted; there was a large rug upon the floor; from a small vessel depending from the centre of the ceiling a soft light illuminated the interior as brightly as might sunlight flooding through an open window, but there was no glare.

The other men had entered and closed the door, which they fastened by a device that was not apparent to me at the time; then one of them pointed to a chair and motioned me to be seated. Under the bright light they examined me intently, and I them. My clothing appeared to puzzle them most; they examined and discussed its material, texture, and weave, if I could judge correctly by their gestures and inflections.

Finding the heat unendurable in my fleece lined coveralls, I removed them and my leather coat and polo shirt. Each newly revealed article aroused their curiosity and comment. My light skin and blond hair also received their speculative attention.

Presently one of them left the chamber, and while he was absent another removed the various articles that had lain upon the table. These consisted of what I took to be books bound in wooden and in leather covers, several ornaments, and a dagger in a beautifully wrought sheath.

When the man who had left the room returned, he brought food and drink which he placed upon the table; and by signs the three indicated that I might eat. There were fruits and nuts in highly polished, carved wooden bowls; there was something I took to be bread, on a golden platter; and there was honey in a silver jug. A tall, slender goblet contained a whitish liquid that resembled milk. This last receptacle was a delicate, translucent ceramic of an exquisite blue shade. These things and the appointments of the room bespoke culture, refinement, and good taste, making the savage apparel of their owners appear incongruous.

The fruits and nuts were unlike any with which I was familiar, both in appearance and flavour; the bread was coarse but delicious; and the honey, if such it were, suggested candied violets to the taste. The milk (I can find no other earthly word to describe it) was strong and almost pungent, yet far from unpleasant. I imagined at the time that one might grow to be quite fond of it.

The table utensils were similar to those with which we are familiar in civilized portions of the earth; there were hollowed instruments with which to dip or scoop, sharp ones with which to cut, and others with tines with which to impale. There was also a handled pusher, which I recommend to earthly hostesses. All these were of metal.

While I ate, the three men conversed earnestly, one or another of them occasionally offering me more food. They seemed hospitable and courteous, and I felt that if they were typical of the inhabitants of Venus I should find my life here a pleasant one. That it would not be a bed of roses, however, was attested by the weapons that the men constantly wore; one does not carry a sword and a dagger about with him unless he expects to have occasion to use them, except on dress parade.

When I had finished my meal, two of the men escorted me from the room by a rear doorway, up a flight of circular stairs, and ushered me into a small chamber. The stairway and corridor were illuminated by a small lamp similar to that which hung in the room where I had eaten, and light from this lamp shone through the heavy wooden grating of the door, into the room where I was now locked and where my captors left me to my own devices.

Upon the floor was a soft mattress over which were spread coverings of a silky texture. It being very warm, I removed all of my clothing except my undershorts and lay down to sleep. I was tired after my arduous descent of the giant tree and dozed almost immediately. I should have been asleep at once had I not been suddenly startled to wakefulness by a repetition of that hideous scream with which the beast that had pursued me through the tree had announced its rage and chagrin when I had eluded it.

However, it was not long before I fell asleep, my dozing mind filled with a chaos of fragmentary recollections of my stupendous adventure.

## Chapter 4

# To the House of the King

When I awoke, it was quite light in the room, and through a window I saw the foliage of trees, lavender and heliotrope and violet in the light of a new day. I arose and went to the window. I saw no sign of sunlight, yet a brightness equivalent to sunlight pervaded everything. The air was warm and sultry. Below me I could see sections of various causeways extending from tree to tree. On some of these I caught glimpses of people. All the men were naked, except for loincloths, nor did I wonder at their scant apparel, in the light of my experience of the temperatures on Venus. There were both men and women; and all the men were armed with swords and daggers, while the women carried daggers only. All those whom I saw seemed to be of the same age; there were neither children nor old people among them. All appeared comely.

From my barred window I sought a glimpse of the ground, but as far down as I could see there was only the amazing foliage of the trees, lavender, heliotrope, and violet. And what trees! From my window I could see several enormous boles fully two hundred feet in diameter. I had thought the tree I descended a giant, but compared with these, it was only a sapling.

As I stood contemplating the scene before me, there was a noise at the door behind me. Turning, I saw one of my captors entering the room. He greeted me with a few words, which I could not understand, and a pleasant smile, that I could. I returned his smile and said, "Good morning!"

He beckoned to me to follow him from the room, but I made signs indicating that I wished to don my clothes first. I knew I should be hot and uncomfortable in them; I was aware that no one I had seen here wore any clothing, yet so powerful are the inhibitions of custom and habit that I shrank from doing the sensible thing and wearing only my undershorts.

At first, when he realized what I wished to do, he motioned me to leave my clothes where they were and come with him as I was; but eventually he gave in with another of his pleasant smiles. He was a man of fine physique, a little shorter than I; by daylight, I could see that his skin was about that shade of brown that a heavy sun tan imparts to people of my own race; his eyes were dark brown, his hair black. His appearance formed a marked contrast to my light skin, blue eyes, and blond hair.

When I had dressed, I followed him downstairs to a room adjoining the one I had first entered the previous night. Here the man's two companions and two women were seated at a table on which were a number of vessels containing food. As I entered the room the women's eyes were turned upon me curiously; the men smiled and greeted me as had their fellow, and one of them motioned me to a chair. The women appraised me frankly but without boldness, and it was evident that they were discussing me freely between themselves and with the men. They were both uncommonly good-looking, their skins being a shade lighter than those of the men, while their eyes and hair were of about the same colour as those of their male companions. Each wore a single garment of a silken material similar to that of which my bed cover had been made and in the form of a long sash, which was wrapped tightly around the body below the armpits, confining the breasts. From this point it was carried half way around the body downward to the waist, where it circled the body again, the loose end then passing between the legs from behind and up through the sash in front, after the manner of a G string, the remainder falling in front to the knees.

In addition to these garments, which were beautifully embroidered in colours, the women wore girdles from which depended pocket pouches and sheathed daggers, and both were plentifully adorned with ornaments such as rings, bracelets, and hair ornaments. I could recognize gold and silver among the various materials of which these things were fabricated, and there were others that might have been ivory and coral; but what impressed me most was the exquisite workmanship they displayed, and I imagined that they were valued more for this than for the intrinsic worth of the materials that composed them. That this conjecture might be in accordance with fact was borne out by the presence among their ornaments of several of the finest workmanship, obviously carved from ordinary bone.

On the table was bread different from that which I had had the night before, a dish that I thought might be eggs and meat baked together, several which I could not recognize either by appearance or taste, and the familiar milk and honey that I had encountered before. The foods varied widely in range of flavour, so that it would have been a difficult palate indeed that would not have found something to its liking.

During the meal they engaged in serious discussion, and I was certain from their glances and gestures that I was the subject of their debate. The two girls enlivened the meal by attempting to carry on a conversation with me, which appeared to afford them a great deal of merriment, nor could I help joining in their laughter, so infectious was it. Finally one of them hit upon the happy idea of teaching me their language. She pointed to herself and said, "Zuro," and to the other girl and said, "Alzo"; then the men became interested, and I soon learned that the name of him who seemed to be the head of the house, the man who had first challenged me the preceding night, was Duran, the other two Olthar and Kamlot.

But before I had mastered more than these few words and the names of some of the foods on the table, breakfast was over and the three men had conducted me from the house. As we proceeded along the causeway that passed in front of the house of Duran, the interest and curiosity of those we passed were instantly challenged as their eyes fell upon me; and it was at once evident to me that I was a type either entirely unknown on Venus or at least rare, for my blue eyes and blond hair caused quite as much comment as my clothing, as I could tell by their gestures and the direction of their gaze.

We were often stopped by curious friends of my captors, or hosts (I was not sure yet in which category they fell); but none offered me either harm or insult, and if I were the object of their curious scrutiny, so were they of mine. While no two of them were identical in appearance, they were all handsome and all apparently of about the same age. I saw no old people and no children.

Presently we approached a tree of such enormous diameter that I could scarcely believe the testimony of my eyes when I saw it. It was fully five hundred feet in diameter. Stripped of branches for a hundred feet above and below the causeway, its surface was dotted with windows and doors and encircled by wide balconies or verandas. Before a large and elaborately carved doorway was a group of armed men before whom we halted while Duran addressed one of their number.

I thought at the time that he called this man Tofar, and such I learned later was his name. He wore a necklace from which depended a metal disc bearing a hieroglyphic in relief; otherwise he was not accoutred differently from his companions. As he and Duran conversed, he appraised me carefully from head to feet. Presently he and Duran passed through the doorway into the interior of the tree, while the others continued to examine me and question Kamlot and Olthar.

While I waited there, I embraced the opportunity to study the elaborate carvings that surrounded the portal, forming a frame fully five feet wide. The motif appeared historical, and I could easily imagine that the various scenes depicted important events in the life of a dynasty or a nation. The workmanship was exquisite, and it required no stretch of the imagination to believe that each delicately carved face was the portrait of some dead or living celebrity. There was nothing grotesque in the delineation of the various figures, as is so often the case in work of a similar character on earth, and only the borders that framed the whole and separated contiguous plaques were conventional.

I was still engrossed by these beautiful examples of the wood carver's art when Duran and Tofar returned and motioned Olthar and Kamlot and me to follow them into the interior of the great tree. We passed through several large chambers and along wide corridors, all carved from the wood of the living tree, to the head of a splendid stairway, which we descended to another level. The chambers near the periphery of the tree received their light through windows, while the interior chambers and corridors were illuminated by lamps similar to those I had already seen in the house of Duran.

Near the foot of the stairway we had descended we entered a spacious chamber, before the doorway to which stood two men armed with spears and swords, and before us, across the chamber, we saw a man seated at a table near a large window. Just inside the doorway we halted, my companions standing in respectful silence until the man at the table looked up and spoke to them; then they crossed the room, taking me with them, and halted before the table, upon the opposite side of which the man sat facing us.

He spoke pleasantly to my companions, calling each by name, and when they replied they addressed him as Jong. He was a fine-looking man with a strong face and a commanding presence. His attire was similar to that worn by all the other male Venusians I had seen, differing only in that he wore about his head a fillet that supported a circular metal disc in the centre of his forehead. He appeared much interested in me and watched me intently while listening to Duran, who, I had no doubt, was narrating the story of my strange and sudden appearance the night before.

When Duran had concluded, the man called Jong addressed me. His manner was serious, his tones kindly. Out of courtesy, I replied, though I knew that he could understand me no better than I had understood him. He smiled and shook his head; then he fell into a discussion with the others. Finally he struck a metal gong that stood near him on the table; then he arose and came around the table to where I stood. He examined my clothing carefully, feeling its texture and apparently discussing the materials and the weave with the others. Then he examined the skin of my hands and face, felt of my hair, and made me open my mouth that he might examine my teeth. I was reminded of the horse market and the slave block. "Perhaps," I thought, "the latter is more apropos."

A man entered now whom I took to be a servant and, receiving instructions from the man called Jong, departed again, while I continued to be the object of minute investigation. My beard, which was now some twenty-four hours old, elicited considerable comment. It is not a beautiful beard at any age, being sparse and reddish, for which reason I am careful to shave daily when I have the necessary utensils.

I cannot say that I enjoyed this intimate appraisal, but the manner in which it was conducted was so entirely free from any suggestion of intentional rudeness or discourtesy, and my position here was so delicate that my better judgment prevented me from openly resenting the familiarities of the man called Jong. It is well that I did not.

Presently a man entered through a doorway at my right. I assumed that he had been summoned by the servant recently dispatched. As he came forward, I saw that he was much like the others; a handsome man of about thirty. There are those who declaim against monotony; but for me there can never be any monotony of beauty, not even if the beautiful things were all identical, which the Venusians I had so far seen were not. All were beautiful, but each in his own way.

The man called Jong spoke to the newcomer rapidly for about five minutes, evidently narrating all that they knew about me and giving instructions. When he had finished, the other motioned me to follow him; and a few moments later I found myself in another room on the same level. It had three large windows and was furnished with several desks, tables, and chairs. Most of the available wall space was taken up by shelves on which reposed what I could only assume to be books—thousands of them.

The ensuing three weeks were as delightful and interesting as any that I have ever experienced. During this time, Danus, in whose charge I had been placed, taught me the Venusian language and told me much concerning the planet, the people among whom I had fallen, and their history. I found the language easy to master, but I shall not at this time attempt to describe it fully. The alphabet consists of twenty-four characters, five of which represent vowel sounds, and these are the only vowel sounds that the Venusian vocal chords seem able to articulate. The characters of the alphabet all have the same value, there being no capital letters. Their system of punctuation differs from ours and is more practical; for example, before you start to read a sentence you know whether it is exclamatory, interrogative, a reply to an interrogation, or a simple statement. Characters having values similar to the comma and semicolon are used much as we use these two; they have no colon; their character that functions as does our period follows each sentence, their question mark and exclamation point preceding the sentences the nature of which they determine.

A peculiarity of their language that renders it easy to master is the absence of irregular verbs; the verb root is never altered for voice, mode, tense, number, or person, distinctions that are achieved by the use of several simple, auxiliary words.

While I was learning to speak the language of my hosts, I also learned to read and write it, and I spent many enjoyable hours delving into the large library of which Danus is the curator while my tutor was absent attending to his other duties, which are numerous. He is chief physician and surgeon of his country, physician and surgeon to the king, and head of a college of medicine and surgery.

One of the first questions that Danus had asked me when I had acquired a working knowledge of his language was where I came from, but when I told him I had come from another world more than twenty-six million miles from his familiar Amtor, which is the name by which the Venusians know their world, he shook his head sceptically.

"There is no life beyond Amtor," he said. "How can there be life where all is fire?"

"What is your theory of the—" I started, but I had to stop. There is no Amtorian word for universe, neither is there any for sun, moon, star, or planet. The gorgeous heavens that we see are never seen by the inhabitants of Venus, obscured as they perpetually are by the two great cloud envelopes that surround the planet. I started over again. "What do you believe surrounds Amtor?" I asked.

He stepped to a shelf and returned with a large volume, which he opened at a beautifully executed map of Amtor. It showed three concentric circles. Between the two inner circles lay a circular belt designated as Trabol, which means warm country. Here the boundaries of seas, continents, and islands were traced to the edges of the two circles that bounded it, in some places crossing these boundaries as though marking the spots at which venturesome explorers had dared the perils of an unknown and inhospitable land.

"This is Trabol," explained Danus, placing a finger upon that portion of the map I have briefly described. "It entirely surrounds Strabol which lies in the centre of Amtor. Strabol is extremely hot, its land is covered with enormous forests and dense undergrowth, and is peopled by huge land animals, reptiles, and birds, its warm seas swarm with monsters of the deep. No man has ventured far into Strabol and lived to return.

"Beyond Trabol," he continued, placing his finger on the outer band designated as Karbol (Cold Country), "lies Karbol. Here it is as cold as Strabol is hot. There are strange animals there too, and adventurers have returned with tales of fierce human beings clothed in fur. But it is an inhospitable land into which there is no occasion to venture and which few dare penetrate far for fear of being precipitated over the rim into the molten sea."

"Over what rim?" I asked.

He looked at me in astonishment. "I can well believe that you come from another world when you ask me such questions as you do," he remarked. "Do you mean to tell me that you know nothing of the physical structure of Amtor?"

"I know nothing of your theory concerning it," I replied.

"It is not a theory; it is a fact," he corrected me gently. "In no other way may the various phenomena of nature be explained. Amtor is a huge disc with an upturned rim, like a great saucer; it floats upon a sea of molten metal and rock, a fact that is incontrovertibly proved by the gushing forth of this liquid mass occasionally from the summits of mountains, when a hole has been burned in the bottom of Amtor. Karbol, the cold country, is a wise provision of nature that tempers the terrific heat that must constantly surge about the outer rim of Amtor.

"Above Amtor, and entirely surrounding her above the molten sea, is a chaos of fire and flame. From this our clouds protect us. Occasionally there have occurred rifts in the clouds, and at such times the heat from the fires above, when the rifts occurred in the daytime, has been so intense as to wither vegetation and destroy life, while the light that shone through was of blinding intensity. When these rifts occurred at night there was no heat, but we saw the sparks from the fire shining above us."

I tried to explain the spherical shape of the planets and that Karbol was only the colder country surrounding one of Amtor's poles, while Strabol, the hot country, lay in the equatorial region; that Trabol was merely one of two temperate zones, the other one being beyond the equatorial region, which was a band around the middle of a globe and not, as he supposed, a circular area in the centre of a disc. He listened to me politely, but only smiled and shook his head when I had finished.

At first I could not comprehend that a man of such evident intelligence, education, and culture should cling to such a belief as his, but when I stopped to consider the fact that neither he nor any of his progenitors had ever seen the heavens, I began to realize that there could not be much foundation for any other theory, and even theories must have foundations. I also realized, even more than I had before, something of what astronomy has meant to the human race of earth in the advancement of science and civilization. Could there have been such advancement had the heavens been perpetually hidden from our view? I wonder.

But I did not give up. I drew his attention to the fact that if his theory were correct, the boundary between Trabol and Strabol (the temperate and the equatorial zones) should be much shorter than that separating Trabol from Karbol, the polar region, as was shown on the map, but could not have been proved by actual survey; while my theory would require that the exact opposite be true, which was easily demonstrable and must have been demonstrated if surveys had ever been made, which I judged from the markings on the map to be the case.

He admitted that surveys had been made and that they had shown the apparent discrepancy that I had pointed out, but he explained this ingeniously by a purely Amtorian theory of the relativity of distance, which he proceeded to elucidate.

"A degree is one thousandth part of the circumference of a circle," he commenced. (This is the Amtorian degree, her savants not having had the advantage of a visible sun to suggest another division of the circumference of a circle as did the Babylonians, who hit upon three hundred sixty as being close enough.) "And no matter what the length of the circumference, it measures just one thousand degrees. The circle which separates Strabol from Trabol is necessarily one thousand degrees in length. You will admit that?"

"Certainly," I replied.

"Very good! Then, will you admit that the circle which separates Trabol from Karbol measures exactly one thousand degrees?"

I nodded my assent.

"Things which equal the same thing equal each other, do they not? Therefore, the inner and outer boundaries of Trabol are of equal length, and this is true because of the truth of the theory of relativity of distance. The degree is our unit of linear measure. It would be ridiculous to say that the farther one was removed from the centre of Amtor the longer the unit of distance became; it only appears to become longer; in relation to the circumference of the circle and in relation to the distance from the centre of Amtor it is precisely the same.

"I know," he admitted, "that on the map it does not appear to be the same, nor do actual surveys indicate that it is the same; but it must be the same, for if it were not, it is obvious that Amtor would be larger around the closer one approached the centre and smallest of all at the perimeter, which is so obviously ridiculous as to require no refutation.

"This seeming discrepancy caused the ancients considerable perturbation until about three thousand years ago, when Klufar, the great scientist, expounded the theory of relativity of distance and demonstrated that the real and apparent measurements of distance could be reconciled by multiplying each by the square root of minus one."

I saw that argument was useless and said no more; there is no use arguing with a man who can multiply anything by the square root of minus one.

## Chapter 5

# The Girl in the Garden

For some time I had been aware that I was in the house of Mintep, the king, and that the country was called Vepaja. Jong, which I had originally thought to be his name, was his title; it is Amtorian for king. I learned that Duran was of the house of Zar and that Olthar and Kamlot were his sons; Zuro, one of the women I had met there, was attached to Duran; the other, Alzo, was attached to Olthar; Kamlot had no woman. I use the word attached partially because it is a reasonably close translation of the Amtorian word for the connection and partially because no other word seems exactly to explain the relationship between these men and women.

They were not married, because the institution of marriage is unknown here. One could not say that they belonged to the men, because they were in no sense slaves or servants, nor had they been acquired by purchase or feat of arms. They had come willingly, following a courtship, and they were free to depart whenever they chose, just as the men were free to depart and seek other connections; but, as I was to learn later, these connections are seldom broken, while infidelity is as rare here as it is prevalent on earth.

Each day I took exercise on the broad veranda that encircled the tree at the level upon which my apartment was located; at least, I assumed that it encircled the tree, but I did not know, as that portion assigned to me was but a hundred feet long, a fifteenth part of the circumference of the great tree. At each end of my little segment was a fence. The section adjoining mine on the right appeared to be a garden, as it was a mass of flowers and shrubbery growing in soil that must have been brought up from that distant surface of the planet that I had as yet neither set foot upon nor seen. The section on my left extended in front of the quarters of several young officers attached to the household of the king. I call them young because Danus told me they were young, but they appear to be about the same age as all the other Amtorians I have seen. They were pleasant fellows, and after I learned to speak their language we occasionally had friendly chats together.

But in the section at my right I had never seen a human being; and then one day, when Danus was absent and I was walking alone, I saw a girl among the flowers there. She did not see me; and I only caught the briefest glimpse of her, but there was something about her that made me want to see her again, and thereafter I rather neglected the young officers on my left.

Though I haunted the end of my veranda next to the garden for several days, I did not again see the girl during all that time. The place seemed utterly deserted until one day I saw the figure of a man among the shrubbery. He was moving with great caution, creeping stealthily; and presently, behind him, I saw another and another, until I had counted five of them all together.

They were similar to the Vepajans, yet there was a difference. They appeared coarser, more brutal, than any of the men I had as yet seen; and in other ways they were dissimilar to Danus, Duran, Kamlot, and my other Venusian acquaintances. There was something menacing and sinister, too, in their silent, stealthy movements.

I wondered what they were doing there; and then I thought of the girl, and for some reason the conclusion was forced upon me that the presence of these men here had something to do with her, and that it boded her harm. Just in what way I could not even surmise, knowing so little of the people among whom fate had thrown me; but the impression was quite definite, and it excited me. Perhaps it rather overcame my better judgment, too, if my next act is any index to the matter.

Without thought of the consequences and in total ignorance of the identity of the men or the purpose for which they were in the garden, I vaulted the low fence and followed them. I made no noise. They had not seen me originally because I had been hidden from their view by a larger shrub that grew close to the fence that separated the garden from my veranda. It was through the foliage of this shrub that I had observed them, myself unobserved.

Moving cautiously but swiftly, I soon overtook the hindmost man and saw that the five were moving toward an open doorway beyond which, in a richly furnished apartment, I saw the girl who had aroused my curiosity and whose beautiful face had led me into this mad adventure. Almost simultaneously, the girl glanced up and saw the leading man at the doorway. She screamed, and then I knew that I had not come in vain.

Instantly I leaped upon the man in front of me, and as I did so I gave a great shout, hoping by that means to distract the attention of the other four from the girl to me, and in that I was wholly successful. The other four turned instantly. I had taken my man so completely by surprise that I was able to snatch his sword from its scabbard before he could recover his wits; and as he drew his dagger and struck at me, I ran his own blade through his heart; then the others were upon me.

Their faces were contorted by rage, and I could see that they would give me no quarter.

The narrow spaces between the shrubbery reduced the advantage which four men would ordinarily have had over a single antagonist, for they could attack me only singly; but I knew what the outcome must eventually be if help did not reach me, and as my only goal was to keep the men from the girl, I backed slowly toward the fence and my own veranda as I saw that all four of the men were following me.

My shout and the girl's scream had attracted attention; and presently I heard men running in the apartment in which I had seen the girl, and her voice directing them toward the garden. I hoped they would come before the fellows had backed me against the wall, where I was confident that I must go down in defeat beneath four swords wielded by men more accustomed to them than I. I thanked the good fortune, however, that had led me to take up fencing seriously in Germany, for it was helping me now, though I could not long hold out against these men with the Venusian sword which was a new weapon to me.

I had reached the fence at last and was fighting with my back toward it. The fellow facing me was cutting viciously at me. I could hear the men coming from the apartment. Could I hold out? Then my opponent swung a terrific cut at my head, and, instead of parrying it, I leaped to one side and simultaneously stepped in and cut at him. His own swing had carried him off balance, and, of course, his guard was down. My blade cut deep into his neck, severing his jugular. From behind him another man was rushing upon me.

Relief was coming. The girl was safe. I could accomplish no more by remaining there and being cut to pieces, a fate I had only narrowly averted in the past few seconds. I hurled my sword, point first, at the oncoming Venusian; and as it tore into his breast I turned and vaulted the fence into my own veranda.

Then, as I looked back, I saw a dozen Vepajan warriors overwhelm the two remaining intruders, butchering them like cattle. There was no shouting and no sound other than the brief clash of swords as the two sought desperately but futilely to defend themselves. The Vepajans spoke no word. They seemed shocked and terrified, though their terror had most certainly not been the result of any fear of their late antagonists. There was something else which I did not understand, something mysterious in their manner, their silence, and their actions immediately following the encounter.

Quickly they seized the bodies of the five strange warriors that had been killed and, carrying them to the outer garden wall, hurled them over into that bottomless abyss of the forest the terrific depths of which my eyes had never been able to plumb. Then, in equal silence, they departed from the garden by the same path by which they had entered it.

I realized that they had not seen me, and I knew that the girl had not. I wondered a little how they accounted for the deaths of the three men I had disposed of, but I never learned. The whole affair was a mystery to me and was only explained long after in the light of ensuing events.

I thought that Danus might mention it and thus give me an opportunity to question him; but he never did, and something kept me from broaching the subject to him, modesty perhaps. In other respects, however, my curiosity concerning these people was insatiable; and I fear that I bored Danus to the verge of distraction with my incessant questioning, but I excused myself on the plea that I could only learn the language by speaking it and hearing it spoken; and Danus, that most delightful of men, insisted that it was not only a pleasure to inform me but his duty as well, the jong having requested him to inform me fully concerning the life, customs, and history of the Vepajans.

One of the many things that puzzled me was why such an intelligent and cultured people should be living in trees, apparently without servants or slaves and with no intercourse, as far as I had been able to discover, with other peoples; so one evening I asked him.

"It is a long story," replied Danus; "much of it you will find in the histories here upon my shelves, but I can give you a brief outline that will at least answer your question.

"Hundreds of years ago the kings of Vepaja ruled a great country. It was not this forest island where you now find us, but a broad empire that embraced a thousand islands and extended from Strabol to Karbol; it included broad land masses and great oceans; it was graced by mighty cities and boasted a wealth and commerce unsurpassed through all the centuries before or since.

"The people of Vepaja in those days were numbered in the millions; there were millions of merchants and millions of wage earners and millions of slaves, and there was a smaller class of brain workers. This class included the learned professions of science, medicine, and law, of letters and the creative arts. The military leaders were selected from all classes. Over all was the hereditary jong.

"The lines between the classes were neither definitely nor strictly drawn; a slave might become a free man, a free man might become anything he chose within the limits of his ability, short of jong. In social intercourse the four principal classes did not intermingle with each other, due to the fact that members of one class had little in common with members of the other classes and not through any feeling of superiority or inferiority. When a member of a lower class had won by virtue of culture, learning, or genius to a position in a higher class, he was received upon an equal footing, and no thought was given to his antecedents.

"Vepaja was prosperous and happy, yet there were malcontents. These were the lazy and incompetent. Many of them were of the criminal class. They were envious of those who had won to positions which they were not mentally equipped to attain. Over a long period of time they were responsible for minor discord and dissension, but the people either paid no attention to them or laughed them down. Then they found a leader. He was a labourer named Thor, a man with a criminal record.

"This man founded a secret order known as Thorists and preached a gospel of class hatred called Thorism. By means of lying propaganda he gained a large following, and as all his energies were directed against a single class, he had all the vast millions of the other three classes to draw from, though naturally he found few converts among the merchants and employers which also included the agrarian class.

"The sole end of the Thorist leaders was personal power and aggrandizement; their aims were wholly selfish, yet, because they worked solely among the ignorant masses, they had little difficulty in deceiving their dupes, who finally rose under their false leaders in a bloody revolution that sounded the doom of the civilization and advancement of a world.

"Their purpose was the absolute destruction of the cultured class. Those of the other classes who opposed them were to be subjugated or destroyed; the jong and his family were to be killed. These things accomplished, the people would enjoy absolute freedom; there would be no masters, no taxes, no laws.

They succeeded in killing most of us and a large proportion of the merchant class; then the people discovered what the agitators already knew, that some one must rule, and the leaders of Thorism were ready to take over the reins of government. The people had exchanged the beneficent rule of an experienced and cultured class for that of greedy incompetents and theorists.

Now they are all reduced to virtual slavery. An army of spies watches over them, and an army of warriors keeps them from turning against their masters; they are miserable, helpless, and hopeless.

Those of us who escaped with our jong sought out this distant, uninhabited island. Here we constructed tree cities, such as this, far above the ground, from which they cannot be seen. We brought our culture with us and little else; but our wants are few, and we are happy. We would not return to the old system if we might. We have learned our lesson, that a people divided amongst themselves cannot be happy. Where there are even slight class distinctions there are envy and jealousy. Here there are none; we are all of the same class.

We have no servants; whatever there is to do we do better than servants ever did it. Even those who serve the jong are not servants in the sense that they are menials, for their positions are considered posts of honour, and the greatest among us take turns in filling them."

"But I still do not understand why you choose to live in trees, far above the ground," I said.

"For years the Thorists hunted us down to kill us," he explained, "and we were forced to live in hidden, inaccessible places; this type of city was the solution of our problem. The Thorists still hunt us; and there are still occasional raids, but now they are for a very different purpose. Instead of wishing to kill us, they now wish to capture as many of us as they can.

"Having killed or driven away the brains of the nation, their civilization has deteriorated, disease is making frightful inroads upon them which they are unable to check, old age has reappeared and is taking its toll; so they seek to capture the brains and the skill and the knowledge which they have been unable to produce and which we alone possess."

"Old age is reappearing! What do you mean?" I asked.

"Have you not noticed that there are no signs of old age among us?" he inquired.

"Yes, of course," I replied, "nor any children. I have often meant to ask you for an explanation."

"These are not natural phenomena," he assured me; "they are the crowning achievements of medical science. A thousand years ago the serum of longevity was perfected. It is injected every two years and not only provides immunity from all diseases but insures the complete restoration of all wasted tissue.

"But even in good there is evil. As none grew old and none died, except those who met with violent deaths, we were faced with the grave dangers of overpopulation. To combat this, birth control became obligatory. Children are permitted now only in sufficient numbers to replace actual losses in population. If a member of a house is killed, a woman of that house is permitted to bear a child, if she can; but after generations of childlessness there is a constantly decreasing number of women who are capable of bearing children. This situation we have met by anticipating it.

"Statistics compiled over a period of a thousand years indicate the average death rate expectancy per thousand people; they have also demonstrated that only fifty per cent of our women are capable of bearing children; therefore, fifty per cent of the required children are permitted yearly to those who wish them, in the order in which their applications are filed."

"I have not seen a child since I arrived in Amtor," I told him.

"There are children here," he replied, "but, of course, not many."

"And no old people," I mused. "Could you administer that serum to me, Danus?"

He smiled. "With Mintep's permission, which I imagine will not be difficult to obtain. Come," he added, "I'll take some blood tests now to determine the type and attenuation of serum best adapted to your requirements." He motioned me into his laboratory.

When he had completed the tests, which he accomplished with ease and rapidity, he was shocked by the variety and nature of malignant bacteria they revealed.

"You are a menace to the continued existence of human life on Amtor," he exclaimed with a laugh.

"I am considered a very healthy man in my own world," I assured him.

"How old are you?" he asked.

"Twenty-seven."

"You would not be so healthy two hundred years from now if all those bacteria were permitted to have their way with you."

"How old might I live to be if they were eradicated?" I asked.

He shrugged. "We do not know. The serum was perfected a thousand years ago. There are people among us today who were of the first to receive injections. I am over five hundred years old; Mintep is seven hundred. We believe that, barring accidents, we shall live forever; but, of course, we do not know. Theoretically, we should."

He was called away at this juncture; and I went out on the veranda to take my exercise, of which I have found that I require a great deal, having always been athletically inclined. Swimming, boxing, and wrestling had strengthened and developed my muscles since I had returned to America with my mother when I was eleven, and I became interested in fencing while I was travelling in Europe after she died. During my college days I was amateur middle-weight boxer of California, and I captured several medals for distance swimming; so the enforced inactivity of the past two months had galled me considerably. Toward the end of my college days I had grown into the heavy-weight class, but that had been due to an increase of healthy bone and sinew; now I was at least twenty pounds heavier and that twenty pounds was all fat.

On my one hundred feet of veranda I did the best I could to reduce. I ran miles, I shadow boxed, I skipped rope, and I spent hours with the old seventeen setting-up exercises of drill regulations. Today I was shadow boxing near the right end of my veranda when I suddenly discovered the girl in the garden observing me. As our eyes met I halted in my tracks and smiled at her. A frightened look came into her eyes, and she turned and fled. I wondered why.

Puzzled, I walked slowly back toward my apartment, my exercises forgotten. This time I had seen the girl's full face, looked her squarely in the eyes, and I had been absolutely dumfounded by her beauty. Every man and woman I had seen since I had come to Venus had been beautiful; I had come to expect that. But I had not expected to see in this or any other world such indescribable perfection of colouring and features, combined with character and intelligence, as that which I had just seen in the garden beyond my little fence. But why had she run away when I smiled?

Possibly she had run away merely because she had been discovered watching me for, after all, human nature is about the same everywhere. Even twenty-six million miles from earth there are human beings like ourselves and a girl, with quite human curiosity, who runs away when she is discovered. I wondered if she resembled earthly girls in other respects, but she seemed too beautiful to be just like anything on earth or in heaven. Was she young or old? Suppose she were seven hundred years old!

I went to my apartment and prepared to bathe and change my loincloth; I had long since adopted the apparel of Amtor. As I glanced in a mirror that hangs in my bathroom I suddenly understood why the girl may have looked frightened and run away—my beard! It was nearly a month old now and might easily have frightened anyone who had never before seen a beard.

When Danus returned I asked him what I could do about it. He stepped into another room and returned with a bottle of salve.

"Rub this into the roots of the hair on your face," he directed, "but be careful not to get it on your eyebrows, lashes, or the hair on your head. Leave it there a minute and then wash your face."

I stepped into my bathroom and opened the jar; its contents looked like Vaseline and smelled like the devil, but I rubbed it into the roots of my beard as Danus had directed. When I washed my face a moment later my beard came off, leaving my face smooth and hairless. I hurried back to the room where I had left Danus.

"You are quite handsome after all," he remarked. "Do all the people of this fabulous world of which you have told me have hair growing on their faces?"

"Nearly all," I replied, "but in my country the majority of men keep it shaved off."

"I should think the women would be the ones to shave," he commented. "A woman with hair on her face would be quite repulsive to an Amtorian."

"But our women do not have hair on their faces," I assured him.

"And the men do! A fabulous world indeed."

"But if Amtorians do not grow beards, what was the need of this salve that you gave me?" I asked.

"It was perfected as an aid to surgery," he explained. "In treating scalp wounds and in craniectomies it is necessary to remove the hair from about the wound. This unguent serves the purpose better than shaving and also retards the growth of new hair for a longer time."

"But the hair will grow out again?" I asked.

"Yes, if you do not apply the unguent too frequently," he replied.

"How frequently?" I demanded.

"Use it every day for six days and the hair will never again grow on your face. We used to use it on the heads of confirmed criminals. Whenever one saw a bald-headed man or a man wearing a wig he watched his valuables."

"In my country when one sees a bald-headed man," I said, "he watches his girls. And that reminds me; I have seen a beautiful girl in a garden just to the right of us here. Who is she?"

"She is one whom you are not supposed to see," he replied. "Were I you, I should not again mention the fact that you have seen her. Did she see you?"

"She saw me," I replied.

"What did she do?" His tone was serious.

"She appeared frightened and ran."

"Perhaps you had best keep away from that end of the veranda," he suggested.

There was that in his manner which precluded questions, and I did not pursue the subject further. Here was a mystery, the first suggestion of mystery that I had encountered in the life of Vepaja, and naturally it piqued my curiosity. Why should I not look at the girl? I had looked at other women without incurring displeasure. Was it only this particular girl upon whom I must not look, or were there other girls equally sacrosanct? It occurred to me that she might be a priestess of some holy order, but I was forced to discard that theory because of my belief that these people had no religion, at least none that I could discover in my talks with Danus. I had attempted to describe some of our earthly religious beliefs to him, but he simply could not perceive either their purpose or meaning any more than he could visualize the solar system of the universe.

Having once seen the girl, I was anxious to see her again; and now that the thing was proscribed, I was infinitely more desirous than ever to look upon her divine loveliness and to speak with her. I had not promised Danus that I would heed his suggestions, for I was determined to ignore them should the opportunity arise,

I was commencing to tire of the virtual imprisonment that had been my lot ever since my advent upon Amtor, for even a kindly jailer and a benign prison regime are not satisfactory substitutes for freedom. I had asked Danus what my status was and what they planned for me in the future, but he had evaded a more direct answer by saying that I was the guest of Mintep, the jong, and that my future would be a matter of discussion when Mintep granted me an audience.

Suddenly now I felt more than before the restrictions of my situation, and they galled me. I had committed no crime. I was a peaceful visitor to Vepaja. I had neither the desire nor the power to harm anyone. These considerations decided me. I determined to force the issue.

A few minutes ago I had been contented with my lot, willing to wait the pleasure of my hosts; now I was discontented. What had induced this sudden change? Could it be the mysterious alchemy of personality that had transmuted the lead of lethargy to the gold of ambitious desire? Had the aura of a vision of feminine loveliness thus instantly reversed my outlook upon life?

I turned toward Danus. "You have been very kind to me," I said, "and my days here have been happy, but I am of a race of people who desire freedom above all things. As I have explained to you, I am here through no intentional fault of my own; but I am here, and being here I expect the same treatment that would be accorded you were you to visit my country under similar circumstances."

"And what treatment would that be?" he asked.

"The right to life, liberty, and the pursuit of happiness—freedom," I explained. I did not think it necessary to mention chambers of commerce dinners, Rotary and Kiwanis luncheons, triumphal parades and ticker tape, keys to cities, press representatives and photographers, nor news reel cameramen, the price that he would undoubtedly have had to pay for life, liberty, and the pursuit of happiness.

"But, my dear friend, one would think from your words that you are a prisoner here!" he exclaimed.

"I am, Danus," I replied, "and none knows it better than you."

He shrugged. "I am sorry that you feel that way about it, Carson."

"How much longer is it going to last?" I demanded.

"The jong is the jong," he replied. "He will send for you in his own time; until then, let us continue the friendly relations that have marked our association up to now."

"I hope they will never be changed, Danus," I told him, "but you may tell Mintep, if you will, that I cannot accept his hospitality much longer; if he does not send for me soon, I shall leave on my own accord."

"Do not attempt that, my friend," he warned me.

"And why not?"

"You would not live to take a dozen steps from the apartments that have been assigned you," he assured me seriously.

"Who would stop me?"

"There are warriors posted in the corridors," he explained; "they have their orders from the jong."

"And yet I am not a prisoner!" I exclaimed with a bitter laugh.

"I am sorry that you raised the question," he said, "as otherwise you might never have known."

Here indeed was the iron hand in the velvet glove I hoped it was not wielded by a wolf in sheep's clothing. My position was not an enviable one. Even had I the means to escape, there was no place that I could go. But I did not want to leave Vepaja—I had seen the girl in the garden.

## Chapter 6

# Gathering Tarel

A week passed, a week during which I permanently discarded my reddish whiskers and received an injection of the longevity serum. The latter event suggested that possibly Mintep would eventually liberate me, for why bestow immortality upon a potential enemy who is one's prisoner; but then I knew that the serum did not confer absolute immortality—Mintep could have me destroyed if he wished, by which thought was suggested the possibility that the serum had been administered for the purpose of lulling me into a sense of security which I did not, in reality, enjoy. I was becoming suspicious.

While Danus was injecting the serum, I asked him if there were many doctors in Vepaja.

"Not so many in proportion to the population as there were a thousand years ago," he replied.

"All the people are now trained in the care of their bodies and taught the essentials of health and longevity. Even without the serums we use to maintain resistance to disease constantly in the human body, our people would live to great ages. Sanitation, diet, and exercise can accomplish wonders by themselves.

"But we must have some doctors. Their numbers are limited now to about one to each five thousand citizens, and in addition to administering the serum, the doctors attend those who are injured by the accidents of daily life, in the hunt, and in duels and war.

"Formerly there were many more doctors than could eke out an honest living, but now there are various agencies that restrict their numbers. Not only is there a law restricting these, but the ten years of study required, the long apprenticeship thereafter, and the difficult examinations that must be passed have all tended to reduce the numbers who seek to follow this profession; but another factor probably achieved more than all else to rapidly reduce the great number of doctors that threatened the continuance of human life on Amtor in the past.

"This was a regulation that compelled every physician and surgeon to file a complete history of each of his cases with the chief medical officer of his district. From diagnosis to complete recovery or death, each detail of the handling of each case had to be recorded and placed on record for the public to consult. When a citizen requires the services of a physician or surgeon now, he may easily determine those who have been successful and those who have not. Fortunately, today there are few of the latter. The law has proved a good one."

This was interesting, for I had had experience with physicians and surgeons on earth. "How many doctors survived the operation of this new law?" I asked.

"About two per cent," he replied.

"There must have been a larger proportion of good doctors on Amtor than on earth," I commented.

Time hung heavily upon my hands. I read a great deal, but an active young man cannot satisfy all his varied life interests with books alone. And then there was the garden at my right. I had been advised to avoid that end of my veranda, but I did not, at least not when Danus was absent. When he was away I haunted that end of the veranda, but it seemed deserted. And then one day I caught a glimpse of her; she was watching me from behind a flowering shrub.

I was close to the fence that separated my runway from her garden; it was not a high fence, perhaps slightly under five feet. She did not run this time, but stood looking straight at me, possibly thinking that I could not see her because of the intervening foliage. I could not see her plainly enough, that is true; and, God, how I wanted to see her!

What is that inexplicable, subtle attraction that some woman holds for every man? For some men there is only one woman in the world who exercises this influence upon him, or perhaps if there are more, the others do not cross his path; for other men there are several; for some none. For me there was this girl of an alien race, upon an alien planet. Perhaps there were others, but if there were, I had never met them. In all my life before I had never been moved by such an irresistible urge. What I did, I did upon the strength of an impulse as uncontrollable as a law of nature; perhaps it was a law of nature that motivated me. I vaulted the fence.

Before the girl could escape me, I stood before her. There were consternation and horror in her eyes. I thought that she was afraid of me.

"Do not be afraid," I said; "I have not come to harm you, only to speak to you."

She drew herself up proudly. "I am not afraid of you," she said; "I—," she hesitated and then started over. "If you are seen here you will be destroyed. Go back to your quarters at once and never dare such a rash act again."

I thrilled to the thought that the fear that I had seen so clearly reflected in her eyes was for my safety. "How may I see you?" I asked.

"You may never see me," she replied.

"But I have seen you, and I intend seeing you again. I am going to see a lot of you, or die in the attempt."

"Either you do not know what you are doing or you are mad," she said and turned her back on me as she started to walk away.

I seized her arm. "Wait," I begged.

She wheeled on me like a tigress and slapped my face, and then she whipped the dagger from the scabbard at her girdle. "How dare you," she cried, "lay a hand upon me! I should kill you."

"Why don't you?" I asked.

"I loathe you," she said, and it sounded as though she meant it.

"I love you," I replied, and I knew that I spoke the truth.

At that declaration her eyes did indeed reflect horror. She wheeled then so quickly that I could not stop her and was gone. I stood for a moment, debating whether I should follow her or not, and then a modicum of reason intervened to save me from such an assininity. An instant later I had vaulted the fence again. I did not know whether anyone had seen me or not, and I did not care.

When Danus returned a short time later, he told me that Mintep had sent him for me. I wondered if the summons was in any way related to my adventure in the garden at the right, but I did not inquire. If it were, I should know in due time. The attitude of Danus was unchanged, but that no longer reassured me. I was beginning to suspect that the Amtorians were masters of dissimulation.

Two young officers from the quarters adjoining mine accompanied us to the chamber where the jong was to question me. Whether or not they were acting as an escort to prevent my escape I could not tell. They chatted pleasantly with me during the short walk along the corridor and up the staircase to the level above; but then the guards usually chat pleasantly with the condemned man, if he feels like chatting. They accompanied me into the room where the jong sat. This time he was not alone; there were a number of men gathered about him, and among these I recognized Duran, Olthar, and Kamlot. For some reason the assemblage reminded me of a grand jury, and I could not help but wonder if they were going to return a true bill.

I bowed to the jong, who greeted me quite pleasantly enough, and smiled and nodded to the three men in whose home I had spent my first night on Venus. Mintep looked me over in silence for a moment or two; when he had seen me before I had been dressed in my earthly clothes, now I was garbed (or ungarbed) like a Vepajan.

"Your skin is not as light in colour as I thought it," he commented.

"Exposure to light on the veranda has darkened it," I replied. I could not say sunlight, because they have no word for sun, of the existence of which they do not dream. However, such was the case, the ultra violet rays of sunlight having penetrated the cloud envelopes surrounding the planet and tanned my body quite as effectively as would exposure to the direct rays of the sun have done.

"You have been quite happy here, I trust," he said.

"I have been treated with kindness and consideration," I replied, "and have been quite as happy as any prisoner could reasonably be expected to be."

The shadow of a smile touched his lips. "You are candid," he commented.

"Candor is a characteristic of the country from which I come," I replied.

"However, I do not like the word prisoner," he said.

"Neither do I, jong, but I like the truth. I have been a prisoner, and I have been awaiting this opportunity to ask you why I am a prisoner and to demand my freedom."

He raised his eyebrows; then he smiled quite openly. "I think that I am going to like you," he said; "you are honest and you are courageous, or I am no judge of men."

I inclined my head in acknowledgment of the compliment. I had not expected that he would receive my blunt demand in a spirit of such generous understanding; but I was not entirely relieved, for experience had taught me that these people could be very suave while being most uncompromising.

"There are some things that I wish to tell you and some questions that I wish to ask you," he continued. "We are still beset by our enemies, who yet send occasional raiding parties against us, who upon numerous occasions have sought to introduce their spies among us. We have three things that they require if they are not to suffer extinction: scientific knowledge, and the brains and experience to apply it Therefore they go to any lengths to abduct our men, whom they purpose holding in slavery and forcing to apply the knowledge that they themselves do not have. They also abduct our women in the hope of breeding children of greater mentality than those which are now born to them.

"The story that you told of crossing millions of miles of space from another world is, of course, preposterous and naturally aroused our suspicions. We saw in you another Thorist spy, cleverly disguised. For this reason you have been under the careful and intelligent observation of Danus for many days. He reports that there is no doubt but that you were totally ignorant of the Amtorian language when you came among us, and as this is the only language spoken by any of the known races of the world, we have come to the conclusion that your story may be, in part, true. The fact that your skin, hair, and eyes differ in colour from those of any known race is further substantiation of this conclusion. Therefore, we are willing to admit that you are not a Thorist, but the questions remain: who are you, and from whence came you?"

"I have told only the truth," I replied; "I have nothing to add other than to suggest that you carefully consider the fact that the cloud masses surrounding Amtor completely obscure your view and therefore your knowledge of what lies beyond."

He shook his head. "Let us not discuss it; it is useless to attempt to overthrow the accumulated scientific research and knowledge of thousands of years. We are willing to accept you as of another race, perhaps, as was suggested by the clothing you wore upon your arrival, from cold and dreary Karbol. You are free to come and go as you please. If you remain, you must abide by the laws and customs of Vepaja, and you must become self-supporting. What can you do?"

"I doubt that I can compete with Vepajans at their own trades or professions," I admitted, "but I can learn something if I am given time."

"Perhaps we can find some one who will undertake your training," said the jong, "and in the meantime you may remain in my house, assisting Danus."

"We will take him into our house and train him," spoke up Duran, "if he cares to help us collect tarel and hunt"

Tarel is the strong, silky fibber from which their cloth and cordage are made. I imagined that collecting it would be tame and monotonous work, but the idea of hunting appealed to me. In no event, however, could I ignore Duran's well-meant invitation, as I did not wish to offend him, and, furthermore, anything would be acceptable that would provide the means whereby I might become self-supporting. I therefore accepted his offer, and, the audience being concluded, I bid goodbye to Danus, who invited me to visit him often, and withdrew with Duran, Olthar, and Kamlot.

As no mention had been made of the subject, I concluded that no one had witnessed my encounter with the girl in the garden, who was still uppermost in my thoughts and the principal cause of my regret that I was to leave the house of the jong.

Once more I was established in the house of Duran, but this time in a larger and more comfortable room. Kamlot took charge of me. He was the younger of the brothers, a quiet, reserved man with the muscular development of a trained athlete. After he had shown me my room, he took me to another apartment, a miniature armoury, in which were many spears, swords, daggers, bows, shields, and almost countless arrows. Before a window was a long bench with racks in which were tools of various descriptions; above the bench were shelves upon which were stacked the raw materials for the manufacture of bows, arrows, and spear shafts. Near the bench were a forge and anvil, and there were sheets and rods and ingots of metal stored near by.

"Have you ever used a sword?" he asked as he selected one for me.

"Yes, but for exercise only," I replied; "in my country we have perfected weapons that render a sword useless in combat."

He asked me about these weapons and was much interested in my description of earthly firearms. "We have a similar weapon on Amtor," he said. "We of Vepaja do not possess them, because the sole supply of the material with which they are charged lies in the heart of the Thorist country. When the weapons are made they are charged with an element that emits a ray of extremely short wave length that is destructive of animal tissue, but the element only emits these rays when exposed to the radiation of another rare element. There are several metals that are impervious to these rays. Those shields that you see hanging on the walls, the ones that are metal covered, are ample protection from them. A small shutter of similar metal is used in the weapon to separate the two elements; when this shutter is raised and one element is exposed to the emanations of the other, the destructive R-ray is released and passes along the bore of the weapon toward the target at which the latter has been aimed.

"My people invented and perfected this weapon," he added ruefully, "and now it has been turned against us; but we get along very well with what we have, as long as we remain in our trees."

"In addition to a sword and dagger, you will need a bow, arrows, and a spear," and as he enumerated them he selected the various articles for me, the last of which was really a short heavy javelin. A swivelled ring was attached to the end of the shaft of this weapon, and attached to the ring was a long, slender cord with a hand loop at its extremity. This cord, which was no heavier than ordinary wrapping twine, Kamlot coiled in a peculiar way and tucked into a small opening in the side of the shaft.

"What is the purpose of that cord?" I asked, examining the weapon.

"We hunt high in the trees," he replied, "and if it were not for the cord we should lose many spears."

"But that cord is not heavy enough for that, is it?" I asked.

"It is of tarel," he replied, "and could support the weight of ten men. You will learn much of the properties and value of tarel before you have been with us long. Tomorrow we shall go out together and gather some. It has been rather scarce of late."

At the evening meal that day I met Zuro and Alzo again, and they were most gracious to me. In the evening they all joined in teaching me the favourite Vepajan game, tork, which is played with pieces that are much like those used in mah jong and bears a startling resemblance to poker.

I slept well that night in my new quarters and when daylight broke I arose, for Kamlot had warned me that we should start early upon our expedition. I cannot say that I looked forward with any considerable degree of enthusiasm to spending the day gathering tarel. The climate of Vepaja is warm and sultry, and I pictured the adventure as being about as monotonous and disagreeable as picking cotton in Imperial Valley.

After a light breakfast, which I helped Kamlot prepare, he told me to get my weapons. "You should always wear your sword and dagger," he added.

"Even in the house?" I asked.

"Always, wherever you are," he replied. "It is not only a custom, but it is the law. We never know when we may be called upon to defend ourselves, our houses, or our jong."

"Those are all that I need bring, I suppose," I remarked as I was leaving the room.

"Bring your spear, of course; we are going to gather tarel," he replied.

Why I should need a spear to gather tarel I could not imagine; but I brought all the weapons that he had mentioned, and when I returned he handed me a bag with a strap that went around my neck to support it at my back.

"Is this for the tarel?" I asked.

He replied that it was.

"You do not expect to gather much," I remarked.

"We may not get any," he replied. "If we get a bagful between us we may do some tall boasting when we return."

I said no more, thinking it best to learn by experience rather than to be continually revealing my lamentable ignorance. If tarel were as scarce as his statement suggested, I should not have much picking to do, and that suited me perfectly. I am not lazy, but I like work that keeps my mind on the alert.

When we were both ready, Kamlot led the way upstairs, a procedure which mystified me, it did not tempt me into asking any more questions. We passed the two upper levels of the house and entered a dark, spiral staircase that led still farther upward into the tree. We ascended this for about fifteen feet, when Kamlot halted and I heard him fumbling with something above me.

Presently the shaft was bathed with light, which I saw came through a small circular opening that had been closed with a stout door. Through this opening Kamlot crawled, and I followed him, to find myself on a limb of the tree. My companion closed and locked the door, using a small key. I now saw that the door was covered on the outside with bark, so that when it was closed it would have been difficult for anyone to have detected it.

With almost monkey like agility, Kamlot ascended, while I, resembling anything but a monkey in this respect, followed, thankful for the lesser gravitational pull of Venus, however little less than that of earth it might be, for I am not naturally arboreal.

After ascending about a hundred feet, Kamlot crossed to an adjacent tree, the branches of which interlocked with those of the one we had been ascending, and again the upward climb commenced. Occasionally the Vepajan stopped to listen as we passed from tree to tree or clambered to higher levels. After we had travelled for an hour or more, he stopped again and waited until I had overtaken him. A finger on his lips enjoined me to silence.

"Tarel," he whispered, pointing through the foliage in the direction of an adjacent tree.

I wondered why he had to whisper it, as my eyes followed the direction of his index finger. Twenty feet away I saw what appeared to be a huge spider web, partially concealed by the intervening foliage.

"Be ready with your spear," whispered Kamlot. "Put your hand through the loop. Follow me, but not too closely; you may need room to cast your spear. Do you see him?"

"No," I admitted. I saw nothing but the suggestion of a spider web; what else I was supposed to see I did not know.

"Neither do I, but he may be hiding. Look up occasionally so that he can't take you by surprise from above."

This was more exciting than picking cotton in Imperial Valley, though as yet I did not know just what there was to be excited about. Kamlot did not appear excited; he was very cool, but he was cautious. Slowly he crept toward the great web, his javelin ready in his hand; and I followed. When we were in full sight of it we saw that it was empty. Kamlot drew his dagger.

"Start cutting it away," he said. "Cut close to the branches and follow the web around; I will cut in the other direction until we meet. Be careful that you do not get enmeshed in it, especially if he happens to return."

"Can't we go around it?" I asked.

Kamlot looked puzzled. "Why should we go around it?" he demanded, a little shortly I thought.

"To get the tarel" I replied.

"What do you suppose this is?" he demanded.

"A spider's web."

"It is tarel."

I subsided. I had thought that the tarel he pointed at was beyond the web, although I had seen nothing; but then of course I had not known what tarel was or what it looked like. We had been cutting away for a few minutes when I heard a noise in a tree near us. Kamlot heard it at the same time.

"He is coming," he said. "Be ready!" He slipped his dagger into its sheath and grasped his spear. I followed his example.

The sound stopped, but I could see nothing through the foliage. Presently there was a rustling among the foliage, and a face appeared some fifteen yards from us. It was a hideous face—the face of a spider tremendously enlarged. When the thing saw that we had discovered it, it emitted the most frightful scream I had ever heard save once before. Then I recognized them—the voice and the face. It had been a creature such as this that had pursued my pursuer the night that I had dropped to the causeway in front of the house of Duran.

"Be ready," cautioned Kamlot; "he will charge."

The words had scarcely crossed the lips of the Vepajan when the hideous creature rushed toward us. Its body and legs were covered with long, black hair, and there was a yellow spot the size of a saucer above each eye. It screamed horribly as it came, as though to paralyze us with terror.

Kamlot's spear hand flew back and forward, and the heavy javelin, rushing to meet the maddened creature, buried itself deeply in the repulsive carcass; but it did not stop the charge. The creature was making straight for Kamlot as I hurled my javelin, which struck it in the side; but even this did not stop it, and to my horror I saw it seize my companion as he fell back upon the great limb upon which he had stood, with the spider on top of him.

The footing was secure enough for Kamlot and the spider, for they were both accustomed to it, but to me it seemed very precarious. Of course the tree limbs were enormous and often the branches were laced together, yet I felt anything but secure. However, I had no time to think of that now. If not already dead, Kamlot was being killed. Drawing my sword, I leaped to the side of the huge arachnid and struck viciously at its head, whereupon it abandoned Kamlot and turned upon me; but it was badly wounded now and moved with difficulty.

As I struck at that hideous face, I was horrified to see that Kamlot lay as though dead. He did not move. But I had only time for that single brief glance. If I were not careful I, too, should soon be dead. The thing confronting me seemed endowed with unsapable vitality. It was oozing sticky blood from several wounds, at least two of which I thought should have been almost instantly lethal; yet still it struggled to reach me with the powerful claws that terminated its forelegs, that it might draw me to those hideous jaws.

The Vepajan blade is a keen, two-edged affair, a little wider and thicker near the point than at the haft, and, while not well balanced to my way of thinking, is a deadly cutting weapon. I found it so in this my first experience with it, for as a great claw reached out to seize me I severed it with a single blow. At this the creature screamed more horribly than ever, and with its last remaining vitality sprang upon me as you have seen spiders spring upon their prey. I cut at it again as I stepped back; and then thrust my point directly into that hideous visage, as the weight of the creature overbore me and I went down beneath it.

As it crashed upon me, my body toppled from the great branch upon which I had been standing, and I felt myself falling. Fortunately, the interlacing, smaller branches gave me some support; I caught at them and checked my fall, bringing up upon a broad, flat limb ten or fifteen feet below. I had clung to my sword, and being unhurt, clambered back as quickly as I could to save Kamlot from further attack, but he needed no protection—the great targo, as the creature is called, was dead.

Dead also was Kamlot; I could find no pulse nor detect any beating of the heart. My own sank within my breast. I had lost a friend, I who had so few here, and I was as utterly lost as one may be. I knew that I could not retrace our steps to the Vepajan city even though my life depended upon my ability to do so, as it doubtless did. I could descend, but whether I was still over the city or not I did not know; I doubted it.

So this was gathering tarel; this was the occupation that I had feared would bore me with its monotony!

## Chapter 7

# By Kamlot's Grave

Having set out to gather tarel I finished the work that Kamlot and I had nearly completed when the targo attacked us; if I succeeded in finding the city, I should at least bring something to show for our efforts. But what about Kamlot? The idea of leaving the body here was repugnant to me. Even in the brief association I had had with the man I had come to like him and to look upon him as my friend. His people had befriended me; the least that I could do would be to take his body back to them. I realized, of course, that that was going to be something of a job, but it must be done. Fortunately, I am extraordinarily muscular, and then, too, the gravitational pull of Venus favoured me more than would that of earth, giving me an advantage of over twenty pounds in the dead weight I should have to carry and even a little better than that in the amount of my own live weight, for I am heavier than Kamlot.

With less difficulty than I had anticipated I succeeded in getting Kamlot's body onto my back and trussed there with the cord attached to his javelin. I had previously strapped his weapons to him with strands of the tare that half filled my bag, for, being unfamiliar with all the customs of the country, I did not know precisely what would be expected of me in an emergency of this nature, and preferred to be on the safe side.

The experiences of the next ten or twelve hours are a nightmare that I should like to forget. Contact with the dead and naked body of my companion was sufficiently gruesome, but the sense of utter bewilderment and futility in this strange world was even more depressing. As the hours passed, during which I constantly descended, except for brief rests, the weight of the corpse seemed to increase. In life Kamlot would have weighed about one hundred eighty pounds on earth, nearly one hundred sixty on Venus, but by the time darkness enveloped the gloomy forest I could have sworn that he weighed a ton.

So fatigued was I that I had to move very slowly, testing each new hand and foothold before trusting my tired muscles to support the burden they were carrying, for a weak hold or a misstep would have plunged me into eternity. Death was ever at my elbow.

It seemed to me that I descended thousands of feet and yet I had seen no sign of the city. Several times I heard creatures moving through the trees at a distance, and twice I heard the hideous scream of a targo. Should one of these monstrous spiders attack me—well, I tried not to think about that. Instead I tried to occupy my mind with recollections of my earthly friends; I visualized my childhood days in India as I studied under old Chand Kabi, I thought of dear old Jimmy Welsh, and I recalled a bevy of girls I had liked and with some of whom I had almost been serious. These recalled the gorgeous girl in the garden of the jong, and the visions of the others faded into oblivion. Who was she? What strange interdiction had forbidden her to see or to speak with me? She had said that she loathed me, but she had heard me tell her that I loved her. That sounded rather silly now that I gave it thought. How could I love a girl the first instant that I laid eyes upon her, a girl concerning whom I knew absolutely nothing, neither her age nor her name? It was preposterous, yet I knew that it was true. I loved the nameless beauty of the little garden.

Perhaps my preoccupation with these thoughts made me careless; I do not know, but my mind was filled with them when my foot slipped a little after night had fallen. I grasped for support, but the combined weights of myself and the corpse tore my hands loose, and with my dead companion I plunged downward into the darkness. I felt Death's cold breath upon my cheek.

We did not fall far, being brought up suddenly by something soft that gave to our combined weights, then bounced up again, vibrating like a safety net such as we have all seen used by aerial performers. In the faint but all pervading light of the Amtorian night I could see what I had already guessed—I had fallen into the web of one of Amtor's ferocious spiders!

I tried to crawl to an edge where I might seize hold of a branch and drag myself free, but each move but entangled me the more. The situation was horrible enough, but a moment later it became infinitely worse, as, glancing about me, I saw at the far edge of the web the huge, repulsive body of a targo.

I drew my sword and hacked at the entangling meshes of the web as the fierce arachnid crept slowly toward me. I recall wondering if a fly entangled in a spider's web suffered the hopelessness and the mental anguish that seized me as I realized the futility of my puny efforts to escape this lethal trap and the ferocious monster advancing to devour me. But at least I had some advantages that no fly enjoys. I had my sword and a reasoning brain; I was not so entirely helpless as the poor fly.

The targo crept closer and closer. It uttered no sound. I presume that it was satisfied that I could not escape and saw no reason why it should seek to paralyze me with fright. From a distance of about ten feet it charged, moving with incredible swiftness upon its eight hairy legs. I met it with the point of my sword.

There was no skill in my thrust; it was just pure luck that my point penetrated the creature's tiny brain. When it collapsed lifeless beside me, I could scarcely believe the testimony of my eyes. I was saved!

Instantly I fell to work severing the strands of tarel that enmeshed me, and in four or five minutes I was free and had lowered myself to a branch below. My heart was still pounding rapidly and I was weak from exhaustion. For a quarter of an hour I remained resting; then I continued the seemingly endless descent out of this hideous forest.

What other dangers confronted me I could not guess. I knew that there were other creatures in this gigantic wood; those powerful webs, capable of sustaining the weight of an ox, had not been built for man alone. During the preceding day I had caught occasional glimpses of huge birds, which might themselves, if carnivorous, prove as deadly menaces as the targo; but it was not them that I feared now, but the nocturnal prowlers that haunt every forest by night.

Down and down I descended, feeling that each next moment must witness the final collapse of my endurance. The encounter with the targo had taken terrific toll of my great strength, already sapped by the arduous experiences of the day, yet I could not stop, I dared not. Yet how much longer could I drive exhausted nature on toward the brink of utter collapse?

I had about reached the end of my endurance when my feet struck solid ground. At first I could not believe the truth, but glancing down and about me I saw that I had indeed reached the floor of the forest; after a month on Venus I had at last placed foot upon her surface. I could see little or nothing—just the enormous boles of great trees in whatever direction I looked. Beneath my feet lay a thick matting of fallen leaves, turned white in death.

I cut the cords that bound the corpse of Kamlot to my back and lowered my poor comrade to the ground; then I threw myself down beside him and was asleep almost immediately.

When I awoke, it was daylight again. I looked about me, but could see nothing but the counterpane of whitened leaves spread between the boles of trees of such gargantuan girth that I almost hesitate to suggest the size of some of them, lest I discredit the veracity of this entire story of my experiences on Venus. But indeed they must need to be huge to support their extraordinary height, for many of them towered over six thousand feet above the surface of the ground, their lofty pinnacles enshrouded forever in the eternal fog of the inner cloud envelope.

To suggest an idea of the size of some of these monsters of the forest, I may say that I walked around the bole of one, counting over a thousand paces in the circuit, which gives, roughly, a diameter of a thousand feet, and there were many such. A tree ten feet in diameter appeared a frail and slender sapling—and there can be no vegetation upon Venus!

What little knowledge of physics I had and a very slight acquaintance with botany argued that trees of such height could not exist, but there must be some special, adaptive forces operating on Venus that permit the seemingly impossible. I have attempted to figure it out in terms of earthly conditions, and I have arrived at some conclusions that suggest possible explanations for the phenomenon. If vertical osmosis is affected by gravity, then the lesser gravity of Venus would favour the growth of taller trees, and the fact that their tops are forever in the clouds would permit them to build up an ample supply of carbohydrates from the abundant water vapour, provided there was the requisite amount of carbon dioxide in the atmosphere of Venus to promote this photosynthetic process.

I must admit, however, that at the time I was not greatly interested in these intriguing speculations; I had to think about myself and poor Kamlot. What was I to do with the corpse of my friend? I had done my best to return him to his people, and failed. I doubted now that I could ever find his people. There remained but a single alternative; I must bury him.

This decided, I started to scrape away the leaves beside him, that I might reach the ground beneath and dig a grave. There were about a foot of leaves and leaf meld and below that a soft, rich soil which I loosened easily with the point of my spear and scooped out with my hands. It did not take me long to excavate a nice grave; it was six feet long, two feet wide, and three feet deep. I gathered some freshly fallen leaves and carpeted its bottom with them, and then I gathered some more to place around and over Kamlot after I had lowered him to his final resting place.

While I worked I tried to recall the service for the dead; I wanted Kamlot to have as decent and orderly a burial as I could contrive. I wondered what God would think about it, but I had no doubt but that he would receive this first Amtorian soul to be launched into the unknown with a Christian burial and welcome him with open arms.

As I stooped and put my arms about the corpse to lower it into the grave, I was astounded to discover that it was quite warm. This put an entirely new aspect on the matter. A man dead for eighteen hours should be cold. Could it be that Kamlot was not dead? I pressed an ear to his chest; faintly I heard the beating of his heart. Never before had I experienced such an access of relief and joy. I felt as one reborn to new youth, to new hopes, to new aspirations. I had not realized until that instant the depth of my loneliness.

But why was Kamlot not dead? and how was I to resuscitate him? I felt that I should understand the former before I attempted the latter. I examined the wound again. There were two deep gashes on his chest just below the presternum. They had bled but little, and they were discoloured, as I now noticed, by a greenish tint. It was this, meaningless though it may be, that suggested an explanation of Kamlot's condition. Something about that greenish tint suggested poison to my mind, and at once I recalled that there were varieties of spiders that paralyzed their victims by injecting a poison into them that preserved them in a state of suspended animation until they were ready to devour them. The targo had paralyzed Kamlot!

My first thought was to stimulate circulation and respiration, and to this end I alternately massaged his body and applied the first aid measures adapted to the resuscitation of the drowned. Which of these accomplished the result I do not know (perhaps each helped a little), but at any rate I was rewarded after a long period of effort with evidences of returning animation. Kamlot sighed and his eyelids fluttered. After another considerable period, during which I nearly exhausted myself, he opened his eyes and looked at me.

At first his gaze was expressionless and I thought that perhaps his mind had been affected by the poison; then a puzzled, questioning look entered his eyes and eventually recognition. I was witnessing a resurrection.

"What happened?" he asked in a whisper, and then, "Oh, yes, I recall; the targo got me." He sat up, with my assistance, and looked around. "Where are we?" he demanded.

"On the ground," I replied, "but where on the ground I do not know."

"You saved me from the targo," he said. "Did you kill it? But you must have, or you never could have gotten me away from it. Tell me about it."

Briefly, I told him. "I tried to get you back to the city, but I became lost and missed it. I have no idea where it lies."

"What is this?" he asked, glancing at the excavation beside him.

"Your grave," I replied. "I thought that you were dead."

"And you carried a corpse half a day and half a night! But why?"

"I do not know all the customs of your people," I replied; "but your family has been kind to me, and the least that I could do was to bring your body back to them, nor could I leave a friend up there to be devoured by birds and beasts."

"I shall not forget," he said quietly. He tried to rise then, but I had to assist him. "I shall be all right presently," he assured me, "after I have exercised a little. The effects of the targo's poison wear off in about twenty-four hours even without treatment. What you have done for me has helped to dissipate them sooner, and a little exercise will quickly eradicate the last vestiges of them." He stood looking about as though in an effort to orient himself, and as he did so his eyes fell upon his weapons, which I had intended burying with him and which lay on the ground beside the grave. "You even brought these!" he exclaimed. "You are a jong among friends!"

After he had buckled his sword belt about his hips, he picked up his spear, and together we walked through the forest, searching for some sign that would indicate that we had reached a point beneath the city, Kamlot having explained that trees along the important trails leading to the location of the city were marked in an inconspicuous and secret manner, as were certain trees leading upward to the hanging city.

"We come to the surface of Amtor but seldom," he said, "though occasionally trading parties descend and go to the coast to meet vessels from the few nations with which we carry on a surreptitious commerce. The curse of Thorism has spread far, however, and there are few nations of which we have knowledge that are not subject to its cruel and selfish domination. Once in a while we descend to hunt the basto for its hide and flesh."

"What is a basto?" I inquired.

"It is a large, omnivorous animal with powerful jaws armed with four great fangs in addition to its other teeth. On its head grow two heavy horns. At the shoulder it is as tall as a tall man. I have killed them that weighed thirty-six hundred tob."

A tob is the Amtorian unit of weight, and is the equivalent of one third of an English pound; all weights are computed in tobs or decimals thereof, as they use the decimal system exclusively in their tables of weights and measures. It seems to me much more practical than the confusing earthly collection of grains, grams, ounces, pounds, tons, and the other designations in common use among the various nations of our planet.

From Kamlot's description I visualized the basto as an enormous boar with horns, or a buffalo with the jaws and teeth of a carnivore, and judged that its twelve hundred pounds of weight would render it a most formidable beast. I asked him with what weapons they hunted the animal.

"Some prefer arrows, others spears," he explained, "and it is always handy to have a low branched tree near by," he added with a grin.

"They are bellicose?" I asked.

"Very. When a basto appears upon the scene, man is as often the hunted as the hunter, but we are not hunting bastos now. What I should most like to find is a sign that would tell me where we are."

We moved on through the forest, searching for the tiny road signs of the Vepajans, which Kamlot had described to me as well as explaining the location in which they are always placed. The sign consists of a long, sharp nail with a flat head bearing a number in relief. These nails are driven into trees at a uniform height from the ground. They are difficult to find, but it is necessary to have them so, lest the enemies of the Vepajans find and remove them, or utilize them in their search for the cities of the latter.

The method of the application of these signs to the requirements of the Vepajans is clever. They would really be of little value to any but a Vepajan as guide posts, yet each nail tells a remarkable story to the initiated; briefly it tells him precisely where he is on the island that comprises the kingdom of Mintep, the jong. Each nail is placed in position by a surveying party and its exact location is indicated on a map of the island, together with the number on the head of the nail. Before a Vepajan is permitted to descend to the ground alone, or to lead others there, he must memorize the location of every sign nail in Vepaja. Kamlot had done so. He told me that if we could find but a single nail he would immediately know the direction of and distance to those on either side of it, our exact position upon the island, and the location of the city; but he admitted that we might wander a long time before we discovered a single nail.

The forest was monotonously changeless. There were trees of several species, some with branches that trailed the ground, others bare of branches for hundreds of feet from their bases. There were boles as smooth as glass and as straight as a ship's mast, without a single branch as far up as the eye could see. Kamlot told me that the foliage of these grew in a single enormous tuft far up among the clouds.

I asked him if he had ever been up there, and he said he had climbed, he believed, to the top of the tallest tree, but that he had nearly frozen to death in the attempt.

"We get our water supply from these trees," he remarked. "They drink in the water vapour among the clouds and carry it down to their roots. They are unlike any other tree. A central, porous core carries the water from the clouds to the roots, from whence it rises again in the form of sap that carries the tree's food upward from the ground. By tapping one of these trees anywhere you may obtain a copious supply of clear, cool water—a fortunate provision of . . . . ."

"Something is coming, Kamlot," I interrupted. "Do you hear it?"

He listened intently for a moment. "Yes," he replied. "We had better take to a tree, at least until we see what it is."

As he climbed into the branches of a nearby tree, I followed him, and there we waited. Distinctly I could hear something moving through the forest as it approached us. The soft carpet of leaves beneath its feet gave forth but little sound—just a rustling of the dry leaves. Nearer and nearer it came, apparently moving leisurely; then, suddenly, its great head came into view from behind the bole of a tree a short distance from us.

"A basto," whispered Kamlot, but from his previous description of the beast I had already guessed its identity.

It looked like a basto, only more so. From the eyes up its head resembled that of an American bison, with the same short, powerful horns. Its poll and forehead were covered with thick, curly hair, its eyes were small and red-rimmed. Its hide was blue and of about the same texture as that of an elephant, with sparsely growing hairs except upon the head and at the tip of the tail. It stood highest at the shoulders and sloped rapidly to its rump. Its front legs were short and stocky and ended in broad, three-toed feet; its hind legs were longer and the hind feet smaller, a difference necessitated by the fact that the forelegs and feet carried fully three quarters of the beast's weight. Its muzzle was similar to that of a boar, except that it was broader, and carried heavy, curved tusks.

"Here comes our next meal," remarked Kamlot in an ordinary tone of voice. The basto stopped and looked about as he heard my companion's voice. "They are mighty good eating," added Kamlot, "and we have not eaten for a long while. There is nothing like a basto steak grilled over a wood fire."

My mouth commenced to water. "Come on," I said, and started to climb down from the tree, my spear ready in my hand.

"Come back!" called Kamlot. "You don't know what you are doing."

The basto had located us and was advancing, uttering a sound that would have put to shame the best efforts of a full-grown lion. I do not know whether to describe it as a bellow or a roar. It started with a series of grunts and then rose in volume until it shook the ground.

"He seems to be angry," I remarked; "but if we are going to eat him we must kill him first, and how are we to kill him if we remain in the tree?"

"I am not going to remain in the tree," replied Kamlot, "but you are. You know nothing about hunting these beasts, and you would probably not only get yourself killed but me into the bargain. You stay where you are. I will attend to the basto."

This plan did not suit me at all, but I was forced to admit Kamlot's superior knowledge of things Amtorian and his greater experience and defer to his wishes, but nevertheless I held myself ready to go to his assistance should occasion require.

To my surprise, he dropped his spear to the ground and carried in its stead a slender leafy branch which he cut from the tree before descending to engage the bellowing basto. He did not come down to the floor of the forest directly in front of the beast, but made his way part way around the tree before descending, after asking me to keep the basto's attention diverted, which I did by shouting and shaking a branch of the tree

Presently, to my horror, I saw Kamlot out in the open a dozen paces in rear of the animal, armed only with his sword and the leafy branch which he carried in his left hand. His spear lay on the ground not far from the enraged beast and his position appeared utterly hopeless should the basto discover him before he could reach the safety of another tree. Realizing this, I redoubled my efforts to engage the creature's attention until Kamlot shouted to me to desist.

I thought that he must have gone crazy and should not have heeded him had not his voice attracted the attention of the basto and frustrated any attempt that I might have made to keep the beast's eyes upon me. The instant that Kamlot called to me the great head turned ponderously in his direction and the savage eyes discovered him. The creature wheeled and stood for a moment eyeing the rash but puny man-thing; then it trotted toward him.

I waited no longer but dropped to the ground with the intention of attacking the thing from the rear. What happened thereafter happened so quickly that it was over almost in the time it takes to tell it. As I started in pursuit, I saw the mighty basto lower its head and charge straight for my companion, who stood there motionless with his puny sword and the leafy branch grasped one in either hand. Suddenly, at the very instant that I thought the creature was about to impale him on those mighty horns, he waved the leaf covered branch in its face and leaped lightly to one side, simultaneously driving the keen point of his blade downward from a point in front of the left shoulder until the steel was buried to the hilt in the great carcass

The basto stopped, its four legs spread wide for an instant it swayed, and then it crashed to the ground at the feet of Kamlot. A shout of admiration was on my lips when I chanced to glance upward. What attracted my attention I do not know, perhaps the warning of that inaudible voice which we sometimes call a sixth sense. What I saw drove the basto and the feat of Kamlot from my thoughts.

"My God!" I cried in English, and then in Amtorian, "Look, Kamlot! What are those?"

## Chapter 8

# On Board the Sofal

Hovering just above us, I saw what at first appeared to be five enormous birds; but which I soon recognized, despite my incredulity, as winged men. They were armed with swords and daggers, and each carried a long rope at the end of which dangled a wire noose.

"Voo klangan!" shouted Kamlot. (The birdmen!)

Even as he spoke a couple of wire nooses settled around each of us. We struggled to free ourselves, striking at the snares with our swords, but our blades made no impression upon the wires, and the ropes to which they were attached were beyond our reach. As we battled futilely to disengage ourselves, the klangan settled to the ground, each pair upon opposite sides of the victim they had snared. Thus they held us so, that we were helpless, as two cowboys hold a roped steer, while the fifth angan approached us with drawn sword and disarmed us. (Perhaps I should explain that angan is singular, klangan plural, plurals of Amtorian words being formed by prefixing kloo to words commencing with a consonant and kl to those commencing with a vowel.)

Our capture had been accomplished so quickly and so deftly that it was over, with little or no effort on the part of the birdmen, before I had had time to recover from the astonishment that their weird appearance induced. I now recalled having heard Danus speak of voo klangan upon one or two occasions, but I had thought that he referred to poultry breeders or something of that sort. How little could I have dreamed of the reality!

"I guess we are in for it," remarked Kamlot gloomily.

"What will they do with us?" I inquired. "Ask them," he replied.

"Who are you?" demanded one of our captors.

For some reason I was astonished to hear him speak, although I do not know why anything should have astonished me now. "I am a stranger from another world," I told him. "My friend and I have no quarrel with you. Let us go."

"You are wasting your breath," Kamlot advised me.

"Yes, he is wasting his breath," agreed the angan. "You are Vepajans, and we have orders to bring Vepajans to the ship. You do not look like a Vepajan," he added, surveying me from head to feet, "but the other does."

"Anyway, you are not a Thorist, and therefore you must be an enemy," interjected another.

They removed the nooses from about us and tied ropes around our necks and other ropes about our bodies beneath our arms; then two klangan seized the ropes attached to Kamlot and two more those attached to me, and, spreading their wings, rose into the air, carrying us with them. Our weight was supported by the ropes beneath our arms, but the other ropes were a constant suggestion to us of what might happen if we did not behave ourselves.

As they flew, winding their way among the trees, our bodies were suspended but a few feet above the ground, for the forest lanes were often low ceiled by overhanging branches. The klangan talked a great deal among themselves, shouting to one another and laughing and singing, seemingly well satisfied with themselves and their exploit. Their voices were soft and mellow, and their songs were vaguely reminiscent of Negro spirituals, a similarity which may have been enhanced by the colour of their skins, which were very dark.

As Kamlot was carried in front of me, I had an opportunity to observe the physical characteristics of these strange creatures into whose hands we had fallen. They had low, receding foreheads, huge, beaklike noses, and undershot jaws; their eyes were small and close set, their ears flat and slightly pointed. Their chests were large and shaped like those of birds, and their arms were very long, ending in long-fingered, heavy-nailed hands. The lower part of the torso was small, the hips narrow, the legs very short and stocky, ending in three-toed feet equipped with long, curved talons. Feathers grew upon their heads instead of hair. When they were excited, as when they attacked us, these feathers stand erect, but ordinarily they lie flat. They are all alike; commencing near the root they are marked with a band of white, next comes a band of black, then another of white, and the tip is red. Similar feathers also grow at the lower extremity of the torso in front, and there is another, quite large bunch just above the buttocks—a gorgeous tail which they open into a huge pompon when they wish to show off.

Their wings, which consist of a very thin membrane supported on a light framework, are similar in shape to those of a bat and do not appear adequate to the support of the apparent weight of the creatures' bodies, but I was to learn later that this apparent weight is deceptive, since their bones, like the bones of true birds, are hollow.

The creatures carried us a considerable distance, though how far I do not know. We were in the air fully eight hours; and, where the forest permitted, they flew quite rapidly. They seemed utterly tireless, though Kamlot and I were all but exhausted long before they reached their destination. The ropes beneath our arms cut into our flesh, and this contributed to our exhaustion as did our efforts to relieve the agony by seizing the ropes above us and supporting the weight of our bodies with our hands.

But, as all things must, this hideous journey ended at last. Suddenly we broke from the forest and winged out across a magnificent landlocked harbour, and for the first time I looked upon the waters of a Venusian sea. Between two points that formed the harbour's entrance I could see it stretching away as far as the eye could reach—mysterious, intriguing, provocative. What strange lands and stranger people lay off there beyond the beyond? Would I ever know?

Suddenly now my attention and my thoughts were attracted to something in the left foreground that I had not before noticed; a ship lay at anchor on the quiet waters of the harbour and just beyond it a second ship. Toward one of them our captors were winging. As we approached the nearer and smaller, I saw a craft that differed but little in the lines of its hull from earthly ships. It had a very high bow, its prow was sharp and sloped forward in a scimitar like curve; the ship was long and narrow of beam. It looked as though it might have been built for speed. But what was its motive power? It had no masts, sails, stacks, nor funnels. Aft were two oval houses—a smaller one resting upon the top of a larger; on top of the upper house was an oval tower surmounted by a small crow's nest. There were doors and windows in the two houses and the tower. As we came closer, I could see a number of open hatches in the deck and people standing on the walkways that surrounded the tower and the upper house and also upon the main deck. They were watching our approach.

As our captors deposited us upon the deck, we were immediately surrounded by a horde of jabbering men. A man whom I took to be an officer ordered the ropes removed from us, and while this was being done he questioned the klangan who had brought us.

All the men that I saw were similar in colour and physique to the

Vepajans, but their countenances were heavy and unintelligent; very few of them were good-looking, and only one or two might have been called handsome. I saw evidences of age among them and of disease—the first I had seen on Amtor.

After the ropes had been removed, the officer ordered us to follow him, after detailing four villainous-looking fellows to guard us, and conducted us aft and up to the tower that surmounted the smaller house. Here he left us outside the tower, which he entered.

The four men guarding us eyed us with surly disfavour. "Vepajans, eh!" sneered one. "Think you're better than ordinary men, don't you? But you'll find out you ain't, not in The Free Land of Thora; there everybody's equal. I don't see no good in bringing your kind into the country anyway. If I had my way you'd get a dose of this," and he tapped a weapon that hung in a holster at his belt.

The weapon, or the grip of it, suggested a pistol of some kind, and I supposed that it was one of those curious firearms discharging deadly rays, that Kamlot had described to me. I was about to ask the fellow to let me see it when the officer emerged from the tower and ordered the guard to bring us in.

We were escorted into a room in which sat a scowling man with a most unprepossessing countenance. There was a sneer on his face as he appraised us, the sneer of the inferior man for his superior, that tries to hide but only reveals the inferiority complex that prompts it. I knew that I was not going to like him.

"Two more klooganfal!" he exclaimed. (A ganfal is a criminal.) "Two more of the beasts that tried to grind down the workers; but you didn't succeed, did you? Now we are the masters. You'll find that out even before we reach Thora. Is either of you a doctor?"

Kamlot shook his head. "Not I," he said.

The fellow, whom I took to be the captain of the ship, eyed me closely. "You are no Vepajan," he said. "What are you, anyway? No one ever saw a man with yellow hair and blue eyes before."

"As far as you are concerned," I replied, "I am a Vepajan. I have never been in any other country in Amtor."

"What do you mean by saying as far as I am concerned?" he demanded.

"Because it doesn't make any difference what you think about it," I snapped. I did not like the fellow, and when I do not like people I have difficulty in hiding the fact. In this case I did not try to hide it.

He flushed and half rose from his chair. "It doesn't, eh?" he cried.

"Sit down," I advised him. "You're here under orders to bring back

Vepajans Nobody cares what you think about them, but you'll get into trouble if you don't bring them back."

Diplomacy would have curbed my tongue, but I am not particularly diplomatic, especially when I am angry, and now I was both angry and disgusted, for there had been something in the attitude of all these people toward us that bespoke ignorant prejudice and bitterness. Furthermore, I surmised from scraps of information I had picked up from Danus, as well as from the remarks of the sailor who had announced that he would like to kill us, that I was not far wrong in my assumption that the officer I had thus addressed would be exceeding his authority if he harmed us. However, I realized that I was taking chances, and awaited with interest the effect of my words.

The fellow took them like a whipped cur and subsided after a single weakly blustering, "We'll see about that." He turned to a book that lay open before him. "What is your name?" he asked, nodding in Kamlot's direction. Even his nod was obnoxious.

"Kamlot of Zar," replied my companion.

"What is your profession?"

"Hunter and wood carver."

"You are a Vepajan?"

"Yes."

"From what city of Vepaja?"

"From Kooaad," replied Kamlot. "And you?" demanded the officer, addressing me.

"I am Carson of Napier," I replied, using the Amtorian form; "I am a Vepajan from Kooaad."

"What is your profession?" "I am an aviator," I replied, using the English word and English pronunciation.

"A what?" he demanded. "I never heard of such a thing." He tried to write the word in his book and then he tried to pronounce it, but he could do neither, as the Amtorians have no equivalents for many of our vowel sounds and seem unable even to pronounce them. Had I written the word for him in Amtorian he would have pronounced it ah-vy-ah-tore, as they cannot form the long a and short o sounds, and their i is always long.

Finally, to cover his ignorance, he wrote some thing in his book, but what it was I did not know; then he looked up at me again. "Are you a doctor?"

"Yes," I replied, and as the officer made the notation in his book, I glanced at Kamlot out of the corner of an eye and winked.

"Take them away," the man now directed, "and be careful of this one," he added, indicating me; "he is a doctor."

We were taken to the main deck and led forward to the accompaniment of jeers and jibes from the sailors congregated on the deck. I saw the klangan strutting around, their tail feathers erect. When they saw us, they pointed at Kamlot, and I heard them telling some of the sailors that he was the one who had slain the basto with a single sword thrust, a feat which appeared to force their admiration, as well it might have.

We were escorted to an open hatch and ordered below into a dark, poorly ventilated hole, where we found several other prisoners. Some of them were Thorans undergoing punishment for infractions of discipline; others were Vepajan captives like ourselves, and among the latter was one who recognized Kamlot and hailed him as we descended into their midst.

"Jodades, Kamlot!" he cried, voicing the Amtorian greeting "luck-to-you."

"Ra jodades," replied Kamlot; "what ill fortune brings Honan here?"

"'Ill fortune' does not describe it," replied Honan; "catastrophe would be a better word. The klangan were seeking women as well as men; they saw Duare" (pronounced Doo-ah'-ee) "and pursued her; as I sought to protect her they captured me."

"Your sacrifice was not in vain," said Kamlot; "had you died in the performance of such a duty it would not have been in vain."

"But it was in vain; that is the catastrophe."

"What do you mean?" demanded Kamlot.

"I mean that they got her," replied Honan dejectedly.

"They captured Duare!" exclaimed Kamlot in tones of horror. "By the life of the jong, it cannot be."

"I wish it were not," said Honan.

"Where is she? on this ship?" demanded Kamlot.

"No; they took her to the other, the larger one."

Kamlot appeared crushed, and I could only attribute his dejection to the hopelessness of a lover who has irretrievably lost his beloved. Our association had not been either sufficiently close nor long to promote confidences, and so I was not surprised that I had never heard him mention the girl, Duare, and, naturally, under the circumstances, I could not question him concerning her. I therefore respected his grief and his silence, and left him to his own sad thoughts.

Shortly after dawn the following morning the ship got under way. I wished that I might have been on deck to view the fascinating sights of this strange world, and my precarious situation as a prisoner of the hated Thorists engendered less regret than the fact that I, the first earth man to sail the seas of Venus, was doomed to be cooped up in a stuffy hole below deck where I could see nothing. But if I had feared being kept below for the duration of the voyage, I was soon disillusioned, for shortly after the ship got under way we were all ordered on deck and set to scrubbing and polishing.

As we came up from below, the ship was just passing between the two headlands that formed the entrance to the harbour, in the wake of the larger vessel; and I obtained an excellent view of the adjacent land, the shore that we were leaving, and the wide expanse of ocean stretching away to the horizon.

The headlands were rocky promontories clothed with verdure of delicate hues and supporting comparatively few trees, which were of a smaller variety than the giants upon the mainland. These latter presented a truly awe inspiring spectacle from the open sea to the eyes of an earth man, their mighty boles rearing their weirdly collared foliage straight up for five thousand feet, where they were lost to view among the clouds. But I was not permitted to gaze for long upon the wonders of the scene. I had not been ordered above for the purpose of satisfying the aesthetic longings of my soul.

Kamlot and I were set to cleaning and polishing guns. There were a number of these on either side of the deck, one at the stern, and two on the tower deck. I was surprised when I saw them, for there had been no sign of armament when I came on board the preceding day; but I was not long in discovering the explanation—the guns were mounted on disappearing carriages, and when lowered, a sliding hatch, flush with the deck, concealed them.

The barrels of these pieces were about eight inches in diameter, while the bore was scarcely larger than my little finger; the sights were ingenious and complicated, but there was no breech block in evidence nor any opening into a breech, unless there was one hidden beneath a hoop that encircled the breech, to which it was heavily bolted. The only thing that I could discover that might have been a firing device projected from the rear of the breech and resembled the rotating crank that is used to revolve the breech block in some types of earthly guns.

The barrels of the guns were about fifteen feet long and of the same diameter from breech to muzzle. When in action they can be extended beyond the rail of the ship about two thirds of their length, thus affording a wider horizontal range and more deck room, which would be of value on a ship such as that on which I was a captive, which was of narrow beam.

"What do these guns fire?" I asked Kamlot, who was working at my side.

"T-rays," he replied.

"Do those differ materially from the R-rays you described when you were telling me about the small arms used by the Thorans?"

"The R-ray destroys only animal tissue," he replied, "while there is nothing that the T-ray may not dissipate. It is a most dangerous ray to work with because even the material of the gun barrel itself is not wholly impervious to it, and the only reason that it can be used at all is that its greatest force is expended along the line of least resistance, which in this case naturally is the bore of the gun. But eventually it destroys the gun itself."

"How is it fired?" I asked.

He touched the crank at the end of the breech. "By turning this, a shutter is raised that permits radiations from element 93 to impinge on the charge, which consists of element 97, thus releasing the deadly T-ray."

"Why couldn't we turn this gun about and rake the ship above deck," I suggested, "thus wiping out the Thorans and giving us our freedom?"

He pointed to a small, irregular hole in the end of the crank shaft. "Because we haven't the key that fits this," he replied.

"Who has the key?"

"The officers have keys to the guns they command," he replied. "In the captain's cabin are keys to all the guns, and he carries a master key that will unlock any of them. At least that was the system in the ancient Vepajan navy, and it is doubtless the same today in the Thoran navy."

"I wish we could get hold of the master key," I said.

"So do I," he agreed, "but that is impossible."

"Nothing is impossible," I retorted.

He made no answer, and I did not pursue the subject, but I certainly gave it a lot of thought.

As I worked, I noted the easy, noiseless propulsion of the ship and asked Kamlot what drove it. His explanation was long and rather technical; suffice it to say that the very useful element 93 (vik-ro) is here again employed upon a substance called lor, which contains a considerable proportion of the element yor-san (105). The action of vik-ro upon yor-san results in absolute annihilation of the lor, releasing all its energy. When you consider that there is eighteen thousand million times as much energy liberated by the annihilation of a ton of coal than by its combustion you will appreciate the inherent possibilities of this marvellous Venusian scientific discovery. Fuel for the life of the ship could be carried in a pint jar.

I noticed as the day progressed that we cruised parallel to a coast line, after crossing one stretch of ocean where no land was in sight, and thereafter for several days I noted the same fact—land was almost always in sight. This suggested that the land area of Venus might be much greater in proportion to its seas; but I had no opportunity to satisfy my curiosity on that point, and of course I took no stock in the maps that Danus had shown me, since the Amtorians' conception of the shape of their world precluded the existence of any dependable maps.

Kamlot and I had been separated, he having been detailed to duty in the ship's galley, which was located in the forward part of the main deck house aft. I struck up a friendship with Honan; but we did not work together, and at night we were usually so tired that we conversed but little before falling asleep on the hard floor of our prison. One night, however, the sorrow of Kamlot having been brought to my mind by my own regretful recollections of the nameless girl of the garden, I asked Honan who Duare was.

"She is the hope of Vepaja," he replied, "perhaps the hope of a world."

## CHAPTER 9

# Soldiers of Liberty

Constant association breeds a certain camaraderie even between enemies. As the days passed, the hatred and contempt which the common sailors appeared to have harboured for us when we first came aboard the ship were replaced by an almost friendly familiarity, as though they had discovered that we were not half bad fellows after all; and, for my part, I found much to like in these simple though ignorant men. That they were the dupes of unscrupulous leaders is about the worst that may be said of them. Most of them were kindly and generous; but their ignorance made them gullible, and their emotions were easily aroused by specious arguments that would have made no impression upon intelligent minds.

Naturally, I became better acquainted with my fellow prisoners than with my guards, and our relations were soon established upon a friendly basis. They were greatly impressed by my blond hair and blue eyes which elicited inquiries as to my genesis. As I answered their questions truthfully, they became deeply interested in my story, and every evening after the day's work was completed I was besieged for tales of the mysterious, far distant world from which I came. Unlike the highly intelligent Vepajans, they believed all that I told them, with the result that I was soon a hero in their eyes; I should have been a god had they had any conception of deities of any description.

In turn, I questioned them; and discovered, with no surprise, that they were not at all contented with their lots. The former free men among them had long since come to the realization that they had exchanged this freedom, and their status of wage earners, for slavery to the state, that could no longer be hidden by a nominal equality.

Among the prisoners were three to whom I was particularly attracted by certain individual characteristics in each. There was Gamfor, for instance, a huge, hulking fellow who had been a farmer in the old days under the jongs. He was unusually intelligent, and although he had taken part in the revolution, he was now bitter in his denunciation of the Thorists, though this he was careful to whisper to me in secrecy.

Another was Kiron, the soldier, a clean-limbed, handsome, athletic fellow who had served in the army of the jong, but mutinied with the others at the time of the revolution. He was being disciplined now for insubordination to an officer who had been a petty government clerk before his promotion.

The third had been a slave. His name was Zog. What he lacked in intelligence he made up in strength and good nature. He had killed an officer who had struck him and was being taken back to Thora for trial and execution. Zog was proud of the fact that he was a free man, though he admitted that the edge was taken off his enthusiasm by the fact that every one else was free and the realization that he had enjoyed more freedom as a slave than he did now as a freeman.

"Then," he explained, "I had one master; now I have as many masters as there are government officials, spies, and soldiers, none of whom cares anything about me, while my old master was kind to me and looked after my welfare."

"Would you like to be really free?" I asked him, for a plan had been slowly forming in my mind.

But to my surprise he said, "No, I should rather be a slave."

"But you'd like to choose your own master, wouldn't you?" I demanded.

"Certainly," he replied, "if I could find some one who would be kind to me and protect me from the Thorists."

"And if you could escape from them now, you would like to do so?"

"Of course! But what do you mean? I cannot escape from them."

"Not without help," I agreed, "but if others would join you, would you make the attempt?"

"Why not? They are taking me back to Thora to kill me. I could be no worse off, no matter what I did. But why do you ask all these questions?"

"If we could get enough to join us, there is no reason why we should not be free," I told him. "When you are free, you may remain free or choose a master to your liking." I watched closely for his reaction.

"You mean another revolution?" he asked. "It would fail. Others have tried, but they have always failed."

"Not a revolution," I assured him, "just a break for liberty."

"But how could we do it?"

"It would not be difficult for a few men to take this ship," I suggested. "The discipline is poor, the night watches consist of too few men; they are so sure of themselves that they would be taken completely by surprise."

Zog's eyes lighted. "If we were successful, many of the crew would join us," he said. "Few of them are happy; nearly all of them hate their officers. I think the prisoners would join us almost to a man, but you must be careful of spies—they are everywhere. That is the greatest danger you would have to face. There can be no doubt but there is at least one spy among us prisoners."

"How about Gamfor," I asked; "is he all right?"

"You can depend upon Gamfor," Zog assured me. "He does not say much, but in his eyes I can read his hatred of them."

"And Kiron?"

"Just the man!" exclaimed Zog. "He despises them, and he does not care who knows it; that is the reason he is a prisoner. This is not his first offence, and it is rumoured that he will be executed for high treason."

"But I thought that he only talked back to an officer and refused to obey him," I said.

"That is high treason—if they wish to get rid of a man," explained Zog. "You can depend on Kiron. Do you wish me to speak to him about the matter?"

"No," I told him. "I will speak to him and to Gamfor; then if anything goes wrong before we are ready to strike, if a spy gets wind of our plot, you will not be implicated."

"I do not care about that," he exclaimed. "They can kill me for but one thing, and it makes no difference which thing it is they kill me for."

"Nevertheless, I shall speak to them, and if they will join us, we can then decide together how to approach others."

Zog and I had been working together scrubbing the deck at the time, and it was not until night that I had an opportunity to speak with Gamfor and Kiron. Both were enthusiastic about the plan, but neither thought that there was much likelihood that it would succeed. However, each assured me of his support; and then we found Zog, and the four of us discussed details throughout half the night. We had withdrawn to a far corner of the room in which we were confined and spoke in low whispers with our heads close together.

The next few days were spent in approaching recruits—a very ticklish business, since they all assured me that it was almost a foregone conclusion that there was a spy among us. Each man had to be sounded out by devious means, and it had been decided that this work should be left to Gamfor and Kiron. I was eliminated because of my lack of knowledge concerning the hopes, ambitions, and the grievances of these people, or their psychology; Zog was eliminated because the work required a much higher standard of intelligence than he possessed.

Gamfor warned Kiron not to divulge our plan to any prisoner who too openly avowed his hatred of the Thorists. "This is a time-worn trick that all spies adopt to lull the suspicions of those they suspect of harbouring treasonable thoughts, and to tempt them into avowing their apostasy. Select men whom you know to have a real grievance, and who are moody and silent," he counselled.

I was a little concerned about our ability to navigate the ship in the event that we succeeded in capturing her, and I discussed this matter with both Gamfor and Kiron. What I learned from them was illuminating, if not particularly helpful.

The Amtorians have developed a compass similar to ours. According to Kiron, it points always toward the centre of Amtor—that is, toward the centre of the mythical circular area called Strabol, or Hot Country. This statement assured me that I was in the southern hemisphere of the planet, the needle of the compass, of course, pointing north toward the north magnetic pole. Having no sun, moon, nor stars, their navigation is all done by dead reckoning; but they have developed instruments of extreme delicacy that locate land at great distances, accurately indicating this distance and the direction; others that determine speed, mileage, and drift, as well as a depth gauge wherewith they may record soundings anywhere within a radius of a mile from the ship.

All of their instruments for measuring distances utilize the radioactivity of the nuclei of various elements to accomplish their ends. The gamma ray, for which they have, of course, another name, being uninfluenced by the most powerful magnetic forces, is naturally the ideal medium for their purposes. It moves in a straight line and at uniform speed until it meets an obstruction, where, even though it may not be deflected, it is retarded, the instrument recording such retardation and the distance at which it occurs. The sounding device utilizes the same principle. The instrument records the distance from the ship at which the ray encounters the resistance of the ocean's bottom; by constructing a right triangle with this distance representing the hypotenuse it is simple to compute both the depth of the ocean and the distance from the ship at which bottom was found, for they have a triangle of which one side and all three angles are known.

Owing to their extremely faulty maps, however, the value of these instruments has been greatly reduced, for no matter what course they lay, other than due north, if they move in a straight line they are always approaching the Antarctic regions. They may know that land is ahead and its distance, but they are never sure what land it is, except where the journey is a short and familiar one. For this reason they cruise within sight of land wherever that is practical, with the result that journeys that might otherwise be short are greatly protracted. Another result is that the radius of Amtorian maritime exploration has been greatly circumscribed; so much so that I believe there are enormous areas in the south temperate zone that have never been discovered by the Vepajans or the Thorists, while the very existence of the northern hemisphere is even unguessed by them. On the maps that Danus showed me considerable areas contained nothing but the single word joram, ocean.

However, notwithstanding all this (and possibly because of it), I was confident that we could manage to navigate the ship quite as satisfactorily as her present officers, and in this Kiron agreed.

"At least we know the general direction of Thora," he argued; "so all we have to do is sail in the other direction."

As our plans matured, the feasibility of the undertaking appeared more and more certain. We had recruited twenty prisoners, five of whom were Vepajans, and this little band we organized into a secret order with passwords, which were changed daily, signs, and a grip, the last reminiscent of my fraternity days in college. We also adopted a name. We called ourselves Soldiers of Liberty. I was chosen vookor, or captain. Gamfor, Kiron, Zog, and Honan were my principal lieutenants, though I told them that Kamlot would be second in command if we were successful in taking the ship.

Our plan of action was worked out in detail; each man knew exactly what was expected of him. Certain men were to overpower the watch, others were to go to the officers' quarters and secure their weapons and keys; then we would confront the crew and offer those who chose an opportunity to join us. The others—well, there I was confronted with a problem. Almost to a man the Soldiers of Liberty wanted to destroy all those who would not join us, and really there seemed no alternative; but I still hoped that I could work out a more humane disposition of them.

There was one man among the prisoners of whom we were all

suspicious. He had an evil face, but that was not his sole claim upon our suspicions—he was too loud in his denunciation of Thorism. We watched him carefully, avoiding him whenever we could, and each member of the band was warned to be careful when talking to him. It was evident to Gamfor first that this fellow, whose name was Anoos, was suspicious. He persisted in seeking out various members of our group and engaging them in conversation which he always led around to the subject of Thorism and his hatred of it, and he constantly questioned each of us about the others, always insinuating that he feared certain ones were spies. But of course we had expected something of this sort, and we felt that we had guarded against it. The fellow might be as suspicious of us as he wished; so long as he had no evidence against us I did not see how he could harm us.

One day Kiron came to me evidently labouring under suppressed excitement. It was at the end of the day, and our food had just been issued to us for the evening meal—dried fish and a hard, dark-collared bread made of coarse meal.

"I have news, Carson," he whispered.

"Let us go off in a corner and eat," I suggested, and we strolled away together, laughing and talking of the day's events in our normal voices. As we seated ourselves upon the floor to eat our poor food, Zog joined us.

"Sit close to us, Zog," directed Kiron; "I have something to say that no one but a Soldier of Liberty may hear."

He did not say Soldier of Liberty, but "kung, kung, kung," which are the Amtorian initials of the order's title. Kung is the name of the Amtorian character that represents the k sound in our language, and when I first translated the initials I was compelled to smile at the similarity they bore to those of a well-known secret order in the United States of America.

"While I am talking," Kiron admonished us, "you must laugh often, as though I were telling a humorous tale; then, perhaps, no one will suspect that I am not.

"Today I was working in the ship's armoury, cleaning pistols," he commenced. "The soldier who guarded me is an old friend of mine; we served together in the army of the jong. He is as a brother to me. For either the other would die. We talked of old times under the banners of the jong and compared those days with these, especially we compared the officers of the old regime with those of the present. Like me and like every old soldier, he hates his officers; so we had a pleasant time together.

"Finally he said to me, quite suddenly, 'What is this I hear of a conspiracy among the prisoners?'

"That almost took me off my feet; but I showed no emotion, for there are times when one must not trust even a brother. 'What have you heard?' I asked.

"'I overheard one of the officers speaking to another,' he told me. 'He said that a man named Anoos had reported the matter to the captain, and that the captain had told Anoos to get the names of all the prisoners whom he knew to be involved in the conspiracy and to learn their plans if he possibly could.'

"'And what did Anoos say?' I asked my friend.

"'He said that if the captain would give him a bottle of wine he believed that he could get one of the conspirators drunk and worm the story from him. So the captain gave him a bottle of wine. That was today.'

"My friend looked at me very closely, and then he said, 'Kiron, we are more than brothers. If I can help you, you have but to ask.'

"I knew this, and knowing how close to discovery we already were, I decided to confide in him and enlist his aid; so I told him. I hope you do not feel that I did wrong, Carson."

"By no means," I assured him. "We have been forced to tell others of our plans whom we knew and trusted less well than you know and trust your friend. What did he say when you had told him?"

"He said that he would help us, and that when we struck he would join us. He promised, too, that many others of the soldiers would do likewise; but the most important thing he did was to give me a key to the armoury."

"Good!" I exclaimed. "There is no reason now why we should not strike at once."

"Tonight?" asked Zog eagerly.

"Tonight!" I replied. "Pass the word to Gamfor and Honan, and you four to the other Soldiers of Liberty."

We all laughed heartily, as though some one had told a most amusing story, and then Kiron and Zog left me, to acquaint Gamfor and Honan with our plan.

But upon Venus as upon earth, the best laid plans of mice and men "gang aft a-gley," which is slang for haywire. Every night since we had sailed from the harbour of Vepaja the hatch had been left off our ill-smelling prison to afford us ventilation, a single member of the watch patrolling near to see that none of us came out; but tonight the hatch was closed.

"This," growled Kiron, "is the result of Anoos's work."

"We shall have to strike by daylight," I whispered, "but we cannot pass the word tonight. It is so dark down here that we should certainly be overheard by some one outside our own number if we attempted it."

"Tomorrow then," said Kiron.

I was a long time getting to sleep that night, for my mind was troubled by fears for our entire plan. It was obvious now that the captain was suspicious, and that while he might not know anything of the details of what we purposed, he did know that something was in the air, and he was taking no chances.

During the night, as I lay awake trying to plan for the morrow, I heard some one prowling around the room, and now and again a whisper. I could only wonder who it was and try to guess what he was about. I recalled the bottle of wine that Anoos was supposed to have, and it occurred to me that he might be giving a party, but the voices were too subdued to bear out that theory. Finally I heard a muffled cry, a noise that sounded like a brief scuffle, and then silence again fell upon the chamber.

"Some one had a bad dream," I thought and fell asleep.

Morning came at last, and the hatch was removed, letting a little light in to dissipate the gloom of our prison. A sailor lowered a basket containing the food for our meagre breakfast. We gathered about it and each took his share, and moved away to eat it, when suddenly there was a cry from the far side of the room.

"Look what's here!" the man shouted. "Anoos has been murdered!"

# Chapter 10
# Mutiny

Yes, Anoos had been murdered, and there was a great hue and cry, much more of a hue and cry, it seemed to me, than the death of an ordinary prisoner should have aroused. Officers and soldiers swarmed in our quarters. They found Anoos stretched out on his back, a bottle of wine at his side. His throat was discoloured where powerful fingers had crushed it. Anoos had been choked to death.

Soon they herded us on deck, where we were searched for weapons following an order from the captain of the ship, who had come forward to conduct an investigation. He was angry and excited and, I believe, somewhat frightened. One by one, he questioned us. When it was my turn to be questioned, I did not tell him what I had heard during the night; I told him that I had slept all night on the far side of the room from where Anoos's body was discovered.

"Were you acquainted with the dead man?" he asked.

"No more so than with any of the other prisoners," I replied.

"But you are very well acquainted with some of them," he said rather pointedly, I thought. "Have you ever spoken with the man?"

"Yes, he has talked to me on several occasions."

"About what?" demanded the captain.

"Principally about his grievances against the Thorists."

"But he was a Thorist," exclaimed the captain.

I knew that he was trying to pump me to discover if I harboured any suspicions concerning the actual status of Anoos, but he was not clever enough to succeed. "I certainly would never had suspected it from his conversation," I replied. "If he were a Thorist, he must have been a traitor to his country, for he continually sought to enlist my interest in a plan to seize the ship and murder all her officers. I think he approached others, also." I spoke in a tone loud enough to be heard by all, for I wanted the Soldiers of Liberty to take the cue from me. If enough of us told the same story it might convince the officers that Anoos's tale of a conspiracy was hatched in his own brain and worked up by his own efforts in an attempt to reap commendation and reward from his superiors, a trick by no means foreign to the ethics of spies.

"Did he succeed in persuading any of the prisoners to join him?" asked the captain.

"I think not; they all laughed at him."

"Have you any idea who murdered him?"

"Probably some patriot who resented his treason," I lied glibly.

As he questioned the other men along similar lines, I was pleased to discover that nearly every one of the Soldiers of Liberty had been approached by the perfidious Anoos, whose traitorous overtures they had virtuously repulsed. Zog said that he had never talked with the man, which, to the best of my knowledge, was the truth.

When the captain finished his investigation, he was farther from the truth than when he commenced it, for I am certain that he went aft convinced that there had been no truth in the tales that Anoos had carried to him.

I had been considerably worried at the time we were being searched, for fear that the key to the armoury would be discovered on Kiron, but it had not been, and later he told me that he had hidden it in his hair the night before as a precaution against just such an eventuality as had occurred.

The Amtorian day consists of 26 hours, 56 minutes, 4 seconds of earth time, which the Amtorians divide into twenty equal periods called te, which, for clarity, I shall translate into its nearest earthly equivalent, hour, although it contains 80.895 earth minutes. On shipboard, the hours are sounded by a trumpeter, there being a distinguishing bar of music for each hour of the day. The first hour, or one o'clock, corresponds to mean sunrise. It is then that the prisoners are awakened and given food; forty minutes later they start work, which continues until the tenth hour, with a short recess for food in the middle of the day. Occasionally we were allowed to quit work at the ninth and even the eighth hour, according to the caprices of our masters.

On this day the Soldiers of Liberty congregated during the midday rest period, and, my mind being definitely determined on immediate action, I passed the word around that we would strike during the afternoon at the moment the trumpeter sounded the seventh hour. As many of us as were working aft near the armoury were to make a dash for it with Kiron, who would unlock it in the event that it were locked. The remainder were to attack the soldiers nearest them with anything that they could use as weapons, or with their bare hands if they had no weapons, and take the soldiers' pistols and swords from them. Five of us were to account for the officers. Half of our number was to constantly shout our battle cry, "For liberty!" The other half was instructed to urge the remaining prisoners and the soldiers to join us.

It was a mad scheme and one in which only desperate men could have found hope.

The seventh hour was chosen because at that time the officers were nearly all congregated in the wardroom, where a light meal and wine were served them daily. We should have preferred launching our plan at night, but we feared a continuation of the practice of locking us below deck would prevent, and our experience with Anoos had taught us that we might expect the whole conspiracy to be divulged by another spy at any time; therefore we dared not wait.

I must confess to a feeling of increasing excitement as the hour approached. As, from time to time, I glanced at the other members of our little band, I thought that I could note signs of nervousness in some of them, while others worked on as placidly as though nothing unusual was about to occur. Zog was one of these. He was working near me. He never glanced toward the tower deck from which the trumpeter would presently sound the fateful notes, though it was with difficulty that I kept my eyes from it at all. No one would have thought that Zog was planning to attack the soldier lolling near him, nor have imagined that the night before he had murdered a man. He was humming a tune, as he polished the barrel of the big gun on which he was working.

Gamfor and, fortunately, Kiron were working aft, scrubbing the deck, and I saw that Kiron kept scrubbing closer and closer to the door of the armoury. How I wished for Kamlot as the crucial moment approached! He could have done so much to insure the success of our coup, and yet he did not even know that such a stroke was contemplated, much less that it was so soon to be launched.

As I glanced about, I met Zog's gaze. Very solemnly he closed his left eye. At last he had given a sign that he was alert and ready. It was a little thing, but it put new heart into me. For some reason, during the past half hour I had felt very much alone.

The time was approaching the zero hour. I moved closer to my guard, so that I stood directly in front of him with my back toward him. I knew precisely what I was going to do, and I knew that it would be successful. Little did the man behind me dream that in a minute, or perhaps a few seconds, he would be lying senseless on the deck, or that the man he guarded would be carrying his sword, his dagger, and his pistol as the last notes of the seventh hour floated sweetly out across the calm waters of this Amtorian sea.

My back was now toward the deck houses. I could not see the trumpeter when he emerged from the tower to sound the hour, but I knew that it could not be long now before he stepped out onto the tower deck. Yet when the first note sounded I was as startled as though I had expected it never to sound. I presume it was the reaction after the long period of nervous tension.

My nervousness, however, was all mental; it did not affect my physical reactions to the needs of the moment. As the first note came softly down to my awaiting ears, I pivoted on a heel and swung my right for the chin of my unsuspecting guard. It was one of those blows that is often described as a haymaker, and it made hay. The fellow dropped in his tracks. As I stooped to recover his arms, pandemonium broke loose upon the deck. There were shrieks and groans and curses, and above all rose the war cry of the Soldiers of Liberty—my band had struck, and it had struck hard.

For the first time now, I heard the weird staccato hiss of Amtorian firearms. You have heard an X-ray machine in operation? It was like that, but louder and more sinister. I had wrenched the sword and pistol from the scabbard and holster of my fallen guard, not taking the time to remove his belt. Now I faced the scene for which I had so long waited. I saw the powerful Zog wrest the weapons from a soldier, and then lift the man's body above his head and cast it overboard. Evidently Zog had no time for proselyting.

At the door to the armoury a battle was being waged; men were trying to enter, and soldiers were shooting them down. I ran in that direction. A soldier leaped in front of me, and I heard the hiss of the death rays that must have passed close to my body, as he tried to stop me. He must have been either nervous or a very poor shot, for he missed me. I turned my own weapon upon him and pressed the lever. The man slumped to the deck with a hole in his chest, and I ran on.

The fight at the door of the armoury was hand to hand with swords, daggers, and fists, for by now the members of the two factions were so intermingled that none dared use a firearm for fear of injuring a comrade. Into this melee I leaped. Tucking the pistol into the band of my G string, I ran my sword through a great brute who was about to knife Honan; then I grabbed another by the hair and dragged him from the door, shouting to Honan to finish him—it took too long to run a sword into a man and then pull it out again. What I wanted was to get into the armoury to Kiron's side and help him.

All the time I could hear my men shouting, "For liberty!" or urging the soldiers to join us—as far as I had been able to judge, all the prisoners had already done so. Now another soldier barred my way. His back was toward me, and I was about to seize him and hurl him back to Honan and the others who were fighting at his side, when I saw him slip his dagger into the heart of a soldier in front of him and, as he did so, cry, "For liberty!" Here was one convert at least. I did not know it then, but at that time there were already many such.

When I finally got into the armoury, I found Kiron issuing arms as fast as he could pass them out. Many of the mutineers were crawling through the windows of the room to get weapons, and to each of these Kiron passed several swords and pistols, directing the men to distribute them on deck.

Seeing that all was right here, I gathered a handful of men and started up the companionway to the upper decks, from which the officers were firing down upon the mutineers and, I may say, upon their own men as well. In fact, it was this heartless and stupid procedure that swung many of the soldiers to our side. Almost the first man I saw as I leaped to the level of the second deck was Kamlot. He had a sword in one hand and a pistol in the other, and he was firing rapidly at a group of officers who were evidently attempting to reach the main deck to take command of the loyal soldiers there.

You may be assured that it did my heart good to see my friend again, and as I ran to his side and opened fire on the officers, he flashed me a quick smile of recognition.

Three of the five officers opposing us had fallen, and now the remaining two turned and fled up the companionway to the top deck. Behind us were twenty or more mutineers eager to reach the highest deck, where all the surviving officers had now taken refuge, and I could see more mutineers crowding up the companionway from the main deck to join their fellows. Kamlot and I led the way to the next deck, but at the head of the companionway the surging mob of howling, cursing mutineers brushed past us to hurl themselves upon the officers.

The men were absolutely out of control, and as there were but few of my original little band of Soldiers of Liberty among them, the majority of them knew no leader, with the result that it was every man for himself. I wished to protect the officers, and it had been my intention to do so; but I was helpless to avert the bloody orgy that ensued with a resulting loss of life entirely disproportionate to the needs of the occasion.

The officers, fighting for their lives with their backs against a wall, took heavy toll of the mutineers, but they were eventually overwhelmed by superior numbers. Each of the common soldiers and sailors appeared to have a special grudge to settle either with some individual officer or with them all as a class and for the time all were transformed into maniacal furies, as time and again they charged the last fortress of authority, the oval tower on the upper deck.

Each officer that fell, either killed or wounded, was hurled over the rail to the deck below, where willing hands cast the body to the main deck from which, in turn, it was thrown into the sea. And then, at last, the mutineers gained access to the tower, from which they dragged the remaining officers, butchering them on the upper deck or hurling them to their shrieking fellows below.

The captain was the last to be dragged out. They had found him hiding in a cupboard in his cabin. At sight of him arose such a scream of hate and rage as I hope never to hear again. Kamlot and I were standing at one side, helpless witnesses of this holocaust of hate. We saw them literally tear the captain to pieces and cast him into the sea.

With the death of the captain the battle was over, the ship was ours. My plan had succeeded, but the thought suddenly assailed me that I had created a terrible power that it might be beyond me to control. I touched Kamlot on the arm. "Follow me," I directed and started for the main deck.

"Who is at the bottom of this?" asked Kamlot as we forced our way among the excited mutineers.

"The mutiny was my plan, but not the massacre," I replied. "Now we must attempt to restore order out of chaos."

"If we can," he remarked dubiously.

As I made my way toward the main deck, I collected as many of the original band of Soldiers of Liberty as we passed, and when I finally reached my destination, I gathered most of them about me. Among the mutineers I had discovered the trumpeter who had unknowingly sounded the signal for the outbreak, and him I caused to sound the call that should assemble all hands on the main deck. Whether or not the notes of the trumpet would be obeyed, I did not know, but so strong is the habit of discipline among trained men that immediately the call sounded the men began to pour onto the deck from all parts of the vessel.

I mounted the breech of one of the guns, and, surrounded by

my faithful band, I announced that the Soldiers of Liberty had taken over the ship, that those who wished to accompany us must obey the vookor of the band; the others would be put ashore.

"Who is vookor?" demanded a soldier whom I recognized as one of those who had been most violent in the attack upon the officers.

"I am," I replied.

"The vookor should be one of us," he growled.

"Carson planned the mutiny and carried it to success," shouted Kiron. "Carson is vookor."

From the throats of all my original band and from a hundred new recruits rose a cheer of approval, but there were many who remained silent or spoke in grumbling undertones to those nearest them. Among these was Kodj, the soldier who had objected to my leadership, and I saw that already a faction was gathering about him.

"It is necessary," I said, "that all men return at once to their duties, for the ship must be handled, no matter who commands. If there is any question about leadership, that can be settled later. In the meantime, I am in command; Kamlot, Gamfor, Kiron, Zog, and Honan are my lieutenants; with me, they will officer the ship. All weapons must be turned over immediately to Kiron at the armoury, except those carried by men regularly detailed by him for guard duty."

"No one is going to disarm me," blustered Kodj. "I have as much right to carry weapons as anyone. We are all free men now. I take orders from no one."

Zog, who had edged closer to him as he spoke, seized him by the throat with one of his huge hands and with the other tore the belt from about his hips. "You take orders from the new vookor or you go overboard," he growled, as he released the man and handed his weapons to Kiron.

For a moment there was silence, and there was a tenseness in the situation that boded ill; then some one laughed and cried, "No one is going to disarm me," mimicking Kodj. That brought a general laugh, and I knew that for the time being the danger was over. Kiron, sensing that the moment was ripe, ordered the men to come to the armoury and turn in their weapons, and the remainder of the original band herded them aft in his wake.

It was an hour before even a semblance of order or routine had been re-established. Kamlot, Gamfor, and I were gathered in the chart room in the tower. Our consort was hull down below the horizon, and we were discussing the means that should be adopted to capture her without bloodshed and rescue Duare and the other Vepajan prisoners aboard her. The idea had been in my mind from the very inception of the plan to seize our own ship, and it had been the first subject that Kamlot had broached after we had succeeded in quieting the men and restoring order; but Gamfor was frankly dubious concerning the feasibility of the project.

"The men are not interested in the welfare of Vepajans," he reminded us, "and they may resent the idea of endangering their lives and risking their new-found liberty in a venture that means nothing whatever to them."

"How do you feel about it, personally?" I asked him.

"I am under your orders," he replied; "I will do anything that you command, but I am only one—you have two hundred whose wishes you must consult."

"I shall consult only my officers," I replied; "to the others, I shall issue orders."

"That is the only way," said Kamlot in a tone of relief.

"Inform the other officers that we shall attack the Sovong at daybreak," I instructed them.

"But we dare not fire on her," protested Kamlot, "lest we endanger the life of Duare."

"I intend boarding her," I replied. "There will be no one but the watch on deck at that hour. On two other occasions the ships have been brought close together on a calm sea; so our approach will arouse no suspicion. The boarding party will consist of a hundred men who will remain concealed until the command to board is given when the ships are alongside one another. At that hour in the morning the sea is usually calm; if it is not calm tomorrow morning we shall have to postpone the attack until another morning.

"Issue strict orders that there is to be no slaughter; no one is to be killed who does not resist. We shall remove all of the Sovong's small arms and the bulk of her provisions, as well as the Vepajan prisoners, to the Sofal."

"And then what do you propose doing?" asked Gamfor.

"I am coming to that," I replied, "but first I wish to ascertain the temper of the men aboard the Sofal. You and Kamlot will inform the other officers of my plans insofar as I have explained them; then assemble the original members of the Soldiers of Liberty and explain my intentions to them. When this has been done, instruct them to disseminate the information among the remainder of the ship's company, reporting to you the names of all those who do not receive the plan with favour. These we shall leave aboard the Sovong with any others who may elect to transfer to her. At the eleventh hour muster the men on the main deck. At that time I will explain my plans in detail."

After Kamlot and Gamfor had departed to carry out my orders, I returned to the chart room. The Sofal, moving ahead at increased speed, was slowly overhauling the Sovong, though not at a rate that might suggest pursuit. I was certain that the Sovong knew nothing of what had transpired upon her sister ship, for the Amtorians are unacquainted with wireless communication, and there had been no time for the officers of the Sofal to signal their fellows aboard the Sovong, so suddenly had the mutiny broken and so quickly had it been carried to a conclusion.

As the eleventh hour approached, I noticed little groups of men congregated in different parts of the ship, evidently discussing the information that the Soldiers of Liberty had spread among them. One group, larger than the others, was being violently harangued by a loud-mouthed orator whom I recognized as Kodj. It had been apparent from the first that the fellow was a trouble maker. Just how much influence he had, I did not know; but I felt that whatever it was, it would be used against me. I hoped to be rid of him after we had taken the Sovong.

The men congregated rapidly as the trumpeter sounded the hour, and I came down the companionway to address them. I stood just above them, on one of the lower steps, where I could overlook them and be seen by all. Most of them were quiet and appeared attentive. There was one small group muttering and whispering—Kodj was its centre.

"At daybreak we shall board and take the Sovong," I commenced. "You will receive your orders from your immediate officers, but I wish to emphasize one in particular—there is to be no unnecessary killing. After we have taken the ship we shall transfer to the Sofal such provisions, weapons, and prisoners as we wish to take with us. At this time, also, we shall transfer from the Sofal to the Sovong all of you who do not wish to remain on this ship under my command, as well as those whom I do not care to take with me," and as I said this, I looked straight at Kodj and the malcontents surrounding him.

"I shall explain what I have in mind for the future, so that each of you may be able to determine between now and daybreak whether he cares to become a member of my company. Those who do will be required to obey orders but they will share in the profits of the cruise, if there are profits. The purposes of the expedition are twofold: To prey on Thorist shipping and to explore the unknown portions of Amtor after we have returned the Vepajan prisoners to their own country.

"There will be excitement and adventure; there will be danger, too; and I want no cowards along, nor any trouble makers. There should be profits, for I am assured that richly laden Thorist ships constantly ply the known seas of Amtor; and I am informed that we can always find a ready market for such spoils of war as fall into our hands—and war it shall be, with the Soldiers of Liberty fighting the oppression and tyranny of Thorism.

"Return to your quarters now, and be prepared to give a good account of yourselves at daybreak."

## Chapter 11

# Duare

I got little sleep that night. My officers were constantly coming to me with reports. From these I learned, what was of the greatest importance to me, the temper of the crew. None was averse to taking the Sovong, but there was a divergence of opinion as to what we should do thereafter. A few wanted to be landed on Thoran soil, so that they could make their way back to their homes; the majority was enthusiastic about plundering merchant ships; the idea of exploring the unknown waters of Amtor filled most of them with fear; some were averse to restoring the Vepajan prisoners to their own country; and there was an active and extremely vocal minority that insisted that the command of the vessel should be placed in the hands of Thorans. In this I could see the hand of Kodj even before they told me that the suggestion had come from the coterie that formed his following.

"But there are fully a hundred," said Gamfor, "upon whose loyalty you may depend. These have accepted you as their leader, and they will follow you and obey your commands."

"Arm these," I directed, "and place all others below deck until after we have taken the Sovong. How about the klangan? They took no part in the mutiny. Are they for us or against us?"

Kiron laughed. "They received no orders one way or the other," he explained. "They have no initiative. Unless they are motivated by such primitive instincts as hunger, love, or hate, they do nothing without orders from a superior."

"And they don't care who their master is," interjected Zog. "They serve loyally enough until their master dies, or sells them, or gives them away, or is overthrown; then they transfer the same loyalty to a new master."

"They have been told that you are their new master," said Kamlot, "and they will obey you."

As there were only five of the birdmen aboard the Sofal, I had not been greatly exercised about their stand; but I was glad to learn that they would not be antagonistic.

At the twentieth hour I ordered the hundred upon whom we could depend assembled and held in the lower deck house, the others having all been confined below earlier in the night, in the accomplishment of which a second mutiny was averted only by the fact that all the men had been previously disarmed except the loyal Soldiers of Liberty.

All during the night we had been gradually gaining upon the unsuspecting Sovong until now we were scarcely a hundred yards astern of her, slightly aport. Across our starboard bow I could see her looming darkly in the mysterious nocturnal glow of the moonless Amtorian night, her lanterns white and collared points of light, her watch dimly visible upon her decks.

Closer and closer the Sofal crept toward her prey. A Soldier of Liberty, who had once been an officer in the Thoran navy, was at the wheel; no one was on deck but the members of the watch; in the lower deck house a hundred men were huddled waiting for the command to board; I stood beside Honan in the chart room (he was to command the Sofal while I led the boarding party), my eyes upon the strange Amtorian chronometer. I spoke a word to him and he moved a lever. The Sofal crept a little closer to the Sovong. Then Honan whispered an order to the helmsman and we closed in upon our prey.

I hastened down the companionway to the main deck and gave the signal to Kamlot standing in the doorway of the deck house. The two ships were close now and almost abreast. The sea was calm; only a gentle swell raised and lowered the softly gliding ships. Now we were so close that a man could step across the intervening space from the deck of one ship to that of the other.

The officer of the watch aboard the Sovong hailed us. "What are you about?" he demanded. "Sheer off, there!"

For answer I ran across the deck of the Sofal and leaped aboard the other ship, a hundred silent men following in my wake. There was no shouting and little noise—only the shuffling of sandaled feet and the subdued clank of arms.

Behind us the grappling hooks were thrown over the rail of the Sovong. Every man had been instructed as to the part he was to play. Leaving Kamlot in command on the main deck, I ran to the tower deck with a dozen men, while Kiron led a score of fighting men to the second deck where most of the officers were quartered.

Before the officer of the watch could gather his scattered wits, I had him covered with a pistol. "Keep quiet," I whispered, "and you will not be harmed." My plan was to take as many of them as possible before a general alarm could be sounded and thus minimize the necessity for bloodshed; therefore, the need for silence. I turned him over to one of my men after disarming him; and then I sought the captain, while two of my detachment attended to the helmsman.

I found the officer for whom I sought reaching for his weapons. He had been awakened by the unavoidable noise of the boarding party, and, suspecting that something was amiss, had seized his weapons as he arose and uncovered the lights in his cabin.

I was upon him as he raised his pistol, and struck it from his hand before he could fire; but he stepped back with his sword on guard, and thus we stood facing one another for a moment.

"Surrender," I told him, "and you will not be harmed."

"Who are you?" he demanded, "and where did you come from?"

"I was a prisoner on board the Sofal," I replied, "but now I command her. If you wish to avoid bloodshed, come out on deck with me and give the command to surrender."

"And then what?" he demanded. "Why have you boarded us if not to kill?"

"To take off provisions, weapons, and the Vepajan prisoners," I explained.

Suddenly the hissing staccato of pistol fire came up to us from the deck below.

"I thought there was to be no killing!" he snapped.

"If you want to stop it, get out there and give the command to surrender," I replied.

"I don't believe you," he cried. "It's a trick," and he came at me with his sword.

I did not wish to shoot him down in cold blood, and so I met his attack with my own blade. The advantage was on his side in the matter of skill, for I had not yet fully accustomed myself to the use of the Amtorian sword; but I had an advantage in strength and reach and in some tricks of German swordplay that I had learned while I was in Germany. The Amtorian sword is primarily a cutting weapon, its weight near the tip making it particularly effective for this method of attack, though it lessens its effectiveness in parrying thrusts, rendering it a rather sluggish defensive weapon. I therefore found myself facing a savage cutting attack against which I had difficulty in defending myself. The officer was an active man and skilful with the sword. Being experienced, it did not take him long to discover that I was a novice, with the result that he pressed his advantage viciously, so that I soon regretted my magnanimity in not resorting to my pistol before the encounter began; but it was too late now—the fellow kept me so busy that I had no opportunity to draw the weapon.

He forced me back and around the room until he stood between me and the doorway, and then, having me where no chance for escape remained he set to work to finish me with dispatch. The duel, as far as I was concerned, was fought wholly on the defensive. So swift and persistent was his attack that I could only defend myself, and not once in the first two minutes of the encounter did I aim a single blow at him.

I wondered what had become of the men who had accompanied me; but pride would not permit me to call upon them for help, nor did I learn until later that it would have availed me nothing, since they were having all that they could attend to in repelling the attack of several officers who had run up from below immediately behind them.

The teeth of my antagonist were bared in a grim and ferocious smile, as he battered relentlessly at my guard, as though he already sensed victory and was gloating in anticipation. The clanging of steel on steel now drowned all sounds from beyond the four walls of the cabin where we fought; I could not tell if fighting were continuing in other parts of the ship, nor, if it were, whether it were going in our favour or against us. I realized that I must know these things, that I was responsible for whatever took place aboard the Sovong, and that I must get out of that cabin and lead my men either in victory or defeat.

Such thoughts made my position even more impossible than as though only my life were at stake and drove me to attempt heroic measures for releasing myself from my predicament and my peril. I must destroy my adversary, and I must do so at once!

He had me now with my back almost against the wall. Already his point had touched me upon the cheek once and twice upon the body, and though the wounds were but scratches, I was covered with blood. Now he leaped upon me in a frenzy of determination to have done with me instantly, but this time I did not fall back. I parried his cut, so that his sword passed to the right of my body which was now close to his; and then I drew back my point, and, before he could recover himself, drove it through his heart.

As he sagged to the floor, I jerked my sword from his body and ran from his cabin. The entire episode had required but a few minutes, though it had seemed much longer to me, yet in that brief time much had occurred on the decks and in the cabins of the Sovong. The upper decks were cleared of living enemies; one of my own men was at the wheel, another at the controls; there was still fighting on the main deck where some of the Sovong's officers were making a desperate last stand with a handful of their men. But by the time I reached the scene of the battle, it was over; the officers, assured by Kamlot that their lives would be spared, had surrendered—the Sovong was ours. The Sofal had taken her first prize!

As I sprang into the midst of the excited warriors on the main deck, I must have presented a sorry spectacle, bleeding, as I was, from my three wounds; but my men greeted me with loud cheers. I learned later that my absence from the fighting on the main deck had been noticed and had made a poor impression on my men, but when they saw me return bearing the scars of combat, my place in their esteem was secured. Those three little scratches proved of great value to me, but they were as nothing in comparison with the psychological effect produced by the wholly disproportionate amount of blood they had spilled upon my naked hide.

We now quickly rounded up our prisoners and disarmed them. Kamlot took a detachment of men and released the Vepajan captives whom he transferred at once to the Sofal. They were nearly all women, but I did not see them as they were taken from the ship, being engaged with other matters. I could imagine, though, the joy in the hearts of Kamlot and Duare at this reunion, which the latter at least had probably never even dared to hope for.

Rapidly we transferred all of the small arms of the Sovong to the Sofal, leaving only sufficient to equip the officers of the ill-starred vessel. This work was entrusted to Kiron and was carried out by our own men, while Gamfor, with a contingent of our new-made prisoners, carried all of the Sovong's surplus provisions aboard our own ship. This done, I ordered all the Sovong's guns thrown overboard—by that much at least I would cripple the power of Thora. The last act in this drama of the sea was to march our one hundred imprisoned malcontents from the Sofal to the Sovong and present them to the latter's new commander with my compliments. He did not seem greatly pleased, however, nor could I blame him. Neither were the prisoners pleased. Many of them begged me to take them back aboard the Sofal; but I already had more men than I felt were needed to navigate and defend the ship; and each of the prisoners had been reported as having expressed disapproval of some part or all of our plan; so that I, who must have absolute loyalty and cooperation, considered them valueless to me.

Kodj, strange to say, was the most persistent. He almost went on his knees as he pleaded with me to permit him to remain with the Sofal, and he promised me such loyalty as man had never known before; but I had had enough of Kodj and told him so. Then, when he found that I could not be moved, he turned upon me, swearing by all his ancestors that he would get even with me yet, even though it took a thousand years.

Returning to the deck of the Sofal, I ordered the grappling hooks cast off, and presently the two ships were under way again, the Sovong proceeding toward the Thoran port that was her destination, the Sofal back toward Vepaja. Now, for the first time, I had opportunity to inquire into our losses and found that we had suffered four killed and twenty-one wounded, the casualties among the crew of the Sovong having been much higher.

For the greater part of the remainder of the day I was busy with my officers organizing the personnel of the Sofal and systematizing the activities of this new and unfamiliar venture, in which work Kiron and Gamfor were of inestimable value; and it was not until late in the afternoon that I had an opportunity to inquire into the welfare of the rescued Vepajan captives. When I asked Kamlot about them, he said that they were none the worse for their captivity aboard the Sovong.

"You see, these raiding parties have orders to bring the women to Thora unharmed and in good condition," he explained. "They are destined for more important persons than ships' officers, and that is their safeguard.

"However, Duare said that notwithstanding this, the captain made advances to her. I wish I might have known it while I was still aboard the Sovong, that I might have killed him for his presumption." Kamlot's tone was bitter and he showed signs of unusual excitement.

"Let your mind rest at ease," I begged him; "Duare has been avenged."

"What do you mean?"

"I killed the captain myself," I explained.

He clapped a hand upon my shoulder, his eyes alight with pleasure. "Again you have won the undying gratitude of Vepaja," he cried. "I wish that it might have been my good fortune to have killed the beast and thus wiped out the insult upon Vepaja, but if I could not be the one, then I am glad that it was you, Carson, rather than another."

I thought that he took the matter rather seriously and was placing too much importance upon the action of the Sovong's captain, since it had resulted in no harm to the girl; but then, of course, I realized that love plays strange tricks upon a man's mental processes, so that an affront to a mistress might be magnified to the proportions of a national calamity.

"Well, it is all over now," I said, "and your sweetheart has been returned to you safe and sound."

At that he looked horrified. "My sweetheart!" he exclaimed. "In the name of the ancestors of all the jongs! Do you mean to tell me that you do not know who Duare is?"

"I thought of course that she was the girl you loved," I confessed. "Who is she?"

"Of course I love her," he explained; "all Vepaja loves her—she is the virgin daughter of a Vepajan jong!"

Had he been announcing the presence of a goddess on shipboard, his tone could have been no more reverential and awed. I endeavoured to appear more impressed than I was, lest I offend him.

"Had she been the woman of your choice," I said, "I should have been even more pleased to have had a part in her rescue than had she been the daughter of a dozen jongs."

"That is nice of you," he replied, "but do not let other Vepajans hear you say such things. You have told me of the divinities of that strange world from which you come; the persons of the jong and his children are similarly sacred to us."

"Then, of course, they shall be sacred to me," I assured him.

"By the way, I have word for you that should please you—a Vepajan would consider it a high honour. Duare desires to see you, that she may thank you personally. It is irregular, of course; but then circumstances have rendered strict adherence to the etiquette and customs of our country impracticable, if not impossible. Several hundred men already have looked upon her, many have spoken to her, and nearly all of them were enemies; so it can do no harm if she sees and speaks with her defenders and her friends."

I did not understand what he was driving at, but I assented to what he had said and told him that I would pay my respects to the princess before the day was over.

I was very busy; and, if the truth must be told, I was not particularly excited about visiting the princess. In fact, I rather dreaded it, for I am not particularly keen about fawning and kowtowing to royalty or anything else; but I decided that out of respect for Kamlot's feelings I must get the thing over as soon as possible, and after he had left to attend to some duty, I made my way to the quarters allotted to Duare on the second deck.

The Amtorians do not knock on a door—they whistle. It is rather an improvement, I think, upon our custom. One has one's own distinctive whistle. Some of them are quite elaborate airs. One soon learns to recognize the signals of one's friends. A knock merely informs you that some one wishes to enter; a whistle tells you the same thing and also reveals the identity of your caller.

My signal, which is very simple, consists of two short low notes followed by a higher longer note; and as I stood before the door of Duare and sounded this, my mind was not upon the princess within but upon another girl far away in the tree city of Kooaad, in Vepaja. She was often in my mind—the girl whom I had glimpsed but twice, to whom I had spoken but once and that time to avow a love that had enveloped me as completely, spontaneously, and irrevocably as would death upon some future day.

In response to my signal a soft, feminine voice bade me enter. I stepped into the room and faced Duare. At sight of me her eyes went wide and a quick flush mounted her cheeks. "You!" she exclaimed.

I was equally dumfounded—she was the girl from the garden of the jong!

## Chapter 12

# "A Ship!"

What a strange contretemps! Its suddenness left me temporarily speechless; the embarrassment of Duare was only too obvious. Yet it was that unusual paradox, a happy contretemps—for me at least.

I advanced toward her, and there must have been a great deal more in my eyes than I realized, for she shrank back, flushing even more deeply than before.

"Don't touch me!" she whispered. "Don't dare!"

"Have I ever harmed you?" I asked.

That question seemed to bring her confidence. She shook her head. "No," she admitted, "you never have—physically. I sent for you to thank you for the service you have already rendered me; but I did not know it was you. I did not know that the Carson they spoke of was the man who—" She stopped there and looked at me appealingly.

"The man who told you in the garden of the jong that he loved you," I prompted her.

"Don't!" she cried. "Can it be that you do not realize the offensiveness, the criminality of such a declaration?"

"Is it a crime to love you?" I asked.

"It is a crime to tell me so," she replied with something of haughtiness.

"Then I am a confirmed criminal," I replied, "for I cannot help telling you that I love you, whenever I see you."

"If that is the case, you must not see me again, for you must never again speak those words to me," she said decisively. "Because of the service you have rendered me, I forgive you your past offences; but do not repeat them."

"What if I can't help it?" I inquired.

"You must help it," she stated seriously; "it is a matter of life and death to you."

Her words puzzled me. "I do not understand what you mean," I admitted.

"Kamlot, Honan, any of the Vepajans aboard this ship would kill you if they knew," she replied. "The jong, my father, would have you destroyed upon our return to Vepaja—it would all depend upon whom I told first."

I came a little closer to her and looked straight into her eyes. "You would never tell," I whispered.

"Why not? What makes you think that?" she demanded, but her voice quavered a little.

"Because you want me to love you," I challenged her.

She stamped her foot angrily. "You are beyond reason or forbearance or decency!" she exclaimed. "Leave my cabin at once; I do not wish ever to see you again."

Her bosom was heaving, her beautiful eyes were flashing, she was very close to me, and an impulse seized me to take her in my arms. I wanted to crush her body to mine, I wanted to cover her lips with kisses; but more than all else I wanted her love, and so I restrained myself, for fear that I might go too far and lose the chance to win the love that I felt was hovering just below the threshold of her consciousness. I do not know why I was so sure of that, but I was. I could not have brought myself to force my attentions upon a woman to whom they were repugnant, but from the first moment that I had seen this girl watching me from the garden in Vepaja, I had been impressed by an inner consciousness of her interest in me, her more than simple interest. It was just one of those things that are the children of old Chand Kabi's training, a training that has made me infinitely more intuitive than a woman. "I am sorry that you are sending me away into virtual exile," I said. "I do not feel that I deserve that, but of course the standards of your world are not the standards of mine. There, a woman is not dishonoured by the love of a man, or by its avowal, unless she is already married to another," and then of a sudden a thought occurred to me that should have occurred before. "Do you already belong to some man?" I demanded, chilled by the thought. "Of course not!" she snapped. "I am not yet nineteen." I wondered that it had never before occurred to me that the girl in the garden of the jong might be already married.

I did not know what that had to do with it, but I was glad to learn that she was not seven hundred years old. I had often wondered about her age, though after all it could have made no difference, since on Venus, if anywhere in the universe, people are really no older than they look—I mean, as far as their attractiveness is concerned.

"Are you going?" she demanded, "or shall I have to call one of the Vepajans and tell them that you have affronted me?"

"And have me killed?" I asked. "No, you cannot make me believe that you would ever do that."

"Then I shall leave," she stated, "and remember that you are never to see me or speak to me again."

With that parting and far from cheering ultimatum she quit the room, going into another of her suite. That appeared to end the interview; I could not very well follow her, and so I turned and made my way disconsolately to the captain's cabin in the tower.

As I thought the matter over, it became obvious to me that I not only had not made much progress in my suit, but that there was little likelihood that I ever should. There seemed to be some insuperable barrier between us, though what it was I could not imagine. I could not believe that she was entirely indifferent to me; but perhaps that was just a reflection of my egotism, for I had to admit that she had certainly made it plain enough both by words and acts that she wished to have nothing to do with me. I was unquestionably persona non grata.

Notwithstanding all this, or maybe because of it, I realized that this second and longer interview had but served to raise my passion to still greater heat, leaving me in a fine state of despair. Her near presence on board the Sofal was constantly provocative, while her interdiction of any relations between us only tended to make me more anxious to be with her. I was most unhappy, and the monotony of the now uneventful voyage back toward Vepaja offered no means of distraction. I wished that we might sight another vessel, for any ship that we sighted would be an enemy ship. We were outlaws, we of the Sofal—pirates, buccaneers, privateers. I rather leaned toward the last and most polite definition of our status. Of course we had not as yet been commissioned by Mintep to raid shipping for Vepaja, but we were striking at Vepaja's enemies, and so I felt that we had some claim upon the dubious respectability of privateerism. However, either of the other two titles would not have greatly depressed me. Buccaneer has a devil-may-care ring to it that appeals to my fancy; it has a trifle more haut ton than pirate.

There is much in a name. I had liked the name of the Sofal from the first. Perhaps it was the psychology of that name that suggested the career upon which I was now launched. It means killer. The verb meaning kill is fal. The prefix so has the same value as the suffix er in English; so sofal means killer. Vong is the Amtorian word for defend; therefore, Sovong, the name of our first prize, means defender; but the Sovong had not lived up to her name.

I was still meditating on names in an effort to forget Duare, when Kamlot joined me, and I decided to take the opportunity to ask him some questions concerning certain Amtorian customs that regulated the social intercourse between men and maids. He opened a way to the subject by asking me if I had seen Duare since she sent for me.

"I saw her," I replied, "but I do not understand her attitude, which suggested that it was almost a crime for me to look at her."

"It would be under ordinary circumstances," he told me, "but of course, as I explained to you before, what she and we have passed through has temporarily at least minimized the importance of certain time-honoured Vepajan laws and customs.

"Vepajan girls attain their majority at the age of twenty; prior to that they may not form a union with a man. The custom, which has almost the force of a law, places even greater restrictions upon the daughters of a jong. They may not even see or speak to any man other than their blood relatives and a few well-chosen retainers until after they have reached their twentieth birthday. Should they transgress, it would mean disgrace for them and death for the man."

"What a fool law!" I ejaculated, but I realized at last how heinous my transgression must have appeared in the eyes of Duare.

Kamlot shrugged. "It may be a fool law," he said, "but it is still the law; and in the case of Duare its enforcement means much to Vepaja, for she is the hope of Vepaja."

I had heard that title conferred upon her before, but it was meaningless to me. "Just what do you mean by saying that she is the hope of Vepaja?" I asked.

"She is Mintep's only child. He has never had a son, though a hundred women have sought to bear him one. The life of the dynasty ends if Duare bears no son; and if she is to bear a son, then it is essential that the father of that son be one fitted to be the father of a jong."

"Have they selected the father of her children yet?" I asked.

"Of course not," replied Kamlot. "The matter will not even be broached until after Duare has passed her twentieth birthday."

"And she is not even nineteen yet," I remarked with a sigh.

"No," agreed Kamlot, eyeing me closely, "but you act as though that fact were of importance to you."

"It is," I admitted.

"What do you mean?" he demanded.

"I intend to marry Duare!"

Kamlot leaped to his feet and whipped our his sword. It was the first time that I had ever seen him show marked excitement. I thought he was going to kill me on the spot.

"Defend yourself!" he cried. "I cannot kill you until you draw."

"Just why do you wish to kill me at all?" I demanded. "Have you gone crazy?"

The point of Kamlot's sword dropped slowly toward the floor. "I do not wish to kill you," he said rather sadly, all the nervous excitement gone from his manner. "You are my friend, you have saved my life—no, I would rather die myself than kill you, but the thing you have just said demands it."

I shrugged my shoulders; the thing was inexplicable to me. "What did I say that demands death?" I demanded.

"That you intend to marry Duare."

"In my world," I told him, "men are killed for saying that they do not intend marrying some girl." I had been sitting at the desk in my cabin at the time that Kamlot had threatened me, and I had not arisen; now I stood up and faced him. "You had better kill me, Kamlot," I said, "for I spoke the truth."

He hesitated for a moment, standing there looking at me; then he returned his sword to its scabbard. "I cannot," he said huskily. "May my ancestors forgive me! I cannot kill my friend.

"Perhaps," he added, seeking some extenuating circumstance, "you should not be held accountable to customs of which you had no knowledge. I often forget that you are of another world than ours. But tell me, now that I have made myself a party to your crime by excusing it, what leads you to believe that you will marry Duare? I can incriminate myself no more by listening to you further."

"I intend to marry her, because I know that I love her and believe that she already half loves me."

At this Kamlot appeared shocked and horrified again. "That is impossible," he cried. "She never saw you before; she cannot dream what is in your heart or your mad brain."

"On the contrary, she has seen me before; and she knows quite well what is in my 'mad brain,'" I assured him. "I told her in Kooaad; I told her again today."

"And she listened?"

"She was shocked," I admitted, "but she listened; then she upbraided me and ordered me from her presence."

Kamlot breathed a sigh of relief. "At least she has not gone mad. I cannot understand on what you base your belief that she may return your love."

"Her eyes betrayed her; and, what may be more convincing, she did not expose my perfidy and thus send me to my death."

He pondered that and shook his head. "It is all madness," he said; "I can make nothing of it. You say that you talked with her in Kooaad, but that would have been impossible. But if you had ever even seen her before, why did you show so little interest in her fate when you knew that she was a prisoner aboard the Sovong? Why did you say that you thought that she was my sweetheart?"

"I did not know until a few minutes ago," I explained, "that the girl I saw and talked with in the garden at Kooaad was Duare, the daughter of the jong."

A few days later I was again talking with Kamlot in my cabin when we were interrupted by a whistle at the door; and when I had bade him do so, one of the Vepajan prisoners that we had rescued from the Sovong entered. He was not from Kooaad but from another city of Vepaja, and therefore none of the other Vepajans aboard knew anything concerning him. His name was Vilor, and he appeared to be a decent sort of fellow, though rather inclined to taciturnity. He had manifested considerable interest in the klangans and was with them often, but had explained this idiosyncrasy on the grounds that he was a scholar and wished to study the birdmen, specimens of which he had never before seen.

"I have come," he explained in response to my inquiry, "to ask you to appoint me an officer. I should like to join your company and share in the work and responsibilities of the expedition."

"We are well officered now," I explained, "and have all the men we need. Furthermore," I added frankly, "I do not know you well enough to be sure of your qualifications. By the time we reach Vejapa, we shall be better acquainted; and if I need you then, I will tell you."

"Well, I should like to do something," he insisted. "May I guard the janjong until we reach Vepaja?"

He referred to Duare, whose title, compounded of the two words daughter and king, is synonymous to princess. I thought that I noticed just a trace of excitement in his voice as he made the request.

"She is well guarded now," I explained.

"But I should like to do it," he insisted. "It would be a service of love and loyalty for my jong. I could stand the night guard; no one likes that detail ordinarily."

"It will not be necessary," I said shortly; "the guard is already sufficient."

"She is in the after cabins of the second deck house, is she not?" he asked.

I told him that she was.

"And she has a special guard?"

"A man is always before her door at night," I assured him.

"Only one?" he demanded, as though he thought the guard insufficient.

"In addition to the regular watch, we consider one man enough; she has no enemies aboard the Sofal." These people were certainly solicitous of the welfare and safety of their royalty, I thought; and, it seemed to me, unnecessarily so. But finally Vilor gave up and departed, after begging me to give his request further thought.

"He seems even more concerned about the welfare of Duare than you," I remarked to Ramlot after Vilor had gone.

"Yes, I noticed that," replied my lieutenant.

"There is no one more concerned about her than I," I said, "but I cannot see that any further precautions are necessary."

"Nor I," agreed Kamlot; "she is quite well protected now."

We had dropped Vilor from our minds and were discussing other matters, when we heard the voice of the lookout in the crow's nest shouting, "Voo notar!" ("A ship!") Running to the tower deck, we got the bearings of the stranger as the lookout announced them the second time, and, sure enough, almost directly abeam on the starboard side we discerned the superstructure of a ship on the horizon.

For some reason which I do not clearly understand, the visibility on Venus is usually exceptionally good. Low fogs and haze are rare, notwithstanding the humidity of the atmosphere. This condition may be due to the mysterious radiation from that strange element in the planet's structure which illuminates her moonless nights; I do not know.

At any rate, we could see a ship, and almost immediately all was excitement aboard the Sofal. Here was another prize, and the men were eager to be at her. As we changed our course and headed for our victim, a cheer rose from the men on deck. Weapons were issued, the bow gun and the two tower guns were elevated to firing positions. The Sofal forged ahead at full speed.

As we approached our quarry, we saw that it was a ship of about the same size as the Sofal and bearing the insignia of Thora. Closer inspection revealed it to be an armed merchantman.

I now ordered all but the gunners into the lower deck house, as I planned on boarding this vessel as I had the Sovong and did not wish her to see our deck filled with armed men before we came alongside. As before, explicit orders were issued; every man knew what was expected of him; all were cautioned against needless killing. If I were to be a pirate, I was going to be as humane a pirate as possible. I would not spill blood needlessly.

I had questioned Kiron, Gamfor, and many another Thoran in my company relative to the customs and practices of Thoran ships of war until I felt reasonably familiar with them. I knew for instance that a warship might search a merchantman. It was upon this that I based my hope of getting our grappling hooks over the side of our victim before he could suspect our true design.

When we were within hailing distance of the ship, I directed Kiron to order her to shut down her engines, as we wished to board and search her; and right then we ran into our first obstacle. It came in the form of a pennant suddenly hoisted at the bow of our intended victim. It meant nothing to me, but it did to Kiron and the other Thorans aboard the Sofal.

"We'll not board her so easily after all," said Kiron. "She has an ongyan on board, and that exempts her from search. It probably also indicates that she carries a larger complement of soldiers than a merchantman ordinarily does."

"Whose friend?" I asked, "Yours?" for ongyan means great friend, in the sense of eminent or exalted.

Kiron smiled. "It is a title. There are a hundred klongyan in the oligarchy; one of them is aboard that ship. They are great friends unquestionably, great friends of themselves, they rule Thora more tyrannically than any jong and for themselves alone."

"How will the men feel about attacking a ship bearing so exalted a personages" I enquired.

"They will fight among themselves to be the first aboard and to run a sword through him."

"They must not kill him," I replied. "I have a better plan."

They will be hard to control once they are in the thick of a fight," Kiron assured me; "I have yet to see the officer who can do it. In the old days, in the days of the jongs, there were order and discipline; but not now."

"There will be aboard the Sofal," I averred. "Come with me; I am going to speak to the men."

Together we entered the lower deck house where the majority of the ship's company was massed, waiting for the command to attack. There were nearly a hundred rough and burly fighting men, nearly all of whom were ignorant and brutal. We had been together as commander and crew for too short a time for me to gauge their sentiments toward me; but I realized that there must be no question in any mind as to who was captain of the ship, no matter what they thought of me.

Kiron had called them to attention as we entered, and now every eye was on me as I started to speak. "We are about to take another ship," I began, "on board which is one whom Kiron tells me you will want to kill. He is an ongyan. I have come here to tell you that he must not be killed." Growls of disapproval greeted this statement, but, ignoring them, I continued, "I have come here to tell you something else, because I have been informed that no officer can control you after you enter battle. There are reasons why it will be better for us to hold this man prisoner than to kill him, but these have nothing to do with the question; what you must understand is that my orders and the orders of your other officers must be obeyed.

"We are embarked upon an enterprise that can succeed only if discipline be enforced. I expect the enterprise to succeed. I will enforce discipline. Insubordination or disobedience will be punishable by death. That is all."

As I left the room, I left behind me nearly a hundred silent men. There was nothing to indicate what their reaction had been. Purposely, I took Kiron out with me; I wanted the men to have an opportunity to discuss the matter among themselves without interference by an officer. I knew that I had no real authority over them, and that eventually they must decide for themselves whether they would obey me; the sooner that decision was reached the better for all of us.

Amtorian ships employ only the most primitive means of intercommunication. There is a crude and cumbersome hand signalling system in which flags are employed; then there is a standardized system of trumpet calls which covers a fairly wide range of conventional messages, but the most satisfactory medium and the most used is the human voice.

Since our quarry had displayed the pennant of the ongyan, we had held a course parallel to hers and a little distance astern. On her main deck a company of armed men was congregated She mounted four guns, which had been elevated into firing position. She was ready, but I think that as yet she suspected nothing wrong in our intentions.

Now I gave orders that caused the Sofal to close in upon the other ship, and as the distance between them lessened I saw indications of increasing excitement on the decks of our intended victim.

"What are you about?" shouted an officer from her tower deck. "Stand off there! There is an ongyan aboard us."

As no reply was made to him, and as the Sofal continued to draw nearer, his excitement waxed. He gesticulated rapidly as he conversed with a fat man standing at his side; then he screamed, "Stand off! or some one will suffer for this"; but the Sofal only moved steadily closer. "Stand off, or I'll fire!" shouted the captain.

For answer I caused all our starboard guns to be elevated into firing position. I knew he would not dare fire now, for a single broadside from the Sofal would have sunk him in less than a minute, a contingency which I wished to avoid as much as he.

"What do you want of us?" he demanded.

"We want to board you," I replied, "without bloodshed if possible."

"This is revolution! This is treason!" shouted the fat man at the captain's side. "I order you to stand off and leave us alone. I am the ongyan, Moosko," and then to the soldiers on the main deck he screamed, "Repel them! Kill any man who sets foot upon that deck!"

## Chapter 13

# Catastrophe

At the same moment that the ongyan, Moosko, ordered his soldiers to repel any attempt to board his ship, her captain ordered full speed ahead and threw her helm to starboard. She veered away from us and leaped ahead in an effort to escape. Of course I could have sunk her, but her loot would have been of no value to me at the bottom of the sea; instead I directed the trumpeter at my side to sound full speed ahead to the officer in the tower, and the chase was on.

The Yan, whose name was now discernible across her stern, was much faster than Kiron had led me to believe; but the Sofal was exceptionally speedy, and it soon became obvious to all that the other ship could not escape her. Slowly we regained the distance that we had lost in the first, unexpected spurt of the Yan; slowly but surely we were closing up on her. Then the captain of the Yan did just what I should have done had I been in his place; he kept the Sofal always directly astern of him and opened fire on us with his after tower gun and with a gun similarly placed in the stern on the lower deck. The manoeuvre was tactically faultless, since it greatly reduced the number of guns that we could bring into play without changing our course, and was the only one that might offer him any hope of escape.

There was something eerie in the sound of that first heavy Amtorian gun that I had heard. I saw nothing, neither smoke nor flame; there was only a loud staccato roar more reminiscent of machine gun fire than of any other sound. At first there was no other effect; then I saw a piece of our starboard rail go and two of my men fall to the deck.

By this time our bow gun was in action. We were in the swell of the Yan's wake, which made accurate firing difficult. The two ships were racing ahead at full speed; the prow of the Sofal was throwing white water and spume far to either side; the sea in the wake of the

Yan was boiling, and a heavy swell that we were quartering kept the ships rolling. The thrill of the chase and of battle was in our blood, and above all was the venomous rattle of the big guns.

I ran to the bow to direct the fire of the gun there, and a moment later we had the satisfaction of seeing the crew of one of the Yan's guns crumple to the deck man by man, as our gunner got his sights on them and mowed them down.

The Sofal was gaining rapidly upon the Yan, and our guns were concentrating on the tower gun and the tower of the enemy. The ongyan had long since disappeared from the upper deck, having doubtlessly sought safety in a less exposed part of the ship, and in fact there were only two men left alive upon the tower deck where he had stood beside the captain; these were two of the crew of the gun that was giving us most trouble.

I did not understand at the time why the guns of neither ship were more effective. I knew that the T-ray was supposedly highly destructive, and so I could not understand why neither ship had been demolished or sunk; but that was because I had not yet learned that all the vital parts of the ships were protected by a thin armour of the same metal of which the large guns were composed, the only substance at all impervious to the T-ray. Had this not been true, our fire would have long since put the Yan out of commission, as our T-rays, directed upon her after tower gun, would have passed on through the tower, killing the men at the controls and destroying the controls themselves. Eventually this would have happened, but it would have been necessary first to have destroyed the protective armour of the tower.

At last we succeeded in silencing the remaining gun, but if we were to draw up alongside the Yan we must expose ourselves to the fire of other guns located on her main deck and the forward end of the tower. We had already suffered some losses, and I knew that we must certainly expect a great many more if we put ourselves in range of those other guns; but there seemed no other alternative than to abandon the chase entirely, and that I had no mind to do.

Giving orders to draw up along her port side, I directed the fire of the bow gun along her rail where it would rake her port guns one by one as we moved up on her, and gave orders that each of our starboard guns in succession should open fire similarly as they came within range of the Yan's guns. Thus we kept a steady and continuous fire streaming upon the unhappy craft as we drew alongside her and closed up the distance between us.

We had suffered a number of casualties, but our losses were nothing compared to those of the Yan, whose decks were now strewn with dead and dying men. Her plight was hopeless, and her commander must at last have realized it, for now he gave the signal of surrender and stopped his engines. A few minutes later we were alongside and our boarding party had clambered over her rail.

As Kamlot and I stood watching these men who were being led by Kiron to take possession of the prize and bring certain prisoners aboard the Sofal, I could not but speculate upon what their answer was to be to my challenge for leadership. I knew that their freedom from the constant menace of their tyrannical masters was so new to them that they might well be expected to commit excesses, and I dreaded the result for I had determined to make an example of any men who disobeyed me, though I fell in the attempt. I saw the majority of them spread over the deck under the command of the great Zog, while Kiron led a smaller detachment to the upper decks in search of the captain and the ongyan.

Fully five minutes must have elapsed before I saw my lieutenant emerge from the tower of the Yan with his two prisoners. He conducted them down the companionway and across the main deck toward the Sofal, while a hundred members of my pirate band watched them in silence. Not a hand was raised against them as they passed.

Kamlot breathed a sigh of relief as the two men clambered over the rail of the Sofal and approached us. "I think that our lives hung in the balance then, quite as much as theirs," he said, and I agreed with him, for if my men had started killing aboard the Yan in defiance of my orders, they would have had to kill me and those loyal to me to protect their own lives.

The ongyan was still blustering when they were halted in front of me, but the captain was awed. There was something about the whole incident that mystified him, and when he got close enough to me to see the colour of my hair and eyes, I could see that he was dumfounded.

"This is an outrage," shouted Moosko, the ongyan. "I will see that every last man of you is destroyed for this." He was trembling, and purple with rage.

"See that he does not speak again unless he is spoken to," I instructed Kiron, and then I turned to the captain. "As soon as we have taken what we wish from your ship," I told him, "you will be free to continue your voyage. I am sorry that you did not see fit to obey me when I ordered you to stop for boarding; it would have saved many lives. The next time you are ordered to lay to by the Sofal, do so; and when you return to your own country, advise other shipmasters that the Sofal is abroad and that she is to be obeyed."

"Do you mind telling me," he asked, "who you are and under what flag you sail?"

"For the moment I am a Vepajan," I replied, "but we sail under our own flag. No country is responsible for what we do, nor are we responsible to any country."

Pressing the crew of the Yan into service, Kamlot, Kiron, Gamfor, and Zog had all her weapons, such of her provisions as we wished, and the most valuable and least bulky portion of her cargo transferred to the Sofal before dark. We then threw her guns overboard and let her proceed upon her way.

Moosko I retained as a hostage in the event that we should ever need one; he was being held under guard on the main deck until I could determine just what to do with him. The Vepajan women captives we had rescued from the Sovong, together with our own officers who were also quartered on the second deck, left me no vacant cabin in which to put Moosko, and I did not wish to confine him below deck in the hole reserved for common prisoners.

I chanced to mention the matter to Kamlot in the presence of Vilor, when the latter immediately suggested that he would share his own small cabin with Moosko and be responsible for him. As this seemed an easy solution of the problem, I ordered Moosko turned over to Vilor, who took him at once to his cabin.

The pursuit of the Yan had taken us off our course, and now, as we headed once more toward Vepaja, a dark land mass was dimly visible to starboard. I could not but wonder what mysteries lay beyond that shadowy coast line, what strange beasts and men inhabited that terra incognita that stretched away into Strabol and the unexplored equatorial regions of Venus. To partially satisfy my curiosity, I went to the chart room, and after determining our position as accurately as I could by dead reckoning, I discovered that we were off the shore of Noobol. I remembered having heard Danus mention this country, but I could not recall what he had told me about it.

Lured by imaginings, I went out onto the tower deck and stood alone, looking out across the faintly illuminated nocturnal waters of Amtor toward mysterious Noobol. The wind had risen to almost the proportions of a gale, the first that I had encountered since my coming to the Shepherd's Star; heavy seas were commencing to run, but I had every confidence in the ship and in the ability of my officers to navigate her under any circumstances; so I was not perturbed by the increasing violence of the storm. It occurred to me though that the women aboard might be frightened, and my thoughts, which were seldom absent from her for long, returned to Duare. Perhaps she was frightened!

Even no excuse is a good excuse to the man who wishes to see the object of his infatuation; but now I prided myself that I had a real reason for seeing her and one that she herself must appreciate, since it was prompted by solicitude for her welfare. And so I went down the companionway to the second deck with the intention of whistling before the door of Duare; but as I had to pass directly by Vilor's cabin, I thought that I would take the opportunity to look in on my prisoner.

There was a moment's silence following my signal, and then Vilor bade me enter. As I stepped into the cabin, I was surprised to see an angan sitting there with Moosko and Vilor. Vilor's embarrassment was obvious; Moosko appeared ill at ease and the birdman frightened. That they were disconcerted did not surprise me, for it is not customary for members of the superior race to fraternize with klangan socially. But if they were embarrassed, I was not. I was more inclined to be angry. The position of the Vepajans aboard the Sofal was a delicate one. We were few in numbers, and our ascendancy depended wholly upon the respect we engendered and maintained in the minds of the Thorans, who constituted the majority of our company, and who looked up to the Vepajans as their superiors despite the efforts of their leaders to convince them of the equality of all men.

"Your quarters are forward," I said to the angan; "you do not belong here."

"It is not his fault," said Vilor, as the birdman rose to leave the cabin. "Moosko, strange as it may seem, had never seen an angan; and I fetched this fellow here merely to satisfy his curiosity. I am sorry if I did wrong."

"Of course," I said, "that puts a slightly different aspect on the matter, but I think it will be better if the prisoner inspects the klangan on deck where they belong. He has my permission to do so tomorrow."

The angan departed, I exchanged a few more words with Vilor, and then I left him with his prisoner and turned toward the after cabin where Duare was quartered, the episode that had just occurred fading from my mind almost immediately, to be replaced by far more pleasant thoughts.

There was a light in Duare's cabin as I whistled before her door, wondering if she would invite me in or ignore my presence. For a time there was no response to my signal, and I had about determined that she would not see me, when I heard her soft, low voice inviting me to enter.

"You are persistent," she said, but there was less anger in her voice than when last she had spoken to me.

"I came to ask if the storm has frightened you and to assure you that there is no danger."

"I am not afraid," she replied. "Was that all that you wished to say?"

It sounded very much like a dismissal. "No," I assured her, "nor did I come solely for the purpose of saying it."

She raised her eyebrows. "What else could you have to say to me—that you have not already said?"

"Perhaps I wished to repeat," I suggested.

"You must not!" she cried.

I came closer to her. "Look at me, Duare; look me in the eyes and tell me that you do not like to hear me tell you that I love you!"

Her eyes fell. "I must not listen!" she whispered and rose as though to leave the room.

I was mad with love for her; her near presence sent the hot blood boiling through my veins; I seized her in my arms and drew her to me; before she could prevent it, I covered her lips with mine. Then she partially tore away from me, and I saw a dagger gleaming in her hand.

"You are right," I said. "Strike! I have done an unforgivable thing. My only excuse is my great love for you; it swept away reason and honour."

Her dagger hand dropped to her side. "I cannot," she sobbed, and, turning, fled from the room.

I went back to my own cabin, cursing myself for a beast and a cad. I could not understand how it had been possible for me to have committed such an unpardonable act. I reviled myself, and at the same time the memory of that soft body crushed against mine and those perfect lips against my lips suffused me with a warm glow of contentment that seemed far removed from repentance.

I lay awake for a long time after I went to bed, thinking of Duare, recalling all that had ever passed between us. I found a hidden meaning in her cry, "I must not listen!" I rejoiced in the facts that once she had refused to consign me to death at the hands of others and that again she had refused to kill me herself. Her "I cannot" rang in my ears almost like an avowal of love. My better judgment told that I was quite mad, but I found joy in hugging my madness to me.

The storm increased to such terrific fury during the night that the screeching of the wind and the wild plunging of the Sofal awakened me just before dawn. Arising immediately, I went on deck, where the wind almost carried me away. Great waves lifted the Sofal on high, only to plunge her the next moment into watery abysses. The ship was pitching violently; occasionally a huge wave broke across her bow and flooded the main deck; across her starboard quarter loomed a great land mass that seemed perilously close. The situation appeared fraught with danger.

I entered the control room and found both Honan and Gamfor with the helmsman. They were worried because of our proximity to land. Should either the engines or the steering device fail, we must inevitably be driven ashore. I told them to remain where they were, and then I went down to the second deck house to arouse Kiron, Kamlot, and Zog.

As I turned aft from the foot of the companionway on the second deck, I noticed that the door of Vilor's cabin was swinging open and closing again with each roll of the vessel; but I gave the matter no particular thought at the time and passed on to awaken my other lieutenants. Having done so, I kept on to Duare's cabin, fearing that, if awake, she might be frightened by the rolling of the ship and the shrieking of the wind. To my surprise, I found her door swinging on its hinges.

Something, I do not know what, aroused my suspicion that all was not right far more definitely than the rather unimportant fact that the door to her outer cabin was unlatched. Stepping quickly inside, I uncovered the light and glanced quickly about the room. There was nothing amiss except, perhaps, the fact that the door to the inner cabin where she slept was also open and swinging on its hinges. I was sure that no one could be sleeping in there while both those doors were swinging and banging. It was possible, of course, that Duare was too frightened to get up and close them.

I stepped to the inner doorway and called her name aloud. There was no reply. I called again, louder; again, silence was my only answer. Now I was definitely perturbed. Stepping into the room, I uncovered the light and looked at the bed. It was empty—Duare was not there! But in the far corner of the cabin lay the body of the man who had stood guard outside her door.

Throwing conventions overboard, I hastened to each of the adjoining cabins where the rest of the Vepajan women were quartered. All were there except Duare. They had not seen her; they did not know where she was. Frantic from apprehension, I ran back to Kamlot's cabin and acquainted him with my tragic discovery. He was stunned.

"She must be on board," he cried. "Where else can she be?"

"I know she must be," I replied, "but something tells me she is not. We must search the ship at once—from stem to stern."

Zog and Kiron were emerging from their cabins as I came from Kamlot's. I told them of my discovery and ordered the search commenced; then I hailed a member of the watch and sent him to the crow's nest to question the lookout. I wanted to know whether he had seen anything unusual transpiring on the ship during his watch, for from his lofty perch he could overlook the entire vessel.

"Muster every man," I told Kamlot; "account for every human being on board; search every inch of the ship."

As the men left to obey my instructions, I recalled the coincidence of the two cabin doors swinging wide—Duare's and Vilor's. I could not imagine what relation either fact had to the other, but I was investigating everything, whether it was of a suspicious nature or not; so I ran quickly to Vilor's cabin, and the moment that I uncovered the light I saw that both Vilor and Moosko were missing. But where were they? No man could have left the Sofal in that storm and lived, even could he have launched a boat, which would have been impossible of accomplishment, even in fair weather, without detection.

Coming from Vilor's cabin, I summoned a sailor and dispatched him to inform Kamlot that Vilor and Moosko were missing from their cabin and direct him to send them to me as soon as he located them; then I returned to the quarters of the Vepajan women for the purpose of questioning them more carefully.

I was puzzled by the disappearance of Moosko and Vilor, which, taken in conjunction with the absence of Duare from her cabin, constituted a mystery of major proportions; and I was trying to discover some link of circumstance that might point a connection between the two occurrences, when I suddenly recalled Vilor's insistence that he be permitted to guard Duare. Here was the first, faint suggestion of a connecting link. However, it seemed to lead nowhere. These three people had disappeared from their cabins, yet reason assured me that they would be found in a short time, since it was impossible for them to leave the ship, unless—

It was that little word "unless" that terrified me most of all. Since I had discovered that Duare was not in her cabin, a numbing fear had assailed me that, considering herself dishonoured by my avowal of love, she had hurled herself overboard. Of what value now the fact that I constantly upbraided myself for my lack of consideration and control? Of what weight my vain regrets?

Yet now I saw a tiny ray of hope. If the absence ofVilor and Moosko from their cabin and Duare from hers were more than a coincidence, then it were safe to assume that they were together and ridiculous to believe that all three had leaped overboard.

With these conflicting fears and hopes whirling through my brain, I came to the quarters of the Vepajan women, which I was about to enter when the sailor I had sent to question the lookout in the crow's nest came running toward me in a state of evident excitement.

"Well," I demanded, as, breathless, he halted before me, "what did the lookout have to say?"

"Nothing, my captain," replied the man, his speech retarded by excitement and exertion.

"Nothing! and why not?" I snapped.

"The lookout is dead, my captain," gasped the sailor.

"Dead!"

"Murdered."

"How?" I asked.

"A sword had been run through his body—from behind, I think. He lay upon his face."

"Go at once and inform Kamlot; tell him to replace the lookout and investigate his death, then to report to me."

Shaken by this ominous news, I entered the quarters of the women. They were huddled together in one cabin, pale and frightened, but outwardly calm.

"Have you found Duare?" one of them asked immediately.

"No," I replied, "but I have discovered another mystery—the ongyan, Moosko, is missing and with him the Vepajan, Vilor."

"Vepajan!" exclaimed Byea, the woman who had questioned me concerning Duare. "Vilor is no Vepajan."

"What do you mean?" I demanded. "If he is not a Vepajan, what is he?"

"He is a Thoran spy," she replied. "He was sent to Vepaja long ago to steal the secret of the longevity serum, and when we were captured the klangan took him, also, by mistake. We learned this, little by little, aboard the Sovong."

"But why was I not informed when he was brought aboard?" I demanded.

"We supposed that everyone knew it," explained Byea, "and thought that Vilor was transferred to the Sofal as a prisoner."

Another link in the chain of accumulating evidence! Yet I was as far as ever from knowing where either end of the chain lay.

## Chapter 14

# Storm

After questioning the women, I went to the main deck, too impatient to await the reports of my lieutenants in the tower where I belonged. I found that they had searched the ship and were just coming to me with their report. None of those previously discovered missing had been found, but the search had revealed another astounding fact—the five klangan also were missing!

Searching certain portions of the ship had been rather dangerous work, as she was rolling heavily, and the deck was still occasionally swept by the larger seas; but it had been accomplished without mishap, and the men were now congregated in a large room in the main deck house. Kamlot, Gamfor, Kiron, Zog, and I had also entered this same room, where we were discussing the whole mysterious affair. Honan was in the control room of the tower.

I told them that I had just discovered that Vilor was not Vepajan but a Thoran spy, and had reminded Kamlot of the man's request that he be allowed to guard the janjong. "I learned something else from Byea while I was questioning the women," I added. "During their captivity aboard the Sovong, Vilor persisted in annoying Duare with his attentions; he was infatuated with her."

"I think that gives us the last bit of evidence we need to enable us to reconstruct the hitherto seemingly inexplicable happenings of the past night," said Gamfor. "Vilor wished to possess Duare; Moosko wished to escape from captivity. The former had fraternized with the klangan and made friends of them; that was known to everyone aboard the Sofal. Moosko was an ongyan; during all their lives, doubtless, the klangan have looked upon the klongyan as the fountain heads of supreme authority. They would believe his promises, and they would obey his commands.

"Doubtless Vilor and Moosko worked out the details of the plot together. They dispatched an angan to kill the lookout, lest their movements arouse suspicion and be reported before they could carry their plan to a successful conclusion. The lookout disposed of, the other klangan congregated in Vilor's cabin; then Vilor, probably accompanied by Moosko, went to the cabin of Duare, where they killed the guard and seized her in her sleep, silenced her with a gag, and carried her to the gangway outside, where the klangan were waiting.

"A gale was blowing, it is true, but it was blowing toward land which lay but a short distance to starboard; and the klangan are powerful fliers.

"There you have what I believe to be a true picture of what happened aboard the Sofal while we slept."

"And you believe that the klangan carried these three people to the shores of Noobol?" I asked.

"I think there can be no question but that such is the fact," replied Gamfor.

"I quite agree with him," interjected Kamlot.

"Then there is but one thing to do," I announced. "We must turn back and land a searching party on Noobol."

"No boat could live in this sea," objected Kiron.

"The storm will not last forever," I reminded him. "We shall lie off the shore until it abates. I am going up to the tower; I wish you men would remain here and question the crew; it is possible that there may be some one among them who has overheard something that will cast new light on the subject. The klangan are great talkers, and they may have dropped some remark that will suggest the ultimate destination Vilor and Moosko had in mind."

As I stepped out onto the main deck, the Sofal rose upon the crest of a great wave and then plunged nose downward into the watery abyss beyond, tilting the deck forward at an angle of almost forty-five degrees. The wet and slippery boards beneath my feet gave them no hold, and I slid helplessly forward almost fifty feet before I could check my descent. Then the ship buried her nose in a mountainous wave and a great wall of water swept the deck from stem to stern, picking me up and whirling me helplessly upon its crest.

For a moment I was submerged, and then a vagary of the Titan that had seized me brought my head above the water, and I saw the Sofal rolling and pitching fifty feet away.

Even in the immensity of interstellar space I had never felt more helpless nor more hopeless than I did at that moment on the storm-lashed sea of an unknown world, surrounded by darkness and chaos and what terrible creatures of this mysterious deep I could not even guess. I was lost! Even if my comrades knew of the disaster that had overwhelmed me, they were helpless to give me aid. No boat could live in that sea, as Kiron had truly reminded us, and no swimmer could breast the terrific onslaught of those racing, wind-driven mountains of water that might no longer be described by so puny a word as wave.

Hopeless! I should not have said that; I am never without hope. If I could not swim against the sea, perhaps I might swim with it; and at no great distance lay land. I am an experienced distance swimmer and a powerful man. If any man could survive in such a sea, I knew that I could; but if I could not, I was determined that I should at least have the satisfaction of dying fighting.

I was hampered by no clothes, as one could scarcely dignify the Amtorian loincloth with the name of clothing; my only impediment was my weapons; and these I hesitated to discard, knowing that my chances for survival on that unfriendly shore would be slight were I unarmed. Neither the belt, nor the pistol, nor the dagger inconvenienced me, and their weight was negligible; but the sword was a different matter. If you have never tried swimming with a sword dangling from your middle, do not attempt it in a heavy sea. You might think that it would hang straight down and not get in the way, but mine did not. The great waves hurled me about mercilessly, twisting and turning me; and now my sword was buffeting me in some tender spot, and now it was getting between my legs, and once, when a wave turned me completely over, it came down on top of me and struck me on the head; yet I would not discard it.

After the first few minutes of battling with the sea, I concluded that I was in no immediate danger of being drowned. I could keep my head above the waves often enough and long enough to insure sufficient air for my lungs; and, the water being warm, I was in no danger of being chilled to exhaustion, as so often occurs when men are thrown into cold seas. Therefore, as closely as I could anticipate any contingency in this unfamiliar world, there remained but two major and immediate threats against my life. The first lay in the possibility of attack by some ferocious monster of the Amtorian deeps; the second, and by far the more serious, the storm-lashed shore upon which I must presently attempt to make a safe landing.

This in itself should have been sufficient to dishearten me, for I had seen seas breaking upon too many shores to lightly ignore the menace of those incalculable tons of hurtling waters pounding, crashing, crushing, tearing their way even into the rocky heart of the eternal hills.

I swam slowly in the direction of the shore, which, fortunately for me, was in the direction that the storm was carrying me. I had no mind to sap my strength by unnecessarily overexerting myself; and so, as I took it easily, content to keep afloat as I moved slowly shoreward, daylight came; and as each succeeding wave lifted me to its summit, I saw the shore with increasing clearness. It lay about a mile from me, and its aspect was most forbidding. Huge combers were breaking upon a rocky coast line, throwing boiling fountains of white spume high in air; above the howling of the tempest, the thunder of the surf rolled menacingly across that mile of angry sea to warn me that death lay waiting to embrace me at the threshold of safety.

I was in a quandary. Death lay all about me; it remained but for me to choose the place and manner of the assignation; I could drown where I was, or I could permit myself to be dashed to pieces on the rocks. Neither eventuality aroused any considerable enthusiasm in my breast. As a mistress, death seemed sadly lacking in many essentials. Therefore, I decided not to die.

Thoughts may be, as has been said, things; but they are not everything. No matter how favourably I thought of living, I knew that I must also do something about it. My present situation offered me no chance of salvation; the shore alone could give me life; so I struck out for the shore. As I drew nearer it, many things, some of them quite irrelevant, passed through my mind; but some were relevant, among them the Burial Service. It was not a nice time to think of this, but then we cannot always control our thoughts; however, "In the midst of life we are in death" seemed wholly appropriate to my situation. By twisting it a bit, I achieved something that contained the germ of hope—in the midst of death there is life. Perhaps—

The tall waves, lifting me high, afforded me for brief instants vantage points from which I could view the death ahead in the midst of which I sought for life. The shore line was becoming, at closer range, something more than an unbroken line of jagged rocks and white water; but details were yet lacking, for each time I was allowed but a brief glimpse before being dropped once more to the bottom of a watery chasm.

My own efforts, coupled with the fury of the gale driving me shoreward, brought me rapidly to the point where I should presently be seized by the infuriated seas and hurled upon the bombarded rocks that reared their jagged heads bleakly above the swirling waters of each receding comber.

A great wave lifted me upon its crest and carried me forward—the end had come! With the speed of a race horse it swept me toward my doom; a welter of spume engulfed my head; I was twisted and turned as a cork in a whirlpool; yet I struggled to lift my mouth above the surface for an occasional gasp of air; I fought to live for a brief moment longer, that I might not be dead when I was dashed by the merciless sea against the merciless rocks—thus dominating is the urge to live.

I was carried on; moments seemed an eternity! Where were the rocks? I almost yearned for them now to end the bitterness of my futile struggle. I thought of my mother and of Duare. I even contemplated, with something akin to philosophic calm, the strangeness of my end. In that other world that I had left forever no creature would ever have knowledge of my fate. Thus spoke the eternal egotism of man, who, even in death, desires an audience.

Now I caught a brief glimpse of rocks. They were upon my left! when they should have been in front of me. It was incomprehensible. The wave tore on, carrying me with it; and still I lived, and there was only water against my naked flesh.

Now the fury of the sea abated. I rose to the crest of a diminishing comber to look with astonishment upon the comparatively still waters of an inlet. I had been carried through the rocky gateway of a landlocked cove, and before me I saw a sandy crescent beach. I had escaped the black fingers of death; I had been the beneficiary of a miracle!

The sea gave me a final fillip that rolled me high upon the sands to mingle with the wrack and flotsam she had discarded. I stood up and looked about me. A more devout man would have given thanks, but I felt that as yet I had little for which to give thanks. My life had been spared temporarily, but Duare was still in peril.

The cove into which I had been swept was formed by the mouth of a canyon that ran inland between low hills, the sides and summits of which were dotted with small trees. Nowhere did I see any such giants as grow in Vepaja; but perhaps, I mused, what I see here are not trees on Venus but only underbrush. However, I shall call them trees, since many of them were from fifty to eighty feet in height.

A little river tumbled down the canyon's bottom to empty into the cove; pale violet grass, starred with blue and purple flowers, bordered it and clothed the hills. There were trees with red boles, smooth and glossy as lacquer. There were trees with azure boles. Whipping in the gale was the same weird foliage of heliotrope and lavender and violet that had rendered the forests of Vepaja so unearthly to my eyes. But beautiful and unusual as was the scene, it could not claim my undivided attention. A strange freak of fate had thrown me upon this shore to which, I had reason to believe, Duare must undoubtedly have been carried; and now my only thought was to take advantage of this fortunate circumstance and attempt to find and succour her.

I could only assume that in the event her abductors had brought her to this shore their landing must have been made farther along the coast to my right, which was the direction from which the Sofal had been moving. With only this slight and unsatisfactory clue, I started immediately to scale the side of the canyon and commence my search.

At the summit I paused a moment to survey the surrounding country and get my bearings. Before me stretched a rolling tableland, tree-dotted and lush with grass, and beyond that, inland, rose a range of mountains, vague and mysterious along the distant horizon. My course lay to the east, along the coast (I shall use the earthly references to points of compass); the mountains were northward, toward the equator. I am assuming of course that I am in the southern hemisphere of the planet. The sea was south of me. I glanced in that direction, looking for the Sofal; there she was, far out and moving toward the east. Evidently my orders were being carried out, and the Sofal was lying off shore waiting for calm weather that would permit a landing.

Now I turned my steps toward the east. At each elevation I stopped and scanned the tableland in all directions, searching for some sign of those I sought. I saw signs of life, but not of human life. Herbivorous animals grazed in large numbers upon the flower-starred violet plain. Many that were close enough to be seen plainly appeared similar in form to earthly animals, but there was none exactly like anything I had ever seen on earth. Their extreme wariness and the suggestion of speed and agility in their conformations suggested that they had enemies; the wariness, that among these enemies was man; the speed and agility, that swift and ferocious carnivores preyed upon them.

These observations served to warn me that I must be constantly on the alert for similar dangers that might threaten me, and I was glad that the table-land was well supplied with trees growing at convenient intervals. I had not forgotten the ferocious basto that Kamlot and I had encountered in Vepaja, and, though I had seen nothing quite so formidable as yet among the nearer beasts, there were some creatures grazing at a considerable distance from me whose lines suggested a too great similarity to those bison like omnivores to insure ease of mind.

I moved rather rapidly, as I was beset by fears for Duare's safety and felt that if I did not come upon some clue this first day my search might prove fruitless. The klangan, I believed, must have alighted near the coast, where they would have remained at least until daylight, and my hope was that they might have tarried longer. If they had winged away immediately, my chances of locating them were slight; and now my only hope lay in the slender possibility that I might come across them before they took up their flight for the day.

The table-land was cut by gullies and ravines running down to the sea. Nearly all of these carried streams varying in size from tiny rivulets to those which might be dignified by the appellation of river, but none that I encountered offered any serious obstacle to my advance, though upon one or two occasions I was forced to swim the deeper channels. If these rivers were inhabited by dangerous reptiles, I saw nothing of them, though I admit that they were constantly on my mind as I made my way from bank to bank.

Once, upon the table-land, I saw a large, catlike creature at a distance, apparently stalking a herd of what appeared to be a species of antelope; but either it did not see me or was more interested in its natural prey, for although I was in plain sight, it paid no attention to me.

Shortly thereafter I dropped into a small gully, and when I had regained the higher ground upon the opposite side the beast was no longer in sight; but even had it been, it would have been driven from my thoughts by faint sounds that came to me out of the distance far ahead. There were what sounded like the shouts of men and the unmistakable hum of Amtorian pistol fire.

Though I searched diligently with my eyes to the far horizon, I could see no sign of the authors of these noises; but it was enough for me to know that there were human beings ahead and that there was fighting there. Being only human, I naturally pictured the woman I loved in the centre of overwhelming dangers, even though my better judgment told me that the encounter reverberating in the distance might have no connection with her or her abductors.

Reason aside, however, I broke into a run; and as I advanced the sounds waxed louder. They led me finally to the rim of a considerable canyon, the bottom of which formed a level valley of entrancing loveliness, through which wound a river far larger than any I had yet encountered.

But neither the beauty of the valley nor the magnitude of the river held my attention for but an instant. Down there upon the floor of that nameless canyon was a scene that gripped my undivided interest and left me cold with apprehension. Partially protected by an outcropping of rock at the river's edge, six figures crouched or lay. Five of them were klangan, the sixth a woman. It was Duare!

Facing them, hiding behind trees and rocks, were a dozen hairy, manlike creatures hurling rocks from slings at the beleaguered six or loosing crude arrows from still cruder bows. The savages and the klangan were hurling taunts and insults at one another, as well as missiles; it was these sounds that I had heard from a distance blending with the staccato hum of the klangan's pistols.

Three of the klangan lay motionless upon the turf behind their barrier, apparently dead. The remaining klangan and Duare crouched with pistols in their hands, defending their position and their lives. The savages cast their stone missiles directly at the three whenever one of them showed any part of his body above the rocky breastwork, but the arrows they discharged into the air so that they fell behind the barrier.

Scattered about among the trees and behind rocks were the bodies of fully a dozen hairy savages who had fallen before the fire of the klangan, but, while Duare's defenders had taken heavy toll of the enemy, the outcome of the unequal battle could have been only the total destruction of the klangan and Duare had it lasted much longer.

The details which have taken long in the telling I took in at a single glance, nor did I waste precious time in pondering the best course of action. At any moment one of those crude arrows might pierce the girl I loved; and so my first thought was to divert the attention of the savages, and perhaps their fire, from their intended victims to me.

I was slightly behind their position, which gave me an advantage, as also did the fact that I was above them. Yelling like a Comanche, I leaped down the steep side of the canyon, firing my pistol as I charged. Instantly the scene below me changed. The savages, taken partially from the rear and unexpectedly menaced by a new enemy, leaped to their feet in momentary bewilderment; and simultaneously the two remaining klangan, recognizing me and realizing that succour was at hand, sprang from the shelter of their barrier and ran forward to complete the demoralization of the savages.

Together we shot down six of the enemy before the rest finally turned and fled, but they were not routed before one of the klangan was struck full between the eyes by a jagged bit of rock. I saw him fall, and when we were no longer menaced by a foe I went to him, thinking that he was only stunned; but at that time I had no conception of the force with which these primitive, apelike men cast the missiles from their slings. The fellow's skull was crushed, and a portion of the missile had punctured his brain. He was quite dead when I reached him.

Then I hastened to Duare. She was standing with a pistol in her hand, tired and dishevelled, but otherwise apparently little worse for the harrowing experiences through which she had passed. I think that she was glad to see me, for she certainly must have preferred me to the hairy ape-men from which I had been instrumental in rescuing her; yet a trace of fear was reflected in her eyes, as though she were not quite sure of the nature of the treatment she might expect from me. To my shame, her fears were justified by my past behaviour; but I was determined that she should never again have cause to complain of me. I would win her confidence and trust, hoping that love might follow in their wake.

There was no light of welcome in her eyes as I approached her, and that hurt me more than I can express. Her countenance rejected more a pathetic resignation to whatever new trials my presence might portend.

"You have not been harmed?" I asked. "You are all right?"

"Quite," she replied. Her eyes passed beyond me, searching the summit of the canyon wall down which I had charged upon the savages. "Where are the others?" she asked in puzzled and slightly troubled tones.

"What others?" I inquired.

"Those who came with you from the Sofal to search for me."

"There were no others; I am quite alone."

Her countenance assumed an even deeper gloom at this announcement. "Why did you come alone?" she asked fearfully.

"To be honest with you, it was through no fault of my own that I came at all at this time," I explained. "After we missed you from the Sofal, I gave orders to stand by off the coast until the storm abated and we could land a searching party. Immediately thereafter I was swept overboard, a most fortunate circumstance as it turned out; and naturally when I found myself safely ashore my first thought was of you. I was searching for you when I heard the shouts of the savages and the sound of pistol fire."

"You came in time to save me from them," she said, "but for what? What are you going to do with me now?"

"I am going to take you to the coast as quickly as possible," I replied, "and there we will signal the Sofal. She will send a boat to take us off."

Duare appeared slightly relieved at this recital of my plans. "You will win the undying gratitude of the jong, my father, if you return me to Vepaja unharmed," she said. "To have served his daughter shall be reward enough for me," I replied, "even though I succeed in winning not even her gratitude."

"That you already have for what you have just done at the risk of your life," she assured me, and there was more graciousness in her voice than before.

"What became ofVilor and Moosko?" I asked.

Her lip curled in scorn. "When the kloonobargan attacked us, they fled."

"Where did they go?" I asked.

"They swam the river and ran away in that direction." She pointed toward the east.

"Why did the klangan not desert you also?"

"They were told to protect me. They know little else than to obey their superiors, and, too, they like to fight. Having little intelligence and no imagination, they are splendid fighters."

"I cannot understand why they did not fly away from danger and take you with them when they saw that defeat was certain. That would have insured the safety of all."

"By the time they were assured of that, it was too late," she explained. "They could not have risen from behind our protection without being destroyed by the missiles of the kloonobargan."

This word, by way of parenthesis, is an interesting example of the derivation of an Amtorian substantive. Broadly, it means savages; literally, it means hairy men. In the singular, it is nobargan. Gan is man; bar is hair. No is a contraction of not (with), and is used as a prefix with the same value that the suffix y has in English; therefore nobar means hairy, nobargan, hairy man. The prefix kloo forms the plural, and we have kloonobargan (hairy men), savages.

After determining that the four klangan were dead, Duare, the remaining angan, and I started down the river toward the ocean. On the way Duare told me what had occurred on board the Sofal the preceding night, and I discovered that it had been almost precisely as Gamfor had pictured it.

"What was their object in taking you with them?" I asked.

"Vilor wanted me," she replied.

"And Moosko merely wished to escape?"

"Yes. He thought that he would be killed when the ship reached Vepaja."

"How did they expect to survive in a wild country like this?" I asked. "Did they know where they were?"

"They said that they thought that the country was Noobol," she replied, "but they were not positive. The Thorans have agents in Noobol who are fomenting discord in an attempt to overthrow the government. There are several of these in a city on the coast, and it was Moosko's intention to search for this city, where he was certain that he would find friends who would be able to arrange transportation for himself, Vilor, and me to Thora."

We walked on in silence for some time. I was just ahead of Duare, and the angan brought up the rear. He was crestfallen and dejected. His head and tail feathers drooped. The klangan are ordinarily so vociferous that this preternatural silence attracted my attention, and, thinking that he might have been injured in the fight, I questioned him. "I was not wounded, my captain," he replied.

"Then what is the matter with you? Are you sad because of the deaths of your comrades?"

"It is not that," he replied; "there are plenty more where they came from. It is because of my own death that I am sad."

"But you are not dead!"

"I shall be soon," he averred.

"What makes you think so?" I demanded.

"When I return to the ship, they will kill me for what I did last night. If I do not return, I shall be killed here. No one could live alone for long in such a country as this."

"If you serve me well and obey me, you will not be killed if we succeed in reaching the Sofal again," I assured him.

At that he brightened perceptibly. "I shall serve you well and obey you, my captain," he promised, and presently he was smiling and singing again as though he had not a single care in the world and there was no such thing as death.

On several occasions, when I had glanced back at my companions, I had discovered Duare's eyes upon me, and in each instance she had turned them away quickly, as though I had surprised and embarrassed her in some questionable act. I had spoken to her only when necessary, for I had determined to atone for my previous conduct by maintaining a purely official attitude toward her that would reassure her and give her no cause for apprehension as to my intentions.

This was a difficult role for me to play while I yearned to take her into my arms and tell her again of the great love that was consuming me; but I had succeeded so far in controlling myself and saw no reason to believe that I should not be able to continue to do so, at least as long as Duare continued to give me no encouragement. The very idea that she might give me encouragement caused me to smile in spite of myself.

Presently, much to my surprise, she said, "You are very quiet. What is the matter?"

It was the first time that Duare had ever opened a conversation with me or given me any reason to believe that I existed for her as a personality; I might have been a clod of earth or a piece of furniture, for all the interest she had seemed to take in me since those two occasions upon which I had surprised her as she watched me from the concealing foliage of her garden.

"There is nothing the matter with me," I assured her. "I am only concerned with your welfare and the necessity for getting you back to the Sofal as quickly as possible."

"You do not talk any more," she complained. "Formerly, when I saw you, you used to talk a great deal."

"Probably altogether too much," I admitted, "but you see, now I am trying not to annoy you."

Her eyes fell to the ground. "It would not annoy me," she said almost inaudibly, but now that I was invited to do the very thing that I had been longing to do, I became dumb; I could think of nothing to say. "You see," she continued in her normal voice, "conditions are very different now from any that I have ever before encountered. The rules and restrictions under which I have lived among my own people cannot, I now realize, be expected to apply to situations so unusual or to people and places so foreign to those whose lives they were intended to govern.

"I have been thinking a great deal about many things—and you. I commenced to think these strange thoughts after I saw you the first time in the garden at Kooaad. I have thought that perhaps it might be nice to talk to other men than those I am permitted to see in the house of my father, the jong. I became tired of talking to these same men and to my women, but custom had made a slave and a coward of me. I did not dare do the things I most wished to do. I always wanted to talk to you, and now for the brief time before we shall be again aboard the Sofal, where I must again be governed by the laws of Vepaja, I am going to be free; I am going to do what I wish; I am going to talk to you."

This naive declaration revealed a new Duare, one in the presence of whom it was going to be most difficult to maintain an austere Platonicism; yet I continued to steel myself to the carrying out of my resolve.

"Why do you not talk to me?" she demanded when I made no immediate comment on her confession.

"I do not know what to talk about," I admitted, "unless I talk about the one thing that is uppermost in my mind."

She was silent for a moment, her brows knit in thought, and then she asked with seeming innocence, "What is that?"

"Love," I said, looking into her eyes.

Her lids dropped and her lips trembled. "No!" she exclaimed. "We must not talk of that; it is wrong; it is wicked."

"Is love wicked on Amtor?" I asked.

"No, no; I do not mean that," she hastened to deny; "but it is wrong to speak to me of love until after I am twenty."

"May I then, Duare?" I asked.

She shook her head, a little sadly I thought. "No, not even then," she answered. "You may never speak to me of love, without sinning, nor may I listen without sinning, for I am the daughter of a jong."

"Perhaps it would be safer were we not to talk at all," I said glumly.

"Oh, yes, let us talk," she begged. "Tell me about the strange world you are supposed to come from."

To amuse her, I did as she requested; and walking beside her I devoured her with my eyes until at last we came to the ocean. Far out I saw the Sofal, and now came the necessity for devising a scheme by which we might signal her.

On either side of the canyon, through which the river emptied into the ocean, were lofty cliffs. That on the west side, and nearer us, was the higher, and to this I made my way, accompanied by Duare and the angan. The ascent was steep, and most of the way I found it, or made it, necessary to assist Duare, so that often I had my arm about her as I half carried her upward.

At first I feared that she might object to this close contact; but she did not, and in some places where it was quite level and she needed no help, though I still kept my arm about her, she did not draw away nor seem to resent the familiarity. At the summit of the cliff I hastily gathered dead wood and leaves with the assistance of the angan, and presently we had a signal fire sending a smoke column into the air. The wind had abated, and the smoke rose far above the cliff before it was dissipated. I was positive that it would be seen aboard the Sofal, but whether it would be correctly interpreted, I could not know.

A high sea was still running that would have precluded the landing of a small boat, but we had the angan, and if the Sofal were to draw in more closely to shore, he could easily transport us to her deck one at a time. However, I hesitated to risk Duare in the attempt while the ship was at its present considerable distance from shore, as what wind there was would have been directly in the face of the angan.

From the summit of this cliff we could overlook the cliff on the east side of the canyon, and presently the angan called my attention to something in that direction. "Men are coming," he said.

I saw them immediately, but they were still too far away for me to be able to identify them, though even at a distance I was sure that they were not of the same race as the savages which had attacked Duare and the klangan.

Now indeed it became imperative that we attract the attention of the Sofal immediately, and to that end I built two more fires at intervals from the first, so that it might be obvious to anyone aboard the ship that this was in fact a signal rather than an accidental fire or a camp fire.

Whether or not the Sofal had seen our signal, it was evident that the party of men approaching must have; and I could not but believe that, attracted by it, they were coming to investigate. Constantly they were drawing nearer, and as the minutes passed we saw that they were armed men of the same race as the Vepajans.

They were still some distance away when we saw the Sofal change her course and point her bow toward shore. Our signal had been seen, and our comrades were coming to investigate; but would they be in time? For us it was a thrilling race The wind had sprung up again and the sea was rising once more. I asked the angan if he could breast the gale, for I had determined to send Duare off at once if I received a favourable reply.

"I could alone," he said, "but I doubt that I could if I were carrying another."

We watched the Sofal plunging and wallowing in the rising sea as it forged steadily closer, and we watched the men drawing near with equal certainty. There was no doubt in my mind as to which would reach us first; my only hope now was that the Sofal could lessen the distance in the meantime sufficiently so that it would be safe for the angan to attempt to carry Duare to her.

Now the men had reached the summit of the cliff on the opposite side of the canyon, and here they halted and observed us while carrying on a discussion of some nature.

"Vilor is with them!" exclaimed Duare suddenly.

"And Moosko," I added. "I see them both now."

"What shall we do?" cried Duare. "Oh, they must not get me again!"

"They shall not," I promised her.

Down the canyon side they came now. We watched them swim the river and cross to the foot of the cliff where we were standing. We watched the Sofal creeping slowly shoreward. I went to the edge of the cliff and looked down upon the ascending men. They were half way up now. Then I returned to Duare and the angan.

"We can wait no longer," I said, and then to the angan, "Take the janjong and fly to the ship. She is closer now; you can make it; you must make it!"

He started to obey, but Duare drew away from him. "I will not go," she said quietly. "I will not leave you here alone!"

For those words I would gladly have laid down my life. Here again was still another Duare. I had expected nothing like this, for I did not feel that she owed me any such loyalty. It was not as though she had loved me; one might expect such self-sacrifice on the part of a woman for the man she loves. I was swept completely from my feet, but only for an instant. The enemy, if such it were, must by now be almost to the summit of the cliff, in a moment they would be upon us, and even as the thought touched my mind, I saw the first of them running toward us.

"Take her!" I cried to the angan. "There is no time to waste now."

He reached for her, but she attempted to elude him; and then I caught her, and as I touched her, all my good resolutions were swept away, as I felt her in my arms. I pressed her to me for an instant; I kissed her, and then I gave her over to the birdman.

"Hurry!" I cried. "They come!"

Spreading his powerful wings, he rose from the ground, while Duare stretched her hands toward me. "Do not send me away from you, Carson! Do not send me away! I love you!"

But it was too late; I would not have called her back could I have done so, for the armed men were upon me.

Thus I went into captivity in the land of Noobol an adventure that is no part of this story; but I went with the knowledge that the woman I loved, loved me, and I was happy.

The Second Adventure

# Lost on Venus

# Foreword

When Carson Napier left my office to fly to Guadalupe Island and take off for Mars in the giant rocket that he had constructed there for that purpose, I was positive that I should never see him again in the flesh. That his highly developed telepathic powers, through the medium of which he hoped to communicate with me, might permit me to envisage him and communicate with him I had no doubts; but I expected no messages after he had detonated the first rocket. I thought that Carson Napier would die within a few seconds of the initiation of his mad scheme.

But my fears were not realized. I followed him through his mad, month—long journey through space, trembling with him as the gravitation of the Moon drew the great rocket from its course and sent it hurtling toward the Sun, holding my breath as he was gripped by the power of Venus, and thrilling to his initial adventures upon that mysterious, cloud-enwrapped planet—Amtor, as it is known to its human inhabitants.

His love for the unattainable Duare, daughter of a king, their capture by the cruel Thorians, his self-sacrificing rescue of the girl, held me enthralled. I saw the strange, unearthly bird-man bearing Duare from the rockbound shore of Noobol to the ship that was to bear her back to her native land just as Carson Napier was overwhelmed and made prisoner by a strong band of Thorians.

I saw–but now let Carson Napier tell his own story in his own words while I retire again to the impersonality of my role of scribe.

## Chapter 1

# The Seven Doors

Leading my captors, but taking no part in the capture, were Moosko, the Ongyan, and Vilor, the Thorist spy, who had together conceived and carried out the abduction of Duare from aboard the Sofal.

They had reached the mainland, carried there by the flying angans, those strange winged humans of Venus. (To make the story simpler to understand, I am abandoning the Amtorian plural prefix, "kl" or akloo," and am forming the plural of nouns in the regular Earth fashion–by adding "s.") The pair had left Duare to her fate when the party was attacked by the hairy wild men from whom I had fortunately been able to rescue her with the aid of the angan who had so heroically defended her.

But now, though they had abandoned her to almost certain death, they were furious with me for having caused her to be carried from their clutches back to the deck of the Sofal by the last survivor of the angans; and having me within their power, after some one else had disarmed me, they became courageous again and attacked me violently.

I think they would have killed me on the spot had not a better idea suggested itself to another member of the Thorist party that had captured me.

Vilor, who had been unarmed, seized a sword from one of his fellows and set upon me with the evident intention of hacking me to pieces, when this man intervened.

"Wait!" he cried. "What has this man done that he should be killed swiftly and without suffering?"

"What do you mean?" demanded Vilor, lowering the point of his weapon.

This country in which we were was almost as strange to Vilor as to me, for he was from the distant mainland of Thora proper, while the party who had assisted in my capture were natives of this land of Noobol who had been induced to join the Thorists in their world-wide attempt to foment discord and overthrow all established forms of government and replace them with their own oligarchy of ignorance.

As Vilor hesitated, the other explained. "In Kapdor," he said, "we have far more interesting ways of disposing of enemies than spitting them on a sword."

"Explain," commanded the Ongyan, Moosko. "This man does not deserve the mercy of a quick death. A prisoner aboard the Sofal, with other Vepajans, he led a mutiny in which all the ship's officers were murdered; then he seized the Sovang, liberated her prisoners, looted her, threw her big guns into the sea, and sailed away upon a piratical expedition.

"In the Sofal, he overhauled the Yan, a merchant ship on which I, an ongyan, was a passenger. Ignoring my authority, he opened fire upon the Yan and then boarded her. After looting her and destroying her armament, he took me prisoner aboard the Sofal. He treated me with the utmost disrespect, threatening my life and destroying my liberty.

"For these things he must die, and if you have a death commensurate with his crimes you shall not go unrewarded by those who rule Thora."

"Let us take him back to Kapdor with us," said the man. "There we have the room with seven doors, and I promise you that if he be an intelligent being he will suffer more agony within its circular walls than any prick of a sword point might inflict upon him."

"Good!" exclaimed Vilor, handing his sword back to the man from whom he had borrowed it. "The creature deserves the worst."

They led me back along the coast in the direction from which they had come, and during the march I discovered from their conversation to what unfortunate chance I could attribute the ill fortune that had befallen me at the very moment when it seemed possible that Duare and I might easily return to the Sofal and our loyal friends.

This armed party from Kapdor had been searching for an escaped prisoner when their attention had been attracted by the fight between the hairy wild men and the angans who were defending Duare, just as I had similarly been attracted to the scene while searching for the beautiful daughter of Mintep, the jong of Vepaja.

As they were coming to investigate, they met Moosko and Vilor fleeing from the engagement, and these two had accompanied them back to the scene just as Duare, the remaining angan, and I had sighted the Sofal off shore and were planning on signalling to her.

As the birdman could transport but one of us at a time, I had commanded him, much against his will, to carry Duare to the ship. She refused to desert me, and the angan feared to return to the Sofal, from which he had aided in the abduction of the princess; but I at length compelled him to seize Duare and fly away with her just as the party of Thorists were upon us.

There had been a stiff gale blowing from the sea; and I was much worried for fear that the angan might not have been able to beat his way against it to the deck of the Sofal, but I had known that death beneath the waters of the sea would be far less horrible to Duare than captivity among the Thorists and especially in the power of Moosko.

My captors had watched the birdman battling his way against the gale with his burden, but only for a few minutes; then they had started upon the return march to Kapdor when Moosko had suggested that Kamlot, who was now in command of the Sofal, would doubtless land a force and pursue them as soon as Duare acquainted him with the fact of my capture. And so, as our path dropped behind the rocky pinnacles of the shore line, the angan and Duare were lost to our view; and I felt that I was doomed to go through whatever brief hours of life remained to me without knowledge of the fate of the gorgeous Venusian girl whom fate had decreed to be my first love.

The fact that I should have chanced to fall in love with this particular girl, in the land of Vepaja where there were so many beautiful girls, was in itself a tragedy. She was the virgin daughter of a jong, or king, whom custom rendered sacrosanct.

During the eighteen years of her life she had been permitted neither to see nor to speak to any man other than members of the royal family and a few trusted servitors until I had invaded her garden and forced my unwelcome attentions upon her. And then, shortly thereafter, the worst had befallen her. A raiding party of Thorists had succeeded in abducting her, members of the same party that had captured Kamlot and me.

She had been shocked and terrified at my avowal of my love, but she had not informed against me. She had seemed to despise me up until the last moment upon the summit of the rocky cliffs overlooking the raging Venusian sea, when I had ordered the angan to carry her to the Sofal; then, with outstretched hands, she had implored, "Do not send me away from you, Carson! Do not send me away! I love you!"

Those word, those unbelievable words, still rang in my ears, leaving me elated even in the face of the nameless death that I knew awaited me in the mysterious chamber of seven doors.

The Thorists from Kapdor who formed my escort were much intrigued by my blond hair and blue eyes, for such were unknown to any of the Venusians I had yet encountered. They questioned Vilor concerning me; but he insisted that I was a Vepajan, and as the Vepajans are the deadliest enemies of the Thorists he could not more effectually have sealed my doom even had I not been guilty of the offences charged against me by Moosko.

"He says that he comes from another world far from Amtor; but he was captured in Vepaja in company with another Vepajan, and he was well known to Duare, the daughter of Mintep, the jong of Vepaja."

"What other world could there be but Amtor?" scoffed one of the soldiers.

"None, of course," assented another; "beyond Amtor lie only boiling rocks and fire."

The cosmic theory of the Amtorians is as wrapped in impenetrable fog as is their world by the two great cloud envelopes that surround it. From the spouting lava of their volcanoes they visualize a sea of molten rock upon which floats Amtor, a vast disk; the occasional rents in the enveloping clouds, through which they glimpse the fiery sun and feel his consuming heat assure them that all is fire above; and when these rents occur at night they believe the myriad stars to be sparks from the eternal, fiery furnace that fuses the molten sea beneath their world.

I was almost exhausted by what I had passed through since the screeching of the hurricane and the plunging of the Sofal had awakened me the preceding night. After the great wave had swept me overboard I had had a battle with the great waves that would have wholly sapped the strength of a less powerful man than I; and then, after I had reached shore, I had walked far in search of Duare and her abductors only to have my strength further sapped by a strenuous battle with the savage nobargans, the hairy beast-men, who had attacked her abductors.

And now I was about all in as, topping a rise, there burst upon my view a walled city lying close to the sea at the mouth of a little valley. I guessed that this was Kapdor, our destination; and though I knew that death awaited me there I could not but look forward to the city with anticipation, since I guessed that food and drink might also await me behind those substantial walls.

The city gate through which we entered was well guarded, suggesting that Kapdor had many enemies; and all the citizens were armed–with swords, or daggers, or pistols, the last similar to those I had first become acquainted with in the house of Duran, the father of

Kamlot, in the tree-city of Kooaad, which is the capitol of Mintep's island kingdom, Vepaja.

These weapons discharge the lethal r-ray, which destroys animal tissue, and are far more deadly than the .45 automatics with which we are familiar, since they discharge a continuous stream of the destructive rays as long as the mechanism which generates them is kept in action by the pressure of a finger.

There were many people on the streets of Kapdor, but they seemed dull and apathetic. Even the sight of a blond haired, blue eyed prisoner aroused no interest within their sodden brains. To me they appeared like beasts of burden, performing their dull tasks without the stimulus of imagination or of hope. It was these that were armed with daggers, and there was another class that I took to be the soldier class who carried swords and pistols. These seemed more alert and cheerful, for evidently they were more favoured, but had no appearance of being more intelligent than the others.

The buildings for the most part were mean hovels of a single story, but there were others that were more pretentious–two and even three story buildings. Many were of lumber, for forests are plentiful in this portion of Amtor, though I had seen none of the enormous trees such as grow upon the island of Vepaja and which afforded me my first introduction of Venus.

There were a number of stone buildings facing the streets along which I was conducted; but they were all boxlike, unprepossessing structures with no hint of artistic or imaginative genius.

Presently my captors led me into an open square surrounded by larger if not more beautiful buildings that we had previously passed. Yet even here were squalor and indications of inefficiency and incompetence.

I was led into a building the entrance to which was guarded by soldiers. Vilor, Moosko, and the leader of the party that had captured me accompanied me into the interior, where, in a bare room, a large, gross appearing man was asleep in a chair with his feet on a table that evidently served him both as desk and dining table, for its top was littered with papers and the remains of a meal.

Disturbed by our entrance, the sleeper opened his eyes and blinked dully at us for a moment.

"Greetings, Friend Sov!" exclaimed the officer who accompanied me.

"Oh, it is you, Friend Hokal?" mumbled Sov, sleepily. "And who are these others?"

"The Ongyan Moosko from Thora, Vilor, another friend, and a Vepajan prisoner I captured." At the mention of Moosko's title, Sov arose, for an ongyan is one of the oligarchy and a great man. "Greetings, Ongyan Moosko!" he cried. "So you have brought us a Vepajan? Is he a doctor, by chance?"

"I do not know and I do not care," snapped Moosko. "He is a cutthroat and a scoundrel; and, doctor or no doctor, he dies."

"But we need doctors badly," insisted Sov. "We are dying of disease and old age. If we do not have a doctor soon, we shall all be dead."

"You heard what I said, did you not, Friend Sov?" demanded Moosko testily.

"Yes, Ongyan," replied the officer, meekly; "he shall die. Shall I have him destroyed at once?"

"Friend Hokal tells me that you have a slower and pleasanter way of dispatching villains than by gun or sword. I am interested. Tell me about it."

"I referred to the room of the seven doors," explained Hokal. "You see, this man's offences were great; he made the great Ongyan a prisoner and even threatened his life."

"We have no death adequate to such a crime," cried the horrified Sov; "but the room of the seven doors, which is the best that we have to offer, shall be made ready."

"Describe it, describe it," snapped Moosko. "What is it like? What will happen to him? How will he die?"

"Let us not explain it in the presence of the prisoner," said Hokal, "if you would reap the full pleasure of the room of the seven doors."

"Yes, lock him up; lock him up!" ordered Moosko. "Put him in a cell."

Sov summoned a couple of soldiers, who conducted me to a rear room and shoved me down into a dark windowless cellar. They slammed down and locked the heavy trap door above me and left me to my gloomy thoughts.

The room of the seven doors. The title fascinated me. I wondered what awaited me there, what strange form of horrible death. Perhaps it might not be so terrible after all; perhaps they were attempting to make my end more terrible by suggestion.

So this was to be the termination of my mad attempt to reach Mars! I was to die alone in this far-flung outpost of the Thorists in the land of Noobol that was scarcely more than a name to me. And there was so much to see upon Venus, and I had seen so little.

I recalled all that Danus had told me, the things concerning Venus that had so stimulated my imagination–sketchy tales, little more than fables, of Karbol, the cold country, where roamed strange and savage beasts and even more strange and more savage men; and Trabol, the warm country, where lay the island of Vepaja toward which chance had guided the rocket in which I had journeyed from Earth. Most of all had I been interested in Strabol, the hot country, for I was positive that this corresponded with the equatorial regions of the planet and that beyond it lay a vast, unexplored region entirely unguessed of by the inhabitants of the southern hemisphere–the north temperature zone.

One of my hopes when I seized the Sofal and set myself up as a pirate chieftain was that I might find an ocean passage north to this terra incognita. What strange races, what new civilizations might I not discover there! But now I had reached the end, not only of hope, but of life as well.

I determined to stop thinking about it. It was going to be too easy to feel sorry for myself if I were to keep on in that vein, and that would never do; it unnerves a man.

I had enough pleasant memories stored away inside my head, and these I called to my aid. The happy days that I had spent in India before my English father died were food for glorious recollection. I thought of old Chand Kabi, my tutor, and of all that I had learned from him outside of school books; not the least of which was that satisfying philosophy which I found it expedient to summon to my aid in this, my last extremity. It was Chand Kabi who had taught me to use my mind to the fullest extent of its resources and to project it across illimitable space to another mind attuned to receive its message, without which power the fruits of my strange adventure must die with me in the room of the seven doors.

I had other pleasant recollections to dissolve the gloom that shrouded my immediate future; they were of the good and loyal friends I had made during my brief sojourn on this distant planet: Kamlot, my best friend on Venus, and those "three musketeers" of the Sofal, Gamfor, the farmer; Kiron, the soldier; and Zog, the slave. These had been friends indeed!

And then, pleasantest memory of all, there was Duare. She was worth all that I had risked; her last words to me compensated even for death. She had told me that she loved me–she, the incomparable, the unattainable–she, the hope of a world, the daughter of a king. I could scarcely believe that my ears had not tricked me, for always before, in the few words she had deigned to fling me, she had sought to impress upon me the fact that not only was she not for such as I, but that she abhorred me. Women are peculiar.

How long, I remained in that dark hole, I do not know. It must have been several hours; but at last I heard footsteps in the room above, and then the trap door was raised and I was ordered to come up.

Several soldiers escorted me back to the filthy office of Sov, where I found that officer seated in conversation with Moosko, Vilor, and Hokal. A jug and glasses, together with the fumes of strong drink, attested the manner in which they had enlivened their conference.

"Take him to the room of the seven doors," Sov directed the soldiers who guarded me; and as I was escorted into the open square, the four who had condemned me to death followed.

A short distance from Sov's office the soldiers turned into a narrow, crooked alley; and presently we came to a large open space in the centre of which were several buildings, one a circular tower rising above the others from the centre of a large enclosure that was surrounded by a high stone wall.

Through a small gate we passed into a covered passageway, a gloomy tunnel, at the end of which was a stout door which one of the soldiers opened with a great key that Hokal passed to him; then the soldiers stood aside and I entered the room, followed by Sov, Moosko, Vilor, and Hokal.

I found myself in a circular apartment in the walls of which were seven identical doors placed at regular intervals about the circumference; so that there was no way of distinguishing one door from another.

In the centre of the room was a circular table upon which were seven vessels containing seven varieties of food and seven cups containing liquids. Depending above the centre of the table was a rope with a noose in the end of it, the upper end of the rope being lost in the shadows of the high ceiling, for the chamber was but dimly lighted.

Suffering with thirst, as I was, and being half famished for food, the sight of that laden table aroused my flagging spirits. It was evident that even if I were about to die I should not die hungry. The Thorists might be cruel and heartless in some respects, but it was clear that there was some kindliness in them, else they would never furnish such an abundance of food to a condemned man.

"Attend!" snapped Sov, addressing me. "Listen well to what I shall say to you." Moosko was inspecting the room with a gloating smile on his thick lips. "We shall leave you here alone presently," continued Sov. "If you can escape from this building your life will be spared.

"As you see, there are seven doors leading from this room; none of them has bolt or bar. Beyond each is a corridor identical to that through which we just approached the chamber. You are free to open any of the doors and enter any of these corridors. After you pass through a door, a spring will close it; and you cannot open it again from the opposite side, the doors being so constructed that from the corridor there is nothing to lay hold upon wherewith to open them, with the exception of the secret mechanism of that one which let us into the room; through that one door lies life; beyond the others, death.

"In the corridor of the second door you will step upon a hidden spring that will cause long, sharp spikes to be released upon you from all directions; and upon these you will be impaled and die.

"In the third corridor a similar spring will ignite a gas that will consume you in flames. In the fourth, r-rays will be loosed upon you, and you will die instantly. In the fifth, another door will open at the far end and admit a tharban."

"What is a tharban?" I asked.

Sov looked at me in astonishment. "You know as well as I," he growled.

"I have told you that I am from another world," I snapped. "I do not know what the word means."

"It will do no harm to tell him," suggested Vilor: "for if, by chance, he does not know, some of the horror of the room of the seven doors may be lost upon him."

"Not a bad thought," interjected Moosko. "Describe the tharban, Friend Sov."

"It is a terrible beast," explained Sov, "a huge and terrible beast. It is covered with stiff hair, like bristles, and is of a reddish colour with white stripes running lengthwise of its body, its belly being of a bluish tinge. It has great jaws and terrible talons, and it eats naught but flesh."

At that instant a terrific roar that seemed to shake the building broke upon our ears.

"That is the tharban," said Hokal with a grin. "He has not eaten for three days, and he is not only very hungry, but he is very angry."

"And what lies beyond the sixth door?" I demanded.

"In the corridor beyond the sixth door hidden jets will deluge you with a corrosive acid. It will fill your eyes and burn them out; and it will consume your flesh slowly, but you will not die too quickly. You will have ample time in which to repent the crimes that brought you to the room of the seven doors. The sixth door, I think, is the most terrible of all."

"To my mind the seventh is worse," remarked Hokal.

"Perhaps," admitted Sov. "In the seventh, death is longer in coming, and the mental agony is protracted. When you step upon the concealed spring in the corridor beyond the seventh door the walls commence to move slowly toward you. Their movement is so slow as to be almost imperceptible, but eventually they will reach you and slowly crush you between them."

"And what is the purpose of the noose above the table?" I asked.

"In the agony of indecision as to which door is the door to life," explained Sov, "you will be tempted to destroy yourself, and the noose is there for that purpose. But it is cunningly arranged at such a distance above the table that you cannot utilize it to break your neck and bring death quickly; you can only strangle to death."

"It appears to me that you have gone to considerable pains to destroy your enemies," I suggested.

"The room of the seven doors was not designed primarily to inflict death," explained Sov. "It is used as a means for converting unbelievers to Thorism, and you would be surprised to know how efficacious it has been."

"I can imagine," I replied. "And now that you have told me the worst, may I be permitted to satisfy my hunger and thirst before I die?"

"All within this room is yours to do with as you please during your last hours on earth, but before you eat let me explain that of the seven varieties of food upon this table all but one are poisoned. Before you satisfy your thirst, you may be interested in knowing that of the seven delicious beverages sparkling in those seven containers, six are poisoned. And now, murderer, we leave you. For the last time in life you are looking upon fellow human beings."

"If life held only the hope of continuing to look upon you, I would gladly embrace death."

In single file they left the room by that door to life. I kept my eyes upon that door to mark it well; and then the dim light went out.

Quickly I crossed the chamber in a straight line toward the exact spot where I knew the door to be, for I had been standing facing it squarely. I smiled to myself to think how simple they were to imagine that I should instantly lose my bearings because the light had been extinguished. If they had not been lying to me, I should be out of that room almost as soon as they to claim the life they had promised me.

With outstretched hands I approached the door. I felt unaccountably dizzy. I was having difficulty in keeping my balance. My fingers came in contact with a moving surface; it was the wall, passing across my hands toward the left. I felt a door brush past them and then another and another; then I guessed the truth–the floor upon which I stood was revolving. I had lost the door to life.

## CHAPTER 2

# Coiled Fury

As I stood there, plunged for the moment into despondency, the light came on again; and I saw the wall and the procession of doors passing slowly before me. Which was the door to life? Which was the door to choose?

I felt very tired and rather hopeless; the pangs of hunger and thirst assailed me. I walked to the table in the centre of the room. Wines and milk mocked me from the seven cups. One of the seven was harmless and would quickly satisfy the gnawing craving for drink that was become almost a torture. I examined the contents of each receptacle, testing each with my nose. There were two cups of water, the contents of one of which had a cloudy appearance; I was positive that the other was the one unpoisoned liquid.

I lifted it in my hands. My parched throat begged for one little drink. I raised the cup to my lips, and then doubts assailed me. While there was a single remote chance for life I must not risk death. Resolutely I replaced the cup upon the table.

Glancing about the room, I saw a chair and a couch in I the shadows against the wall beyond the table; at least, if I could not eat nor drink, I could rest and, perhaps, sleep. I would rob my captors of the fulfilment of their expectations as long as possible, and with this idea in mind I approached the couch.

The light in the room was poor, but as I was about to throw myself upon the couch it was sufficient to enable me to discern that its bed was composed of needle-sharp metal spikes, and my vision of restful sleep was dispelled. An examination of the chair revealed the fact that it was similarly barbed.

What ingenious fiendishness the Thorists had displayed in the conception of this room and its appurtenances! There was nothing about it that I might use that was not feral, with the single exception of the floor; and I was so tired as I stretched myself at full length upon it that for the moment it seemed a luxurious couch.

It is true that the discomfort of its hardness became more and more appreciable; yet, so exhausted was I, I was upon the verge of sleep, half dozing, when I felt something touch my naked back–something cold and clammy.

Instantly apprehending some new and devilish form at torture, I sprang to my feet. Upon the floor, wriggling and writhing toward me, were snakes of all kinds and sizes, many of them unearthly reptiles of horrifying appearance–snakes with sabre-like fangs, snakes with horns, snakes with ears, snakes of blue, of red, of green, of white, of purple. They were coming from holes near the bottom of the wall, spreading out across the floor as though they were seeking what they might devour–seeking me.

Now even the floor, that I had considered my sole remaining hope, was denied me. I sprang to the table top amidst the poisoned food and drink, and there I squatted watching the hideous reptiles squirming about.

Suddenly the food began to tempt me, but now for a reason apart from hunger. I saw in it escape from the hopelessness and torture of my situation. What chance had I for life? My captors had known, when they put me in here, that I would never come out alive. What a vain and foolish thing was hope under such circumstances!

I thought of Duare; and I asked myself, what of her? Even were I to escape through some miracle, what chance had I of ever seeing Duare again? I, who could not even guess the direction in which lay Vepaja, the land of her people, the land to which Kamlot was most assuredly returning her even now.

I had harboured a half, faint-hearted hope immediately after my capture that Kamlot would land the fighting crew of the Sofal in an attempt to rescue me; but I had long since abandoned it, for I knew that his first duty was to Duare, the daughter of his kind; and that no consideration would tempt him to delay an instant the return voyage to Vepaja.

As, immersed in thought, I watched the snakes, there came faintly to my ears what sounded like a woman's scream; and I wondered, indifferently, what new horror was occurring in this hateful city. Whatever it was, I could neither know nor prevent, and so it made little impression upon me, especially in view of a sudden, new interest in the snakes.

One of the larger of them, a great, hideous creature some twenty feet in length, had raised his head to the level of the table and was watching me with its lidless, staring eyes. It seemed to me that I could almost read that dim, reptilian brain reacting to the presence of food.

It laid its head flat upon the table; and, its body undulating slowly, it glided toward me across the table top.

I glanced quickly about the room, vainly seeking some avenue of escape. There, evenly spaced in the periphery of the chamber, were the seven doors, stationary now; for the floor had ceased to revolve shortly after the light had come on again. Behind one of those identical doors lay life; behind each of the other six, death. Upon the floor, between them and me, were the snakes. They had not distributed themselves evenly over the entire area of the flagging. There were spaces across which one might run swiftly without encountering more than an occasional reptile; yet a single one, were it venomous, would be as fatal as a score of them; and I was harassed by knowledge of my ignorance of the nature of a single one of the numerous species represented.

The hideous head of the serpent that had raised itself to the table top was gliding slowly toward me; the greater part of its length extended along the floor, moved in undulating waves as it crept after the head. As yet it had given no indication of the method of its attack. I did not know if it might be expected to strike first with poison fangs, to crush within its constricting folds, or merely to seize in widespread jaws and swallow as I had seen snakes, in my boyhood, swallowing frogs and birds. In any event the outlook was far from pleasing.

I shot a quick glance toward the doors. Should I risk all on a single cast of the die with fate?

The repulsive head was moving closer and closer to me; I turned away from it, determined to run for the door the way to which was clearest of snakes. As I glanced quickly about the room I saw a comparatively open avenue leading toward a door just beyond the spiked couch and chair.

One door was as good as another–I had one chance in seven! And there was no way to differentiate one door from another. Life might lie behind this door, or death. Here was, at least, a chance. To remain where I was, the certain prey of that hideous reptile, offered no chance whatever.

I have always enjoyed more than my share of the lucky "breaks" of life, and now something seemed to tell me that fate was driving me toward the one door beyond which lay life and liberty. So it was with the optimism of almost assured success that I leaped from the table and the yawning jaws of the great snake and ran toward that fateful door.

Yet I was not unmindful of that sound advice, "Put your trust in God, my boys; and keep your powder dry!" In this event I might have paraphrased it to read, "Put your trust in fate, but keep an avenue of retreat open!"

I knew that the doors swung outward from the circular room and that once I had passed through one of them and it had closed behind me there could be no returning. But how could I circumvent this?

All this that I take so long to tell occupied but a few seconds. I ran swiftly across the room, eluding the one or two snakes that were in my path; but I could not be unaware of the hissing and screaming that arose about me nor fail to see the snakes writhing and wriggling forward to intercept or pursue me.

What prompted me to seize the spiked chair as I passed it I do not know–the idea seemed to come to me like an inspiration. Perhaps, subconsciously, I hoped to use it as a weapon of defence; but it was not thus that it was to serve me.

As the nearer snakes were closing upon me I reached the door. There was no time now for further deliberation. I pushed the door open and stepped into the gloomy corridor beyond It was exactly like the corridor through which I had been brought to the room of the seven doors. Hope sprang high within my breast, but I braced the door open with the spiked chair–I was keeping my powder dry!

I had taken but a few steps beyond the doorway when my blood was frozen by the most terrifying roar that I have ever heard, and in the gloom ahead I saw two blazing balls of fire. I had opened the door of the fifth corridor that led to the lair of the tharban!

I did not hesitate. I knew that death awaited me in the darkness of that gloomy hole. No, it was not awaiting me; it was coming charging toward me. I turned and fled for the temporary safety that the light and space of the larger room would give me, and as I passed through the doorway I sought to snatch the chair away and let the door close in the face of the savage beast that was pursuing me. But something went wrong. The door, impelled by a powerful spring, closed too quickly–before I could drag the chair out of the way, wedging it tightly so that I could not free it, and there it stuck, holding the door half open.

I had been in tight places before, but nothing like this. Before me were the snakes and, dominating them, the huge creature that had sought me on the table; behind me was the roaring tharban. And now the only haven that I could think of was that very table top from which I had so thankfully escaped a few seconds before.

To the right of the doorway was a small open space in which there were no snakes; and, hurdling those hissing and striking at me from the threshold, I leaped to it at the very instant that the tharban sprang into the room.

For the instant I was held in the power of a single urge—to reach the top of the table. How futile and foolish the idea may have been did not occur to me; my mind clung to it to the effacement of all other thoughts. And perhaps because of my very singleness of purpose I would have reached my goal in any event, but when I stood again among the dishes and cups of poisoned food and drink and turned to face my fate I saw that another factor had intervened to save me for the moment and permit me to attain the questionable sanctuary of the table top.

Halfway between the door and the table the tharban, a fighting, rearing, roaring monster, was being set upon by the snakes. He snapped and struck and clawed, ripping them to pieces, tearing them in halves; but still they came for him, hissing, striking, entwining. Bodies cut in two, heads severed still sought to reach him; and from all parts of the room came ten to replace each that he disposed of.

Immense and threatening, standing out above them all, rose the huge reptile that had sought to devour me; and the tharban seemed to realize that in this creature lay a foe worthy of its mettle, for while he brushed away the lesser snakes with irritable contempt, he always faced the great one and launched his most vicious attacks against it. But of what avail! With lightning-like movements the sinuous coils darted hither and thither, eluding every blow like some practiced boxer and striking with terrific force at every opening, burying its fangs deep in the bloody flesh of the tharban.

The roars and screams of the carnivore mingled with the hisses of the reptiles to produce the most horrid din that the mind of man might imagine, or at least so it seemed to me, cooped up in this awful room filled with implacable engines of death.

Which would win this struggle of the Titans? What difference could it make to me other than the difference as to which belly I should eventually fill? Yet I could not help watch the encounter with the excited interest of a disinterested spectator at some test of strength and skill.

It was a bloody encounter, but the blood was all that of the tharban and the lesser snakes. The huge creature that was championing my cause that it might later devour me was so far unscathed. How it manipulated its huge body with sufficient quickness to avoid the savage rushes of the tharban is quite beyond me, though perhaps an explanation lies in the fact that it usually met a charge with a terrific blow of its head that sent the tharban reeling back half stunned and with a new wound.

Presently the tharban ceased its offensive and began to back away. I watched the weaving, undulating head of the great snake following every move of its antagonist. The lesser snakes swarmed over the body of the tharban; it seemed not to notice them. Then, suddenly, it wheeled and sprang for the entrance to the corridor that led to its lair.

This, evidently, was the very thing for which the snake had been waiting. It lay half coiled where it had been fighting; and now like a giant spring suddenly released it shot through the air; and so quickly that I could scarcely perceive the action, it wrapped a dozen coils about the body of the tharban, raised its gaping jaws above the back of the beast's neck, and struck!

A horrible scream burst from the distended jaws of the stricken carnivore as the coils tightened suddenly about it, then it was limp.

I breathed a sigh of relief as I thought for how long an entire tharban might satisfy the hunger of this twenty foot snake and distract its mind from other sources of food supply, and as I anticipated this respite the mighty victor unwound its coils from about the body of its victim and turned its head slowly in my direction.

I gazed spellbound for a moment into those cold, lidless eyes, then I was horror-stricken as I saw the creature gliding slowly toward the table. It did not move swiftly as in battle, but very slowly. There was a seemingly predetermined finality, an inevitableness, in that undulating approach that was almost paralyzing in its frightfulness.

I saw it raise its head to the level of the table top; I saw the head glide among the dishes toward me. I could stand it no longer. I turned to run–where, made no difference–anywhere, if only the length of the room, to get away even for a moment from the cold glitter of those baleful eyes.

## CHAPTER 3

# The Noose

As I turned, two things happened: I heard again, faintly, the screams of a woman; and my face struck the noose dangling from the dense shadows of the rafters.

The screams made little impression upon me, but the noose gave birth to a new thought–not the thought that it was placed there to arouse, but another. It suggested an avenue of momentary escape from the snakes; nor was I long in availing myself of it.

I felt the snout of the snake touch my bare leg as I sprang upward and seized the rope above the noose; I heard a loud hiss of rage as I clambered, hand over hand, toward the gloomy shadows where I hoped to find at least temporary refuge.

The upper end of the rope was fastened to a metal eye-bolt set in a great beam. Onto this beam I clambered and looked down. The mighty serpent was hissing and writhing below me. He had raised a third of his body upward and was endeavouring to coil about the dangling rope and follow me upward, but it swung away and eluded his efforts.

I doubted that a snake of his great girth could ascend this relatively tiny strand; but, not caring to take chance, I drew the rope up and looped it over the beam. For the moment, at least, I was safe, and I breathed a deep sigh of relief. Then I looked about me.

The shadows were dense and almost impenetrable, yet it appeared that the ceiling of the room was still far above me; about me was a maze of beams and braces and trusses. I determined to explore this upper region of the room of the seven doors.

Standing upright upon the beam, I moved cautiously toward the wall. At the end of the beam I discovered a narrow walkway that, clinging to the wall, apparently encircled the room. It was two feet wide and had no handrail. It seemed to be something in the nature of a scaffolding left by the workmen who had constructed the building.

As I took my exploratory way along it, feeling each step carefully and brushing the wall with my hand, I again heard the agonized scream that had twice before attracted my attention if not my keenest interest; for I was still more interested in my troubles than in those of some unknown female of this alien race.

And a moment later my fingers came in contact with something that drove all thoughts of screaming women from my mind. By feel, it was the frame of a door or of a window. With both hands I examined my find. Yes, it was a door! It was a narrow door about six feet in height.

I felt the hinges; I searched for a latch–and at last I found it. Cautiously I manipulated it and presently I felt the door move toward me.

What lay beyond? Some new and fiendishly conceived form of death or torture, perhaps; perhaps freedom. I could not know without opening that portal of mystery.

I hesitated, but not for long. Slowly I drew the door toward me, an eye close to the widening crack. A breath of night air blew in upon me; I saw the faint luminosity of a Venusian night.

Could it be possible that with all their cunning the Thorists had inadvertently left this avenue of escape from this lethal chamber? I could scarcely credit it, yet there was naught that I could do but go on and chance whatever lay beyond.

I opened the door and stepped out upon a balcony which extended in both directions until it passed from the range of my vision beyond the curve of the circular wall to which it clung.

At the outer edge of the balcony was a low parapet behind which I now crouched while I reconnoitred my new situation. No new danger seemed to threaten me, yet I was still suspicious. I moved cautiously forward upon a tour of investigation, and again an agonized scream rent the silence of the night. This time it seemed quite close; previously, the walls of the building in which I had been imprisoned had muffled it.

I was already moving in the direction of the sound, and I continued to do so. I was searching for an avenue of descent to the ground below, not for a damsel in distress. I am afraid that at that moment I was callous and selfish and far from chivalric; but, if the truth be known, I would not have cared had I known that every inhabitant of Kapdor, male and female, was being destroyed.

Rounding the curve of the tower, I came in sight of another building standing but a few yards distant; and at the same instant I saw something that greatly aroused my interest and even my hope. It was a narrow causeway leading from the balcony on which I stood to a similar balcony on the adjoining structure.

Simultaneously the screams were renewed; they seemed to be coming from the interior of the building I had just discovered. It was not the screams, however, that lured me across the causeway, but the hope that I might find there the means of descent to the ground.

Crossing quickly to the other balcony, I followed it to the nearest corner; and as I rounded it I saw a light apparently shining from windows on a level with it.

At first I was of a mind to turn back lest, in passing the windows, I be discovered; but once again that scream burst upon my ears, and this time it was so close that I knew it must come from the apartment from which the light shone.

There was such a note of hopelessness and fear in it that I could no longer ignore the demand it made upon my sympathies; and, setting discretion aside, I approached the window nearest me.

It was wide open, and in the room beyond I saw a woman in the clutches of a man. The fellow was holding her down upon a couch and with a sharp dagger was pricking her. Whether he had it in his mind to kill her eventually or not was not apparent, his sole purpose at the moment seeming to be torture.

The fellow's back was toward me, and his body hid the features of the woman; but when he pricked her and she screamed, he laughed–a hideous, gloating laugh. I guessed at once the psychopathic type he represented, deriving pleasure from the infliction of pain upon the object of his maniacal passion.

I saw him stoop to kiss her, and then she struck him in the face; and as she did so he half turned his head to avoid the blow, revealing his profile to me; and I saw that it was Moosko, the Ongyan.

He must have partially released his hold upon her as he shrank aside, for the girl half rose from the couch in an effort to escape him. As she did so her face was revealed to me, and my blood froze in rage and horror. It was Duare!

With a single bound I cleared the sill and was upon him. Grasping him by the shoulder, I whirled him about; and when he saw my face he voiced a cry of terror and shrank back, drawing his pistol from its holster. Instantly I closed with him, grasping the weapon and turning its muzzle toward the ceiling. He toppled backward across the couch, carrying me with him, both of us falling on top of Duare.

Moosko had dropped his dagger as he reached for his pistol, and now I tore the latter from his grasp and hurled it aside; then my fingers sought his throat.

He was a large, gross man, not without strength; and the fear of death seemed to increase the might of his muscles. He fought with the desperation of the doomed.

I dragged him from the couch, lest Duare be injured, and we rolled upon the floor, each intent upon winning a death hold upon the other. He was screaming for help now, and I redoubled my efforts to shut off his wind before his cries attracted the aid of any of his fellows.

He was snapping at me like a savage beast as he screamed, alternately striking at my face and seeking to close upon my throat. I was exhausted from all that I had passed through and from loss of sleep and lack of food. I realized that I was weakening rapidly, while Moosko seemed to my frenzied imagination to be growing stronger.

I knew that if I were not to be vanquished and Duare lost, I must overcome my antagonist without further loss of time, and so, drawing away from him to get greater distance for a blow, I drove my fist full into his face with all my remaining strength.

For an instant he wilted, and in that instant my fingers closed upon his throat. He struggled and writhed and struck me terrific blows; but, dizzy and half stunned though I was, I clung to him until at last he shuddered convulsively, relaxed, and sank to the floor.

If ever a man were dead, Moosko appeared so as I arose and faced Duare, who, half sitting, had crouched upon the cot where she had been a silent witness to this brief duel for possession of her.

"You!" she cried. "It cannot be!"

"It is," I assured her.

Slowly she arose from the couch as I approached it and stood facing me as I opened my arms to press her to me. She took a step forward; her hands went up; then she stopped in confusion.

"No!" she cried. "It is all a mistake."

"But you told me that you loved me, and you know that I love you," I said, bewildered.

"That is the mistake," she said. "I do not love you. Fear, gratitude, sympathy, nerves distraught by all that I had passed through, brought strange words to my lips that I might not—not have meant."

I felt suddenly cold and weary and forlorn. All hope of happiness was crushed in my breast. I turned away from her. I no longer cared what happened to me. But only for an instant did this mood possess me. No matter whether she loved me or not, my duty remained plain before me; I must get her out of Kapdor, out of the clutches of the Thorists and, if possible, return her to her father, Mintep, king of Vepaja.

I stepped to the window and listened. Moosko's cries had not attracted succour in so far as I could perceive; no one seemed to be coming. And if they had not come in response to Duare's screams, why should they be attracted by Moosko's? I realized that there was now little likelihood that any one would investigate.

I returned to the body of Moosko and removed his harness to which was attached a sword that he had had no opportunity to draw against me; then I retrieved his dagger and pistol. I now felt much better, far more efficient. It is strange what the possession of weapons will do even for one not accustomed to bearing them, and until I had come to Venus I had seldom if ever carried a lethal weapon.

I took the time now to investigate the room, on the chance that it might contain something else of use or value to us in our bid for liberty. It was a rather large room. An attempt had been made to furnish it ornately, but the result was a monument to bad taste. It was atrocious.

At one end, however, was something that attracted my keenest interest and unqualified approval; it was a table laden with food.

I turned to Duare. "I am going to try to take you away from Noobol," I told her. "I shall try also to return you to Vepaja. I may not succeed, but I shall do my best. Will you trust me and come with me?"

"How can you doubt it?" she replied. "If you succeed in returning me to Vepaja you will be well repaid by the honours and rewards that will be heaped upon you if my wishes prevail."

That speech angered me, and I turned upon her with bitter words on my lips; but I did not utter them. What was the use? I once more focused my attention upon the table. "What I started to say," I continued, "is that I shall try to save you, but I can't do it on an empty stomach. I am going to eat before we leave this room. Do you care to join me?"

"We shall need strength," she replied. "I am not hungry, but it is wiser that we both eat. Moosko ordered the food for me, but I could not eat it while he was present."

I turned away and approached the table where she joined me presently, and we ate in silence.

I was curious to know how Duare had come to the Thorist city of Kapdor, but her cruel and incomprehensible treatment of me made me hesitate to evince any further interest in her. Yet presently I realized how childish was my attitude–how foolish it was of me not to realize that the strictness and seclusion of her previous life probably accounted for her frightened and distant manner now–and I asked her to tell me all that had happened since I had despatched the angan with her toward the Sofal and the moment that I had discovered her in the clutches of Moosko.

"There is not much to tell," she replied. "You will recall how fearful the angan was of returning to the ship lest he be punished for the part he had taken in my abduction? They are very low creatures, with illy developed minds that react only to the most primitive forces of nature–self preservation, hunger, fear.

"When we were almost above the deck of the Sofal, the angan hesitated and then turned back toward the shore. I asked him what he was doing, why he did not continue on and place me aboard the ship; and he replied that he was afraid. He said they would kill him because he had helped to steal me.

"I promised him that I would protect him and that no harm would befall him, but he would not believe me. He replied that the Thorists, who had been his original masters, would reward him if he brought me back to them. That much he knew, but he had only my word that Kamlot would not have him killed. He doubted my authority with Kamlot.

"I pleaded and threatened but all to no purpose. The creature flew directly to this hideous city and delivered me to the Thorists. When Moosko learned that I had been brought here he exercised his authority and claimed me as his own. The rest you know."

"And now," I said, "we must find a way out of Kapdor and back to the coast. Perhaps the Sofal has not departed. It is possible that Kamlot has landed a party to search for us."

"It will not be easy to escape from Kapdor," Duare reminded me. "As the angan brought me here, I saw high walls and hundreds of sentries. There is not much hope for us."

## CHAPTER 4

# "Open the Gates!"

First we must get out of this building, I said. Do you recall any of its details as you were brought through it?"

"Yes. There is a long hallway from the front of the building on the ground floor leading directly to stairs that lie at the back of the first floor. There are several rooms opening from each side of the hall. There were people in the two front rooms, but I could not see into the others as the doors were closed."

"We shall have to investigate, and if there are sounds of life below we must wait until all are asleep. In the meantime I am going out on the balcony and see if I can discover some safer way to the ground."

When I went to the window I found that it had started to rain. I crept around the building until I could look down onto the street that passed before it. There was no sign of life there; it was likely that the rain had driven all within doors. In the distance I could dimly make out the outlines of the city wall at the end of the street. Everything was faintly illumined by the strange night light that is so peculiar a feature of the Amtorian scene. There was no stairway or ladder leading from the balcony to the ground. Our only avenue of descent was by way of the interior stairs.

I returned to Duare. Come," I said. "We might as well try it now as later."

"Wait!" she exclaimed. "I have a thought. It just occurred to me from something I overheard on board the Sofal relative to the customs of the Thorists. Moosko is an ongyan."

"Was," I corrected her, for I thought him dead.

"That is immaterial. The point is that he was one of the rulers of the so-called Free Land of Thora. His authority, especially here, where there is no other member of the oligarchy, would be absolute. Yet he was unknown to any of the natives of Kapdor. What proof did he bring of his identity or his high position?"

"I do not know," I admitted.

"I believe that you will find upon the index finger of his right hand a great ring that is the badge of his office."

"And you think that we could use this ring as authority to pass the sentries?"

"It is possible," replied Duare.

"But not probable," I demurred. "Not by the wildest flight of fancy could any one mistake me for Moosko—unless my conceit flatters me."

A faint smile touched Duare's lips. "I am believing that it will not be necessary for you to look like him," she explained. These people are very ignorant. Probably only a few of the common warriors saw Moosko when he arrived. Those same men would not be on watch now. Furthermore, it is night, and with the darkness and the rain the danger that your imposture will be discovered is minimized."

"It is worth trying," I agreed; and, going to the body of Moosko, I found the ring and removed it from his finger. It was too large for me, as the ongyan had gross, fat hands; but if any one was stupid enough to accept me as the ongyan he would not notice so minor a discrepancy as an ill-fitting ring.

Now Duare and I crept silently out of the chamber to the head of the stairs, where we paused, listening. All was dark below, but we heard the sound of voices, muffled, as though coming from behind a closed door. Slowly, stealthily, we descended the stairs. I felt the warmth of the girl's body as it brushed mine, and a great longing seized me to take her in my arms and crush her to me; but I only continued on down the stairway as outwardly cool and possessed as though no internal fire consumed me.

We had reached the long hallway and had groped our way about half the distance to the door that opened upon the street, a feeling of optimism enveloping me, when suddenly a door at the front end of the corridor opened and the passageway was illuminated by the light from the open doorway. I saw a portion of the figure of a man standing in the doorway of the room he was about to quit, he had paused and was conversing with someone from the room beyond. In another moment he might step into the corridor.

At my elbow was a door. Gingerly I tripped the latch and pushed the door open; the room beyond was in darkness, but whether or not it was occupied I could not tell. Stepping through the doorway I drew

Duare in after me and partially closed the door again, standing close to the aperture, watching and listening.

Presently I heard the man who had been standing in the other doorway say, "Until tomorrow, friends, and may you sleep in peace," then the door slammed and the hallway was plunged into darkness again.

Now I heard footsteps; they were coming in our direction. Very gingerly I drew the sword of Moosko, the ongyan. On came the footsteps; they seemed to hesitate before the door behind which I waited; but perhaps it was only my imagination. They passed on; I heard them ascending the stairway.

Now a new fear assailed me. What if this man should enter the room in which lay the dead body of Moosko! He would spread the alarm. Instantly I recognized the necessity for immediate action.

"Now Duare!" I whispered, and together we stepped into the corridor and almost ran to the front door of the building.

A moment later we were in the street. The drizzle had become a downpour. Objects were indiscernible a few yards distant, and for this I was thankful.

We hastened along the street in the direction of the wall and the gate, passing no one, seeing no one. The rain increased in violence.

"What are you going to say to the sentry?" asked Duare.

"I do not know," I replied candidly.

"He will be suspicious, for you can have no possible excuse for wishing to leave the safety of a walled city on a night like this and go out without an escort into a dangerous country where savage beasts and savage men roam."

"I shall find a way," I said, "because I must."

She made no reply, and we continued on toward the gate. It was not at a great distance from the house from which we had escaped and presently we came upon it looming large before us through the falling rain.

A sentry, standing in the shelter of a niche in the wall, discovered us and demanded what we were doing aboard at this hour of such a night. He was not greatly concerned, since he did not know that it was in our minds to pass through the gateway; he merely assumed, I presume, that we were a couple of citizens passing by on our way to our home.

"Is Sov here?" I demanded.

"Sov here!" he exclaimed in astonishment. "What would Sov be doing here on a night like this?"

"He was to meet me here at this hour," I said. "I instructed him to be here."

"You instructed Sov to be here!" The fellow laughed. "Who are you to give instructions to Sov?"

"I am the ongyan, Moosko," I replied.

The man looked at me in astonishment. "I do not know where Sov is," he said, a little sullenly, I thought.

"Well, never mind," I told him; "he will be here presently; and in the meantime, open up the gate, for we shall want to hurry on as soon as he arrives."

"I cannot open the gate without orders from Sov," replied the sentry.

"You refuse to obey an ongyan?" I demanded in the most ferocious tones I could command.

"I have never seen you before," he parried. "How do I know you are an ongyan?"

I held out my hand with the ring of Moosko on the index finger. "Do you know what that is?" I demanded.

He examined it closely. "Yes, ongyan," he said fearfully, "I know."

"Then open the gate, and be quick about it," I snapped.

"Let us wait until Sov comes," he suggested. "There will be time enough then."

"There is no time to be lost, fellow. Open up, as I command. The Vepajan prisoner has just escaped, and Sov and I are going out with a party of warriors to search for him."

Still the obstinate fellow hesitated; and then we heard a great shouting from the direction from which we had come, and I guessed that the fellow who had passed us in the corridor had discovered the dead body of Moosko and given the alarm.

We could hear men running. There was no more time to be lost.

"Here comes Sov with the searching party," I cried. "Throw open the gates, you fool, or it will go ill with you." I drew my sword, intending to run him through if he did not obey.

As finally, he turned to do my bidding, I heard the excited voices of the approaching men grow louder as they neared us. I could not see them yet for the rain, but as the gate swung open I glimpsed the oncoming figures through the murk.

Taking Duare by the arm I started through the gate. The sentry was still suspicious and wanted to stop us, but he was not sure of himself.

"Tell Sov to hurry," I said, and before the man could bolster his courage to do his duty, Duare and I hastened into the outer darkness and were lost to his view in the rain.

It was my intention to reach the coast and follow along it until daylight, when, I hoped and prayed, we should sight the Sofal off shore and be able to contrive a means of signalling to her.

We groped our way through the darkness and the rain during all that terrible night. No sound of pursuit reached our ears, nor did we come upon the ocean.

The rain ceased about dawn, and when full daylight came we looked eagerly for the sea, but only low hills and rolling country dotted with trees and a distant forest where we had thought the sea to be rewarded our straining eyes.

"Where is the sea?" asked Duare.

"I do not know," I admitted.

Only at sunrise and at sunset, for a few minutes, is it possible to differentiate between the points of the compass on Venus; then the direction of the sun is faintly indicated by a slightly intensified light along the eastern or the western horizon.

And now the sun was rising at our left, when it should have been upon our right were we going in the direction that I believed the ocean to be.

My heart sank in my breast, for I knew that we were lost.

## CHAPTER 5

# Cannibals

Dutare, who had been watching my face intently, must have read the truth in the despair of my expression.

"You do not know where the sea lies?" she asked.

"I shook my head. "No."

"Then we are lost?"

"I am afraid so. I am sorry, Duare; I was so sure that we would find the Sofal and that you would soon be out of danger. It is all my fault, the fault of my stupidity and ignorance."

"Do not say that; no one could have known the direction he was going during the darkness of last night. Perhaps we shall find the sea yet."

"Even if we could, I am afraid that it will be too late to ensure your safety."

What do you mean–that the Sofal will be gone?" she asked.

"There is that danger, of course; but what I most fear is that we may be recaptured by the Thorists. They will certainly search along the coast for us in the locality where they found us yesterday. They are not so stupid as not to guess that we will try to reach the Sofal."

"If we can find the ocean, we might hide from them," she suggested, "until they tire of the search and return to Kapdor; then, if the Sofal is still there, we may yet be saved."

"And if not, what?" I asked. "Do you know anything about Noobol? Is there not some likelihood that we may find a friendly people somewhere in this land who will aid us to reach Vepaja again?"

She shook her head. "I know little about Noobol," she replied, "but what little I have heard is not good. It is a sparsely settled land reaching, it is supposed, far into Strabol, the hot country, where no man may live. It is filled with wild beasts and savage tribes. There are scattered settlements along the coast, but most of these have been captured or reduced by the Thorists; the others, of course, would be equally dangerous, for the inhabitants would consider all strangers as enemies."

"The outlook is not bright," I admitted, "but we will not give up; we will find a way."

"If any man can, I am sure that it is you," she said.

Praise from Duare was sweet. In all the time that I had known her she had said only one other kind thing to me, and later she had retracted that.

"I could work miracles if only you loved me, Duare."

She straightened haughtily. "You will not speak of that," she said.

"Why do you hate me, Duare, who have given you only love?" I demanded.

"I do not hate you," she replied, "but you must not speak of love to the daughter of a jong. We may be together for a long time, and you must remember that I may not listen to love from the lips of any man. Our very speaking together is a sin, but circumstances have made it impossible to do otherwise.

"Before I was stolen from the house of the jong no man had ever addressed me other than the members of my own family, except a few loyal and privileged members of my father's household, and until I should be twenty it were a sin in me and a crime in any man who should disregard this ancient law of the royal families of Amtor."

"You forget," I reminded her, "that one man did address you in the house of your father."

"An impudent knave," she said, "who should have died for his temerity."

"Yet you did not inform on me."

"Which made me equally guilty with you," she replied, flushing. "It is a shameful secret that will abide with me until my death."

"A glorious memory that will always sustain my hope," I told her.

"A false hope that you would do well to kill," she said, and then, "Why did you remind me of that day?" she demanded. "When I think of it, I hate you; and I do not want to hate you."

"That is something," I suggested.

"Your effrontery and your hope feed on meagre fare."

Which reminds me that it might be well for me to see if I can find something in the way of food for our bodies, too."

"There may be game in that forest," she suggested, indicating the wood toward which we had been moving.

"We'll have a look," I said, stand then turn back and search for the elusive sea."

A Venusian forest is a gorgeous sight. The foliage itself is rather pale–orchid, heliotrope and violet predominate–but the boles of the trees are gorgeous. They are of brilliant colours and often so glossy as to give the impression of having been lacquered.

The wood we were approaching was of the smaller varieties of trees, ranging in height from two hundred to three hundred feet, and in diameter from twenty to thirty feet. There were none of the colossi of the island of Vepaja that reared their heads upward five thousand feet to penetrate the eternal inner cloud envelope of the planet.

The interior of the forest was illuminated by the mysterious Venusian ground glow, so that, unlike an earthly forest of similar magnitude upon a cloudy day, it was far from dark or gloomy. Yet there was something sinister about it. I cannot explain just what, nor why it should have been.

"I do not like this place," said Duare, with a little shudder; there is no sight of animal, no sound of bird."

"Perhaps we frightened them away," I suggested.

"I do not think so; it is more likely that there is something else in the forest that has frightened them."

I shrugged. "Nevertheless, we must have food," I reminded her, and I continued on into the forbidding, and at the same time gorgeous, wood that reminded me of a beautiful but wicked woman.

Several times I thought I saw a suggestion of movement among the boles of distant trees, but when I reached them there was nothing there. And so I pressed on, deeper and deeper; and constantly a sense of impending evil grew stronger as I advanced.

"There!" whispered Duare suddenly, pointing. "There is something there, behind that tree. I saw it move."

Something, just glimpsed from the corner of my eye, caught my attention to the left of us; and as I turned quickly in that direction something else dodged behind the bole of a large tree.

Duare wheeled about. "There are things all round us!"

"Can you make out what they are?" I asked.

"I thought that I saw a hairy hand, but I am not sure. They move quickly and keep always out of sight. Oh, let us go back! This is an evil place, and I am afraid."

"Very well," I agreed. "Anyway, this doesn't seem to be a particularly good hunting ground; and after all that is all that we are looking for."

As we turned to retrace our steps a chorus of hoarse shouts arose upon all sides of us–half human, half bestial, like the growls and roars of animals blending with the voices of men; and then, suddenly, from behind the boles of trees a score of hairy, manlike creatures sprang toward us.

Instantly I recognized them—nobargans—the same hairy, manlike creatures that had attacked the abductors of Duare, whom I had rescued from them. They were armed with crude bows and arrows and with slings from which they hurled rocks; but, as they closed upon us, it appeared that they wished to take us alive, for they launched no missiles at us.

But I had no mind to be thus taken so easily, nor to permit Duare to fall into the hands of these savage beast-men. Raising my pistol, I loosed the deadly r-ray upon them; and as some fell others leaped behind the boles of the trees.

"Do not let them take me," said Duare in a level voice unshaken by emotion. When you see there is no further hope of escape, shoot me."

The very thought of it turned me cold, but I knew that I should do it before permitting her to fall into the hands of these degraded creatures.

A nobargan showed himself, and I dropped him with my pistol; then they commenced to hurl rocks at me from behind. I wheeled and fired, and in the same instant a rock felled me to the ground unconscious.

When I regained consciousness I was aware first of an incredible stench, and then of something rough rubbing against my skin, and of a rhythmic jouncing of my body. These sensations were vaguely appreciable in the first dim light of returning reason. With the return of full control of my faculties they were accounted for; I was being carried across the shoulder of a powerful nobargan.

The door from his body was almost suffocating in its intensity, and the rough hair abrading my skin was only a trifle more annoying than the motion that his stride imparted to my body.

I sought to push myself from his shoulder; and, realizing that I was no longer unconscious, he dropped me to the ground. All about me were the hideous faces and hairy bodies of the nobargans and permeating the air the horrid stench that emanated from them.

They are, I am sure, the filthiest and most repulsive creatures I have ever seen. Presumably they are one of evolution's first steps from beast to man; but they are no improvement upon the beast. For the privilege of walking upright upon two feet, thus releasing their hands from the mean servitude of ages, and for the gift of speech they have sacrificed all that is fine and noble in the beast.

It is true, I believe, that man descended from the beasts; and it took him countless ages to rise to the level of his progenitors. In some respects he has not succeeded yet, even at the height of his vaunted civilization.

As I looked about, I saw Duare being dragged along by her hair by a huge nobargan. It was then that I discovered that my weapons had been taken from me. So low in the scale of intelligence are the nobargans, they cannot use the weapons of civilized man that fall into their hands, so they had simply thrown mine aside.

But even though I was disarmed, I could not see Duare suffering this ignominy and abuse without making an effort to aid her.

I sprang forward before the beasts at my side could prevent and hurled myself upon the creature that dared to maltreat this daughter of a jong, this incomparable creature who had aroused within my breast the first exquisite tortures of love.

I seized him by one hairy arm and swung him around until he faced me, and then I struck him a terrific blow upon the chin that felled him. Instantly his fellows broke into loud laughter at his discomfiture; but that did not prevent them from falling upon me and subduing me, and you may be assured that their methods were none too gentle.

As the brute that I had knocked down staggered to his feet his eyes fell upon me, and with a roar of rage he charged me. It might have fared badly with me had not another of them interfered. He was a burly creature, and when he interposed himself between me and my antagonist the latter paused.

"Stop!" commanded my ally, and had I heard a gorilla speak I could not have been more surprised. It was my introduction to a remarkable ethnological fact: All the races of mankind on Venus (at least those that I have come in contact with) speak the same tongue. Perhaps you can explain it; I cannot. When I have questioned Amtorian savants on the matter, they were merely dumfounded by the question; they could not conceive of any other condition; therefore there had never been any occasion to explain it.

Of course the languages differ in accordance with the culture of the nations; those with the fewest wants and the fewest experiences have the fewest words. The language of the nobargans is probably the most limited; a vocabulary of a hundred words may suffice them. But the basic root-words are the same everywhere.

The creature that had protected me, it presently developed, was the jong, or king, of this tribe; and I later learned that his act was not prompted by humanitarian considerations but by a desire to save me for another fate.

My act had not been entirely without good results, for during the balance of the march Duare was no longer dragged along by her hair. she thanked me for championing her; and that in itself was something worth being manhandled for, but she cautioned me against antagonizing them further.

Having discovered that at least one of these creatures could speak at least one word of the Amtorian language with which I was familiar, I sought to delve farther in the hope that I might ascertain the purpose for which they had captured us.

"Why have you seized us?" I inquired of the brute that had spoken that single word.

He looked at me in surprise, and those near enough to have overheard my question commenced to laugh and repeat it. Their laugh is far from light, airy, or reassuring. They bare their teeth in a grimace and emit a sound that is for all the world like the retching of mal de mer, and there is no laughter in their eyes. It took quite a stretch of my imagination to identify this as laughter.

"Albargan not know?" asked the jong. Albargan is, literally, no-hair-man, or without-hair-man, otherwise, hairless man.

"I do not know," I replied. "We were not harming you. We were searching for the sea coast where our people are."

"Albargan find out soon," and then he laughed again.

I tried to think of some way to bribe him into letting us go; but inasmuch as he had thrown away as useless the only things of value that we possessed, it seemed rather hopeless.

"Tell me what you want most," I suggested, "and perhaps I can get it for you if you will take us to the coast."

"We have what we want," he replied, and that answer made them all laugh.

I was walking close to Duare now, and she looked up at me with a hopeless expression. "I am afraid we are in for it," she said.

"It is all my fault. If I had had brains enough to find the ocean this would never have happened."

"Don't blame yourself. No one could have done more to protect and save me than you have. Please do not think that I do not appreciate it."

That was a lot for Duare to say, and it was like a ray of sunshine in the gloom of my despondency. That is a simile entirely earthly, for there is no sunshine upon Venus. The relative proximity of the sun lights up the inner cloud envelope brilliantly, but it is a diffused light that casts no well defined shadows nor produces contrasting highlights. There is an all pervading glow from above that blends with the perpetual light emanations from the soil, and the resultant scene is that of a soft and beautiful pastel.

Our captors conducted us into the forest for a considerable distance; we marched practically all day. They spoke but seldom and then usually in monosyllables. They did not laugh again, and for that I was thankful. One can scarcely imagine a more disagreeable sound.

We had an opportunity to study them during this long march, and there is a question if either of us was quite sure in his own mind as to whether they were beast-like men or man-like beasts. Their bodies were entirely covered with hair; their feet were large and flat, and their toes were armed, like the fingers, with thick, heavy, pointed nails that resembled talons. They were large and heavy, with tremendous shoulders and necks.

Their eyes were extremely close set in a baboon-like face; so that in some respects their heads bore a more striking similarity to the heads of dogs than to men. There was no remarkable dissimilarity between the males and the females, several of which were in the party; and the latter deported themselves the same as the bulls and appeared to be upon a plane of equality with these, carrying bows and arrows and slings for hurling rocks, a small supply of which they carried in skin pouches slung across their shoulders.

At last we reached an open space beside a small river where there stood a collection of the rudest and most primitive of shelters. These were constructed of branches of all sizes and shapes thrown together without symmetry and covered with a thatch of leaves and grasses. At the bottom of each was a single aperture through which one might crawl on hands and knees. They reminded me of the nests of pack rats built upon a Gargantuan scale.

Here were other members of the tribe, including several young, and at sight of us they rushed forward with excited cries. It was with difficulty that the jong and other members of the returning party kept them from tearing us to pieces.

The former hustled us into one of their evil smelling nests and placed a guard before the entrance, more to protect us from his fellows, I suspect, than to prevent our escape.

The hut in which we were was filthy beyond words, but in the dim light of the interior I found a short stick with which I scraped aside the foul litter that covered the floor until I had uncovered a space large enough for us to lie down on the relatively clean earth.

We lay with our heads close to the entrance that we might get the benefit of whatever fresh air should find its way within. Beyond the entrance we could see a number of the savages digging two parallel trenches in the soft earth; each was about seven feet long and two feet wide.

"Why are they doing that, do you suppose?" asked Duare.

"I do not know," I replied, although I had my suspicions; they looked remarkably like graves.

Perhaps we can escape after they have gone to sleep tonight," suggested Duare.

"We shall certainly take advantage of the first opportunity," I replied, but there was no hope within me. I had a premonition that we should not be alive when the nobargans slept next.

"Look what they're doing said Duare, presently; "they're filling the trenches with wood and dry leaves. You don't suppose–?" she exclaimed, and caught her breath with a lithe gasp.

I placed a hand on one of hers and pressed it. "We must not conjure unnecessary horrors in our imaginations," but I feared what she had guessed what I had already surmised–that my graves had become pits for cooking fires.

In silence we watched the creatures working about the two trenches. They built up walls of stone and earth about a foot high along each of the long sides of each pit; When they laid poles at intervals of a few inches across the tops of each pair of walls. Slowly before our eyes we saw two grilles take shape.

"It is horrible," whispered Duare.

Night came before the preparations were completed; then the savage jong came to our prison and commanded us to come forth. As we did so we were seized by several shes and bulls who carried the long stems of tough jungle vines.

They drew us down and wound the vines about us. They were very clumsy and inept, not having sufficient intelligence to tie knots; but they accomplished their purpose in binding us by wrapping these fibber ropes around and around us until it seemed that it would be impossible to extricate ourselves even were we given the opportunity.

They bound me more securely than they did Duare, but even so the job was a clumsy one. Yet I guessed that it would be adequate to their purpose as they lifted us and laid us on the two parallel grilles.

This done, they commenced to move slowly about us in a rude circle, while near us, and also inside the circle, squatted a bull that was engaged in the business of making fire in the most primitive manner, twirling the end of a sharpened stick in a tinder-filled hole in a log.

From the throats of the circling tribesmen issued strange sounds that were neither speech nor song, yet I guessed that they were groping blindly after song just as in their awkward circling they were seeking self-expression in the rhythm of the dance.

The gloomy wood, feebly illumined by the mysterious ground glow, brooded darkly above and about the weird and savage scene. In the distance the roar of a beast rumbled menacingly.

As the hairy men-things circled about us the bull beside the log at last achieved fire. A slow wisp of smoke rose lazily from the tinder. The bull added a few dry leaves and blew upon the feeble spark. A tiny flame burst forth, and a savage cry arose from the circling dancers. It was answered from the forest by the roar of the beast we had heard a short time before. Now it was closer, and was followed by the thundering voices of others of its kind.

The nobargans paused in their dancing to look apprehensively into the dark wood, voicing their displeasure in grumblings and low growls; then the bull beside the fire commenced to light torches, a quantity of which lay prepared beside him; and as he passed them out the others resumed their dancing.

The circle contracted, and occasionally a dancer would leap in and pretend to light the faggots beneath us. The blazing torches illumined the weird scene, casting grotesque shadows that leaped and played like gigantic demons.

The truth of our predicament was now all too obvious, though I knew that we both suspected it since long before we had been laid upon the grilles–we were to be barbecued to furnish the flesh for a cannibal feast.

Duare turned her head toward me. "Goodbye, Carson Napier!" she whispered. "Before I go, I want you to know that I appreciate the sacrifice you have made for me. But for me you would be aboard the Sofal now, safe among loyal friends."

"I would rather be here with you, Duare," I replied, "than to be anywhere else in the universe without you."

I saw that her eyes were wet as she turned her face from me, but she did not reply, and then a huge, shaggy bull leaped in with a flaming torch and ignited the faggots at the lower end of the trench beneath her.

## Chapter 6

# Fire

From the surrounding forest came the roars of hungry beasts; but the sounds affected me none, so horrified was I by the hideous fate that had overtaken Duare.

I saw her struggling with her bonds, as I struggled with mine; but in the clumsily wound coils of the tough lianas we were helpless. Little flames below her feet were licking the larger faggots. Duare had managed to wriggle toward the head of the grille, so that the flames were not as yet directly beneath her, and she was still struggling with her bonds.

I had been paying little attention to the nobargans, but suddenly I realized that they had ceased their crude dancing and singing. Glancing toward them, I saw that they were standing looking off into the forest, the torches dangling in their hands, nor had they as yet lighted the faggots beneath me. Now I took note again of the thunderous roars of the beasts; they sounded very close. I saw dim figures slinking amidst the shadows of the trees and blazing eyes gleaming in the half light.

Presently a huge beast slunk out of the forest into the clearing, and I recognized it. I saw the stiff hair, like bristles. It was standing erect along the shoulders, neck, and spine. I saw the white, longitudinal stripes marking the reddish coat, and the bluish belly and the great, snarling jaws. The creature was a tharban.

The nobargans were also watching it. Presently they commenced to cry out against it and cast rocks at it from their slings in an obvious effort to frighten it away; but it did not retreat. Instead it came closer slowly, roaring horribly; and behind it came others–two, three, a dozen, two score–slinking from the concealing shadows of the forest. All were roaring, and the hideous volume of those mighty voices shook the ground.

And now the nobargans fell back. The great beasts invading the village increased their speed, and suddenly the hairy savages turned and fled. After them, roaring and growling, sprang the tharbans.

The speed of the clumsy appearing nobargans was a revelation to me, and as they disappeared into the dark mazes of the forest it was not apparent that the tharbans were gaining on them, though as the latter raced past me they seemed to be moving as swiftly as a charging lion.

The beasts paid no attention to Duare or me. I doubt that they even saw us, their whole attention being fixed upon the fleeing savages.

Now I turned again toward Duare, just in time to see her roll herself from the grille to the ground as the licking flames were about to reach her feet. For the moment she was safe, and I breathed a little prayer of thanksgiving. But what of the future? Must we lie here until inevitably the nobargans returned?

Duare looked up at me. She was struggling steadily with her bonds. "I believe that I can free myself," she said. "I am not bound so tightly as you. If only I can do it before they return!"

I watched her in silence. After what seemed an eternity, she got one arm free. After that the rest was comparatively easy, and when she was free she quickly released me.

Like two phantoms in the eerie light of the Amtorian night we faded into the shadows of the mysterious forest; and you may rest assured that we took a direction opposite to that in which the lions and the cannibals had disappeared.

The momentary elation that escape from the clutches of the nobargans had given me passed quickly as I considered our situation. We two were alone, unarmed, and lost in a strange country that brief experience had already demonstrated to be filled with dangers and that imagination peopled with a hundred menaces even more frightful than those we had encountered.

Raised in the carefully guarded seclusion of the house of a jong, Duare was quite as ignorant of the flora, the fauna, and the conditions existing in the land of Noobol as was I, an inhabitant of a far distant planet; and notwithstanding our culture, our natural intelligence, and my considerable physical strength we were still little better than babes in the woods.

We had been walking in silence, listening and looking for some new menace to our recently won respite from death, when Duare spoke in low tones, as one might who is addressing a question to himself.

"And should I ever return to the house of my father, the jong, who will believe the story that I shall tell? Who will believe that I, Duare, the daughter of the jong, passed through such incredible dangers alive?" She turned and looked up into my face. "Do you believe, Carson Napier, that I ever shall return to Vepaja?"

"I do not know, Duare," I replied honestly. "To be perfectly frank, it seems rather hopeless inasmuch as neither of us knows where we are or where Vepaja is, or what further dangers may confront us in this land.

"And what if we never find Vepaja, Duare? What if you and I go on for many years together? Must it always be as strangers, as enemies? Is there no hope for me, Duare? No hope to win your love?"

"Have I not told you that you must not speak to me of love? It is wicked for a girl under twenty to speak or ever think of love; and for me, the daughter of a jong, it is even worse. If you persist, I will not talk to you at all."

After this we walked on in silence for a long time. We were both very tired and hungry and thirsty, but for the time we subordinated all other desires to that of escaping the clutches of the nobargans; but at last I realized that Duare had about reached the limit of her endurance and I called a halt.

Selecting a tree, and lower branches of which were within easy reach, we climbed upward until I chanced upon a rude nest-like platform that might have been built by some arboreal creature or formed by debris falling from above during a storm. It lay upon two almost horizontal branches that extended from the bole of the tree in about the same plane, and was amply large enough to accommodate both of us.

As we stretched our tired bodies upon this mean yet none the less welcome couch, the growl of some great beast arose from the ground beneath to assure us that we had found sanctuary none too soon. What other dangers menaced us from arboreal creatures I did not know, but any thought of keeping wakeful vigil was dissipated by the utter exhaustion of both my mind and my body. I doubt that I could have kept awake much longer even in the act of walking.

As I was dozing off, I heard Duare's voice. It sounded sleepy and far away. "Tell me, Carson Napier," she said, "what is this thing called love?"

When I awoke, another day had come. I looked up at the mass of foliage Lying motionless in the air above me, and for a moment I had difficulty in recalling my surroundings and the events that had led me to this place. I turned my head and saw Duare Lying beside me, and then it all came back to me. I smiled a little as I recalled that last, sleepy question she had asked me–a question that I realized now I had not answered. I must have fallen asleep as it was propounded.

For two days we moved steadily in what we thought was the direction of the ocean. We subsisted on eggs and fruit, which we found in abundance. There was a great deal of life in the forest–strange birds such as no earthly eye had ever gazed upon before, monkey-like creatures that raced, chattering, through the trees, reptiles, herbivorous and carnivorous animals. Many of the latter were large and predacious. The worst of these that we encountered were the tharbans; but their habit of senseless roaring and growling preserved us from them by warning us of their proximity.

Another creature that caused us some bad moments was the basto. I had met this animal once before, that time that Kamlot and I had gone out upon our disastrous tarel gathering excursion; and so I was prepared to take to the trees with Duare the instant that we sighted one of these beasts.

Above the eyes, the head of a basto resembles the American bison, having the same short powerful horns and the thick hair upon its poll and forehead. Its eyes are small and red rimmed. The hide is blue and about the same texture as that of an elephant, with sparsely growing hairs except upon the head and tip of the tail, where the hair is thicker and longer. The beast stands very high at the shoulders but slopes downward rapidly to the rump. It has a tremendous depth of shoulder and exceedingly short, stocky fore legs, which are supplied with three toed feet. The fore legs carry fully three-quarters of the beast's weight. The muzzle is similar to that of a boar, except that it is broader, with heavy, curved tusks.

The basto is an ill tempered, omnivorous brute, always looking for trouble. Between him and the tharban, Duare and I became most proficient tree climbers during the first few days that we wandered through the forest.

My two greatest handicaps in this encounter with the primitive were lack of weapons and my inability to make fire. The latter was probably the worse, since, without a knife, fire was indispensable to the fashioning of weapons.

At every rest I experimented. Duare became inoculated with the virus of the quest, and fire became our sole aim. We talked about little else and were forever experimenting with different combinations of wood and with bits of rock that we picked up along the way.

All my life I had read of primitive men making fire in various ways, and I tried them all. I blistered my hands twirling firesticks. I knocked bits of flesh off my fingers striking pieces of stone together. At last I was on the point of giving up in disgust.

"I don't believe any one ever made fire," I grumbled.

"You saw the nobargan make it," Duare reminded me.

"There's a catch in it somewhere," I insisted.

"Are you going to give up?" she asked.

"Of course not. It's like golf. Most people never learn to play it, but very few give up trying. I shall probably continue my search for fire until death overtakes me or Prometheus descends to Venus as he did to Earth."

"What is golf and who is Prometheus? demanded Duare.

"Golf is a mental disorder and Prometheus a fable."

"I don't see how they can help you."

I was squatting over a little pile of tinder laboriously knocking together various bits of rock that we had collected during the day.

"Neither do I," I replied, viciously striking two new specimens together. A string of sparks shot from the two rocks and ignited the tinder! "I apologize to Prometheus," I cried; "he is no fable."

With the aid of this fire I was able to fashion a bow and to make and sharpen a spear and arrows. I strung the bow with a fibber from a tough liana, and I feathered my arrows gaily with the plumage of birds.

Duare was much interested in this work. She gathered feathers, split them, and bound them to the arrows with the long blades of a very tough grass that grew in profusion throughout the forest. Our work was facilitated by the use of bits of stone we had found so shaped that they made excellent scrapers.

I cannot express the change that came over me with the possession of weapons. I had come to feel like a hunted beast whose only defence is flight, and that is a most unhappy situation for the man who wished to impress the object of his love with his heroic qualities.

I really cannot say that I had any such intention in my mind at any time, yet with the growing realization of my futility I really did come to wish that I might cut a better figure before Duare.

Now I stepped out with a new stride. I was the hunter rather than the hunted. My pitiful, inadequate little weapons swept all doubts from my mind. I was now equal to any emergency.

"Duare," I exclaimed, "I am going to find Vepaja; I am going to take you home!"

She looked at me questioningly. "The last time we spoke of that," she reminded me, "you said that you hadn't the remotest idea where Vepaja was and that if you had, you couldn't hope to get there."

"That," I said, "was several days ago. Things are different now. Now, Duare, we are going hunting; we are going to have meat for dinner. You walk behind me so as not to frighten the game."

I moved forward with my old assurance and, perhaps, a little incautiously. Duare followed a few paces in the rear. There was considerable undergrowth in this portion of the forest, more than I had encountered before, and I could not see very far in any direction. We were following what appeared to be a game trail, along which I advanced boldly but silently.

Presently I saw a movement in the foliage ahead and then what appeared to be the outlines of some large animal. Almost instantly the silence of the forest was broken by the thunderous bellow of a basto, and there was a great crashing in the undergrowth.

"Take to the trees, Duare!" I cried, and at the same time I turned and ran back to assist her in climbing out of danger; and then Duare stumbled and fell.

Again the basto bellowed, and a quick backward glance revealed the mighty creature in the trail only a few paces in my rear. He was not charging, but he was advancing, and I could see that he would be upon us before we could possibly climb to safety, because of the slight delay occasioned by Duare's fall.

There appeared to be but one course of action open to me–I must delay the beast until Duare had gained a place of safety. I recalled how Kamlot had slain one of the creatures by distracting its attention from himself to a leafy branch held in his left hand and then plunged his keen sword behind the shoulder down into the heart. But I had no leafy branch and only a crude wooden spear.

He was almost upon me, his red rimmed eyes blazing, his white tusks gleaming. He loomed as large as an elephant to my excited imagination. He put his head down, another thunderous roar rumbled from his cavernous chest, and then he charged.

As the basto bore down upon me my only thought was to divert his attention from Duare until she should be safely out of his reach. It all happened so quickly that I imagine I had no time to think of my own almost certain fate.

The brute was so close to me when he started his charge that he attained no great speed. He came straight toward me with head lowered, and so mighty and awe inspiring was he that I did not even consider attempting to stop him with my puny weapons.

Instead, all my thoughts cantered upon one objective –to save myself from being impaled upon those horns.

I grasped them, one with each hand, as the basto struck me, and, thanks to my unusual strength, I succeeded in breaking the force of the impact as well as diverting the horns from my vitals.

The instant that he felt my weight the brute ripped upward with his head in an effort to gore and toss me, and in the latter he succeeded beyond anything that I might have expected and, I imagine, beyond what he intended.

With almost the force of an explosion I was hurtled upward to crash through the foliage and the branches of the tree above, dropping my weapons as I went. Fortunately my head came in contact with no large limb, and so I retained consciousness through it all. I also retained my presence of mind and, clutching frantically, I succeeded in grasping a branch across which my body had fallen. From there I dragged myself to the safety of a larger limb.

My first thought was of Duare. Was she safe? Had she been able to climb out of danger before the basto disposed of me and was upon her, or had he reached and gored her?

My fears were almost immediately allayed by the sound of her voice. "Oh, Carson, Carson! Are you hurt?" she cried. The anguish of her tones was ample reward for any hurts I might have sustained.

"I think not," I replied; "just shaken up a bit. Are you all right? Where are you?"

"Here, in the next tree. Oh, I thought he had killed you!"

I was testing out my joints and feeling of myself for possible injuries; but I discovered nothing more serious than bruises, and scratches, and of these I had plenty.

As I was examining myself, Duare made her way along interlocking branches and presently she was at my side. "You're bleeding," she exclaimed. "You are hurt."

"These are nothing but scratches," I assured her; "only my pride is hurt."

"You have nothing to be ashamed of; you should be very proud of what you did. I saw. I glanced behind me as I got to my feet, and I saw you standing right in the path of that terrible beast so that it would not reach me."

"Perhaps," I suggested, "I was too terrified to run–just paralyzed by fears."

She smiled and shook her head. "I know better than that; I know you too well."

"Any risk would be worth taking if it won your approval."

She was silent for a moment, looking down at the basto. The brute was pawing the ground and bellowing. Occasionally it would pause and look up at us.

"We could get away from it by going through the trees," suggested Duare. "They grow very close together here."

"And abandon my new weapons?" I demanded.

"He'll probably go away in a few minutes, as soon as he realizes we are not coming down."

But he didn't go away in a few minutes. He bellowed and pawed and gored the ground for half an hour, and then he lay down beneath the tree.

"That fellow's an optimist," I remarked. "He thinks that if he waits long enough we'll probably come down of our own volition."

Duare laughed. "Maybe he thinks we'll die of old age and fall down."

"That's a joke on him; he doesn't know that we have been inoculated with the serum of longevity."

"In the meantime, the joke is on us; and I am getting hungry."

"Look, Duare!" I whispered, as I caught sight of something dimly visible through the tangled undergrowth beyond the basto.

"What is it?" she asked.

"I don't know, but it's something large."

"It is creeping silently through the brush, Carson. Do you suppose it is something that has caught our scent, some other terrible beast of prey?"

"Well we are up a tree," I reassured her.

"Yes, and many of these creatures climb trees. I wish you had your weapons."

"If that basto would look the other way for a minute, I'd go down and get them."

"No, you mustn't do that–one or the other of them would get you."

"Here it comes now, Duare! Look!"

It's a tharban," she whispered.

## CHAPTER 7

# Bull Against Lion

The evil face of the fierce carnivore was protruding from the underbrush a short distance beyond and behind the basto. The latter did not see it, nor did his nostrils catch the scent of the great cat-like creature.

"It's not looking at us," I said; "it's watching the basto."

"Do you suppose–" commenced Duare, and then her words were drowned by the most blood-curdling scream I have ever heard.

It came from the savage throat of the tharban at the instant it sprang toward the basto. The latter beast, lumbering to its feet, was caught at a disadvantage. The tharban leaped full upon its back, sinking talons and fangs deep into the tough flesh.

The bellowing of the basto mingled with the roars and growls of the tharban in a hideous diapason of bestial rage that seemed to rock the forest.

The huge bull wheeled in a frenzy of pain and sought to sink its horn in the thing upon its back. The tharban struck viciously at the savage face, raking downward from poll to muzzle, tearing hide and flesh to the bone, one great talon ripping an eye from its socket.

Its head a bloody mass of torn flesh, the basto threw itself upon its back with almost cat-like agility, seeking to crush the life from its tormentor; but the tharban leaped to one side and, as the bull scrambled to its feet, sprang in again.

This time the basto, wheeling with lowered head and incredible swiftness, caught the tharban full upon its horns and tossed it high into the foliage of the tree above.

A screaming, clawing hellion of unrestrained primitive rage and hate, the great carnivore hurtled upward within a few feet of Duare and me; and then, still clawing and screaming, it fell back.

Like a huge cat, that it most closely resembled, it came down feet first. With ready horns and tail stiffly erect, the basto waited to catch it and toss it again. Full on those powerful horns the tharban fell; but when the basto surged upward with all the strength of that mighty, bulging neck, the tharban did not soar upward into the tree again. With powerful claws and mighty jaws it clung to the head and neck of its antagonist. It raked shoulder and throat as the basto attempted to shake it loose. With fearful strokes of its talons it was tearing the basto to shreds.

In a bloody welter of gore, the stricken creature, now totally blinded by the loss of its remaining eye, wheeled in a grotesque and futile pirouette of death; but still its screaming Nemesis clung to it, tearing, striking in mad, blind rage, its hideous cries mingling with the now shrill death bellowings of the stricken bull.

Suddenly the basto stopped in its tracks, its feet spread swaying weakly. Blood was gushing from its neck in such a torrent that I was positive its jugular must have been severed; I knew that the end must be near and only wondered at the unbelievable tenacity with which the creature clung to life.

Nor was the tharban in an enviable state. Once badly gored and now impaled upon those two mighty horns, the blood of his terrible wounds mingling with the blood of his intended victim, his chances of survival were as negligible as those of the weaving bull, already seemingly dead upon its feet.

But how could I guess the inconceivable vitality of these mighty creatures?

With a sudden shake of his horns the bull stiffened; then he lowered his head and charged blindly, apparently with all the strength and vigour of unimpaired vitality.

It was to be a short charge. With terrific impact he struck the bole of the tree in which we were crouching. The branch upon which we sat swayed and snapped like a loose spar in a gale, and Duare and I were toppled from our perch.

Clutching futilely for support, we shot downward on top of the tharban and the basto. For an instant I was terrified for Duare's safety, but there was no need for apprehension. Neither of these mighty engines of destruction turned upon us; neither moved. Except for a few convulsive shudders they lay still in death.

The tharban had been caught between the bole of the tree and massive poll of the basto and crushed to pulp; the basto had died as it wreaked its final, fearful vengeance on the tharban.

Duare and I had rolled to the ground beside the bodies of these mighty Titans; and now, uninjured, we sprang to our feet. Duare was pale and a trifle shaken, but she smiled bravely up into my face.

"Our hunting was more successful than we dreamed," she said. "There is meat enough for many men."

"Kamlot told me that there was nothing like a basto steak grilled over a wood fire."

"They are delicious. My mouth is watering already."

"And mine, too, Duare; but without a knife we are still a long way from the steak. Look at that thick hide."

Duare looked crestfallen. "Did ever two people have such continuous bad luck?" she exclaimed. "But never mind," she added. "Get your weapons, and perhaps we shall find something small enough to tear to pieces or cook whole."

"Wait!" I exclaimed, opening the pocket pouch that hung over my shoulder by a stout cord. "I have a piece of stone with a sharp edge that I use for scraping my bow and arrows. I may be able to hack out a meal with it."

It was a laborious job but I finally succeeded, and while I was engaged upon this crude and ragged butchery Duare gathered tinder and wood and surprised us both by starting a fire. She was very happy and excited over her success, and proud, too. In all her pampered life at home she had never been required to do a practical thing, and the reward of even this small accomplishment filled her with joy.

That meal was a memorable one; it was epochal. It marked the emergence of primitive man from the lower orders of life. He had achieved fire; he had fashioned weapons; he had made his kill (figuratively, in this case); and now for the first time he was eating cooked food. And I liked to carry the metaphor a little further in this instance and think of the partner of his achievements as his mate. I sighed as I thought of the happiness that might be ours did Duare but return my love.

"What's the matter?" demanded Duare. "Why do you sigh?"

"I am sighing because I am not really a primitive man instead of a poor, weak imitation of one."

"Why do you want to be a primitive man she inquired.

"Because primitive man was not bound by silly conventions," I replied. "If he wanted a woman and she did not want him, he grabbed her by the hair and dragged her to his lair."

"I am glad that I did not live in those times," said Duare.

For several days we wandered on through the forest. I knew that we were hopelessly lost, but I was anxious to get out of that gloomy wood. It was getting on our nerves. I managed to kill small game with my spear and my arrows; there was an abundance of fruit and nuts; and water was plentiful. In the matter of food we lived like kings, and we were fortunate in our encounters with the more formidable creatures we met. Luckily for us we saw none that were arboreal, though I am positive that this was merely by the luckiest chance, for the woods of Amtor harbour many terrible creatures that live wholly in the trees.

Duare, notwithstanding all the hardships and dangers she was constantly undergoing, seldom complained. She remained remarkably cheerful in the face of what was now palpably the absolute certainty that we could never hope to find the distant island where her father was king. Sometimes she was sober and silent for long periods, and I guessed that at these times she was sorrowing; but she did not share her sorrows with me. I wished that she would; we often share our sorrows with those we love.

But one day she suddenly sat down and began to cry. I was so surprised that I just stood there for several minutes staring at her before I could think of anything to say, and then I didn't think of anything very brilliant.

"Why, Duare!" I cried. "What's the matter? Are you ill?"

She shook her head and sought to stifle her sobs. I'm sorry," she managed to say at last. "I didn't mean to; I've tried not to; but this forest! Oh, Carson, it's on my nerves; it haunts me even in my sleep. It is endless; it goes on and on forever–gloomy, forbidding, filled with terrible dangers. There!" she exclaimed, and rising she shook her head as though to dispel unwelcome visions. "I'm all right now; I won't do it again." She smiled through her tears.

I wanted to take her in my arms and comfort her oh, how badly I wanted to! But I only laid a hand upon her shoulder. "I know just how you feel," I told her. I've felt the same way for days. I have to take it out by swearing to myself. But it can't last forever, Duare. There must be an end to it pretty soon; and, anyway, you must remember that the forest has fed us and sheltered us and protected us."

"As a jailer feeds and shelters and protects the criminal condemned to die," she responded dully. "Come! Let's not speak of it any more."

Once again the underbrush was thick, and we were following a game trail that was as erratic as most game trails. I think it was this thick brush that depressed Duare even more than the forest itself. I know it always depressed me. The trail was wide and we were walking abreast when suddenly at a turning the forest seemed to disappear in front of us. There was a void staring us in the face, and beyond that, far, far away, the outlines of distant mountains.

## Chapter 8

# Down the Escarpment

Wonderingly we advanced until we stood upon the brink of a lofty escarpment. Far below, at least five thousand feet, a great valley spread before our eyes. Far, far away, across it, we saw the outlines of the distant mountains that hemmed it upon that side; but to the right and left its extent was shrouded in the mists of distance.

During the days that we had been wandering in the forest we must have been climbing steadily, but the ascent had been so gradual that we had scarcely noticed it. Now, the effect of coming suddenly upon this mighty depression was startling. It was as though I were looking into a deep pit that lay far below sea level. This impression, however, was soon dispelled, for in the distance I saw a great river winding along the bed of the valley; and I knew that it must run downward to some sea.

"A new world!" breathed Duare. "How beautiful by contrast with this frightful forest!"

"Let us hope that it will be no less kind to us than the forest has been."

"How could it be otherwise than kind? It is so beautiful," she replied. "There must be people living there, generous, kindly people as lovely as their lovely valley. There could be no evil where there is so much beauty. Perhaps they will help us to return to my Vepaja. I am sure they will."

"I hope so, Duare," I said.

"See!" she exclaimed. "There are little rivers running into the big river, and there are level plains dotted with trees, and there are forests, too, but no terrible forest that stretches on and on seemingly without end as this that we are escaping. Do you see any cities or signs of man, Carson?"

I shook my head. "I cannot be positive. We are very high above the valley; and the large river, where it is probable the cities would be, is far away. Only a very great city with tall buildings would be visible from here, and the haze that hangs over the valley might even hide a large city from us. We shall have to go down into the valley to find out."

"I can scarcely wait," exclaimed Duare.

The trail on which we had approached the edge of the escarpment turned sharply to the left and skirted the brink, but from it a smaller trail branched and dropped over the edge.

This trail was little better than a faintly marked foot path, and it zigzagged down the almost vertical face of the escarpment in a manner calculated to send the cold chills up one's back if he happened to be affected by such things.

"Few creatures go up and down here," remarked Duare, as she looked over the edge of the escarpment at the dizzy trail.

"Perhaps we had better go on farther; there may be an easier way down," I suggested, thinking that she might be fearful.

"No," she demurred. "I wanted to get out of the forest, and here is my chance. Something has gone up and down here; and if something else has, we can."

"Take my hands, then; it is very steep."

She did as I bid, and I also handed her my spear to use as a staff. Thus we started the perilous descent. Even now I hate to recall it. It was not only fraught with danger but it was exceedingly exhausting. A dozen times I thought that we were doomed; seemingly it was impossible to descend farther, and certainly it would have been impossible to retrace our steps to the summit, for there had been places where we had lowered ourselves over ledges that we could not have again scaled.

Duare was very brave. She amazed me. Not only was her courage remarkable, but her endurance was almost unbelievable in one so delicately moulded. And she kept cheerful and good-natured. Often she laughed when she would slip and almost fall, where a fall meant death.

"I said," she recalled, once while we were resting, "that something must have come up and down this trail. Now I wonder what manner of creature it may be."

"Perhaps it is a mountain goat," I suggested. "I can think of nothing else that might do it."

She did not know what a mountain goat was, and I knew of no Venusian animal with which to compare it. She thought that a mistal might easily go up and down such a trail. I had never heard of this animal, but from her description I judged it to be a rat-like animal about the size of a house cat.

As we were starting down again after a rest, I heard a noise below us and looked over the edge of the ledge on which we stood to see what had caused it."

"We are about to have our curiosity satisfied," I whispered to Duare. "Here comes the trail maker."

"Is it a mistal?" she asked.

"No, nor a mountain goat; but it is just the sort of a creature that might most easily cling to this vertical pathway. I don't know what you Amtorians call it. Take a look; perhaps you will recognize it."

It was a huge, hideous lizard about twenty feet in length that was climbing sluggishly upward toward our position.

Leaning on my shoulder, Duare glanced downward over the ledge. She voiced a low gasp of terror.

"I think it is a vere," she said, "and if it is we are in for it. I have never seen one, but I have read of them in books and seen their pictures; this one looks like the pictures I have seen."

"Are they dangerous?" I asked.

"They are deadly," she replied. "We wouldn't have a chance against a vere."

"See if you can climb back out of the way," I said to Duare. "I will try to hold it here until you are safe." Then I turned toward the creature crawling slowly upward.

It was covered with scales of red, black, and yellow arranged in intricate designs. Its coloration and ornamentation were beautiful, but right there its beauty stopped. It had a head not unlike that of a crocodile, and along each side of its upper jaw was a row of gleaming white horns. Across the top and down the sides of its head sprawled a single huge eye of myriad facets.

It had not discovered us yet, but in another half minute it would be upon us. I loosened a bit of rock near my hand and hurled it down, thinking I might turn the creature back. The missile struck it on the snout, and with a grunt it raised its head and saw me.

Its great jaws opened and out shot the most prodigious tongue I had ever seen. Like lightning it curled about me and snapped me toward those gaping jaws from which was issuing a harsh screaming whistle.

All that saved me from being instantly engulfed was the fact that I was a little too large a mouthful for the creature to negotiate with ease. I wedged crosswise of his snout and there I fought with all my strength to keep from being dragged into that rapacious maw.

It was a great slimy, toothless, sucking gullet that I struggled to escape. Evidently the creature swallowed its prey whole, its horns being probably solely for defence. From that repulsive throat issued a fetid door that almost overpowered me. I think that it may have been a poisonous exhalation that was intended to anaesthetize its victims. I felt myself growing weak and dizzy, and then I saw Duare at my side.

She was grasping my spear in both hands and lunging viciously at the horrid face of the vere. All the time she was moaning, "Carson! Carson!"

How small and frail and inadequate she looked to be pitting herself against this fearsome creature!–and how magnificent!

She was risking her life to save mine, and yet she did not love me. Still, it was not incredible–there are noble qualities far more unselfish than love. Loyalty is of these. But I could not permit her to sacrifice her life for loyalty.

"Run, Duare!" I cried. "You can't save me–I am done for. Run while you can, or it will kill us both."

She paid no attention to me, but thrust again. This time the spear tore into the many-faceted eye. With a shrill whistle of pain, the reptile turned upon Duare and sought to strike her with its gleaming horns; but she stood her ground and, thrusting again, drove the weapon between the distended jaws, drove it deep and far into the pink flesh of that repulsive maw.

The spear point must have pierced the tongue, for it suddenly went limp; and I rolled from its encircling grasp to the ground.

Instantly I was on my feet again, and seizing Duare's arm dragged her to one side as the vere charged blindly. It brushed past us, whistling and screaming, and then turned, but in the wrong direction.

It was then that I realized that the creature had been totally blinded by the wound in its eye. Taking a perilous risk, I threw my arm about Duare and slid over the edge of the ledge upon which the brute had encountered us, for to have remained even an instant where we were would have meant being maimed or hurled to our doom by the viciously lashing tail of the frenzied lizard.

Fortune favoured us, and we came safely to rest upon another ledge at a slightly lower level. Above us we could hear the whistling scream of the vere and the thudding of his tail against the rocky escarpment.

Fearing that the creature might descend upon us, we hurried on, taking even greater risks than we had before; nor did we stop until we had reached comparatively level ground near the foot of the escarpment. Then we sat down to rest. We were both panting from our exertions.

"You were wonderful," I said to Duare. "You risked your life to save mine."

"Perhaps I was just afraid to be left alone," she said with some embarrassment. "I may have been entirely selfish."

"I don't believe that," I remonstrated.

The truth was that I didn't want to believe it. Another implication was far sweeter to me.

"Anyhow," remarked Duare, "we found out what made the trail up the escarpment."

"And that our beautiful valley may not be as secure as it looks," I added.

"But the creature was going out of the valley up into the forest," she argued. "That is probably where it lived."

"However, we had best be on our guard constantly."

"And now you have no spear; and that is a real loss, for it is because of the spear that you are alive."

"Down there a little way," I indicated, pointing, "is a winding strip of wood that seems to be following the meanderings of a stream. There we can find material for another spear and also water. I am as dry as a bone."

"So am I," said Duare, "and hungry too. Perhaps you can kill another basto."

I laughed. "This time I shall make you a spear and a bow and arrows, too. From what you have already done, you seem to be better able to kill bastos than I."

Leisurely we walked toward the wood, which was about a mile away, through soft grass of a pale violet hue. Flowers grew in profusion on every hand. There were purple flowers and blue and pale yellow; and their foliage, like the blossoms, was strange and unearthly. There were flowers and leaves of colours that have no name, colours such as no earthly eye had ever seen before.

Such things bear in upon me the strange isolation of our senses. Each sense lives in a world of its own, and though it lives a lifetime with its fellow senses it knows nothing of their worlds.

My eyes see a colour; but my fingers, my ears, my nose, my palate may never know that colour. I cannot even describe it so that any of your senses may perceive it as I perceive it, if it is a new colour that you have never seen. Even less well might I describe an door or a flavour or the feel of some strange substance.

Only by comparison might I make you see the landscape that stretched before our eyes, and there is nothing in your world with which I may compare it–the glowing fog bank overhead, the pale, soft pastels of field and forest and distant misty mountains–no dense shadows and no high lights–strange and beautiful and weird– intriguing, provocative, compelling, always beckoning one on to further investigation, to new adventure.

All about us the plain between the escarpment and the forest was dotted with trees; and, Lying beneath them or grazing in the open, were animals that were entirely new to my experience either here or on Earth. That several distinct families and numerous genera were represented was apparent to even a cursory survey.

Some were large and cumbersome, others were small and dainty. All were too far away for me to note them in detail; and for that I was glad, for I guessed that among that array of wild beasts there must be some at least which might prove dangerous to man. But, like all animals except hungry carnivores and men, they showed no disposition to attack us so long as we did not interfere with them or approach them too closely.

"I see that we shall not go hungry here," remarked Duare.

"I hope some of those little fellows are good to eat," I laughed.

"I am sure that big one under the tree is delicious; the one looking at us," and she pointed to an enormous, shaggy creature as large as an elephant. Duare had a sense of humour.

"Possibly it entertains the same idea concerning us," I suggested; "here it comes!"

The huge beast was walking toward us. The forest was still a hundred yards away.

"Shall we run?" asked Duare.

"I am afraid that would be fatal. You know. it is almost instinctive for a beast to pursue any creature that runs away from it. I think the best course for us to follow is to continue steadily toward the forest without seeming haste. If the thing does not increase its speed we shall reach the trees ahead of it; if we run for it the chances are that it will overtake us, for of all created things mankind seems to be about the slowest."

As we proceeded, we constantly cast backward glances at the shaggy menace trailing us. He lumbered along, exhibiting no signs of excitement; but his long strides were eating up the distance between us. I saw that he would overtake us before we reached the forest. I felt utterly helpless, with my puny bow and my tiny arrows, before this towering mountain of muscle.

"Quicken your pace a little, Duare," I directed.

She did as I bid, but after a few steps she glanced back. "Why don't you come, too?" she demanded.

"Don't argue," I snapped a little shortly. "Do as I bid you."

She stopped and waited for me. I shall do as I please," she informed me, "and it does not please me to let you make this sacrifice for me. If you are to be killed, I shall be killed with you. Furthermore, Carson Napier, please remember that I am the daughter of a jong and am not accustomed to being ordered about."

"If there were not more pressing matters to occupy me I would spank you," I growled.

She looked at me, horrified; then she stamped one little foot in rage and commenced to cry. "You take advantage of me because there is no one to protect me," she sputtered. "I hate you, you–you–"

"But I am trying to protect you, Duare; and you are only making it harder for me."

"I don't want any of your protection; I would rather be dead. It is more honourable to be dead than to be talked to like that–I am the daughter of a jong."

"I think you have mentioned that several times before," I said, coldly.

She threw up her head and walked stiffly on without looking back at me. Even her little shoulders and back radiated offended dignity and stifled rage.

I glanced behind me. The mighty beast was scarce fifty feet away; ahead of us the forest was about the same distance. Duare could not see me. I stopped and faced the colossus. By the time it had dispatched me Duare would probably be close to the safety of the branches of the nearest tree.

I held my bow in one hand, but my arrows remained in the crude quiver. I had fashioned to hold them behind my right shoulder. I had sense enough to realize that the only effect they might have upon this mountain of hairy sinew would be to enrage it.

After I stopped, the beast approached more slowly, almost warily. Two little eyes, set far apart, regarded me intently; two large, mulish ears pricked forward; quivering nostrils dilated.

On it came, very gradually now. A bony protuberance extending from its snout to its forehead commenced to rise until it revealed itself to my astonished gaze as a sharp-pointed horn. The horn rose until it pointed fiercely at me, a terrible weapon of offence.

I did not move. My experience of earthly animals had taught me that few will attack without provocation, and I stake my life on the chance that the same rule prevailed on Venus. But there are other provocations besides those that arouse fear or anger; a most potent one is hunger. However, this creature looked herbivorous; and I hoped that it was a vegetarian. But I could not forget the basto; that somewhat resembled an American bison, yet would eat meat.

Closer and closer came the remarkable beast, very, very slowly, as though its mind were assailed by doubts. It towered above me like a living mountain. I could feel its warm breath upon my almost naked body; but, better still, I could smell its breath–the sweet, inoffensive breath of a grass eater. My hopes rose.

The creature stuck out its muzzle toward me; a low rumbling issued from its cavernous chest; that terrible horn touched me; then the cool, moist muzzle. The beak sniffed at me. Slowly the horn subsided.

Suddenly, with a snort, the animal wheeled about and went galloping off, bucking and jumping as I have seen a playful steer buck and jump, its little tail stiffly erect. It presented a most ludicrous appearance–as would a steam locomotive skipping rope. I laughed, possibly a little hysterically, for my knees were suddenly weak and wobbly. If I had not been near death, I had at least thought that I was.

As I turned back toward the forest I saw Duare standing there looking at me, and as I approached her I perceived that she was wide-eyed and trembling.

You are very brave, Carson," she said with a little catch in her throat. Her anger seemed to have departed. "I know that you remained there so that I might escape."

"There really wasn't much else that I could do," I assured her. "And now that that's over, let's see if we can't find something to eat–something a few sizes smaller than that mountains of steaks and roasts. I think we'll go on until we strike the stream that flows through this forest. We may find a drinking place or a ford that the animals are accustomed to coming to."

"There are many animals out there on the plain that are small," suggested Duare. "Why don't you hunt there?"

"There are plenty of animals, but there are not enough trees," I replied with a laugh. "We may need some trees in our hunting. I don't know enough about these Amtorian beasts as yet to warrant me in taking unnecessary risks."

We moved on into the wood beneath the delicate foliage and among the strangely beautiful boles with their lacquer-like bark of white and red and yellow and blue.

Presently we came in sight of a little river winding leisurely between its violet banks, and at the same instant I saw a small creature drinking. It was about the size of a goat, but it didn't look like a goat. Its sharply pointed ears were constantly moving, as though on the alert for the slightest sound of danger; its tufted tail switched nervously. A collar of short horns encircled its neck just where it joined the head. They pointed slightly forward. There must have been a dozen of them. I could not but wonder what their specific purpose might be until I recalled the vere from whose horrible maw I had so recently escaped. That necklace of short horns would most certainly have discouraged any creature that was in the habit of swallowing its prey whole.

Very gently, I pushed Duare behind a tree and crept forward, fitting an arrow to my bow. As I was preparing to shoot, the creature threw up its head and turned half around. Probably it had heard me. I had been creeping on it from behind, but its change of position revealed its left side to me, and I planted my first arrow squarely in its heart.

So we made our camp beside the river and dined on juicy chops, delicious fruits, and the clear water from the little stream. Our surroundings were idyllic. Strange birds sang to us, arboreal quadrupeds swung through the trees jabbering melodiously in soft sing-song voices.

"It is very lovely here," said Duare, dreamily. "Carson –I wish that I were not the daughter of a jong."

## CHAPTER 9

# The Gloomy Castle

We were both loath to leave this lovely spot, and so we tarried there for two days while I made weapons for Duare and a new spear for myself.

I had constructed a little platform in a tree that overhung the river; and there at night we were comparatively safe from predatory animals while the soft music of the purling water lulled us to sleep, a sleep that might be suddenly broken by the savage roars of hunting beasts or the screams of their victims, to which the distant lowing and bellowing of the vast herds upon the plain furnished a harmonious undertone in this raw aria of life.

It was our last night in this pleasant camp. We were sitting on our little platform watching the fish leaping and jumping in the river below.

"I could be happy here forever–with you, Duare," I said.

"One may not think of happiness alone," she replied; "there is duty also."

"But what if circumstances make us helpless to perform our duties? Aren't we warranted in making the best of our fate and making the most of the chance for happiness where we find it?"

What do you mean?" she asked.

"I mean that there is practically no possibility that we can ever reach Vepaja. We do not know where it is, and if we did it seems to me that there is not even the remotest chance that we should survive the dangers that must lie along that unknown trail that leads back to the house of Mintep, your father."

"I know that you are right," she replied a little wearily, abut it is my duty to try; and I may never cease to seek to return, to the end of my life, no matter how remote I may know the chance of success may be."

"Isn't that being a little unreasonable, Duare?"

"You do not understand, Carson Napier. If I had a brother or sister it might make a difference; but I have neither, and my father and I are the last of our line. It is not for myself nor for my father that I must return but for my country–the royal line of the jongs of Vepaja must not be broken, and there is none to perpetuate it but myself."

"And if we do return–what then?"

"When I am twenty I shall marry a noble selected by my father, and after my father dies I shall be vadjong, or queen, until my oldest son is twenty; then he will be jong."

"But with the longevity serum that your scientists have perfected your father will never die; so why return?"

"I hope he will not die, but there are accidents and battles and assassins. Oh, why discuss it! The royal line must be preserved!"

"And what of me, if we reach Vepaja?" I asked.

"What do you mean?"

"Will there be a chance for me?"

"I do not understand."

"If your father consents, will you marry me?" I blurted.

Duare flushed. "How many times must I tell you that you may not speak of such serious things to me?"

"I can't help it, Duare; I love you. I care nothing for customs nor jongs nor dynasties. I shall tell your father that I love you, and I shall tell him that you love me."

"I do not love you; you have no right to say that. It is sinful and wicked. Because once I was weak and lost my head and said a thing I did not mean you have no right to constantly throw it in my face."

Now that was just like a woman. I had been fighting every impulse to keep from speaking of love during all the time we had been together. I couldn't recall but one other instance when I had lost control of myself, yet she accused me of constantly throwing in her face the one admission of love that she had made.

"Well," I said, sullenly, "I shall do what I said I'd do, if I ever see your father again."

"And do you know what he will do?"

"If he's the right kind of a father he'll say, 'Bless you, my children.'"

"He is a jong before he is a father, and he will have you destroyed. Even if you do not make any such mad admission to him, I shall have to use all of my powers of persuasion to save you from death."

Why should he kill me?"

"No man who has spoken, without royal permission, to a janjong, or princess, is ordinarily permitted to live. That you may be with me alone for months and possibly years before we return to Vepaja will but tend to exaggerate the seriousness of the situation. I shall plead your service to me; that you risked your life innumerable times to preserve mine; and that I think will have sufficient weight to save you from death; but, of course, you will be banished from Vepaja."

"That is a pleasant outlook. I may lose my life, and I am certain to lose you. Under such circumstances, do you think that I will prosecute the search for Vepaja with much enthusiasm or diligence?"

"Perhaps not with enthusiasm; but with diligence, yes. You will do it for me, because of that thing which you call love."

"Possibly you are right," I said, and I knew that she was.

The next day we started, in accordance with a plan we had formulated, to follow the little river down toward the big river along which we would continue to the sea. Where we should go from there was problematical. We decided to wait until we reached the sea before making any further plans. What lay before us we could not guess; had we been able to we might have fled back to the comparative safety of the gloomy forest we had so recently quitted with delight.

Late in the afternoon we were taking a short cut across open ground where the river made a great bend. It was rather rough going, for there were many rocks and boulders and the surface of the land was cut by gullies.

As we clambered up the bank of a particularly deep gully I chanced to glance back and saw a strange animal standing on the opposite rim watching us. It was about the size of a German police dog, but there the similarity ceased. It had a massive, curved beak remarkably similar to that of a parrot; and its body was covered with feathers; but it was no bird, for it went on four legs and had no wings. Forward of its two short ears were three horns, one in front of either ear and the third growing midway between the others. As it turned part way around to look back at something we could not see, I saw that it had no tail. At a distance its legs and feet appeared bird-like.

"Do you see what I see, Duare?" I asked, nodding in the direction of the weird creature; "or am I suffering from a touch of fever?"

"Of course I see it," she replied, "but I don't know what it is. I am sure that there is no such creature on the island of Vepaja."

"There's another of them, and another, and another! I exclaimed. "Lord! there must be a dozen of them."

They were standing in a little knot surveying us when suddenly the one we had first seen raised its grotesque head and voiced a hoarse, wailing scream; then it started down into the gully and headed for us at a rapid gallop, and behind it came its fellows, all now voicing that hideous cry.

"What are we going to do?" asked Duare. "Do you suppose they are dangerous?"

"I don't know whether they are dangerous our not," I replied, "but I wish that there were a tree handy."

"A forest does have its advantages," admitted Duare. "What are we going to do?"

"It would do no good to run; so we might as well stand here and have it out with them. We'll have some advantage as they come up the bank of the gully."

I fitted an arrow to my bow and Duare did likewise; then we stood waiting for them to come within range. They loped easily across the bottom of the gully and started the ascent. They didn't seem to be in much of a hurry; that is, they didn't seem to be extending themselves to their full speed, probably because we were not running away from them.

Perhaps this surprised them, for they presently slowed down to a walk and advanced warily. They had ceased their baying. The feathers along their backs rose stiffly erect as they slunk toward us.

Aiming carefully at the foremost, I loosed an arrow. It struck the beast full in the chest, and with a scream it stopped and tore at the feathered shaft protruding from its body. The others halted and surrounded it. They made a strange cackling sound.

The wounded creature staggered and sank to the ground, and instantly its fellows were upon it, tearing and rending. For a moment it fought fiercely to defend itself, but futilely.

As the others commenced to devour their fallen comrade I motioned Duare to follow me, and we turned and ran toward the trees we could see about a mile away where the river turned back across our line of march. But we hadn't gone far before we heard again the infernal screaming that told us that the pack was on our trail.

This time they overtook us while we were at the bottom of a depression, and once again we made a stand. Instead of attacking us directly, the beasts slunk about just out of range, as though they knew the danger line beyond which they would be safe; then slowly they circled us until we were surrounded.

"If they charge now, all at once," said Duare, "we are sure to be finished."

"Perhaps if we succeed in killing a couple of them the others will stop to devour them, thus giving us another chance to get closer to the wood," I argued with an assumed optimism.

As we waited for the next move of our antagonists, we heard a loud shout in the direction from which we had come. Looking quickly up, I saw a man seated upon the back of a four footed animal at the rim of the depression in which we stood.

At the sound of the human voice, the beasts surrounding us looked in the direction of the interruption and immediately commenced to cackle. The man on the beast rode slowly down toward us, and as he came to the ring of beasts they moved aside and let him pass through their savage ranks.

"It is fortunate for you that I came when I did," said the stranger, as the beast he rode stopped in front of us; "these kazars of mine are a ferocious lot." He was eying us intently, especially Duare. "Who are you, and where are you from?" he demanded.

"We are strangers, and we are lost," I replied. "I am from California." I did not wish to tell him that we were from Vepaja until we knew more of him. If he was a Thorist he was an enemy; and the less he knew about us the better, especially that we were from the country of Mintep, the jong, than whom the Thorists have no more bitter enemy.

"California," he repeated. "I never heard of such a country. Where is it?"

"In North America," I replied, but he only shook his head. "And who are you," I asked, "and what country is this?"

"This is Noobol, but that of course you already know. This part of it is known as Morov. I am Skor, the jong of Morov. But you have not told me your names."

"This is Duare," I replied, "and I am Carson." I did not give surname as they are seldom used on Venus.

"And where were you going?"

"We were trying to find our way to the sea."

"From where did you come?"

"Recently we were in Kapdor," I explained.

I saw his eyes narrow ominously. "So you are Thoristst" he snapped.

"No," I assured him, "we are not. We were prisoners of the Thorists." I hoped that my guess had been a good one and that he was not kindly disposed toward the Thorists. The slender thread upon which I hung my hopes was no more substantial than the frown that had clouded his brow at my admission that we had just come from Kapdor.

To my relief his expression changed. "I am glad that you are not Thorists; otherwise I would not help you. I have no use for the breed."

"You will help us, then?" I asked.

"With pleasure," he replied. He was looking at Duare as he spoke, and I did not exactly relish the tone of his voice nor the expression on his face.

The kazars were circling around us, cackling and whistling. When one of them approached us too close, Skor would flick it with the lash of a long whip he carried; and the creature would retreat, screaming and cackling the louder.

"Come," he said presently, "I will take you to my house; then we may discuss plans for the future. The woman may ride behind me on my zorat."

"I prefer to walk," said Duare. "I am accustomed to it now."

Skor's eyes narrowed a bit. He started to speak, and then he checked himself. Finally he shrugged. "As you will," he said, and turned the head of his mount back in the direction from which he had come.

The creature he rode, which he called a zorat, was unlike any beast that I had ever seen before. It was about the size of a small horse. Its long, slender legs suggested great speed. Its feet were round and nail-less and heavily calloused on the bottoms. Its almost vertical pasterns suggested that it might be a hard gaited beast, but this was not so. Later I learned that almost horizontal femurs and humeri absorbed the jolts and rendered the zorat an easy riding saddle animal.

Above its withers and just forward of its kidneys were soft pads or miniature humps which formed a perfect saddle with natural pommel and cantle. Its head was short and broad, with two large, saucer-like eyes and pendulous ears. Its teeth were those of a grass-eater. Its only means of defence seemed to lie in its fleetness, although, as I afterward had occasion to discover, it could use its jaws and teeth most effectively when its short temper was aroused.

We walked beside Skor on the journey toward his house, the grotesque kazars following docilely behind at the command of their master. The way led toward the great bend of the river, that we had sought to avoid by taking a short cut, and a forest that lined its banks. The proximity of the kazars made me nervous, for occasionally one of them would trot close at our heels; and I was fearful that Duare might be injured by one of the fierce beasts before I could prevent it. I asked Skor what purpose the creatures served.

"I use them for hunting," he replied, "but principally for protection.

I have enemies; and then, too, there are many savage beasts roaming at large in Morov. The kazars are quite fearless and very savage fighters. Their greatest weakness is their predilection for cannibalism; they will abandon a fight to devour one of their own number that has fallen."

Shortly after we entered the forest we came upon a large, gloomy, fortress like building of stone. It was built upon a low rise of ground at the water's edge, the river lapping the masonry upon that side. A stone wall connecting with the river wall of the building enclosed several acres of clear land in front of the structure. A heavy gate closed the only aperture that was visible in this wall.

As we approached, Skor shouted, "Open! It is the jong," and the gates swung slowly outward.

As we entered, several armed men, who had been sitting beneath one of the several trees that had been left standing when the ground was cleared, arose and stood with bowed heads. They were a hard and also a sad looking lot. The feature that struck me most forcibly was the strange hue of their skin, a repulsive, unhealthy pallor, a seeming bloodlessness. I caught the eyes of one that chanced to raise his head as we passed, and I shivered. They were glazed, clammy eyes, without light, without fire. I would have thought the fellow stone blind but for the fact that the instant that my eyes caught his they dropped swiftly. Another had an ugly, open wound across his cheek from temple to chin; it gaped wide, but it did not bleed.

Skor snapped a brief order; and two of the men herded the pack of cackling kazars into a strong enclosure built beside the gateway, as we proceeded on toward the house. Perhaps I should call it castle.

The enclosure across which we passed was barren except for the few trees that had been left standing. It was littered with refuse of all descriptions and was unspeakably disorderly and untidy. Old sandals, rags, broken pottery, and the garbage from the castle kitchens were strewn promiscuously about. The only spot from which any effort had been made to remove the litter was a few hundred square feet of stone flagging before the main entrance to the building.

Here Skor dismounted as three more men similar to those at the gate came lifelessly from the interior of the building. One of these took Skor's mount and led it away, the others stood one on either side of the entrance as we passed in.

The doorway was small, the door that closed it thick and heavy. It seemed to be the only opening on the first floor on this side of the castle. Along the second and third floor levels I had seen small windows heavily barred. At one corner of the building I had noticed a tower rising two more stories above the main part of the castle. This, too, had small windows, some of which were barred.

The interior of the building was dark and gloomy. Coupled with the appearance of the inmates I had already seen it engendered within me a feeling of depression that I could not throw off.

"You must be hungry," suggested Skor. "Come out into the inner court–it is pleasanter there–and I will have food served."

We followed him down a short corridor and through a doorway into a courtyard around which the castle was built. The enclosure reminded me of a prison yard. It was flagged with stone. No living thing grew there. The grey stone walls, cut with their small windows, rose upon four sides. There had been no effort toward architectural ornamentation in the design of the structure, nor any to beautify the courtyard in any way. Here, too, was litter and trash that it had evidently been easier to throw into the inner court than carry to the outer.

I was oppressed by forebodings of ill. I wished that we had never entered the place, but I tried to brush my fears aside. I argued that Skor had given no indications of being other than a kindly and solicitous host. He had seemed anxious to befriend us. That he was a jong I had commenced to doubt, for there was no suggestion of royalty in his mode of living.

In the centre of the court a plank table was flanked by grimy, well worn benches. On the table were the remains of a meal. Skor graciously waved us toward the benches; then he clapped his hands together three times before he seated himself at the head of the table.

"I seldom have guests here," he said. "It is quite a pleasant treat for me. I hope that you will enjoy your stay. I am sure that I shall," and as he spoke he looked at Duare in that way that I did not like.

"I am sure that we might enjoy it could we remain," replied Duare quickly, "but that is not possible. I must return to the house of my father."

"Where is that?" asked Skor.

"In Vepaja," explained Duare.

"I never heard of that country," said Skor. "Where is it?"

"You never heard of Vepaja!" exclaimed Duare incredulously. "Why, all the present country of Thora was called Vepaja until the Thorists rose and took it and drove the remnants of the ruling class to the island that is now all that remains of ancient Vepaja."

"Oh, yes, I had heard of that," admitted Skor; "but it was a long time ago and in distant Trabol."

"Is this not Trabol?" asked Duare.

"No," replied Skor; "this is Strabol."

"But Strabol is the hot country," argued Duare. "No one can live in Strabol."

"You are in Strabol now. It is hot here during a portion of the year, but not so hot as to be unendurable."

I was interested. If what Skor said were true, we had crossed the equator and were now in the northern hemisphere of Venus. The Vepajans had told me that Strabol was uninhabitable–a steaming jungle reeking with heat and moisture and inhabited only by fierce and terrible beasts and reptiles. The entire northern hemisphere was a terra incognita to the men of the southern hemisphere, and for that reason I had been anxious to explore it.

With the responsibility of Duare on my shoulders I could not do much exploring, but I might learn something from Skor; so I asked him of the country farther north.

"It is no good," he snapped. "It is the land of fools. They frown upon true science and progress. They drove me out; they would have killed me. I came here and established the kingdom of Morov. That was many years ago–perhaps a hundred years. I have never returned since to the country of my birth; but sometimes their people come here," and he laughed unpleasantly.

Just then a woman came from the building, evidently in response to Skor's summons. She was middle aged. Her skin was the same repulsive hue as that of the men I had seen, and it was very dirty. Her mouth hung open and her tongue protruded; it was dry and swollen. Her eyes were glazed and staring. She moved with a slow, awkward shuffle. And now, behind her, came two men. They were much as she; there was something indescribably revolting about all three.

"Take these away!" snapped Skor with a wave of the hand toward the soiled dishes. "And bring food."

The three gathered up the dishes and shuffled away. None of them spoke. The look of horror in Duare's eyes could not have gone unnoticed by Skor.

"You do not like my retainers?" demanded Skor testily.

"But I said nothing," objected Duare.

"I saw it in your face." Suddenly Skor broke into laughter. There was no mirth in it, nor was there laughter in his eyes but another expression, a terrible glint that passed as quickly as it had come. "They are excellent servants," he said in normal tones; "they do not talk too much, and they do whatever I tell them to do."

Presently the three returned carrying vessels of food. There was meat, partially raw, partially burned, and wholly unpalatable; there were fruits and vegetables, none of which appeared to have been washed; there was wine. It was the only thing there fit for human consumption.

The meal was not a success. Duare could not eat. I sipped my wine and watched Skor eat ravenously.

Darkness was falling as Skor arose from the table. "I will show you to your rooms," he said. "You must be tired." His tone and manner were those of the perfect host. "Tomorrow you shall set out again upon your journey."

Relieved by this promise we followed him into the house. It was a dark and gloomy abode, chill and cheerless. We followed him up a stairway to the second floor and into a long, dark corridor. Presently he stopped before a door and threw it open.

"May you sleep well," he said to Duare, bowing and motioning her to enter.

Silently Duare crossed the threshold and Skor closed the door behind her; then he conducted me to the end of the corridor, up two flights of stairs and ushered me into a circular room that I guessed was in the tower I had seen when we entered the castle.

"I hope you awaken refreshed," he said politely and withdrew, closing the door behind him.

I heard his footsteps descending the stairs until they were lost in the distance. I thought of Duare down there alone in this gloomy and mysterious pile. I had no reason to believe that she was not safe, but nevertheless I was apprehensive. Anyway, I had no intention of leaving her alone.

I waited until he had had plenty of time to go to his own quarters wherever they might be; then I stepped to the door, determined to go to Duare. I laid my hand upon the latch and sought to open it. It was locked from the outside. Quickly I went to the several windows. Each was heavily barred. Faintly from the distant recesses of that forbidding pile I thought I heard a mocking laugh.

## CHAPTER 10

# The Girl in the Tower

The tower room in which i found myself imprisoned was lighted only by the mysterious night glow that relieves the nocturnal darkness ofVenus, which would otherwise have been impenetrable. Dimly I saw the furnishings of the room–they were meagre. The place had more the aspect of a prison cell than a guest chamber.

I crossed to a chest of drawers and investigated it. It was filled with odds and ends of worn and useless apparel bits of string, a few lengths of rope which, I had an ugly suspicion, might once have served as bonds. I paced the floor worrying about Duare. I was helpless. I could do nothing. It would be vain to pound upon the door or call for release. The will that had incarcerated me was supreme here. Only by the voluntary act of that will could I be released.

Seating myself on a rude bench before a small table I tried to plan; I sought to discover some loophole for escape. Apparently there was none. I arose and once again examined the window bars and the sturdy door; they were impregnable.

Finally I crossed to a rickety couch that stood against the wall and lay down upon the worn and odorous hide that covered it. Absolute silence reigned–the silence of the tomb. For a long time it was unbroken; then I heard a sound above me. I listened, trying to interpret it. It was like the slow padding of naked feet–back and forth, to and fro above my head.

I had thought that I was on the top floor of the tower, but now I realized that there must be another room above the one in which I had been placed–if the sound I heard was that of human feet.

Listening to that monotonous padding had a soporific effect upon my jaded nerves. I caught myself dozing a couple of times. I did not wish to go to sleep; something seemed to warn me that I must remain awake, but at last I must have succumbed.

How long I slept I do not know. I awoke with a start, conscious that something touched me. A dim figure was leaning over me. I started to rise. Instantly strong fingers, clutched my throat–cold, clammy fingers–the fingers of Death they seemed.

Struggling, I sought the throat of my antagonist. I closed upon it–it, too, was cold and clammy. I am a strong man, but the Thing upon my chest was stronger. I struck at it with closed fists. From the doorway came a low, hideous laugh. I felt my scalp stiffen to the horror of it all.

I sensed that death was close, and a multitude of thoughts raced through my mind. But uppermost among them were thoughts of Duare, and harrowing regret that I must leave her here in the clutches of the fiend I was now certain was the instigator of this attack upon me. I guessed that its purpose was to dispose of me and thus remove the only possible obstacle that might stand between himself and Duare.

I was still struggling when something struck me on the head; then came oblivion.

It was daylight when I regained consciousness. I still lay upon the couch, sprawled upon my back. Staring up at the ceiling, trying to collect my thoughts and memories, I perceived a crack just above me such as might have been made by a trap door partially raised; and through the crack two eyes were peering down at me.

Some new horror? I did not move. I lay there fascinated, watching the trap door slowly open. Presently a face was revealed. It was the face of a girl, a very beautiful girl; but it was strained and drawn and the eyes were terrified, frightened eyes.

In a whisper, the girl spoke. "You are alive?" she asked.

I raised myself on an elbow. "Who are you?" I demanded. "Is this some new trick to torture me?"

"No. I am a prisoner, too. He has gone away. Perhaps we can escape."

"How?" I asked. I was still sceptical, believing her a confederate of Skor.

"Can you get up here? There are no bars on my windows; that is because they are so high that no one could jump from them without being killed or badly injured. If we only had a rope!"

I considered the matter for a moment before I replied. What if it was a trick? Could I be any worse off in one room in this accursed castle than in another?

"There is rope down here," I said. "I will get it and come up. Perhaps there is not enough to be of any use to us, but I will bring what there is."

"How will you get up?" she asked.

"That will not be difficult. Wait until I get the rope."

I went to the chest of drawers and took out all the rope and string that I had discovered there the previous night; then I shoved the chest across the floor until it was directly beneath the trap door.

From the top of the chest I could easily reach the edge of the floor above. Handing the rope up to the girl, I quickly drew myself up into the room with her; then she closed the trap and we stood facing each other.

Despite her dishevelled and frightened appearance, I found her even more beautiful than I had at first thought her; and as her fine eyes met mine in mutual appraisal my fears of treachery vanished. I was sure no duplicity lurked behind that lovely countenance.

"You need not doubt me," she said as though she had read my thoughts, "though I cannot wonder that you doubt every one in this terrible place."

"Then how can you trust me?" I asked. "You know nothing of me."

"I know enough," she replied. "From that window I saw you when you and your companion came yesterday with Skor, and I knew that he had two more victims. I heard them bring you to the room below last night. I did not know which one of you it was. I wanted to warn you then, but I was afraid of Skor. I walked the floor for a long time trying to decide what to do."

"Then it was you I heard walking?"

"Yes. Then I heard them come again; I heard sounds of a scuffle and Skor's awful laugh. Oh, how I hate and fear that laugh! After that it was quiet. I thought they had killed you, if it was you, or taken the girl away, if it was she they had imprisoned in the room below. Oh, the poor thing! And she is so beautiful. I hope she got away safely, but I am afraid there can be little hope of that."

"Got away? What do you mean?" I demanded.

"She escaped very early this morning. I do not know how she got out of her room, but from the window I saw her cross the outer courtyard. She climbed the wall on the river side, and she must have dropped into the river. I did not see her again."

"Duare has escaped! You are sure it was she?"

"It was the beautiful girl who came here with you yesterday. About an hour after she got away Skor must have discovered that she was gone. He came out of the castle in a terrible rage. He took with him all of the miserable creatures that watch the gate, and all his fierce kazars, and set out in pursuit. Possibly never again may we have such an opportunity to escape."

"Let's get busy, then!" I exclaimed. "Have you a plan?"

"Yes," she replied. "With the rope we can lower ourselves to the castle roof and from there to the courtyard. There is no one watching the gate; the kazars are gone. If we are discovered we shall have to trust to our legs, but there are only three or four of Skor's retainers left in the castle and they are not very alert when he is not here."

"I have my weapons," I reminded her. "Skor did not take them from me, and if any of his people try to stop us I will kill them."

She shook her head. "You cannot kill them," she whispered, shuddering.

"What do you mean?" I demanded. "Why can I not kill them?"

"Because they are already dead."

I looked at her in astonishment as the meaning of her words slowly filtered to my shocked brain to explain the pitiful creatures that had filled me with such disgust on the previous day.

"But," I exclaimed, "how can they be dead? I saw them move about and obey the commands of Skor."

"I do not know," she replied; "it is Skor's terrible secret. Presently you will be as they, if we do not escape; and the girl who came with you, and I–after a while. He will keep us a little longer in the flesh for the purpose of his experiments. Every day he takes a little blood from me. He is seeking the secret of life. He says that he can reproduce body cells, and with these he has instilled synthetic life into the poor creatures that he has resurrected from the grave. But it is only a parody on life; no blood flows in those dead veins, and the dead minds are animated only by the thoughts that Skor transmits to them by some occult, telepathic means.

"But what he most desires is the power to reproduce germ cells and thus propagate a new race of beings fashioned according to his own specifications. That is why he takes blood from me; that is why he wanted the girl you call Duare. When our blood has become so depleted that death is near, he will kill us and we will be like these others. But he would not keep us here; he would take us to the city where he rules as jong. Here he keeps only a few poor, degraded specimens; but he says that in Kormor he has many fine ones."

"So he is a jong? I doubted it."

"He made himself a jong and created his own subjects," she said.

"And he kept you only to draw blood from you?"

"Yes. He is not like other men; he is not human."

"How long have you been here?"

"A long time; but I am still alive because Skor has been away most of the time in Kormor."

"Well, we must get away, too, before he returns. I want to search for Duare.

I went to one of the windows, none of which was barred, and looked down on the castle roof below, a distance of about twenty feet. Then I got the rope and examined it carefully. There were several pieces, in all about forty feet–more than enough; also it was stout rope. I tied the pieces together and then returned to the window. The girl was at my elbow.

"Can anyone see us from here?" I asked.

"The creatures are not very alert," she replied. "Those that Skor left here are the servants. They remain in a room on the first floor on the other side of the castle. When he is away they just sit. After a while two of them will bring food for us; and we should get away before they come, for sometimes they forget to go back to their quarters; then they sit around outside my door for hours. You will notice that there is a grille in the door; they would see us if we attempted to escape while they were there."

We'll start now," I said. Then I made a loop in one end of the rope and passed it around the girl's body so that she could sit in it while I lowered her to the roof.

Without an instant's hesitation she stepped to the sill of the window and lowered herself over the edge until she was seated securely in the loop. Bracing my feet against the wall, I let her down rapidly until I felt the rope go slack in my hands.

I then dragged her cot close beneath the window, passed the free end of the rope beneath it and out the window, letting it fall toward the roof below. This gave me two strands of rope reaching to the roof with the middle part of the rope passing around the cot which was too large to be dragged through the window by my weight as I descended.

Grasping both strands firmly in my two hands, I slipped through the window and slid quickly to the side of the waiting girl; then I pulled in rapidly on one end of the rope, dragging the free end around the cot until it fell to the roof. Thus I retrieved the rope for use in descending the remainder of the way to the ground.

We crossed the roof quickly to the edge overlooking the outer courtyard into which we expected to descend. There was no one in sight, and I was just about to lower the girl over the edge when a loud shout from behind us startled us both.

Turning, we saw three of Skor's creatures looking at us from an upper window of the castle on the opposite side of the inner court. Almost as we turned, the three left the window and we could hear them shouting through the castle.

"What shall we do?" cried the girl. "We are lost!" They will come to the roof by the tower door, and they will have us trapped. They were not the servants; they were three of his armed men. I thought they had all accompanied him, but I was wrong."

I said nothing, but I seized her hand and started toward the far end of the castle roof. A sudden hope had flared within me, born of an idea suggested by what the girl had told me of Duare's escape.

We ran as fast as we could, and when we reached the edge we looked down upon the river lapping the castle wall two stories below. I passed the rope about the girl's waist. She asked no question; she made no comment. Quickly she climbed over the low parapet, and I commenced lowering her toward the river below.

Hideous mouthings arose behind me. I turned and saw three dead men running toward me across the roof. Then I lowered away so rapidly that the rope burned my fingers, but there was no time to lose. I feared that they would be upon me before I could lower the girl to the dubious safety of the swirling waters.

Nearer and nearer sounded the hurrying footsteps and the incoherent yammerings of the corpses. I heard a splash, and the rope went slack in my fingers. I glanced behind. The nearest of the creatures was already extending his hands to seize me. It was one of those that I noticed at the gate the day before; I recognized it by the bloodless gash across its cheek. Its dead eyes were expressionless–glazed and staring–but its mouth was contorted in a ghastly snarl.

Immediate recapture faced me; there was but a single alternative. I sprang to the top of the parapet and leaped. I have always been a good diver, but I doubt that I ever made a prettier swan dive in my life than I did that day from the parapet of the gloomy castle of Skor, the jong of Morov.

As I rose to the surface of the river, shaking the water from my eyes, I looked about for the girl; she was nowhere to be seen. I knew that she could not have reached the river bank in the short time that had elapsed since I had lowered her into the water, for the masonry of the castle and the walls which extended it both above and below the building offered not even a hand-hold for hundreds of feet in both directions, and the opposite shore was too far away.

I cast about me in all directions as the current carried me down stream, and I saw her head rise above the surface of the water a short distance below me. Swiftly I struck out for her. She went down again just before I reached her, but I dived for her and brought her to the surface. She was still conscious but almost out.

Glancing back at the castle, I saw that my would-be captors had disappeared from the roof; and I guessed that they would shortly appear on the bank of the river ready to seize us when we emerged. But I had no intention of emerging on their side.

Dragging the girl with me, I struck out for the opposite shore. The river here was considerably deeper and broader than at the point we had first encountered it farther up stream. Now it was quite a river. What strange creatures inhabited its depths I had no means of knowing. I could only hope that none would discover us.

The girl lay very quiet; she did not struggle at all. I began to fear that she was dead and I exerted myself still more to reach the bank quickly. The current bore us down stream, and I was glad of that, for it was taking us farther away from the castle and retainers of Skor.

At last I reached the bank and dragged the girl out onto a little patch of pale violet grass and set to work to resuscitate her, but even as I commenced she opened her eyes and looked up at me. A shadow of a smile touched her lips.

"I shall be all right in a minute," she said weakly. "I was so frightened."

"Don't you know how to swim?" I asked.

She shook her head. "No."

"And you let me lower you into the river without telling me!" I was amazed by the sheer bravery of her act.

"There was nothing else to do," she said simply. "Had I told you, you would not have lowered me, and we both should have been recaptured. I do not see even now how you got down before they seized you."

"I dived," I explained.

"You jumped from the top of that castle! It is incredible!"

"You do not come from a land where there is much water," I commented with a laugh.

"What makes you think so?"

"If you did you would have seen enough diving to know that mine was nothing extraordinary."

"My country is in a mountainous district," she admitted, "where the streams are torrents and there is little swimming."

"And where is that?" I asked.

"Oh, it is very far," she replied. "I do not even know where."

"How did you happen to get into Skor's country?"

"During a war in my country I was captured with others by the enemy. They carried us down out of the mountains into a great plain. One night two of us escaped. My companion was a soldier who had been long in the service of my father. He was very loyal. He tried to return me to my country, but we became lost. I do not know how long we wandered, but at last we came to a great river.

"Here were people who went in boats upon the river. They lived in the boats always, fighting. They sought to capture us, and my companion was killed defending me; then they took me. But I was not with them long. The first night several men were quarrelling over me; each of them claimed me as his own. And while they quarrelled, I slipped into a small boat tied to the larger one and floated away down the great river.

"I drifted for many days and nearly starved to death, although I saw fruits and nuts growing along the banks of the river. But the boat was without oars and was so heavy that I could not bring it in to shore.

"Finally it ran aground by itself on a sand bar where the river ran slowly about a great bend, and it chanced that Skor was hunting near and saw me. That is all. I have been here a long time."

## Chapter 11

# The Pygmies

As the girl finished her story I saw the three dead men standing upon the opposite bank. For a moment they hesitated, then they plunged into the river.

I seized the girl by the hand and raised her to her feet. Our only defence lay in flight. Although I had had to abandon my spear, I had saved my bow and arrows, the latter being tied securely in my quiver while the former I had looped across one shoulder before leaving the tower; but of what use were arrows against dead men?

Casting another glance toward our pursuers I saw them floundering in the deep water of the channel, and it became immediately evident that none of them could swim. They were bobbing around helplessly as the current swept them down stream. Sometimes they floated on their backs, sometimes on their faces.

"We haven't much to fear from them," I said; "they will all drown."

"They cannot drown," replied the girl with a shudder.

"I hadn't thought of that," I admitted. "But at least there is little likelihood that they will reach this shore; certainly not before they have been carried a long distance down stream. We shall have plenty of time to escape them."

"Then let's be going. I hate this place. I want to get away from it."

"I cannot go away until I have found Duare," I told her. "I must search for her."

"Yes, that is right; we must try to find her. But where shall we look?"

"She would try to reach the big river and follow it to the sea," I explained, "and I think that she would reason much as we would, that it would be safer to follow this stream down to the larger one inasmuch as then she would have the concealing protection of the forest."

"We shall have to keep careful watch for the dead men," cautioned the girl. "If they wash ashore on this side we shall be sure to meet them."

"Yes; and I want to make sure where they do come ashore, because I intend crossing over and hunting for Duare on the other side."

For some time we moved cautiously down stream in silence, both constantly alert for any sound that might portend danger. My mind was filled with thoughts of Duare and apprehension for her safety, yet occasionally it reverted to the girl at my side; and I could not but recall her courage during our escape and her generous willingness to delay her own flight that we might search for Duare. It was apparent that her character formed a trinity of loveliness with her form and her face. And I did not even know her name!

That fact struck me as being as remarkable as that I had only known her for an hour. So intimate are the bonds of mutual adversity and danger that it seemed I had known her always, that that hour was indeed an eternity.

"Do you realize," I asked, turning toward her, "that neither of us knows the other's name?" And then I told her mine.

"Carson Napier!" she repeated. "That is a strange name."

"And what is yours?"

"Nalte voo man kum Baltoo," she replied, which means Nalte, the daughter of Baltoo. "The people call me Voo Jan, but my friends call me Nalte."

"And what am I to call you?" I asked.

She looked at me in surprise. "Why, Nalte, of course."

"I am honoured by being included among your friends."

"But are you not my best, my only friend now in all Amtor?"

I had to admit that her reasoning was sound, since as far as all the rest of Amtor was concerned we were the only two people on that cloud-girt planet, and we were certainly not enemies.

We were moving cautiously along without sight of the river when Nalte suddenly touched my arm and pointed toward the opposite bank, at the same time dragging me down behind a shrub.

Just opposite us a corpse had washed ashore; and a short distance below, two others. They were our pursuers. As we watched, they slowly crawled to their feet then the one we had first seen called to the others, who presently joined him. The three corpses talked together, pointing and gesticulating. It was horrible. I felt my skin creep.

What would they do? should they continue the search or would they return to the castle? If the former, they would have to cross the river; and they must already have learned that there was little likelihood of their being able to do that. But that was attributing to dead brains the power to reason! It seemed incredible. I asked Nalte what she thought about.

"It is a mystery to me," she replied. "They converse, and they appear to reason. At first I thought they were motivated through the hypnotic influence of Skor's mind solely–that they thought his thoughts, as it were; but they take independent action when Skor is away, as you have seen them do today, which refutes that theory. Skor says that they do reason. He has stimulated their nervous systems into the semblance of life, though no blood flows in their veins; but the past experiences of their lives before they died are less potent in influencing their judgments than the new system of conduct and ethics that Skor has instilled into their dead brains. He admits that the specimens he has at the castle are very dull; but that, he insists, is because they were dull people in life."

The dead men conversed for some time and then started slowly up river in the direction of the castle, and it was with a sigh of relief that we saw them disappear.

"Now we must try to find a good place to cross," I said. "I wish to search the other side for some sign of Duare. She must have left footprints in the soft earth."

"There is a ford somewhere down river," said Nalte. "when Skor captured me we crossed it on our way to the castle. I do not know just where it is, but it cannot be far."

We had descended the river some two miles from the point at which we had seen the dead man emerge upon the opposite bank, without seeing any sign of a crossing, when I heard faintly a familiar cackling that seemed to come from across the river and farther down.

"Do you hear that?" I asked Nalte. She listened intently for a moment as the cackling grew louder. "Yes," she replied—the kazars. We had better hide."

Acting upon Nalte's suggestion we concealed ourselves behind a clump of underbrush and waited. The cackling grew in volume, and we knew that the kazars were approaching.

"Do you suppose that it is Skor's pack?" I asked.

"It must be," she replied. "There is no other pack in this vicinity, according to Skor."

"Nor any wild kazars?"

"No. He says that there are no wild ones on this side of the big river. They range on the opposite side. These must be Skor's!"

We waited in silence as the sounds approached, and presently we saw the new leader of the pack trot into view on the opposite bank. Behind him strung several more of the grotesque beasts, and then came Skor, mounted on his zorat, with the dead men that formed his retinue surrounding him.

"Duare is not there!" whispered Nalte. "Skor did not recapture her."

We watched Skor and his party until they had passed out of sight among the trees of the forest on the other side of the river, and it was with a sigh of relief that I saw what I hoped would be the last of the jong of Morov.

While I was relieved to know that Duare had not been recaptured, I was still but little less apprehensive concerning her fate. Many dangers might beset her, alone and unprotected in this savage land; and I had only the vaguest conception of where to search for her.

After the passing of Skor we had continued on down the river, and presently Nalte pointed ahead to a line of ripples that stretched from bank to bank where the river widened.

"There is the ford," she said, "but there is no use crossing it to look for Duare's trail. If she had escaped on that side of the river the kazars would have found her before now. The fact that they didn't find her is fairly good proof that she was never over there."

I was not so sure of that. I did not know that Duare could swim nor that she could not, but the chances were highly in favour of the latter possibility, since Duare had been born and reared in the tree city of Kooaad.

"Perhaps they found her and killed her," I suggested, horrified at the very thought of such a tragedy.

"No," dissented Nalte. "Skor would have prevented that; he wanted her."

"But something else might have killed her; they might have found her dead body."

"Skor would have brought it back with him and invested it with the synthetic life that animates his retinue of dead," argued Nalte.

Still I was not convinced. "How do the kazars trail?" I asked. "Do they follow the spoor of their quarry by scent?"

Nalte shook her head. "Their sense of smell is extremely poor, but their vision is acute. In trailing, they depend wholly upon their eyes."

"Then it is possible that they might not have crossed Duare's trail at all and so missed her."

"Possible, but not probable," replied Nalte. "What is more probable is that she was killed and devoured by some beast before Skor was able to recapture her."

The explanation had already occurred to me, but I did not wish to even think about it. "Nevertheless," I said, "we might as well cross over to the other bank. If we are going to follow the big river down stream we shall have to cross this affluent sooner or later, and we may not find another ford as it grows broader and deeper toward its mouth."

The ford was broad and well marked by ripples, so we had no difficulty in following it toward the opposite bank. However, we were compelled to keep our eyes on the water most of the time as the ford took two curves that formed a flattened S, and it would have been quite easy to have stepped off into deep water and been swept down stream had we not been careful.

The result of our constant watchfulness approached disaster as we neared the left bank of the stream. The merest chance caused me to look up. I was slightly in advance of Nalte as we walked hand in hand for greater safety. I stopped so suddenly at what I saw that the girl bumped into me. Then she looked up, and a little, involuntary cry of alarm burst from her lips.

"What are they?" she asked.

"I don't know," I replied. "Don't you?"

"No; I never saw such creatures before."

At the edge of the water, awaiting us, were half a dozen manlike creatures, while others like them were coming from the forest, dropping from the trees to shuffle awkwardly toward the ford. They were about three feet tall and entirely covered with long hair. At first I thought that they were monkeys, although they bore a startling resemblance to human beings, but when they saw that we had discovered them one of them spoke, and the simian theory was exploded.

"I am Ul," said the speaker. "Go away from the land of Ul. I am Ul; I kill!"

"We will not harm you," I replied. "We only want to pass through your country."

"Go away!" growled Ul, baring sharp fighting fangs.

By now, fifty of the fierce little men were gathered at the water's edge, growling, menacing. They were without clothing or ornaments and carried no weapons, but their sharp fangs and the bulging muscles of their shoulders and arms bespoke their ability to carry out Ul's threats.

"What are we going to do?" demanded Nalte. "They will tear us to pieces the moment we step out of the water."

"Perhaps I can persuade them to let us pass," I said, but after five minutes of fruitless effort I had to admit defeat. Ul's only reply to my arguments was, "Go away! I kill! I kill!"

I hated to turn back, for I knew that we must cross the river eventually and we might not find such another crossing, but at last, reluctantly, I retraced my steps to the right bank hand in hand with Nalte.

All the remainder of the day I searched for traces of Duare as we followed the course of the river downward, but my efforts were without success. I was disheartened. I felt that I should never see her again. Nalte tried to cheer me up, but inasmuch as she believed that Duare was dead she was not very successful.

Late in the afternoon I succeeded in killing a small animal. As we had eaten nothing all that day we were both famished, so we soon had a fire going and were grilling cuts of the tender meat.

After we had eaten I built a rude platform among the branches of a large tree and gathered a number of huge leaves to serve as mattress and covering, and as darkness fell Nalte and I settled ourselves, not uncomfortably, in our lofty sanctuary.

For a while we were silent, wrapped in our own thoughts. I do not know about Nalte's, but mine were gloomy enough. I cursed the day that I had conceived the idea to build the huge torpedo that had carried me from Earth to Venus, and in the next thought I blessed it because it had made it possible for me to know and to love Duare.

It was Nalte who broke the silence. As though she had read my thoughts, she said, "You loved Duare very much?"

"Yes," I replied.

Nalte sighed. "It must be sad to lose one's mate."

"She was not my mate."

"Not your mate!" Nalte's tone expressed her surprise. "But you loved one another?"

"Duare did not love me," I replied. "At least she said she didn't. You see, she was the daughter of a jong and she couldn't love any one until after she was twenty."

Nalte laughed. "Love does not come or go in accordance with any laws or customs," she said.

"But even if Duare had loved me, which she didn't, she couldn't have said so; she couldn't even talk of love because she was the daughter of a jong and too young. I don't understand it, of course, but that is because I am from another world and know nothing of your customs."

"I am nineteen," said Nalte, "and the daughter of a jong, but if I loved a man I should say so."

"Perhaps the customs of your country and those of Duare's are not the same," I suggested.

"They must be very different," agreed Nalte, "for in my country a man does not speak to a girl of love until she has told him that she loves him; and the daughter of the jong chooses her own mate whenever she pleases."

"That custom may have its advantages," I admitted, "but if I loved a girl I should want the right to tell her so."

"Oh, the men find ways of letting a girl know without putting it into words. I could tell if a man loved me, but if I loved him very much I wouldn't wait for that."

"And what if he didn't love you?" I asked.

Nalte tossed her head. "I'd make him."

I could readily understand that Nalte might be a very difficult young person not to love. She was slender and dark, with an olive skin and a mass of black hair in lovely disorder. Her eyes sparkled with health and intelligence. Her features were regular and almost boyish, and over all was the suggestion of a veil of dignity that bespoke her blood. I could not doubt but that she was the daughter of a jong.

It seemed to be my fate to encounter daughters of jongs. I said as much to Nalte.

"How many have you met?" she asked.

"Two," I replied," you and Duare."

"That is not very many when you consider how many jongs there must be in Amtor and how many daughters they must have. My father has seven."

"Are they all as lovely as you?" I asked.

"Do you think me lovely?"

"You know you are."

"But I like to hear people say so. I like to hear you say it," she added softly.

The roars of hunting beasts came up to us from the dim forest aisles, the screams of stricken prey; then the silence of the night broken only by the murmuring of the river rolling down to some unknown sea.

I was considering a tactful reply to Nalte's ingenuous observation when I dozed and fell asleep.

I felt someone shaking me by the shoulder. I opened my eyes to look up into Nalte's.

"Are you going to sleep all day?" she demanded.

It was broad daylight. I sat up and looked around. "We have survived another night," I said.

I gathered some fruit, and we cooked some more of the meat left from my kill of the previous day. We had a splendid breakfast, and then we set off again down stream in our quest for–what?

"If we do not find Duare today," I said, "I shall have to admit that she is irrevocably lost to me."

"And then what?" asked Nalte.

"You would like to return to your own country?"

"Of course."

"Then we shall start up the big river toward your home."

"We shall never reach it," said Nalte, "but–"

"But what?" I demanded.

"I was thinking that we might be very happy while we were trying to reach Andoo," she said.

"Andoo?" I queried.

"That is my country," she explained. "The mountains of Andoo are very beautiful."

There was a note of wistfulness in her voice; her eyes were contemplating a scene that mine could not see. Suddenly I realized how brave the girl had been, how cheerful she had remained through the hardships and menacing dangers of our flight, all despite the probably hopelessness of her situation. I touched her hand gently.

"We shall do our best to return you to the beautiful mountains of Andoo," I assured her.

Nalte shook her head. "I shall never see them again, Carson. A great company of warriors might not survive the dangers that lie between here and Andoo–a thousand kobs of fierce and hostile country."

"A thousand kobs is a long way," I agreed. "It does seem hopeless, but we'll not give up."

The Amtorians divide the circumference of a circle into a thousand parts to arrive at their hita, or degree; and the kob is one tenth of a degree of longitude at the equator (or what the Amtorians call The Small Circle), roughly about two and a half earth miles; therefore a thousand kobs would be about two thousand five hundred miles.

A little mental arithmetic convinced me that Nalte could not have drifted down the big river two thousand five hundred miles without food, and I asked her if she was sure that Andoo was that far away.

"No," she admitted, "but it seems that far. We wandered a long time before we reached the river, and then I drifted for so long that I lost track of time."

Nevertheless, if we found Duare, I was going to be faced by a problem. One girl must go down the valley in search of her own country, the other up the valley! And only one of them had even a hazy idea of where her country lay!

## Chapter 12

# The Last Second

During the afternoon of the second day of our search for Duare Nalte and I came to the big river that Duare and I had seen from the summit of the escarpment, the same river down which Nalte had drifted into the clutches of Skor.

And it was a big river, comparable to the Mississippi. It ran between low cliffs of gleaming white limestone, flowing silently out of the mystery above, flowing silently toward the mystery below. Upon its broad expanse, from where it swept majestically into sight around a low promontory to where it disappeared again beyond a curve down stream, there was no sign of life, nor on either bank–only the girl, Nalte, and I. I felt the awe of its grandeur and my own insignificance.

I had no words to express my thoughts; and I was glad that Nalte stood in silence that was almost reverential as we viewed the majesty and the desolation of the scene.

Presently the girl sighed. It awoke me to the need of the moment. I could not stand mooning there in the face of the immediate necessity that confronted us.

"Well," I said, "this is not crossing the river." I referred to the affluent that we had followed down from the castle of Skor.

"I am glad that we do not have to cross the big river," remarked Nalte.

"We may have enough trouble crossing this other," I suggested.

It flowed at our left, making a sudden turn before it emptied into the larger stream. below us was a great eddy that had strewn the nearer bank with flotsam—leaves, twigs, branches of all sizes, and even the boles of great trees. These things appeared to have been deposited during a period of high water.

"How are we going to cross?" asked Nalte. "There is no ford, and it seems too wide and swift to swim even if I were a good swimmer."

She looked up at me quickly then as a new thought seemed to strike her. "I am a burden to you," she said. "If you were alone you would doubtless be able to cross easily. Pay no attention to me; I shall remain on this side and start up the river on my journey toward Andoo."

I looked down at her and smiled. "You really do not believe or hope that I will do anything of the sort."

"It would be the sensible thing to do," she said.

"The sensible thing to do is to build a raft with some of that stuff down there and float across the river." I pointed to the debris piled up on the bank.

"Why, we could do that, couldn't we?" she cried.

She was all eagerness and excitement now, and a moment later she pitched in and helped me drag out such pieces as I thought we could use in the construction of a raft.

It was hard work, but at last we had enough material to float us in safety. The next job was to fasten the elements of our prospective raft together so securely that the river could not tear it to pieces before we had gained the opposite bank.

We gathered lianas for that purpose, and though we worked as rapidly as we could it was almost dark before we had completed our rude ferry.

As I contemplated the fruit of our labour, I saw Nalte surveying the swirling waters of the eddy with a dubious eye.

"Are we going to cross now," she asked, "or wait until morning?"

"It is almost dark now," I replied. "I think we had better wait until tomorrow."

She brightened visibly and drew a deep sigh of relief.

"Then we had better think about eating now," she said. I had found the girls of Venus not unlike their earthly sisters in this respect.

The meal that night was a matter of fruit and tubers, but it was sufficient. Once more I constructed a platform among the branches of a tree and prayed that no prowling arboreal carnivore would discover us.

Each morning that I awoke on Venus it was with a sense of surprise that I still lived, and this first morning on the big river was no exception.

As soon as we had eaten we went to our raft, and after some difficulty succeeded in launching it. I had equipped it with several long branches for poling and some shorter ones that we might use as oars after we got into the deep channel, but they were most inadequate makeshifts. I was depending almost exclusively on the eddy to carry us within striking distance of the opposite shore, where I hoped that we would then be able to pole the raft to the bank.

Our craft floated much better than I had anticipated. I had feared that it would be almost awash and most uncomfortable; but the wood was evidently light, with the result that the top of the raft was several inches above the water.

No sooner had we shoved off than the eddy seized us and commenced to bear us up stream and out toward the centre. Our only concern now was to keep from being drawn into the vortex, and by poling frantically we managed to keep near the periphery of the whirlpool until the water deepened to such a degree that our poles would no longer touch bottom; then we seized the shorter branches and paddled desperately. It was gruelling work, yet Nalte never faltered.

At last we swung in toward the left bank, and once more we seized our poles, but, to my astonishment and chagrin, I discovered that the water here was still too deep. The current, too, was much stronger on this side than on the other; and our futile oars were almost useless.

Remorselessly the river held us in its grip and dragged us back toward the vortex. We paddled furiously, and held our own; we were keeping away from the centre of the eddy, but we were being carried farther from the left bank.

Presently we were in mid-channel. We seemed to be hanging on the very edge of the eddy. Both of us were almost exhausted by this time, yet we might not pause for an instant. With a last, supreme effort we tore the raft from the clutches of the current that would have drawn us back into the embrace of the swirling Titan; then the main current of the mid-channel seized us–a fierce, relentless force. Our craft swirled and bobbed about absolutely beyond control, and we were swept down toward the great river.

I laid aside my inadequate paddle. "We have done our best, Nalte," I said, "but it wasn't good enough. Now all that we can do is to hope that this thing will hang together until we drift to one shore or the other somewhere along the big river."

"It will have to be soon," said Nalte.

"Why?" I asked.

"When Skor found me he said that I was fortunate to have come to shore where I did, as farther down the river tumbles over falls."

I looked at the low cliffs that lined the river on both sides. "There isn't any chance of making a landing here," I said.

"Perhaps we shall have better luck lower down," suggested Nalte.

Down we drifted with the current, sometimes borne close to one shore, sometimes close to the other as the channel meandered from bank to bank; or again we rode far out on the centre of the flood. Sometimes we saw little breaks in the cliffs where we might have made a landing; but we always saw them too late, and were carried past before we could manoeuvre our clumsy craft within reach.

As we approached each bend we looked expectantly for some change in the shore line that would offer us some hope of landing, but always we were disappointed. And then, at last, as we swung around a headland, we saw two cities. One lay upon the left bank of the river, the other on the right directly opposite. The former appeared grey and drab even at a distance, while that upon the right bank shone white and beautiful and gay with its limestone walls and towers and its roofs of many colours.

Nalte nodded toward the city on the left bank. "That must be Kormor; this is about the location that Skor told me his city occupied."

"And the other?" I asked.

She shook her head. "Skor never mentioned another city."

"Perhaps it is all one city built upon both banks of the river," I suggested.

"No; I do not think so. Skor told me that the people who dwelt across the river from Kormor were his enemies, but he never said anything about a city. I thought it was just some savage tribe. Why, that is a splendid city–far larger and handsomer than Kormor."

We could not, of course, see the entire expanse of either city, but as we drifted closer it was apparent that the city on our right extended along the river front for several miles. This we could see because at this point the river ran almost as straight as a canal for a greater distance than I could see. But the city on our left, which was Kormor, was much smaller, extending but about a mile along the water front. As far as we could see both cities were walled, a high wall extending along the river side of each. Kormor had a short quay in front of a gate about the centre of this wall, while the quay of the other city appeared to be a long avenue extending as far as I could see.

We had been drifting for some time opposite the right hand city before we came close to Kormor. There were a few fishermen on the long quay of the former city, and others, possibly sentries, on top of the wall behind them. Many of these saw us and pointed at us and seemed to be discussing us, but at no time did we drift close enough to that side of the river so that we could obtain a close view of them.

As we came down toward the quay of Kormor, a small boat pushed out into the river. It contained three men, two of whom were rowing while the third stood in the bow. That they were pulling out to intercept us appeared quite evident.

"They are Skor's men," said Nalte.

"What do you suppose they want of us?" I asked.

"To capture us, of course, for Skor; but they will never capture me!" She stepped toward the edge of the raft.

"What do you mean?" I demanded. "What are you going to do?"

"I am going to jump into the river."

"But you can't swim," I objected. "You will be sure to drown."

"That is what I wish to do. I shall never let Skor take me again."

"Wait, Nalte," I begged. "Why haven't taken us yet. Perhaps they won't."

"Yes, they will," she said hopelessly.

"We must never give up hope, Nalte. Promise me that you will wait. Even in the last second you can still carry out your plan."

"I will wait," she promised, abut in the last second you had better follow my example and join me in death rather than fall into the hands of Skor and become one of those hopeless creatures that you saw at his castle, for then you will be denied even the final escape of death."

The boat was now approaching closer, and I hailed its occupants. "What do you want of us?" I demanded.

"You must come ashore with us," said the man in the bow.

I was close enough now so that I could get a good look at the fellow. I had thought at first that they were some more of Skor's living dead, but now I saw that this fellow's cheeks had the hue of health and blood.

"We will not come with you," I called back to him. "Leave us alone; we are not harming you. Let us go our way in peace."

"You will come ashore with us," said the man, as his boat drew closer.

"Keep away, or I'll kill you." I cried, fitting an arrow to my bow.

The fellow laughed–a dry, mirthless laugh. Then it was that I saw his eyes, and a cold chill swept over me. They were the dead eyes of a corpse!

I loosed an arrow. It drove straight through the creature's chest, but he only laughed again and left the arrow sticking there.

"Do you know," cried Nalte, "that you cannot kill the dead?" She stepped to the far side of the raft. "Goodbye, Carson," she said quietly; "the last second is here!"

"No! No, Nalte!" I cried. "Wait! It is not the last second."

I turned again toward the approaching boat. Its bow was already within a foot of the raft. I leaped upon him. He struck at me with his dead hands; his dead fingers clutched for my throat. But my attack had been too quick and unexpected. I had carried him off his balance, and in the same instant I seized him and threw him overboard.

The two other creatures had been rowing with their backs toward the bow and were unaware that any danger threatened them until I crashed upon their leader. As he went overboard the nearer of the others rose and turned upon me. His skin, too, was painted in the semblance of life, but those dead eyes could not be changed.

With a horrid, inarticulate scream he leaped for me. I met his rush with a right to the jaw that would have knocked a living man down for a long count; and while, of course, I couldn't knock the thing out, I did knock it overboard.

A quick glance at the two in the water convinced me that my guess had not been amiss–like their fellows at the castle, the two could not swim and were floating helplessly down stream with the current. But there was still another, and it was stepping across the thwarts toward me.

I sprang forward to meet it, ripping in a blow toward the side of the jaw that would have sent it after the other two had it connected; but it did not. Our movements caused the boat to rock and threw me off my balance, and before I could regain my equilibrium the creature seized me.

It was very powerful, but it fought without fire or enthusiasm just the cold, deadly application of force. It reached for my throat; to reach for its throat was useless. I could not choke the life from something that had no life. The best that I could do was to try to evade its clutches and wait for an opening that might never come.

I am rather muscular myself; and I did manage to push the thing from me for a moment, but it came right back. It didn't say anything; it didn't make any sound at all. There was no expression in its glazed eyes, but its dry lips were drawn back over yellow teeth in a snarling grimace. The sight of it and the touch of those cold, clammy fingers almost unnerved me–these and the strange door that emanated from it, the strange door that is the door of death.

As it came toward me the second time it came with lowered head and outstretched arms. I leaped for it, and locked my right arm about its head from above. The back of its neck was snug against my armpit as I seized my own right wrist with my left hand and locked my hold tighter. Then I swung quickly around, straightening up as I did so and, incidentally, nearly capsizing the boat. The creature lost its footing as

I swung it about; its arms flailed wildly, as with a last mighty surge I released my hold and sent it stumbling over the gunwale into the river. Like the others, it floated away.

A few yards away, the raft was drifting with Nalte wide-eyed and tense with excitement. Seizing an oar I brought the boat alongside and extending a hand assisted Nalte over the side, I noticed that she was trembling.

Were you frightened, Nalte?" I asked.

"For you, yes. I didn't think that you had a chance against three of them. Even now I can't believe what I saw. It is incredible that one man could have done what you did."

"Luck had a lot to do with it," I replied, "and the fact that I took them by surprise. They weren't expecting anything of the sort."

"How strangely things happen," mused Nalte. "A moment ago I was about to drown myself in sheer desperation, and now everything is changed. The danger is over, and instead of an inadequate raft we have a comfortable boat."

"Which proves that one should never give up hope."

"I shan't again–while you are with me." I had been keeping an eye on the Kormor quay rather expecting to see another boat put out in pursuit of us, but none did.

The fishermen and the sentries on the waterfront of the other city had all stopped what they were doing and were watching us.

"Shall we row over there and see if they will take us in?" I asked.

"I am afraid," replied Nalte. "We have a saying in Andoo that the farther strangers are away the better friends they are."

"You think that they would harm us?" I asked.

Nalte shrugged. "I do not know, but the chances are that they would kill you and keep me."

"Then we won't take the chance, but I would like to remain near here for a while and search for Duare."

"You can't land on the left bank until we are out of sight of Kormor," said Nalte, "or they would be after us in no time."

"And if we land in sight of this other city these people would take after us, if what you fear be true,"

"Let's go down stream until we are out of sight of both cities," suggested the girl, "and then wait until night before coming back near Kormor to search, for that is where you will have to search for Duare."

Following Nalte's suggestion we drifted slowly down stream. We soon passed Kormor, but the white city on the right bank extended on for a couple of miles farther. I should say that its full length along the river front was fully five miles, and along all that length was the broad quay backed by a gleaming white wall pierced by an occasional gate–I counted six or seven along the full length of the water front.

Just below the city the river turned to the right, and almost immediately the cliffs shut off our view of both cities. Simultaneously the aspect of the country changed. The limestone cliffs ended abruptly, the river running between low banks. Here it spread out to considerable width, but farther ahead I could see where it narrowed again and entered a gorge between cliffs much higher than any that we had passed. They were wooded cliffs, and even from a distance I could see that they were not of the white limestone that formed those with which we had now become familiar.

There came to my ears faintly an insistent sound that was at first little more than a murmur, but as we drifted down the river it seemed to grow constantly in volume.

"Do you hear what I hear?" I demanded, "or am I the victim of head noises?"

"That distant roaring?"

"Yes; it has become a roar now. What do you suppose it can be?"

"It must be the falls that Skor told me of," said Nalte.

"By Jove! That's just what it is," I exclaimed. "And the best thing that we can do is to get to shore while we can."

The current had carried us closer to the right bank at this point, and just ahead of us I saw a small stream emptying into the river. There was an open forest on the farther side of the stream and scattered trees on the nearer.

It appeared an ideal location for a camp.

We made the shore easily, for the current here was not swift. I ran the boat into the mouth of the small stream, but there was not water enough to float it. However, I managed to drag it up far enough to tie it to an overhanging limb of a tree where it was out of sight of any possible pursuers from Kormor who might come down the river in search of Nalte and myself.

"Now, I said, "the thing that interests me most at present is securing food."

"That is something that always interests me," admitted Nalte, with a laugh. "Where are you going to hunt? That forest on the other side of this little stream looks as though it should be filled with game."

She was facing the forest as she spoke, while my back was toward it. Suddenly the expression on her face changed, and she seized my arm with a little cry of alarm. "Look, Carson! What is that?"

## CHAPTER 13

# To Live or Die

As I turned at Nalte's warning cry, I thought that I saw something dodge behind low bushes on the opposite bank.

"What was it, Nalte?" I demanded.

"Oh, it couldn't be what I thought I saw," she whispered excitedly. "I must be mistaken."

"What did you think you saw?"

"There's another–there–look!" she cried.

And then I saw it. It stepped from behind the bole of a large tree and stood eying us, its fangs bared in a snarl. It was a man that went on four feet like a beast. Its hind legs were short, and it walked on its hind toes, the heels corresponding to the hocks of animals. Its hands were more human, and it walked flat on the palms of them in front. Its nose was flat, its mouth broad, and its heavy, undershot jaws were armed with powerful teeth. Its eyes were small and close set and extremely savage. Its skin was white and almost hairless except upon its head and jowls. Another one appeared suddenly beside it.

"You don't know what they are?" I asked Nalte.

"We have heard of them in Andoo, but no one ever believed that they existed. They are called zangans. If the stories I have heard are true they are terribly ferocious. They hunt in packs and devour men as well as beasts."

Zangan means beast-man, and no better word could have been coined to describe the creature that faced us across that little stream in far Noobol. And now others came slinking into view from the shelter of bushes and from behind the boles of trees.

"I think we had better hunt elsewhere," I said in a weak effort to be jocose.

"Let's take to the boat again," suggested Nalte.

We had already walked a little distance from the spot where I had moored our craft, and as we turned to retrace our steps I saw several of the zangans enter the water on the opposite side and approach the boat. They were much closer to it than we, and long before I could untie it and drag it into deeper water they could be upon us.

"It is too late!" cried Nalte.

"Let's fall back slowly to that little rise of ground behind us," I said. "Perhaps I can hold them off there."

We retreated slowly, watching the zangans as they crossed the stream toward us. When they came out on shore they shook themselves as dogs do, and then they came slinking after us again. They reminded me of tigers–human tigers–and their gait was much that of a stalking tiger as they approached with flattened heads and snarling lips.

They growled and snapped at one another, revealing a viciousness greater than that of beasts. Momentarily I expected a charge, and I knew that when it came Nalte's troubles and mine would be over forever. We wouldn't have even a fighting chance against that savage pack.

There were about twenty of them, mostly males; but there were a couple of females and two or three half grown cubs. On the back of one of the females rode a baby, its arms tightly hugging the neck of its mother.

Savage as they appeared, they followed us warily as though they were half afraid of us; but their long, easy strides were constantly cutting down the distance between us.

When we reached the little mound toward which we had been retreating they were still fifty yards behind us. As we started to ascend the rise a large male trotted forward, voicing a low roar. It was as though it had just occurred to him that we might be trying to escape and that he ought to try to prevent it.

I stopped and faced him, fitting an arrow to my bow. Drawing the shaft back to the very tip I let him have it squarely in the chest. He stopped in his tracks, roared horribly, and clawed at the feathered end protruding from his body; then he came on again; but he was staggering, and presently he sank to the ground, struggled for a moment, and lay still.

The others had stopped and were watching him. Suddenly a young male ran up to him and bit him savagely about the head and neck; then raised his head and voiced a hideous roar. I guessed that it was a challenge as I saw him look about him at the other members of the pack. Here, perhaps, was a new leader usurping the powers of the one who had fallen

Apparently no one was prepared to question his authority, and now he turned his attention again to us. He did not advance directly toward us, but slunk off to one side. As he did so he turned and growled at his fellows. That he was communicating orders to them at once became evident, for immediately they spread out as though to surround us.

I loosed another arrow then, this time at the new leader. I struck him in the side and elicited such a roar of pain and rage as I hope I may never hear again–at least not under such circumstances.

Reaching back with one hand the beast man seized the shaft and tore it from his body, inflicting a far more serious hurt than the arrow had made in entering; and now his roars and screams fairly shook the ground.

The others paused to watch him, and I saw one large male slink slowly toward the wounded leader. The latter saw him, too; and with bared fangs and ferocious growls charged him. The ambitious one, evidently realizing that his hopes had been premature, wheeled and fled; and the new chief let him go and turned again toward us.

By this time we were three-quarters surrounded. There were nearly twenty ferocious beasts confronting us, and I had less than a dozen arrows.

Nalte touched me on the arm. "Goodbye, Carson," she said, "Now, surely, the last is upon us."

I shook my head. "I am saving the last second in which to die," I replied. "Until then I shall not admit that there is ever to be a last second for me, and then it will be too late to matter."

"I admire your courage if not your reasoning," said Nalte, the ghost of a smile on her lips. "But at least it will be a quick death–did you see how that fellow tore at the throat of the first one you shot? It is better than what Skor would have done to us."

"At least we shall be dead," I observed.

"Here they come!" cried Nalte.

They were closing in on us now from three sides. Arrow after arrow I drove into them, nor once did I miss my mark; but they only stopped those that I hit–the others slunk steadily forward.

They were almost upon us as I loosed my last arrow. Nalte was standing close beside me. I put an arm about her.

"Hold me close," she said. "I am not afraid to die, but I do not want to be alone–even for an instant."

"You are not dead yet, Nalte." I couldn't think of anything else to say. It must have sounded foolish at such a time, but Nalte ignored it.

"You have been very good to me, Carson," she said.

"And you have been a regular brick, Nalte, if you know what that means–which you don't."

"Goodbye, Carson! It is the last second."

"I guess it is, Nalte." I stooped and kissed her. "Goodbye!"

From above us and behind us on the mound came a sudden crackling hum that was like the noise that an X-ray machine makes, but I knew that it was not an X-ray machine. I knew what it was even without the evidence of the crumpling bodies of the zangans dropping to the ground before us–it was the hum of the r-ray rifle of Amtor!

I wheeled and looked up toward the summit of the mound. There stood a dozen men pouring streams of the destructive rays upon the pack. It lasted for but a few seconds, but not one of the ferocious beasts escaped death. Then one of our rescuers (or were they our captors) came toward us.

He, like his companions, was a man of almost perfect physique, with a handsome, intelligent face. My first impression was that if these were fair examples of the citizens of that white city from which I assumed they had come, we must have stumbled upon an Olympus inhabited solely by gods.

In every company of men we are accustomed to seeing some whose proportions or features are ungainly or uncouth; but here, though no two men exactly resembled one another, all were singularly handsome and symmetrically proportioned.

He who approached us wore the customary g-string and military harness of the men of Amtor. His trappings were handsome without being ornate, and I guess from the insigne on the fillet that encircled his brow that he was an officer.

"You had a close call," he said pleasantly.

"Rather too close for comfort," I replied. "We have you to thank for our lives."

"I am glad that I arrived in time. I happened to be on the river wall as you drifted past, and saw your encounter with the men from Kormor. My interest was aroused; and, knowing that you were headed for trouble down river on account of the falls, I hurried down to try to warn you."

"A rather unusual interest in strangers for a man of Amtor," I commented, "but I can assure you that I appreciate it even if I do not understand it."

He laughed shortly. "It was the way you handled those three creatures of Skor," he explained. "I saw possibilities in such a man; and we are always looking for better qualities to infuse into the blood of Havatoo. But come, let me introduce myself. I am Ero Shan."

"And this is Nalte of Andoo," I replied, "and I am Carson Napier of California."

"I have heard of Andoo," he acknowledged. "They raise an exceptionally fine breed of people there, but I never heard of your country. In fact I have never seen a man before with blue eyes and yellow hair. Are all the people of Cal–"

"California," I prompted.

"–of California like you?"

"Oh, no! There are all colours among us, of hair and eyes and skin."

"But how can you breed true to type then?" he demanded.

"We don't," I had to admit. "Rather shocking," he said, half to himself. "Immoral—racially immoral. Well, be that as it may, your system seems to have produced a rather fine type at that; and now, if you will come with me, we shall return to Havatoo.

"May I ask," I inquired, "if we return as guests or as prisoners?"

He smiled, just the shadow of a smile. "Will that make any difference–as to whether you return with me or not?"

I glanced up at the armed men behind him and grinned. "None," I replied.

"Let us be friends," he said. "You will find justice it Havatoo. If you deserve to remain as a guest, you will be treated as a guest—if not—" he shrugged.

As we reached the top of the little hillock we saw, just behind it, a long, low car with transverse seats and no top. It was the first motor car that I had seen on Venus. The severity of its streamlines and its lack of ornamentation suggested that it was a military car.

As we entered the rear seat with Ero Shan his men took their places in the forward seats. Ero Shan spoke a word of command and the car moved forward. The driver was too far from me, and hidden by the men between us, to permit me to see how he controlled the car, which moved forward over the uneven ground smoothly and swiftly.

Presently as we topped a rise of ground we saw the city of Havatoo Lying white and beautiful before us. From our elevation I could see that it was built in the shape of a half circle with the flat side Lying along the water front, and it was entirely walled.

The river curves to the right below the city, and the direct route that we followed returning to it brought us to a gate several miles from the river. The gate itself was of magnificent proportions and an architectural gem, bespeaking a high order of civilization and culture. The city wall, of white limestone, was beautifully carved with scenes that I took to portray the history of the city or of the race that inhabited it, the work having apparently been conceived and executed with the rarest taste; and these carvings extended as far as I could see.

When one considers the fact that the wall on the land side is about eight miles long and on the river side about five miles, and that all of it is elaborately carved, one may understand the vast labour and the time required to complete such an undertaking along both faces of a twenty foot wall.

As we were halted at the gate by the soldiers on guard I saw emblazoned above the portal, in the characters of the universal Amtorian language, *Tag Kuni Voo Klambad*, Gate of the Psychologists.

Beyond the gate we entered a broad, straight avenue that ran directly toward the centre of the water front. It was filled with traffic–cars of various sizes and shapes, running swiftly and quietly in both directions. There was nothing but vehicular traffic on this level, pedestrians being accommodated on walkways at the level of the second stories of the buildings, which were connected by viaducts at all intersections.

There was practically no noise–no tooting of horns, no screeching of brakes–traffic seemed to regulate itself. I asked Ero Shan about it.

"It is very simple," he said. "All vehicles are energized from a central power station from which power emanates in three frequencies; on the control board of each vehicle is a dial that permits the operator to pick up any frequency he desires. One is for avenues running from the outer wall to the centre of the city, another is for transverse avenues, and the third for all traffic outside the city. The first two are cut off and on alternately; when one is on all traffic moving in the opposite direction is stopped at intersections automatically."

"But why doesn't the traffic between intersections stop at the same time?" I asked.

"That is regulated by the third frequency, which is always operative," he explained. "A hundred feet before a vehicle reaches an intersection a photo-electric current moves the dial on the control board to the proper frequency for that lane."

Nalte was thrilled by all that she saw. She was a mountain girl from a small kingdom, and this was the first large city that she had ever seen.

"It is marvellous," she said. "And how beautiful the people are!"

I had noticed that fact myself. Both the men and the women in the cars that passed us were of extraordinary perfection of form and feature.

Ambad Lat. Psychologist Avenue, led us directly to a semicircular civic centre at the water front, from which the principal avenues radiated toward the outer wall like the spokes of a wheel from the hub toward the felloe. Here were magnificent buildings set in a gorgeous park, and here Ero Shan escorted us from the car toward a splendid palace. There were many people in the park, going to or coming from the various buildings. There was no hurry, no bustle, no confusion; nor was there idling or loitering. All suggested well considered, unhurried efficiency. The voices of those who conversed were pleasant, well modulated. Like the people I had seen elsewhere in the city, these were all handsome and well formed.

We followed Ero Shan through an entrance into a wide corridor. Many of those we passed spoke pleasant greetings to our companion, and all of them looked at us with seemingly friendly interest, but without rudeness.

"Beautiful people in a beautiful city," murmured Nalte.

Ero Shan turned toward her with a quick smile. "I am glad that you like us and Havatoo," he said. "I hope that nothing will ever alter this first impression."

"You think that something may?" asked Nalte.

Ero Shan shrugged. "That all depends upon you," he replied, "or rather upon your ancestors."

"I do not understand," said Nalte.

"You will presently."

He stopped before a door and, swinging it open, bade us enter. We were in a small anteroom in which several clerks were employed.

"Please inform Korgan Kantum Mohar that I wish to see him," said Ero Shan to one of the clerks.

The man pressed one of several buttons on his desk and said, "Korgan Sentar Ero Shan wishes to see you." Apparently from the desktop a deep voice replied, "Send him in."

"Come with me," directed Ero Shan, and we crossed the anteroom to another door which a clerk opened. In the room beyond a man faced us from a desk behind which he was seated. He looked up at us with the same friendly interest that had been manifested by the people we had passed in the park and the corridor.

As we were introduced to Korgan Kantum Mohar he arose and acknowledged the introduction with a bow then he invited us to be seated.

"You are strangers in Havatoo," he remarked. "It is not often that strangers enter our gates." He turned to Ero Shan. "Tell me, how did it happen?"

Ero Shan told of witnessing my encounter with the three men from Kormor. I hated to see a man like this go over the falls," he continued, and I felt that it was worth while bringing them into Havatoo for an examination. Therefore I have brought them directly to you, hoping that you will agree with me."

"It can do no harm," admitted Mohar. "The examining board is in session now. Take them over. I will advise the board that I have authorized the examination."

"What is the examination, and what is its purpose?" I asked. "Perhaps we do not care to take it."

Korgan Kantum Mohar smiled. That is not for you to say," he said.

"You mean that we are prisoners?"

"Let us say rather guests by command."

"Do you mind telling me the purpose of this examination?" I asked.

"Not at all. It is to determine whether or not you shall be permitted to live."

## CHAPTER 14

# Havatoo

They were all very polite and pleasant, very professional and efficient. First we were bathed; then blood tests were made, our hearts examined, our blood pressure taken, our reflexes checked. After that we were ushered into a large room where five men sat behind a long table.

Ero Shan accompanied us throughout the examination. Like the others, he was always pleasant and friendly. He encouraged us to hope that we would pass the examination successfully. Even yet I did not understand what it was all about. I asked Ero Shan.

"Your companion remarked upon the beauty of Havatoo and its people," he replied. "This examination is the explanation of that beauty–and of many other things here which you do not yet know of."

The five men seated behind the long table were quite as pleasant as any of the others we had met. They questioned us rapidly for fully an hour and then dismissed us. From the questions propounded I judged that one of them was a biologist, another a psychologist, one a chemist, the fourth a physicist, and the fifth a soldier.

"Korgan Sentar Ero Shan," said he who appeared to be the head of the examining board, "you will take custody of the man until the result of the examination is announced. Hara Es will take charge of the girl." He indicated a woman who had entered the room with us and had been standing beside Nalte.

The latter pressed closer to me. "Oh, Carson! They are going to separate us," she whispered.

I turned toward Ero Shan to expostulate, but he motioned me to be silent. "You will have to obey," he said, "but I think you have no reason to worry."

Then Nalte was led away by Hara Es, and Ero Shan took me with him. A car was waiting for Ero Shan, and in it we were driven into a district of beautiful homes. Presently the car drew up in front of one of these and stopped.

"This is my home," said my companion. "You will be my guest here until the result of the examination is announced. I wish you to enjoy yourself while you are with me. Do not worry; it will do no good. Nalte is safe. She will be well cared for."

"At least they have provided me with a beautiful prison and a pleasant jailer," I remarked.

"Please do not think of yourself as a prisoner," begged Ero Shan. "It will make us both unhappy, and unhappiness is not to be tolerated in Havatoo."

"I am far from unhappy," I assured him. "On the contrary, I am greatly enjoying the experience, but I still cannot understand what crime is charged against Nalte and me that we should have been put on trial for our lives."

"It was not you who were on trial; it was your heredity," he explained.

"An answer," I assured him, "that leaves me as much at sea as I was before."

We had entered the house as we were conversing, and I found myself amid as lovely surroundings as I have ever seen. Good taste and good judgment had evidently dictated, not only the design of the house, but its appointments as well. From the entrance there was a vista of shrubbery and flowers and trees in a beautiful garden at the end of a wide hall.

It was to this garden that Ero Shan led me and then to an apartment that opened upon it.

"You will find everything here for your convenience and comfort," he said. "I shall detail a man to wait upon you; he will be courteous and efficient. But he will also be responsible for your presence when it is again required at the Central Laboratories.

"And now," he said, seating himself in a chair near a window, "let me try to answer your last question more explicitly."

"Havatoo and the race that inhabits it are the result of generations of scientific culture. Originally we were a people ruled by hereditary jongs that various factions sought to dominate for their own enrichment and without consideration for the welfare of the remainder of the people.

"If we had a good jong who was also a strong character we were well ruled; otherwise the politicians misruled us. Half of our people lived in direst poverty, in vice, in filth; and they bred like flies. The better classes, refusing to bring children into such a world, dwindled rapidly. Ignorance and mediocrity ruled.

"Then a great jong came to the throne. He abrogated all existing laws and government and vested both in himself. Two titles have been conferred upon him–one while he lived, the other after his death. The first was Mankar the Bloody; the second, Mankar the Saviour.

"He was a great warrior, and he had the warrior class behind him. With what seemed utter ruthlessness he wiped out the politicians, and to the positions many of them had filled he appointed the greatest minds of Havatoo–physicists, biologists, chemists, and psychologists.

"He encouraged the raising of children by people whom these scientists passed as fit to raise children, and he forbade all others to bear children. He saw to it that the physically, morally, or mentally defective were rendered incapable of bringing their like into the world; and no defective infant was allowed to live.

"Then, before his death, he created a new form of government–a government without laws and without a king. He abdicated his throne and relinquished the destinies of Havatoo to a quintumvirate that but guides and judges.

"Of these five men one is a sentar (biologist), one an ambad (psychologist), one a kalto (chemist), one a kantum (physicist), and one a korgan (soldier). This quintumvirate is called Sanjong (literally, five-king), and the fitness of its members to serve is determined by examinations similar to that which was given you. These examinations are held every two years. Any citizen may take them; any citizen may become one of the Sanjong. It is the highest honour to which a citizen of Havatoo may win, and he may only achieve it through actual merit."

"And these men make the laws and administer justice," I remarked.

Ero Shan shook his head. "There are no laws in Havatoo," he replied. "During the many generations since Mankar we have bred a race of rational people who know the difference between right and wrong, and for such no rules of behaviour are necessary. The Sangjong merely guides."

"Do you have any difficulty in finding the proper men to form the Sanjong?" I asked.

"None whatever. There are thousands of men in Havatoo capable of serving with honour and distinction. There is a tendency to breed Sanjongs among five of the six classes into which the people of Havatoo are naturally divided.

"When you become more familiar with the city you will discover that the semicircular area facing the Central Laboratories is divided into five sections. The section next to the river and above the Central Laboratories is called Kantum. Here reside the physicists. There are no caste distinctions between the physicists and any of the other five classes, but because they all live in the same district and because they associate with one another than with members of other classes. The result is that they more often mate with their own kind–the laws of heredity do the rest, and the breed of physicists in Havatoo is constantly improving.

"The next district is Kalto; here live the chemists. The centre district is Korgan, the district in which I dwell. It is reserved for the warrior class. Next comes Ambad, the section where the psychologists live; and, last, Sentar, for the biologists, lies along the water front and down the river from the Central Laboratories.

"Havatoo is laid out like the half of a wagon wheel, with the Central Laboratories at the hub. The main sections of the city are bounded by four concentric semicircles. Inside the first is the civic centre, where the Central Laboratories are situated; this I have called the hub. Between this and the next semicircle lie the five sub districts. I have just described. Between this and the third semicircle lies the largest district, called Yorgan; here dwell the common people. And in the fourth section, a narrow strip just inside the outer wall, are the shops, markets, and factories."

"It is all most interesting," I said, "and to me the most interesting part of it is that the city is governed without laws."

Without man-made laws," Ero Shan corrected me. "We are governed by natural laws with which all intelligent people are conversant. Of course occasionally a citizen commits an act that is harmful to another or to the peace of the city, for the genes of vicious and nonconformist characteristics have not all been eradicated from the germ cells of all of the citizens of Havatoo.

"If one commits an act that is subversive of the rights of others or of the general welfare of the community he is tried by a court that is not hampered by technicalities nor precedent, and which, taking into consideration all of the facts in the case, including the heredity of the defendant, reaches a decision that is final and without appeal."

"It seems rather drastic to punish a man for the acts of his ancestors," I remarked.

"But let me remind you that we do not punish," explained Ero Shan. "We only seek to improve the race to the end that we shall attain the greatest measure of happiness and contentment."

"Havatoo, with no bad people in it, must be an ideal city in which to live," I said.

"Oh, there are some bad people," replied Ero Shan, "for there are bad genes in all of us; but we are a very intelligent race, and the more intelligent people are the better able are they to control their bad impulses. Occasionally strangers enter Havatoo, bad men from the city across the river. How they accomplish it is a mystery that has never been solved, but we know that they come and steal a man or a woman occasionally. Sometimes we catch them, and when we do we destroy them. Rarely, our own people commit crimes, usually crimes of passion; but occasionally one commits a premeditated crime. The latter are a menace to the race and are not permitted to survive and transmit their characteristics to future generations or influence the present by their bad examples."

As he ceased speaking a very powerfully built man came to the door of the room.

"You sent for me, Korgan Sentar Ero Shan?" he asked.

"Come in, Herlak," said Ero Shan. Then he turned to me. "Herlak will serve and guard you until the result of the examination is announced. You will find him an efficient and pleasant companion.

"Herlak," he continued, addressing my guard, this man is a stranger in Havatoo. He has just been before the examining board. You will be responsible for him until the board's decision has been announced. His name is Carson Napier."

The man inclined his head. "I understand," he said.

"You will both dine with me in an hour," Ero Shan announced as he took his departure.

"If you would like to rest before dinner," said Herlak, "there is a couch in the next room."

I went in and lay down, and Herlak came and sat in a chair in the same room. It was evident that he was not going to let me get out of his sight. I was tired, but not sleepy; so I started a conversation with Herlak.

"Are you employed in Ero Shan's house?" I asked.

"I am a soldier in the unit he commands," he explained.

"An officer?"

"No, a common soldier."

"But he asked you to dine with him. In my world officers do not mingle socially with common soldiers."

Herlak laughed. "Similar social conditions prevailed in Havatoo ages ago," he said, "but not now. There are no social distinctions. We are all far too intelligent, too cultured, and too sure of ourselves to need artificial conventions to determine our importance. Whether a man cleans a street or is a member of the Sanjong is not so important as is how he performs the duties of his position, his civic morality, and his culture.

"In a city where all are intelligent and cultured all men must be more or less companionable, and an officer suffers no loss of authority by mingling with his men socially."

"But don't the soldiers take advantage of this familiarity to impose upon their officers?" I asked.

Herlak looked his surprise. "Why should they?" he demanded. "They know their duties as well as the officer knows his; and it is the aim in life of every good citizen to do his duty, not to evade it."

I shook my head as I thought of the mess that Earthmen have made of government and civilization by neglecting to apply to the human race the simple rules which they observe to improve the breeds of dogs and cows and swine.

"Do the various classes mingle to the extent of intermarrying?" I asked.

"Of course," replied Herlak. "It is thus that we maintain the high moral and mental standards of the people. Were it otherwise, the yorgans must deteriorate while the several other classes diverged so greatly from one another that eventually they would have nothing in common and no basis for mutual understanding and regard."

We talked of many things during that hour while we awaited dinner, and this common soldier of Havatoo discussed the sciences and the arts with far greater understanding and appreciation than I myself possessed. I asked him if he was particularly well educated, and he said that he was not–that all the men and women of Havatoo were schooled alike to a certain point, when a series of elaborate examinations determined the calling for which they were best fitted and in which they would find the greatest happiness.

"But where do you find your street cleaners?" I asked.

"You speak as though some reproach might attach to that calling," he remonstrated.

"But it is work that many might find distasteful," I argued.

"Necessary and useful work is never distasteful to the man best fitted to do it. Of course, highly intelligent people prefer creative work, and so these necessary but more or less mechanical duties, which, by the way, are usually done by means of mechanical contrivances in Havatoo, never become the permanent calling of any man. Any one can do them; so every one takes his turn– that is, every one in the yorgan class. It is his contribution to the public welfare–a tax paid in useful labour."

And now a girl came to summon us to dinner. She was a very lovely girl; her sarong like garment was of fine material, her ornaments of great beauty.

"A member of Ero Shan's family?" I asked Herlak after she had left.

"She is employed in his house," replied Herlak. "Korgan Sentar Ero Shan has no family."

I had heard this Korgan Sentar title attached to Ero Shan's name previously, and had wondered relative to its significance. The two words mean warrior biologist, but they made no sense to me as a title. I questioned Herlak concerning them as we crossed the garden in response to the summons to dinner.

"The title means that he is both a warrior and a biologist; he has passed examinations admitting him to both classes. The fact that he is a member of one of the other four classes as well as a Korgan makes him an officer and eligible to the title. We common soldiers would not care to serve under any but a brilliant man; and believe me it takes a brilliant man to pass the entrance examination to any of the scientific classes, for he has to pass creditably even in the three to which he is not seeking elevation."

Herlak led me to a large apartment where I saw Ero Shan, three other men, and six women laughing and talking together. There was a suggestion of a lull in the conversation as we entered the room, and interested glances were cast in my direction. Ero Shan came forward to meet me and then introduced me to the others.

I should have enjoyed that dinner, with its marvellous food and sparkling conversation, and the kindness showed me by the other guests, but I could not rid my mind of a suspicion that their kindness might be prompted by pity–that they might share my doubt as to my ability to pass the hereditary test.

They knew, as well as I did, that the shadow of death was hovering over me. I thought of Duare, and hoped she was safe.

## Chapter 15

# The Judgment

Herlak slept on a couch near me that night. I called him the death watch, and he was polite enough to enjoy my little joke.

Ero Shan, Herlak and I breakfasted together the next morning. The girl who had summoned us to dinner the night before waited on us. She was so radiantly beautiful that it was almost embarrassing; I felt that I should be waiting on her. She was young, but then every one I had seen in Havatoo appeared young.

Of course I was not greatly surprised by this, for I knew of the longevity serum developed by the scientists of Amtor. I myself had been inoculated against old age, but I remarked on it casually to Ero Shan.

"Yes," he said, "we could live forever if the Sanjong so decreed. At least we would never die of old age or disease, but they have decreed otherwise. Our serum gives immunity for two or three hundred years, depending upon the natural constitution of the individual. When it ceases to be effective death comes quickly. As a rule we anticipate it when we see that the end is coming."

"But why not live forever if you can?" I asked.

"It was quite apparent that if we lived forever the number of children that could be permitted would be too small to result in any considerable improvement of the race, and so we have refused immortality in the interest of future generations and of all Amtor."

As we were finishing breakfast word was brought to Ero Shan directing him to bring me before the examining board immediately; and a short time later, with Herlak accompanying us, we entered Ero Shan's car and drove down the Korgan Lat. or Avenue of Warriors, toward the Central Laboratories that stand in the civic centre of Havatoo.

Both Ero Shan and Herlak were unusually quiet and grave during the drive, and I sensed that they anticipated that the worst was about to befall me. Nor can I say that I was particularly blithe though the least of my worries was occasioned by what lay in store for me; it was Duare I was thinking of, Duare and Nalte.

The stately government buildings, the Sera Tartum or Central Laboratories as they call them, looked very beautiful in the gorgeous setting of Mankar Pol, the park that is named for the great last jong of Havatoo, as we drove in and stopped before the building in which I had been examined the day before.

We did not have to wait after we entered the building, but were immediately ushered into the presence of the examining board. Their grave faces portended bad news, and I prepared myself for the worst. Through my mind raced plans for escape, but something told me that these people did things so well and were so efficient that there would be no escape from whatever fate they decreed for me.

Kantum Shogan, chief of the board, invited me to be seated; and I took a chair facing the august five. Ero Shan sat at my right, Herlak at my left.

"Carson Napier," commenced Kantum Shogan, "our examination of you shows that you are not without merit. Physically you approach that perfection toward which our race is constantly striving; intellectually you are alert but ill trained–you have no culture. While that might be remedied, I regret to advise you that you possess inherent psychological faults that, if transmitted to progeny or allowed to contaminate others through association with you, would work inestimable wrong on future generations.

"You are the unfortunate victim of inherited repressions, complexes, and fears. To a great extent you have risen above these destructive characteristics but the chromosomes of your germ cells are replete with these vicious genes, constituting a potential menace to generations yet unborn.

"With deep regret, therefore, we could but conclude that it would best serve the interests of humanity were you destroyed."

"May I ask," I inquired, "by what right you elect to say whether or not I shall live? I am not a citizen of Havatoo. I did not come to Havatoo of my own free will. If—"

Kantum Shogan raised his hand in a gesture that enjoined silence. "I repeat," he said, "that we regret the necessity, but there is nothing more to be said upon the subject. Your accomplishments are not such as to outweigh your inherited defects. This is unfortunate, but of course Havatoo cannot be expected to suffer because of it."

So I was to die! After all that I had passed through it verged upon the ridiculous that I should die thus tamely simply because one of my ancestors failed to exercise a little intelligence in the selection of his bride. And to come all this long way just to die! It made me smile.

"Why do you smile?" inquired a member of the board. "Does death seem an amusing thing to you? Or do you smile because you expect to escape death through some ruse?"

"I smile," I replied, "when perhaps I should weep—weep at the thought of all the toil and knowledge and energy that were wasted to transport me twenty-six million miles just to die because five men of another world believe that I have inherited some bad genes."

"Twenty-six million miles!" exclaimed a member of the board; and a second:

"Another world! What do you mean?"

"I mean that I came here from another world twenty-six million miles from Amtor," I replied. "A world much further advanced in some respects than yours."

The members of the board stared at each other. I heard one of them remark to another: "This bears out the theory that many of us have long held."

"Most interesting, and not improbable," said another?"

"You say that Amtor is not the only world?" demanded Kantum Shogan; "that there is another?"

"The heavens are filled with countless worlds," I replied. "Your world and mine and at least eight other worlds revolve around a great ball of flaming gases that we call a sun, and this sun with its worlds or planets is called a solar system. The illimitable void of the heavens is starred with countless other suns, many of which are the centres of other solar systems; and no man knows how many worlds there are."

"Wait!" said Kantum Shogan. "You have said enough to suggest that our examination of you may have been faulty in that it presumed that we possessed the sum total of available human knowledge. Now it appears that you may possess knowledge of such vast importance as to outweigh the biological inadequacies inherent in you.

"We shall question you further upon the subject of this theory which you have propounded, and in the meantime the execution of our sentence is postponed. Our final decision as to your future will depend upon the outcome of this further questioning. Science may ignore no possible source of knowledge, and if your theory is sound and opens a new field to science, you shall be free to enjoy Havatoo for life; nor shall you go unhonoured."

Although I had graduated with honours from a college of high scholastic standing I realized as I stood in the presence of these supermen of science that what Kantum Shogan had said to me was true. By comparison with them I was poorly trained and uncultured–my degrees meaningless, my diploma a mere scrap of paper. Yet in one field of science I surpassed them, and as I explained the solar system and drew diagrams of it for them I saw the keen interest and the ready understanding with which they grasped all I said.

Now, for the first time, they were listening to an explanation of the phenomena of the transition from day to night and from night to day, of the seasons, of the tides. Their vision restricted by the cloud envelopes that constantly enshroud Venus, they had been able to see nothing upon which to base a planetary theory; and so it is not strange that astronomy was an unknown science to them, that the sun and the stars did not exist insofar as they were concerned.

For four hours they listened to me and questioned me; then they instructed Ero Shan and Herlak to withdraw to an anteroom with me and wait there until we were again summoned.

We did not have long to wait. In less than fifteen minutes we were recalled before the board.

"It is our unanimous opinion," announced Kantum Shogan, "that your value of humanity far outweighs the danger that it incurs from your inherited defects. You are to live and enjoy the freedom of Havatoo. Your duties will consist of instructing others in that new science which you call astronomy and in applying it for the welfare of humanity.

"As you are now the only member of your class you may live in any section of the city you choose. Your requisitions for all that you require for your personal needs and the advancement of your department will be honoured by the Sera Tartum.

"For the time being I recommend you to the guidance of Korgan Sentar Ero Shan as you are a stranger to Havatoo and will wish to become familiar with our customs and our manners."

With that he dismissed us.

"Before I go may I ask what is to become of the girl, Nalte, who was taken with me yesterday?" I inquired.

"She was considered fit to remain in the yorgan section of Havatoo," he replied. "When her duties have been definitely determined and her living quarters assigned her I will let you know where you may find her."

It was with a feeling of relief that I left the Sera Tartum with Ero

Shan and Herlak. Nalte was safe, and so was I. Now if I could only find Duare!

I spent the following several days familiarizing myself with the city and purchasing such things as I required, an of which were suggested by Ero Shan. Among them was a car. It was very easy—all I had to do was sign a voucher.

"But what check have they on my expenditures?" I asked my friend. I do not even know how much has been placed to my credit."

"Why should they check what you spend?" he asked.

"But I might be dishonest. I might buy things for which I had no need and resell them."

Ero Shan laughed. "They know you will not do that," he assured me. "If the psychologist who examined you had not known that you are an honourable man, not even your knowledge of astronomy would have saved you; that is one vice we will not tolerate in Havatoo. When Mankar destroyed the corrupt and the vicious he almost completely eradicated the breeds in Havatoo, and during the many generations of men that have followed him we have succeeded in completing the work he inaugurated. There are no dishonest men in Havatoo."

I often talked with Ero Shan about Duare. I wanted to cross the river to Kormor and search for her, but he convinced me that it would be suicidal to attempt it. And in view of the fact that I had no reason to believe that she was there I reluctantly put the idea away from me.

"If I had an airplane," I said, "I would find a way to search Kormor."

What is an airplane?" asked Ero Shan, and when I explained it he became very much interested, as flying has never been developed in Amtor, at least in those portions with which I am familiar.

The idea intrigued my companion to such an extent that he could scarcely talk to anything else. I explained the various types of both heavier and lighter than air ships and described the rocket in which I had traversed space from Earth to Venus. In the evening he had me sketch the several types I had explained. His interest seemed to be becoming an obsession.

One evening when I returned to the house I now shared with Ero Shan I found a message awaiting me. It was from an under-clerk of the board of examiners and it gave the address of the house in which Nalte lived.

As I was now familiar with the city I started out in my car after the evening meal to visit Nalte. I went alone as Ero Shan had another engagement.

I found the house in which Nalte lived in the yorgan section of a quiet street not far from the Korgan Lat, the Avenue of Warriors. The house was occupied by women who cleaned the preparatory schools on the Korgan Lat nearby. One of their number admitted me and said that she would call Nalte; then she conducted me to a living room in which were eight or ten women. One of them was playing a musical instrument, the others were painting, embroidering, or reading.

As I entered, they stopped what they were doing and greeted me pleasantly. There was not one among them that was not beautiful, and all were intelligent and cultured. These were the scrub women of Havatoo! Breeding had done for the people of Havatoo what it has done for our prize-winning dairy herds; it has advanced them all toward perfection.

Nalte was glad to see me, and as I wished to visit with her alone I asked her to come for a ride with me.

"I am glad that you passed your examination successfully," I said as we started toward the Korgan Lat.

Nalte laughed joyously. "I just squeezed through," she admitted. "I wonder what they would say back in Andoo if they knew that I, the daughter of their jong, was considered fit only to scrub floors in Havatoo!" and again she laughed happily. It was plain to be seen that her pride had not suffered by reason of her assignment. "But after all," she continued, "it is a high honour to be considered fit to remain on any footing among such a race of supermen.

"And you! I am very proud of you, Carson Napier, for I have been told that you were elevated to a high place among them."

It was my turn to laugh now. "I did not pass the examination at all," I admitted. "I would have been destroyed but for my knowledge of a science that is unknown to Amtor. It was rather a jolt to my self esteem."

We drove along the Korgan Lat. through the great public park and parade ground in the centre of which stands a magnificent stadium, and thus to the Avenue of the Gates which forms a great arc nearly eight miles long just inside the outer wall on the land side of Havatoo.

Here are the factories and the shops in the district included between the Avenue of Gates and the Yorgan Lat. a wide avenue a third of a mile inside the wall, all the principal shops being located along the Avenue of Gates. The avenue and the shops were brilliantly lighted, the street swarmed with vehicles, and the walkways at the level of the second stories were crowded with pedestrians.

We drove twice the full length of the avenue, enjoying the life and beauty of the scene; then we drove into one of the parking places, to which all of the ground floors on the main arteries are devoted, and were lifted by an escalator to the walkway on the level above.

Here shops displayed their wares in show windows, much as is the custom in American cities, though many of the displays aimed solely to please the eye rather than to call attention to the goods for sale within. The scientists of Havatoo have developed a light that is brilliant and at the same time soft with which they attain effects impossible of achievement by our relatively crude lighting methods. At no place is the source of the light apparent; it casts soft shadows and gives forth no heat. Ordinarily it resembles sunlight, but it can also produce soft, pastel shades of various hues.

After we had enjoyed the spectacle for an hour, mingling with the happy crowd upon the walkway, I made a few small purchases, including a gift for Nalte; then we returned to my car, and I took my companion home.

The next morning I was busy organizing my classes in astronomy, and so numerous were those wishing to enrol that I had to organize several large classes, and as only four hours a day are ordinarily devoted to work of any nature it was evident that I should have to devote my time at first to the training of instructors if the new science was to be expounded to all the inhabitants who were interested.

I was greatly flattered by the personnel of the first matriculants. Not only were there scientists and soldiers from the first five classes of Havatoo, but every member of the Sanjong, the ruling quintumvirate of Havatoo, enrolled. The thirst of these people for useful knowledge is insatiable.

Shortly after noon, my work for the day having been completed, I received a summons to call upon Korgan Kanturn Mohar, the warrior physicist who had arranged for the examination of Nalte and myself the day Ero Shan brought us to the city.

I could not but wonder what he wanted of me. Could it be that I must undergo another examination? Always, I presume, I shall connect Mohar's name with examinations.

As I entered his office on the Sera Tartum he greeted me with the same pleasant demeanour that had marked his attitude the day he had told me I was to be examined to ascertain whether or not I should be permitted to live; so his graciousness was not entirely reassuring.

"Come over here and sit down near me," he said. "I have something here that I should like to discuss with you.

As I took a chair beside him I saw spread on his desk the sketches of airships that I had made for Ero Shan.

"These," be said, pointing to the sketches, "were brought to me by Ero Shan who explained them as best he could. He was quite excited and enthusiastic about them, and I must confess that he imparted some of his enthusiasm to me. I am much interested, and would know more concerning these ships that sail through the air."

For an hour I talked to him and answered his questions. I dwelt principally on the practical achievements of aeronautics–the long flights, the great speed, the uses to which ships had been put in times of peace and in times of war.

Korgan Kantum Mohar was deeply interested. The questions that he asked revealed the trained, scientific mind; and the last one that of the soldiers the man of action.

"Can you build one of these ships for me?" he demanded.

I told him that I could but that it might require long experimentation to adapt their motors and materials to the requirements of a successful airplane.

"You have two or three hundred years," he said with a smile, "and the resources of a race of scientists. Materials that we do not now possess we can produce; nothing is impossible to science."

## Chapter 16

# Attack in the Night

I was given a factory close to the gate of the physicists, at the end of Kantum Lat. I chose this location because there was a level plain beyond this gate that would make an excellent flying field, and also so that I would have my finished plane finally assembled where it could easily be wheeled out of the city without interfering with traffic to any great extent.

On the advice of the Sanjong, which took a deep interest in both this new venture into aeronautics and the, to them, new science of astronomy, I divided my time between the two.

My time was fully occupied, and I worked far more than the usual four hours a day. But I enjoyed the work, especially the building of a plane; and engrossing were the day dreams in which I indulged of exploring Venus in a ship of my own.

The necessity for relaxation and entertainment is stressed by the people of Havatoo, and Ero Shan was constantly dragging me away from my drawing board or my conferences with the corps of assistants that had been placed at my disposal by Mohar to take me to this thing or that.

There were theatres, art exhibits, lectures, musicales, concerts, and games of various descriptions in gymnasiums and the great stadium. Many of their games are extremely dangerous, and injury and death often accompany them. In the great stadium at least once a month men fight with wild beasts or with one another to the death, and once a year the great war game is played. Ero Shan, Gara Lo, Ero Shan's friend, Nalte, and I attended this year's game together. To Nalte and I it was all new; we did not know what to expect.

"Probably we shall witness an exhibition of such scientific wonders as only the men of Havatoo are capable," I suggested to her.

"I haven't the faintest conception of what it will be," she replied.

"No one will tell me anything about it. They say, 'Wait and see. You will be thrilled as you have never been before.'"

"The game doubtless hinges on the use of the most modern, scientific instruments of war and strategy," I ventured.

"Well," she remarked, "we shall soon know. It is about time for the games to begin."

The great stadium, seating two hundred thousand people, was crammed to capacity. It was gorgeous with the costumes and the jewels of the women and the handsome trappings of the men, for the intelligence of Havatoo concedes their full value to beauty and to art. But of all that went to make up this splendid spectacle there was nothing more outstanding than the divine beauty of the people themselves.

Suddenly a cry arose, a roar of welcome. "They come! The warriors!"

Onto the field at each end marched two hundred men; a hundred men naked but for white g-strings at one end of the field, a hundred men with red g-strings at the other end of the field.

They carried short swords and shields. For a while they stood inactive, waiting; then two small cars were driven onto the field. Each contained a driver and a young woman.

One of the cars was red, the other white. The red car attached itself to the contingent wearing the red g-strings, the white cars to the whites.

When they were in position the two factions paraded entirely around the field clockwise. As they passed the stands the people cheered and shouted words of encouragement and praise, and when the warriors had completed the circuit they took their places again.

Presently a trumpet sounded, and the reds and the whites approached each other. Now their formations were changed. There was an advance party and a rear guard, there were flankers on either side. The cars remained in the rear, just in front of the rear guard. On running-boards that encircled the cars were a number of warriors.

I leaned toward Ero Shan. "Tell us something of the idea of the game," I begged, "so that we may understand and enjoy it better."

"It is simple," he replied. "They contend for fifteen vir (the equivalent of sixty minutes of earth time), and the side that captures the opponent's queen oftenest is the winner."

I do not know what I expected, but certainly not that which followed. The reds formed a wedge with its apex toward the whites, then charged. In the melee that ensued I saw three men killed and more than a dozen wounded, but the whites held their queen.

When a queen was pressed too closely her car turned and fled, the rear guard coming up to repel the enemy. The tide of battle moved up and down the field. Sometimes the whites seemed about to capture the red queen, again their own was in danger. There were many individual duels and a display of marvellous swordsmanship throughout.

But the whole thing seemed so out of harmony with all that I had heretofore seen in Havatoo that I could find no explanation for it. Here was the highest type of culture and civilization that man might imagine suddenly reverting to barbarism. It was inexplicable. And the strangest part of all of it to me was the almost savage enjoyment with which the people viewed the bloody spectacle.

I must admit that I found it thrilling, but I was glad when it was over. Only one queen was captured during the entire game. At the very last the white queen fell into the hands of the reds, but only after the last of her defenders had fallen.

Of the two hundred men who took part in the game, not one came through unwounded; fifty were killed on the field, and I afterward learned that ten more died of their wounds later.

As we drove from the stadium toward our house I asked Ero Shan how such a savage and brutal exhibition could be tolerated, much less enjoyed, by the refined and cultured inhabitants of Havatoo.

"We have few wars," he replied. "For ages war was man's natural state. It gave expression to the spirit of adventure, which is a part of his inheritance. Our psychologists discovered that man must have some outlet for this age-old urge. If it be not given him by wars or dangerous games he will seek it in the commission of crimes or in quarrels with his fellows. It is better that it is so. Without it man would stagnate, he would die of ennui."

I was now working on my plane with the keenest enthusiasm, for I now saw rapidly taking form such a ship as, I truly believe, might be built nowhere in the universe other than in Havatoo. Here I had at my disposal materials that only the chemists of Havatoo might produce, synthetic wood and steel and fabric that offered incalculable strength and durability combined with negligible weight.

I had also the element, vik-ro, undiscovered on earth, and the substance lor, to furnish fuel for my engine. The action of the element, vik-ro, upon the element, yor-san, which is contained in the substance, lor, results in absolute annihilation of the lor. Some conception of the amount of energy thus released may be obtained by considering the fact that there is eighteen thousand million times as much energy liberated by the annihilation of a ton of coal as by its combustion. Fuel for the life of my ship could be held in the palm of my hand, and with the materials that entered into its construction the probable life of the ship was computed by the physicists working on it to be in the neighbourhood of fifty years. Can you wonder that I looked forward with impatience to the completion of such a marvel ship! With it I would be sure to find Duare.

At last it was finished! I spent the final afternoon checking it over carefully with my large corps of assistants. On the morrow it was to be wheeled out for my trial flight I knew that it would be successful. All my assistants knew that it would be; it was a scientific certainty that it must fly.

That evening I determined to indulge in a little relaxation; and I called Nalte on the wireless, transmitterless, receiverless communicating system that is one of the wonders of Havatoo. I asked her if she would take dinner with me, and she accepted with an alacrity and display of pleasure that warmed my heart.

We dined in a little public garden on the roof of a building at the corner of Yorgan Lat and Havatoo Lat, just inside the river wall.

"It seems good to see you again," said Nalte. "It has been a long time–not since the war games. I thought you had forgotten me."

"Far from it," I assured her, "but I have been working day and night on my airship."

"I have heard some mention of it," she said, "but no one that I have talked with seemed to understand very much about it. Just what is it and what will it do?"

"It is a ship that flies through the air faster than a bird can wing," I replied.

"But what good will that be?" she demanded.

"It will carry people quickly and safely from one place to another," I explained.

"You don't mean to say that people will ride in it!" she exclaimed.

"Why, certainly; why else should I build it?"

"But what will keep it in the air? Will it flap its wings like a bird?"

"No; it will soar like a bird on stationary wings."

"But how will you get through the forests where the trees grow close together?"

"I shall fly over the forests."

"So high? Oh, it will be dangerous," she cried. "Please do not go up in it, Carson."

"It will be very safe," I assured her, "much safer than incurring the dangers of the forest on foot. No savage beasts or men can harm the voyager in an airship."

"But think of being way up above the trees!" she said with a little shudder.

"I shall fly even higher than that," I told her. "I shall fly over the loftiest mountains."

"But you will never fly over the great trees of Amtor; I know that."

She referred to the gigantic trees that raise their tips five thousand feet above the surface of Amtor to drink the moisture from the inner cloud envelope.

"Yes; possibly I shall fly even above those," I replied, "though I will admit that flying blind in that solid bank of clouds does not appeal to me."

She shook her head. "I shall be afraid every time I know that you are up in the thing."

"Oh, no you won't, not after you are familiar with it. Some day soon I am going to take you up with me."

"Not me!"

"We could fly to Andoo," I said. "I have been thinking of that ever since I started to build the ship."

"To Andoo!" she exclaimed. "Home! Oh, Carson, if we only could!"

"But we can–that is if we can find Andoo. This ship will take us anywhere. If we could carry enough food and water we could stay in the air for fifty years, and it certainly wouldn't take that long to find Andoo."

"I love it here in Havatoo," she said, musingly, "but after all, home is home. I want to see my own people, but I would like to come back to Havatoo again. That is, if–"

"If what?" I asked.

"If you are going to be here."

I reached across the table and pressed her hand. "We have been pretty good friends, haven't we, Nalte? I should miss you terribly if I thought that I were not to see you again."

"I think that you are the best friend I ever had," she said, and then she looked up at me quickly and laughed. "Do you know," she continued; but stopped suddenly and looked down, as a slight flush suffused her cheeks.

"Do I know what?" I asked.

"Well, I might as well confess. There was a long time that I thought that I loved you."

"That would have been a great honour, Nalte."

"I tried to hide it because I knew that you loved Duare; and now recently Ero Shan has been coming to see me, and I know that I did not know before what love was.

"You love Ero Shan?"

"Yes."

"I am glad. He is a splendid fellow. I know you will both be happy."

"That might be true but for one thing," she said.

"And what is that?"

"Ero Shan does not love me."

"How do you know that he doesn't? I don't see how he could help it. If I had never known Duare–"

"If he loved me he would tell me," she interrupted. Sometimes I think that he believes that I belong to you. We came here together, you know, and we have been much together since. But what's the good in speculating! If he loved me he would not be able to hide it."

We had finished our dinner, and I suggested that we drive about the city for a while and then go to a concert.

"Let's take a little walk instead of driving," suggested Nalte, and as we rose from our table, "How beautiful the view is from here!"

In the strange glow of the Amtorian night the expanse of the great river stretched into the vanishing visibility above and below the city, while on the opposite shore gloomy Kormor was but a darker blotch against the darkness of the night, with here and there a few dim lights showing feebly in contrast to brilliant Havatoo lying at our feet.

We followed the walkway along Havatoo Lat to a narrow side street that extended away from the river.

"Let's turn here," said Nalte. "I feel like quiet and dim lights tonight, not the brilliance and the crowds of Havatoo Lat."

The street that we turned into was in the yorgan section of the city; it was but dimly lighted, and the walkway was deserted. It was a quiet and restful street even by comparison with the far from noisy main avenues of Havatoo, where raucous noises are unknown.

We had proceeded but a short distance from Havatoo Lat when I heard a door open behind us and footsteps on the walkway. I gave the matter no thought; in fact I scarcely had time to give it thought when some one seized me roughly from behind and as I wheeled about I saw another man grab Nalte, clap a hand over her mouth and drag her into the doorway from which the two had come.

## CHAPTER 17

# City of the Dead

I tried to break away from the man who held me, but he was very strong. I did succeed in turning about so that I could strike him; and this I did repeatedly, hitting him in the face as he sought to reach my throat with his fingers.

We must have made quite a lot of noise in that quiet street although neither of us spoke, for soon a head was put out of a window, and presently men and women came running from their houses. But before any of them reached us I had tripped my assailant and was on top of him clutching his throat. I would have choked the life out of him had not several men dragged me from him.

They were shocked and angry because of this unseemly disturbance and brawl on a street in Havatoo, and they placed us under arrest, nor would they listen to what I tried to tell them. All they would say was: "The judges will listen to you;" "it is not our province to judge."

As every citizen of Havatoo has police powers and there is no other police force, there was no delay as there would have been in an earthly city while waiting for the police to answer a summons.

We were bundled into a large car belonging to one of the citizens, and with an adequate guard we were whisked away toward the Sera Tartum.

They do things with celerity in Havatoo. They may have a jail; I presume they have, but they didn't waste any time or cause the state any expense by putting us in to be boarded and lodged by the taxpayers.

Five men were hastily summoned, one from each of the five upper classes; they were judge, jury, and court of last resort. They sat in a large room that resembled a huge library; they were served by a dozen clerks.

One of the judges asked us our names, and when we had given them two clerks went quickly to the shelves and brought forth books in which they began to search.

Then the judges asked those who had arrested us to explain why they brought us in. During the recital of our violation of the peace of Havatoo one of the clerks, evidently having found what he sought, laid his book open before the judges; the other was still searching.

From the open book one of the judges read aloud my official record since I had come to Havatoo, including the result of the examination that I had undergone and its embarrassing finding.

A judge asked me to state my case. In a few brief words I told of the unprovoked attack upon us and the abduction of Nalte, and in conclusion I said, "Instead of wasting time trying me for being the victim of this unwarranted attack and defending myself against my assailant you should be helping me search for the girl who has been stolen."

"The peace of Havatoo is of more importance than the life of any individual," replied a judge. When we have fixed the responsibility for this breach of the peace the other matter will be investigated."

The second clerk now approached the judges. "The name of the prisoner who calls himself Mal Un does not appear in the records in Havatoo."

All eyes turned toward my assailant, Mal Un, and for the first time I had a good look at him under a bright light. I saw his eyes! Instantly I recalled what I had evidently noticed only subconsciously before–the chill of the flesh of his hands and his throat when I had fought with him. And now those eyes. They were the eyes of a dead man!

I wheeled toward the judges. "I understand it all now," I cried. "When I first came to Havatoo I was told that there were few bad men in the city; but that occasionally, none knew how, bad men came from the city of Kormor across the river and stole men and women from Havatoo. This man is from Kormor. He is not a living man; he is a corpse. He and his companion sought to steal Nalte and me for Skor!"

With calm efficiency the judges made a few brief and simple, but none the less effective, tests upon Mal Un; then they whispered together for a few seconds without leaving the bench. Following this, the one who acted as spokesman for the tribunal cleared his throat.

"Mal Un," he announced, "you will be decapitated and cremated forthwith. Carson Napier, you are exonerated with honour. You are free. You may conduct a search for your companion and call upon any citizen of Havatoo to assist you in any way that you desire assistance."

As I was leaving the room I heard a mirthless laugh burst from the dead mouth of Mal Un. Horribly it rang in my ears as I hastened out into the night. The dead man laughing because he was sentenced to death

Naturally, the first person I thought of in my extremity was Ero Shan, who had rescued me from the ape-men. My own car was parked where I had left it at the corner of Yorgan Lat and Havatoo Lat; so I hailed a public conveyance and was driven rapidly to the house at which Ero Shan was being entertained that evening.

I did not go in but sent word that I wished to speak to him upon a matter of great urgency, and a moment later I saw him coming from the house toward me.

"What brings you here, Carson?" he asked. "I thought you were spending the evening with Nalte."

When I told him what had happened he went very white. "There is no time to be lost!" he cried. "Can you find that house again?"

I told him that I could. That doorway is indelibly burned into my memory."

"Dismiss your car; we will go in mine," he said, and a moment later we were speeding toward the place where I had lost Nalte.

"You have all my sympathy, my friend," said Ero Shan. "To have lost the woman you love, and such a woman! is a calamity beyond any feeble words to express."

"Yes," I replied, "and even if I had loved Nalte I could scarcely be more grieved than I now am."

"'Even if you had loved Nalte'!" he repeated incredulously. "But, man, you do love her, do you not?"

"We were only the best of friends," I replied. "Nalte did not love me."

Ero Shan made no reply, he drove swiftly on in silence. Presently we reached our destination. Ero Shan stopped his car beside the stairway, nearest the house, that led up to the walkway; and a moment later we were before the door.

Repeated summons elicited no response, and then I tried the door and found it unlocked.

Together we entered the dark interior, and I regretted that we had brought no weapons, but in peaceful Havatoo men do not ordinarily go armed. Ero Shan soon located a light switch, and as the room in which we stood was illuminated, we saw that it was entirely unfurnished.

The building rose two stories above the walkway, and of course there was a lower floor on a level with the street. We searched the upper stories first, and then the roof, for in this part of Havatoo most of the roofs are developed as gardens; but we found no sign of recent habitation. Then we went to the ground floor, but with no better results. Here was space for the parking of cars, and in rear of that a number of dark storerooms.

"There is no living creature in this house except ourselves," said Ero Shan. "They must have taken Nalte to some other house. It will be necessary to make a search, and only under the authority of the Sanjong itself may the home of a citizen be searched. Come! we will go and get that authority."

"You go," I said. "I will remain here. We should keep a careful watch on this house."

"You are right," he replied. "I shall not be gone long."

After Ero Shan's departure I commenced another careful investigation of the premises. Once again I went through every room searching for some secret place where a person might be hidden.

I had covered the upper stories of the house thus, and was searching the first floor. The dust of neglect lay heavy upon everything, but I noticed that in one of the back rooms it had been disturbed upon the floor at a point where Ero Shan and I had not walked. Previous this had escaped my notice. It seemed to me that it might be fraught with importance.

I examined the floor carefully. I saw footprints. They approached a wall; and there they stopped; there seemed to be a path worn in the dust of this point in the wall. I examined the wall. It was covered with a form of synthetic wood common in Havatoo, and when I rapped upon it it sounded hollow.

The wall covering was applied in panels about three feet wide, and at the top of the panel I was examining was a small round hole about an inch in diameter. Inserting a forefinger in this hole I discovered just what I had imagined I would discover–a latch. I tripped it; and with a slight pressure the panel swung toward me, revealing a dark aperture beyond it.

At my feet I dimly discerned the top of a flight of steps. I listened intently; no sound came up to me from the gloom into which the stairs disappeared. Naturally, I was convinced that Nalte's abductor had carried her down that stairway.

I should have waited for the return of Ero Shan, but I thought that Nalte might be in danger. I could not think of wasting a single precious instant in delay.

I placed a foot upon the stairs and started to descend; and as I did so the panel closed softly behind me, actuated by a spring. I heard the latch click. I was now in utter darkness. I had to feel my way. At any moment I might come upon Nalte's abductor waiting to dispatch me. It was a most uncomfortable sensation, I can assure you.

The stairway, which was apparently cut from the living limestone that underlies Havatoo, ran straight down to a great depth. From the bottom of the stairway I felt my way along a narrow corridor. Occasionally I stopped and listened. At first I heard not a sound; the silence was the silence of the grave.

Presently the walls commenced to feel moist; and then, occasionally, a drop of water fell upon my head. Now a low, muffled sound like the shadow of a roar seemed to fill the subterranean corridor like a vague, oppressive menace.

On and on I groped my way. I could not advance rapidly, for I was compelled to feel every forward footstep before taking it; I could not know what lay beyond the last.

Thus I continued on for a long distance until finally my extended foot felt an obstruction. Investigating, I found that it was the lowest step of a flight of stairs.

Cautiously I ascended, and at the top I came against a blank wall. But experience had taught me where to search for a latch, for I was confident that what barred my progress was a door.

Presently my fingers found what they sought; a door gave to the pressure of my hand.

I pushed it slowly and cautiously until a narrow crack permitted me to look beyond it.

I saw a portion of a room dimly illuminated by the night light of Amtor. I opened the door a little farther; there was no one in the room. I stepped into it, but before I permitted the door to close I located the opening through which the latch could be tripped from that side.

The room in which I found myself was filthy and littered with debris. It was filled with a revolting, musty door that suggested death and decay.

In the wall opposite me were three openings, a doorway and two windows; but there was no window sash and no door. Beyond the door, to which I now crossed, was a yard enclosed by one side of the building and a high wall.

There were three rooms on the ground floor of the building, and these I searched rapidly; they contained only broken furniture, old rags, and dirt. I went upstairs. Here were three more rooms; they revealed nothing more of interest than those downstairs.

Other than these six rooms there was nothing more to the house, and so I was soon aware that I must search farther for Nalte. Neither she nor any one else was in this house.

From an upper window I looked out over the yard. Beyond the wall I saw a street. It was a dingy, gloomy street. The houses that fronted it were drab and dilapidated, but I did not have to look out upon this scene to know where I was. Long before this I had guessed that I was in Kormor, the city of the cruel jong of Morov. The tunnel through which I had passed from Havatoo had carried me beneath the great river that is called Gerlat kum Rov, River of Death. Now I knew that Nalte had been abducted by the agents of Skor.

From the window I saw an occasional pedestrian on the street that passed the house. They moved with slow, shuffling steps. Somewhere in this city of the dead was Nalte in danger so great that I turned cold at the mere thought of it. I must find her! But how?

Descending to the yard, I passed through a gateway in the wall and out into the street. Only the natural, nocturnal light of Amtor illuminated the scene. I did not know which way to go, yet I knew that I must keep moving if I were not to attract attention to myself.

My judgment and my knowledge of Skor suggested that where Skor was there I would find Nalte, and so I knew that I must find the jong's palace. If I might only stop one of the pedestrians and ask him; but that I did not dare do, for to reveal my ignorance of the location of the jong's palace would be to brand me a stranger and therefore an enemy.

I was approaching two men who were walking in the opposite direction to that which I had chosen. As I passed them I noted their sombre garb, and I saw them half stop as we came abreast and eye me intently. But they did not accost me, and it was with relief that I realized that they had gone on their way.

Now I understood that with my handsome trappings and my brisk, alert step and carriage I would be a marked man in Kormor. It became absolutely imperative, therefore, that I disguise myself; but that was going to be more easily thought of than accomplished. However, it must be done. I could never hope to find and rescue Nalte if I were constantly subject to detection and arrest.

Turning, I retraced my steps to the mean hovel I had just quitted, for there I remembered having seen odds and ends of rags and discarded clothing from among which I hoped that I might select sufficient to cover my nakedness and replace the fine apparel I had purchased in Havatoo.

Nor was I disappointed, and a few moments later I emerged again upon the streets clothed in the cleanest of the foul garments I had had to select from. And now, to carry out my disguise to the fullest, I shuffled slowly along like some carrion from a forgotten grave.

Again I met pedestrians; but this time they gave me no second look, and I knew that my disguise was ample. To all outward appearances, in this unlighted city of the dead, I was just another corpse.

In a few houses dim lights burned; but I heard no noises–no singing, no laughter. Somewhere in this city of horror was Nalte. That so sweet and lovely a creature was breathing this fetid air was sufficiently appalling, but of far greater import was the fact that her life hung in the balance.

If Skor was in the city he might kill her quickly in a fit of mad revenge because she had escaped him once. My sustaining hope was that Skor was at his castle and that his minions would hold Nalte unharmed until he returned to Kormor. But how to learn these things!

I knew that it would be dangerous to question any of the inhabitants; but finally I realized that in no other way might I quickly find the house of Skor, and haste was essential if I were to find Nalte before it was too late.

As I wandered without plan I saw nothing to indicate that I was approaching a better section such as I felt might contain the palace of a jong. The houses were all low and grimy and unlovely in design.

I saw a man standing at the intersection of two streets, and as I came close to him I stopped. He looked at me with his glassy eyes.

"I am lost," I said.

"We are all lost," he replied, his dead tongue thick in his dead mouth.

"I cannot find the house where I live."

"Go into any house; what difference does it make?"

"I want to find my own house," I insisted.

"Go and find it then. How should I know where it is if you do not?"

"It is near the house of the jong," I told him.

"Then go to the house of the jong," he suggested surlily.

"Where is it?" I demanded in the same thick tones.

He pointed down the street that I had been following; and then he turned and shuffled away in the opposite direction, while I continued on in the direction he had indicated. I wished to reach my destination quickly; but I dared not accelerate my speed for fear of attracting attention, and so I shuffled along in the lifeless manner of the other wayfarers.

Somewhere ahead of me lay the palace of Skor, Jong of Morov; there I was certain I would find Nalte. But after I found her–what?

## Chapter 18

# A Surprise

The palace of Skor was a three-storied building of grey stone similar in its ugliness to his castle by the river in the forest, but it was considerably larger. It stood in no spacious plaza. Mean hovels were its near neighbours. All about it was a high wall, and before heavy gates stood a dozen warriors. It looked impregnable.

I shuffled slowly past the gates, observing from the corners of my eyes. It seemed useless to attempt to enter there. The guards were posted for a purpose, and that purpose must be to keep out those who had no business within.

What reason could I give for wishing to enter?–what reason that they would accept?

It was evident that I must seek some other means of ingress. If I failed to find any then I might return to the gates as a last resort, but I can tell you that the outlook seemed most hopeless.

I followed the high wall that enclosed the palace grounds, but nowhere did I find any place to scale it. It was about twelve feet high, just too high for me to reach the top with my fingers by a running jump.

I reached the rear of the palace without discovering any place where I might scale the wall, and I was convinced that there was no place. There was plenty of litter and rubbish in the filthy street that encircled the wall but nothing that I could make use of as a ladder.

Upon the opposite side of the street were mean hovels, many of which appeared deserted. In only a few, dim lights revealed a sign of–life. I was going to say–of occupancy. Directly across from me an open door sagged on a single hinge. It gave me an idea.

I crossed the street. There were no lights in any of the nearby houses. That before which I stood appeared tenantless. Stealthily I crept to the doorway and listened. There was no sound from the gloom of the interior, but I must make sure that no one was there.

Scarcely breathing, I entered the house. It was a one-story hovel of two rooms. I searched them both. The house was unoccupied. Then I returned to the door and examined the remaining hinge. To my delight I discovered that I could easily remove the door, and this I did.

I looked up and down the street. There was no one in sight. Lifting the door, I crossed to the wall and leaned the door against it.

Again I searched the street with my eyes. All was clear.

Cautiously I crawled up the door. From its top, precariously gained, I could reach the top of the wall. Then I threw caution to the winds, drew myself up, and dropped to the ground on the opposite side. I could not take the chance of remaining even for an instant on the summit of the wall in plain view of the palace windows on one side and the street on the other.

I recalled the vicious kazars that Skor kept at his castle, and I prayed that he kept none here. But no kazar attacked me, nor did any evidence suggest that my entry had been noted.

Before me loomed the palace, dark and forbidding even though some lights shone within it. The courtyard was flagged, and as barren as that of the castle in the wood.

Crossing quickly to the building I walked along it seeking an entrance. It was three stories high. I saw at least two towers. Many of the windows were barred, but not all. Behind one of those barred windows, perhaps, was Nalte. The task before me was to discover which.

I dared not go to the front of the palace lest I be questioned by the guard. Presently I discovered a small door; it was the only door on this side of the building, but it was securely locked. Carrying my investigation further, I came to an open window. The room beyond was unlighted. I listened but heard no sound; then I vaulted quietly to the sill and dropped within. At last I was inside the palace of the jong of Morov.

Crossing the room, I found a door on the opposite side; and when I drew it open I saw a dimly lighted corridor beyond. And with the opening of the door sounds from the interior of the palace reached my ears.

The corridor was deserted as I stepped into it and made my way in the direction of the sounds I had heard. At a turning I came to a broader and better lighted corridor, but here dead men and women passed to and fro. Some were carrying dishes laden with food in one direction, others were bearing empty dishes in the opposite direction.

I knew that I risked detection and exposure, but I also knew that it was a risk I must take sooner or later. As well now, I thought, as any time. I noticed that these corpses were painted in the semblance of life and health; only their eyes and their shuffling gait revealed the truth. My eyes I could not change, but I kept them lowered as I shuffled into the corridor behind a man carrying a large platter of food.

I followed him to a large room in which two score men and women were seated at a banquet table. Here at last, I thought, were living people–the masters of Kormor. They did not seem a very gay company, but that I could understand in surroundings such as theirs. The men were handsome, the women beautiful. I wondered what had brought them and what kept them in this horrid city of death.

A remarkable feature of the assemblage was the audience that packed the room, leaving only sufficient space for the servants to pass around the table. These people were so well painted that at first I thought them alive too.

Seeing an opportunity to lose my identity in the crowd, I wormed my way behind the rear rank and then gradually worked my way around the room and toward the front rank of the spectators until I stood directly in rear of a large, throne-like chair that stood at the head of the table and which I assumed to be Skor's chair.

Close contact with the men and women watching the banqueters soon disclosed the fact that I was doubtless the only living creature among them, for no make-up, however marvellous, could alter the expressionlessness of those dead eyes or call back the fire of life or the light of soul. Poor creatures! How I pitied them.

And now, from the lower end of the chamber, came a blare of trumpets; and all the banqueters arose and faced in that direction. Four trumpeters marching abreast entered the banquet hall, and behind them came eight warriors in splendid harness. Following these were a man and a woman, partially hidden from my sight by the warriors and the trumpeters marching in front of them. These two were followed by eight more warriors.

And now the trumpeters and the warriors separated and formed an aisle down which the man and the woman walked. Then I saw them, and my heart stood still. Skor and—Duare!

Duare's head was still high–it would be difficult to break that proud spirit–but the loathing, the anguish, the hopelessness in her eyes, struck me like dagger to the heart. Yet, even so, hope bounded in my breast as I saw them, for they were expressions; and they told me that Skor had not yet worked his worst upon her.

They seated themselves, Skor at the head of the table, Duare at his right, scarce three paces from me; and the guests resumed their seats.

I had come for Nalte, and I had found Duare. How was I to rescue her now that I had found her? I realized that I must do nothing precipitate. Here, faced by overwhelming odds in the stronghold of an enemy, I knew that I might accomplish nothing by force.

I looked about the room. On one side were windows, in the centre of the opposite wall was a small door, at the far end the large doors through which all seemed to be entering or leaving; and behind me was another small doorway. I had no plan, but it was well to note the things that I had noted.

I saw Skor pound on the table with his fist. All the guests looked up. Skor raised a goblet, and the guests did likewise.

"To the jong!" he cried.

"To the jong!" repeated the guests.

"Drink!" commanded Skor, and the guests drank.

Then Skor addressed them. It was not a speech; it was a monologue to which all listened. In it occurred what Skor evidently considered an amusing anecdote. When he had narrated it he paused, waiting. There was only silence. Skor scowled. "Laugh!" he snapped, and the guests laughed–hollow, mirthless laughs. It was then, with those laughs, that my suspicions were aroused.

When Skor finished his monologue there was another silence until he commanded, "Applaud!" Skor smiled and bowed in acknowledgment of the ensuing applause just as though it had been spontaneous and genuine.

"Eat!" he commanded, and the guests ate; then he said, "Talk!" and they commenced to converse.

"Let us be gay!" cried Skor. This is a happy moment for Morov. I bring you your future queen!" He pointed to Duare. There was only silence. "Applaud!" growled Skor, and when they had done his bidding he urged them again to be gay. "Let us have laughter," he bid them. "Starting at my left you will take turns laughing, and when the laughter has passed around the table to the future queen you will start over again."

The laughter commenced. It rose and fell as it passed around the table. God, what a travesty on gayety it was!

I had passed closer until I stood directly behind Skor's chair. Had Duare turned her eyes in my direction she must have seen me, but she did not. She sat staring straight before her.

Skor leaned toward her and spoke. "Are they not fine specimens?"

he demanded. "You see I am coming closer and closer to the fulfilment of my dream. Do you not see how different are all the people of Kormor from the mean creatures at my castle? And look at these, the guests at my table. Even their eyes have the semblance of real life. Soon I shall have it–I shall be able to breathe full life into the dead. Then think what a nation I can create! And I shall be jong, and you shall be vadjong."

"I do not wish to be vadjong," replied Duare. "I only wish my liberty."

A dead man sitting across the table from her said, "That is all that any of us wishes, but we shall never get it." It was then his turn to laugh, and he laughed. It was incongruous, horrible. I saw Duare shudder.

Skor's sallow face paled. He glowered at the speaker.

"I am about to give you life," cried the jong angrily, "and you do not appreciate it."

"We do not wish to live," replied the corpse. "We wish death. Let us have death and oblivion again–let us return to our graves in peace."

At these words, Skor flew into a fit of rage. He half rose, and drawing a sword struck at the face of the speaker. The keen blade laid open an ugly wound from temple to chin. The edges of the wound gaped wide, but no blood flowed.

The dead man laughed. "You cannot hurt the dead," he mocked.

Skor was livid. He sought words, but his rage choked him. Flecks of foam whitened his lips. If ever I have looked upon a madman it was then. Suddenly he turned upon Duare.

"You are the cause of this!" he screamed. "Never say such things again before my subjects. You shall be queen! I will make you queen of Morov, a living queen, or I will make you one of these. Which do you choose?"

"Give me death," replied Duare.

"That you shall never have–not real death, only the counterfeit that you see before you–neither life nor death."

At last the ghastly meal drew to a close. Skor arose and motioned Duare to accompany him. He did not leave the room as he had entered it; no trumpeters nor warriors accompanied him. He walked toward the small doorway at the rear of the room, the spectators giving way before him and Duare as they advanced.

So suddenly had Skor risen and turned that I thought he must surely see me; but if he did he did not recognize me, and a moment later he had passed me, and the danger was over. And as he and Duare moved toward the doorway I fell in behind and followed. Each instant I expected to feel a hand upon my shoulder stopping me, but no one seemed to pay any attention to me. I passed through the doorway behind Skor and Duare without a challenge. Even Skor did not turn as he raised the hangings at the doorway and let them fall again behind him.

I moved softly, making no noise. The corridor in which we were was deserted. It was a very short corridor, ending at a heavy door. As Skor threw this door open I saw a room beyond that at first I thought must be a storeroom. It was large and almost completely filled with a heterogeneous collection of odds and ends of furniture, vases, clothing, arms, and pictures. Everything was confusion and disorder, and everything was covered with dust and dirt.

Skor paused for a moment on the threshold, seemingly viewing the room with pride. "What do you think of it?" he demanded.

"Think of what?" asked Duare.

"This beautiful room," he said. "In all Amtor there cannot be a more beautiful room; nowhere else can there be another such collection of beautiful objects; and now to them I am adding the most beautiful of all–you! This, Duare, is to be your room–the private apartment of the queen of Morov."

I stepped in and closed the door behind me, for I had seen that but for us three there was no one else in the apartment; and now seemed as good a time to act as any.

I had not meant to make any noise as I entered. Skor was armed and I was not, and it had been my intention to throw myself upon him from the rear and overpower him before he could have an opportunity to use his weapons against me. But the lock of the door clicked as I closed it, and Skor wheeled and faced me.

## Chapter 19

# In Hiding

As the eyes of the jong of Morov fell upon me he recognized me, and he voiced a sardonic laugh as he whipped out his sword and brought my charge to a sudden, ignominious stop–one does not finish a charge with the point of a sword in one's belly.

"So!" he exclaimed; "it is you? Well, well. It is good to see you again. I did not expect to be so honoured. I thought Fortune had been very kind to me when she returned the two young women. And now you have come! What a merry party we shall have!"

With the last words his tone, which had been sarcastically bantering, changed; he fairly hissed that gay sentence. And the expression on his face changed too. It became suddenly malevolent, and his eyes glittered with the same mad fire of insanity that I had seen there before.

Behind him stood Duare, her wide eyes fixed upon me with incredulity mixed with terror. "Oh, why did you come, Carson?" she cried. "Now he will kill you."

"I will tell you why he came," said Skor. "He came for the other girl, for Nalte, not for you. You have been here a long time, but he did not come. Tonight one of my people seized the girl, Nalte, in Havatoo; and he came immediately to try to rescue her, the fool. I have known for a long time that they were in Havatoo. My spies have seen them there together. I do not know how he got here, but here he is–and here he stays, forever."

He poked me in the belly with the point of his sword. "How would you like to die, fool?" he snarled. "A quick thrust through the heart, perhaps. That would mutilate you least. You will make a fine specimen. Come, now, what have you to say? Remember this will be the last chance you will have to think with your own brain; hereafter I shall do your thinking for you. You will sit in my banquet hall, and you will laugh when I tell you to laugh. You will see the two women who loved you, but they will shrink from the touch of your clammy hands, from your cold, dead lips. And whenever you see them they will be with Skor in whose veins flows the bright blood of life."

My plight seemed quite hopeless. The sword at my belly was long, keen, and two-edged. I might have grasped it, but its edges were so sharp that it would have slipped through my fingers, severing them as it plunged into my body. Yet that I intended doing. I would not wait like a sheep the lethal blow of the butcher.

"You do not reply," said Skor. "Very well, we will have it over quickly!" He drew back his sword hand for the thrust.

Duare was standing behind him beside a table littered with the sort of junk to which Skor seemed partial–his crazy objects d'art. I was waiting to seize the blade when he thrust. Skor hesitated a moment, I presume to better enjoy my final agony; but in that he was disappointed. I would not give him that satisfaction; and so, to rob him of most of his pleasure, I laughed in his face.

At that moment Duare raised a heavy vase from the table, held it high above her, and crashed it down on Skor's head. Without a sound he sank to the floor.

I leaped across his body to take Duare into my arms, but with a palm against my breast she pushed me away.

"Do not touch me!" she snapped. "If you want to get out of Kormor there is no time to be wasted. Come with me! I know where the girl you came to rescue is imprisoned."

Her whole attitude toward me seemed to have changed, and my pride was piqued. In silence I followed her from the room. She led me into the corridor along which we had approached the room to which I had followed her and Skor. Opening a door at one side, she hurried along another corridor and stopped before a heavily bolted door.

"She is in here," she said.

I drew the bolts and opened the door. Standing in the middle of the room beyond, looking straight at me, was Nalte. As she recognized me she gave a little cry of joy and, running toward me, threw her arms about me.

"Oh, Carson! Carson!" she cried. "I knew that you would come; something told me that you would surely come."

"We must hurry," I told her. "We must get out of here."

I turned toward the door. Duare stood there, her chin in the air, her eyes flashing; but she said nothing. Nalte saw her then and recognized her. "Oh, it is you!" she exclaimed. "You are alive! I am so glad. We thought that you had been killed."

Duare seemed puzzled by the evident sincerity of Nalte's manner, as though she had not expected that Nalte would be glad that she was alive. She softened a little. "If we are to escape from Kormor, though I doubt that we can, we must not remain here," she said. "I think that I know a way out of the castle–a secret way that Skor uses. He showed me the door once during some strange mood of his insanity; but he has the key to the door on his person, and we must get that before we can do anything else."

We returned to the room where we had left Skor's body, and as I entered it I saw the jong of Morov stir and try to rise. He was not dead, though how he had survived that shattering blow I do not know.

I ran toward him and threw him down. He was still only half conscious and made little or no resistance. I suppose I should have killed him, but I shrank from killing a defenceless man–even a fiend like Skor. Instead I bound and gagged him; then I searched him and found his keys.

After that Duare led us to the second floor of the palace and to a large room furnished in the bizarre taste that was Skor's. She crossed the apartment and drew aside a grotesque hanging, revealing a small door behind

"Here is the door," she said; "see if you can find a key to fit the lock."

I tried several keys, and at last found the right one. The opened door revealed a narrow corridor which we entered after rearranging the hangings, and then closed the door behind us. A few steps brought us to the top of a spiral staircase. I went first, carrying Skor's sword which I had taken from him with his keys. The two girls followed closely behind me.

The stairway was lighted, for which I was glad, since it permitted us to move more rapidly and with greater safety. At the bottom was another corridor. I waited there until both girls stood beside me.

"Do you know where this corridor leads?" I asked Duare.

"No," she replied. "All that Skor said was that he could get out of the castle this way without any one seeing him–he always came and went this way. Practically everything that he did, the most common-place things in life, he veiled with mystery and secrecy."

"From the height of that stairway," I said, I believe that we are below the ground level of the palace. I wish that we knew where this corridor ends, but there is only one way to find out. Come on!"

This corridor was but dimly illuminated by the light from the stairway, and the farther we went from the stairway the darker it became. It ran straight for a considerable distance, ending at the foot of a wooden stairway. Up this I groped my way only a few steps, when my head came in contact with a solid substance above me. I reached up and felt of the obstruction. It consisted of planking and was obviously a trap door. I tried to raise it, but could not. Then I searched around its edges with my fingers, and at last I found that which I sought–a latch. Tripping it, I pushed again; and the door gave. I opened it only an inch or two, but no light showed in the crack. Then I opened it wider and raised my head through the aperture.

Now I could see more, but not much more–only the dark interior of a room with a single small window through which the night light of Amtor showed dimly. Grasping the sword of the jong of Morov more tightly I ascended the stairway and entered the room. I heard no sound.

The girls had followed me and now stood just behind me. I could hear them breathing. We stood waiting, listening. Slowly my eyes became accustomed to the darkness, and I made out what I thought was a door beside the single window. I crossed to it and felt; it was a door.

Cautiously I opened it and looked out into one of the sordid streets of Kormor. I peered about in an effort to orient myself and saw that the street was one of those that extended directly away from the palace which I could see looming darkly behind its wall at my right.

"Come!" I whispered, and with the girls behind me I stepped out into the street and turned to the left. "If we meet any one," I cautioned, "remember to walk like the dead, shuffle along as you will see me do. Keep your eyes on the ground; it is our eyes that will most surely betray us."

"Where are we going?" asked Duare in a whisper.

"I am going to try to find the house through which I came into the city," I replied; "but I don't know that I can do so."

"And if you can't?"

"Then we shall have to make an attempt to scale the city wall; but we shall find a way, Duare."

"What difference will it make?" she murmured, half to herself. "If we escape from here there will only be something else. I think I would rather be dead than go on any more."

The note of hopelessness in her voice was so unlike Duare that it shocked me. "You mustn't feel like that, Duare," I expostulated. "If we can get back to Havatoo you will be safe and happy, and I have a surprise there for you that will give you new hope." I was thinking of the plane in which we might hope to find Vepaja, the country that I could see she had about despaired of ever seeing again.

She shook her head. "There is no hope, no hope of happiness, ever, for Duare."

Some figures approaching us along the dusty street put an end to our conversation. With lowered eyes and shuffling feet we neared them.

They passed, and I breathed again in relief.

It would be useless to recount our futile search for the house I could not find. All the remainder of the night we searched, and with the coming of dawn I realized that we must find a place to hide until night came again.

I saw a house with a broken door, no unusual sight in dismal Kormor; and investigation indicated that it was tenantless. We entered and ascended to the second floor. Here, in a back room, we prepared to await the ending of the long day that lay ahead of us.

We were all tired, almost exhausted; and so we lay down on the rough planks and sought to sleep. We did not talk; each seemed occupied with his own dismal thoughts. Presently, from their regular breathing, I realized that the girls were both asleep; and very shortly thereafter I must have fallen asleep myself.

How long I slept I do not know. I was awakened by footsteps in an adjoining room. Some one was moving about, and I heard mutterings as of a person talking to himself.

Slowly I rose to my feet, holding Skor's sword in readiness. Its uselessness against the dead did not occur to me, yet had it, I still would have felt safer with the sword in my hand.

The footsteps approached the door to the room in which we had sought sanctuary, and a moment later an old woman stopped upon the threshold and looked at me in astonishment.

What are you doing here?" she demanded. If she was surprised, no less was I; for old age was something I had never before seen in Amtor. Her voice awakened the girls, and I heard them rising to their feet behind me.

What are you doing here?" repeated the old woman querulously. "Get out of my house, accursed corpses! I'll have none of the spawn of Skor's evil brain in my house!"

I looked at her in astonishment. "Aren't you dead?" I demanded.

"Of course I'm not dead!" she snapped.

"Neither are we," I told her.

"Eh? Not dead?" She came closer. "Let me see your eyes. No, they do not look like dead eyes; but they say that Skor has found some foul way in which to put a false light of life into dead eyes."

"We are not dead," I insisted.

"Then what are you doing in Kormor? I thought that I knew all of the living men and women here, and I do not know you. Are the women alive too?"

"Yes, we are all alive." I thought quickly. I wondered if I might trust her with our secret and seek her aid. She evidently hated Skor, and we were already in her power if she wished to denounce us. I felt that we could not be much worse off in any event. "We were prisoners of Skor. We escaped. We want to get out of the city. We are at your mercy. Will you help us?–or will you turn us over to Skor?"

"I won't turn you over to Skor," she snapped. "I wouldn't turn a dead mistal over to that fiend; but I don't know how I can help you. You can't get out of Kormor. The dead sentries along the wall never sleep."

"I got into Kormor without being seen by a sentry," I said. "If I could only find the house I could get out again."

"What house?" she demanded.

"The house at the end of the tunnel that runs under Gerlat kum Rov to Havatoo."

"A tunnel to Havatoo! I never heard of such a thing. Are you sure?"

"I came through it last night."

She shook her head. "None of us ever heard of it–and if we who live here cannot find it, how could you, a stranger, hope to? But I'll help as much as I can. At least I can hide you and give you food. We always help one another here in Kormor, we who are alive."

"A few," she replied. "Skor has not succeeded in hunting us all down yet. We live a mean life, always hiding; but it is life. If he found us he would make us like those others."

The old woman came closer. "I cannot believe that you are alive," she said. "Perhaps you are tricking me." She touched my face, and then ran her palms over the upper part of my body. "You are warm," she said, and then she felt my pulse. "Yes, you are alive."

Similarly she examined Duare and Nalte, and at last she was convinced that we had told her the truth. "Come," she said, "I will take you to a better place than this. You will be more comfortable. I do not use this house very often."

She led us down stairs and out into a yard at the rear of which stood another house. It was a mean house, poorly furnished. She took us into a back room and told us to remain there.

"I suppose you want food," she said.

"And water," added Nalte. "I have had none since yesterday evening."

"You poor thing," said the old woman. "I'll get it for you. How young and pretty you are. Once I was young and pretty too."

"Why have you aged?" I asked. "I thought that all the people of Amtor held the secret of longevity."

"Aye, but how may one obtain the serum in Kormor? We had it once, before Skor came; but he took it away from us. He said that he would create a new race that would not require it, for they would never grow old. The effects of my last inoculation have worn off, and now I am growing old and shall die. It is not so bad to die–if Skor does not find one's corpse. We of the living here bury our dead in secret beneath the floors of our houses. My mate and our two children lie beneath this floor. But I must go and fetch food and water for you. I shall not be gone long." And with that, she left us.

"Poor old creature," said Nalte. "She has nothing to look forward to except the grave, with the chance that Skor may rob her of even that poor future."

"How strange she looked!" There was a shocked expression in Duare's eyes as she spoke. "So that is old age! I never saw it before. That is the way I should look some day, were it not for the serum! How ghastly Oh, I should rather die than be like that. Old age! Oh, how terrible!"

Here was a unique experience. I was witnessing the reactions of a nineteen-year-old girl who had never before seen the ravages of old age, and I could not but wonder if the subconscious effect of old age on youth accustomed to seeing it was not similar. But these meditations were interrupted by the return of the old woman, and I caught a new insight into the character of Duare.

As the old woman entered the room, her arms laden, Duare ran forward and took the things from her. "You should have let me come with you and help you," she said. "I am younger and stronger."

Then she placed the food and water upon a table, and with a sweet smile she put an arm about the withered shoulders of the old crone and drew her toward a bench. "Sit down," she said. "Nalte and I will prepare the food. You just sit here and rest until it is ready, and then we shall all eat together."

The old woman looked at her in astonishment for a moment and then burst into tears. Duare dropped to the bench beside her and put her arms about her.

"Why do you cry?" she asked.

"I don't know why I cry," sobbed the old creature. "I feel like singing, but I cry. It has been so long since I have heard kind words, since any one has cared whether I was happy or sad, tired or rested."

I saw the tears come to Duare's eyes and to Nalte's, and they had to busy themselves with the preparation of the food to hide their emotions.

That night a dozen of the living of Kormor came to the house of Kroona, the old woman who had befriended us. They were all very old, some of them older than Kroona. They laughed at Kroona's fears that Skor wanted them; and pointed out, as evidently they had many times before, that if it was old bodies Skor wanted he long since could have found them, for their old age was ample evidence that they were of the living. But Kroona insisted that they were all in danger; and I soon realized that it was her pet obsession, without which she would probably be more miserable than she was with it. She got a great thrill out of leading a life of constant danger and hiding first in one house and then in another.

But they were all of one opinion that we were in great danger, and the dear old things pledged themselves to help us in every way they could–to bring us food and water and hide us from our enemies. That was all that they could do, for none of them believed that it was possible to escape from Kormor.

Early the following morning a very old man, one of the visitors of the previous evening, hobbled into the house. He was perturbed and greatly excited. His palsied hands were trembling. "They are searching the city for you," he whispered. "There is a terrible story of what you did to Skor and of what Skor will do to you when he finds you. All night and all day last night be lay bound and helpless where you left him; then one of his creatures found and released him. Now the whole city is being scoured for you. They may be here any minute."

"What can we do?" asked Duare, "Where can we hide?"

"You can do nothing," said the old man, "but wait until they come. There is no place in all Kormor that they will not search."

"We can do something," said Nalte; then she turned to our informant. "Can you get us paints such as the corpses use to make themselves appear like living men?"

"Yes," said the old man.

"Well, go quickly and fetch them," urged Nalte.

The old man hobbled out of the room, mumbling to himself.

"It is the only way, Nalte," I cried. "I believe that if he returns in time we can fool them; dead men are not very bright."

It seemed a long time before the old man came back; but he came finally, and he brought a large box of makeup with him. It was quite an elaborate affair which he said that he had obtained from a friend of his, a living man, whose craft was applying the makeup to corpses.

Quickly Nalte went to work on Duare and soon had transformed her into an old woman with lines and wrinkles and hollows. The hair was the most difficult problem to solve, but we finally succeeded in approximating the results we desired, though we used up all of the cosmetician's white pigment, rubbing it into our hair.

Duare and I together worked on Nalte, for we knew that we had no time to spare, the old man having brought word when he returned with the make-up that the searchers were working in the next block and coming our way; then Nalte and Duare transformed me into a very sad looking old man.

Kroona said that we should each have some task that we could be performing when the searchers arrived, to that we might appear natural. She gave Duare and Nalte some old rags which they might pretend to be fashioning into garments, and she sent me out into the yard to dig a hole. It was fortunate that she did so, because the association of ideas resulting reminded me that I must hide Skor's sword. Were that found we were doomed.

I wrapped it up in a piece of cloth and carried it out into the yard with me, and you may take my word for it that I dug one hole there in record time. When I had covered the sword with dirt I started digging another hole beside it and threw that dirt also on the spot above the weapon.

I had just finished when the yard gate was thrown open and a score of dead men came shuffling in. "We are looking for the strangers who escaped from the palace," said one. "Are they here?"

I cupped my hand behind my ear and said, "Eh?"

The fellow repeated his question, shouting very loud, and again I did the same thing and said, "Eh?" Then he gave up and went on into the house, followed by the others.

I heard them searching in there, and every instant I expected to hear cries of excitement when one of them discovered and pierced the thin disguises of Duare and Nalte.

## Chapter 20

# Under Suspicion

Skor's creature's searched Kroona's house far more carefully than they would have searched that of one of their own kind, for Skor must have assumed that of all the people in Kormor the living would be most likely to aid the living; but at last they came out and went away. And I sat down on the pile of dirt I had dug and mopped the perspiration from my forehead, nor was it the sweat of toil. I think that for fifteen minutes I had come as near to sweating blood as a man can.

When I went into the house I found Duare, Nalte, and Kroona just sitting there in dazed silence. They couldn't seem to realize that we had passed through the ordeal successfully.

"Well," I said, "that's over."

My voice seemed to break the spell.

"Do you know what saved us?" demanded Nalte.

"Why, our disguises, of course," I replied.

"Yes," she admitted, "they helped, but our real salvation was the stupidity of the searchers. They scarcely looked at us. They were hunting for somebody who was hidden, and because we were not hiding they didn't give us a second thought."

"Do you think we might remove the paint now?" asked Duare. "It is very uncomfortable."

"I think we should not remove it at all," I replied. "As we know, they won't find us in this search; so Skor may order another search, and next time we may not have time to disguise ourselves even if we are lucky enough to get the materials again."

"I suppose you are right," said Duare, "and after all the discomfort is not much by comparison to what we have already gone through."

"The disguises have one advantage," said Nalte. "We can move about more freely without danger of detection. We won't have to sit in this stuffy little back room all the time, and I for one am going to the front of the house and get a breath of fresh air."

It was not a bad suggestion, and Duare and I joined Nalte while Kroona went about some household duties. The front room on the second floor, to which we went, overlooked the street. We could hear the searchers ransacking the house next door, and we could see the pedestrians shuffling along the dusty street.

Suddenly Nalte seized my arm and pointed. "See that man?" she exclaimed in an excited whisper.

Shuffling along the street was a large corpse painted in the semblance of life. His trappings were finer than those ordinarily seen in Kormor. Only his peculiar gait revealed to the initiated eye the fact that he was not as alive as we.

"Yes, I see him," I replied. "What about him?"

"He is the man that abducted me from Havatoo!"

"Are you sure?" I demanded.

"Absolutely," replied Nalte. "As long as I live I shall never forget that face."

A plan, perhaps I had better call it an inspiration, shot into my mind. "I am going to follow him," I said. "I shall be back soon; hope for the best." I turned and hurried from the room.

A moment later I was in the street. The fellow was only a short distance ahead of me. If my guess was correct he would lead me eventually to the entrance to the tunnel that leads to Havatoo. Perhaps not today, but if I learned where he lived today; then some other day.

His gait was more rapid than that of the average Kormoran, and he walked as though with a definite purpose in view. I judged that he was one of Skor's more successful experiments and that for this reason he had been chosen as one of the jong's agents in Havatoo, where the ordinary run of Kormoran corpses could not long have passed themselves off as living men.

As I followed him I noted carefully every detail of the street in which we were; so that I would not again be unable to return to my starting point. When presently he turned into a street leading toward the river my hopes rose, and I noted carefully the buildings at the intersection.

Near the river the fellow turned into a small alley, followed it to the next street, and then turned again toward the river. Directly ahead of us, even before he turned into it, I saw and recognized the building beneath which lay the Kormor end of the tunnel.

At the gateway leading into the yard before the house the man turned for the first time and looked behind him, I presume to see if he was being observed. Then he saw me.

There was nothing for me to do but keep on toward him. I kept my eyes on the ground and paid no attention to him as I approached him, though I could almost feel his gaze upon me. It seemed an eternity before I reached him. I was about to breathe a sigh of relief as I passed him, then he spoke to me.

"Who are you and what are you doing here?" he demanded.

"I am looking for another house to live in," I cackled. "The doors and the windows have all fallen off mine." "There are no houses here for you," he snapped. "Your kind is not allowed in this district. Get out of here and never let me see you here again."

"Yes," I replied meekly, and turned back.

To my great joy he let me go, and a moment later I had turned into the alley and was hidden from his view. But I had learned what I wanted to know, and my blood was tingling with happiness. Now only the. worst of ill fortune could prevent me guiding Duare and Nalte back to the safety of Havatoo.

As I made my way through the streets of Kormor toward the house of Kroona my mind was filled with thoughts and plans for escape. I was determined to leave as soon as darkness fell, and already I was looking forward to and planning on what I should do upon my return to Havatoo.

As I entered Kroona's house I saw immediately, even before any one had a chance to speak, that something was amiss. Duare and Nalte both rushed toward me, and it was evident that both were perturbed. Kroona and the old man who had brought us the pigments with which we had disguised ourselves were cackling together excitedly.

"At last you are back!" cried Nalte. "We thought that you would never come."

"Perhaps it is not too late even now," said Duare.

"I wanted them to come with me and let me hide them," croaked Kroona, "but neither one of them would leave without you. They said that if you were to be taken then they would be taken too."

"What in the world are you all talking about?" I demanded. What has happened

"It is soon told," said the old man who had brought us the make-up. "The cosmetician from whom I borrowed the materials to change you into old people has betrayed us in order to curry favour with Skor. A man heard him tell his servant to go to the palace and inform

Skor that he would lead Skor's men to this hiding place of yours. The man was a friend of mine and came and told me. Skor's men may be here at any minute now."

I thought rapidly; then I turned to Duare and Nalte. "Get your make-up off as quickly as you can," I directed, "and I will do the same."

"But then we shall be lost for certain," exclaimer Duare.

"On the contrary," I replied as I commenced to remove the pigment from my blond head.

"They will know us at once without our disguises," insisted Duare, but I was glad to see that both she and Nalte were following my example and removing the paint from their hair and faces.

"Our own youth will be the best disguise we can adopt in this emergency," I explained. "These creatures of Skor are none too intelligent, and having been sent to find three fugitives who have disguised themselves as very old people they will be looking only for those who appear very old. If we can get out of the house before they come I think we have a good chance to avoid detection."

We worked rapidly and soon had the last vestiges of our disguises removed; then we thanked Kroona and the old man, bid them goodbye, and left the house. As we entered the street we saw a body of warriors approaching from the direction of the palace.

"We were not quite in time," said Nalte. "Shall we turn and run for it?"

"No," I replied. "That would only arouse their suspicions immediately and they would pursue and most certainly overtake us. Come! We shall go and meet them."

"What!" demanded Duare in astonishment. "Are we going to give ourselves up?"

"By no means," I replied. "We are going to take a great chance, but there is no alternative. If they see three people walking away from them they will investigate, and if they do that we may be recognized; but if they see us approaching them they will believe that we do not fear anything from them and will be convinced therefore that we are not those whom they seek. Walk with the shuffling gait of the dead, and keep your eyes on the ground. Duare, you walk ahead, Nalte a few paces behind you; I shall cross to the other side of the street. By separating we shall attract less attention; they are looking for three people whom they expect to find together."

"I hope your reasoning is correct," said Duare, but it was evident that she was sceptical. I was none too enthusiastic about the plan myself.

I crossed the street to the side along which the warriors were approaching, knowing that there was less likelihood that any of them would recognize me than that they would know Duare, who had been in Skor's palace for some time.

I must admit that I felt none too comfortable as the distance between me and the warriors steadily lessened, but I kept my eyes on the ground and shuffled slowly along.

As I came abreast of them their leader halted and addressed me. My heart stood still. "Where is the house of Kroona?" he asked.

"I do not know," I replied and shuffled on my way. Momentarily I expected to be seized, but the warriors went on their way and let me go on mine. My ruse had been successful!

As soon as I felt that it was safe I crossed to the opposite side of the street, and as I caught up with the two girls I told them to follow behind me but not too closely.

It still lacked an hour until sunset, and I did not dare risk approaching the entrance to the tunnel until after dark. In the meantime we must find a place to hide and keep off the streets where every moment we were in danger of arousing suspicion.

Turning into a side street I soon found a deserted house, of which there are many in Kormor; and presently we were in hiding again.

Both girls were dejected. I could tell by their silence and listlessness. The future must have seemed hopeless to them, yet they voiced no complaints.

"I have some good news for you," I said.

Duare looked at me with scarcely any indication of interest, as though there never could be any good news for her again. She had been unusually silent since our escape from the palace. She seldom spoke unless directly addressed; and she avoided speech with Nalte as much as possible, although her manner toward her was not definitely unfriendly.

"What is the good news?" demanded Nalte.

"I have found the entrance to the tunnel to Havatoo," I replied.

The effect of that statement upon Nalte was electrical, but it seemed to arouse only passive interest in Duare. "In Havatoo," she said, "I shall be as far as ever from Vepaja."

"But your life will not be in danger," I reminded her.

She shrugged. "I do not know that I care to live," she replied.

"Don't be discouraged, Duare," I begged. "Once we are in Havatoo I am confident that I shall discover a way to find Vepaja and return you to your people." I was thinking of the plane ready and waiting in its hangar on Kantum Lat, but I didn't say anything about it. I wanted to save it as a surprise for her; and, anyway, we were not yet in Havatoo.

The two hours that we waited until complete darkness enveloped the city were as long a two hours as I have ever spent; but at last it seemed safe to attempt to reach the silent, deserted house near the river front, where all our hopes were cantered.

The street was deserted when we left the building where we had been hiding; I was certain of my way to our destination, and without delay or adventure we at last came in sight of the decaying structure that hid the entrance to our avenue of escape.

I led the girls into the buildings, and there we huddled in the dark, listening. I regretted then that I had been unable to retrieve the sword I had taken from Skor and buried in the yard of Kroona's home. It would have given me a feeling of far greater security than I now enjoyed.

Satisfied at last that we were the sole occupants of the building and that no one had followed us, I crossed to the doorway that hid the entrance to the tunnel, Duare and Nalte close behind me.

I had no difficulty in finding the latch, and a moment later we were descending into the dark corridor with liberty and safety almost in our grasp.

There was a chance that we might meet one of Skor's creatures returning from Havatoo; but I felt that everything was in our favour inasmuch as one of them had just crossed in the opposite direction, and there had never been any evidence that they were in Havatoo in great numbers. It was my opinion that the two that set upon Nalte and me were alone in that venture, and if that were true it was also doubtless true that Skor never had more than a couple of his retainers in Havatoo at the same time. I certainly hoped that I was right.

In silence, through the utter darkness, we groped our way along the cold, moist corridor beneath the River of Death. I moved more rapidly than I had when I had come through it to Kormor, for I knew now that no pitfalls lay in my path.

At last I felt the stairs leading upward at the tunnel's end, and a moment later I stopped behind the door that would let us into Havatoo. I did not wait; I did not listen. Nothing could have stopped me then. I would have grappled a dozen of the gruesome corpses of Kormor had they stood in my way, and I believe that I should have overcome them, so desperate was my mood.

But we met neither dead nor living as we stepped out onto the lower floor of the dismal building off the Havatoo Lat. Quickly we crossed to the front of the building and out through the door there to the street beyond, and a moment later we stood in the Havatoo Lat with its brilliant lights and its two streams of traffic.

We were a conspicuous trio in our mean garments of rags with which we had sought to disguise ourselves in Kormor, and many were the suspicious glances cast in our direction.

As quickly as I could I hailed a public conveyance and instructed the driver to take us to the home of Ero Shan, and as we settled down upon the cushions we relaxed for the first time in many a day.

We talked a great deal during the drive, particularly Nalte and I. Duare was very quiet. She spoke of the beauty of Havatoo and the wonders that surrounded us, all strange and new to her, but only briefly and then lapsed into silence again.

Our driver had eyed us suspiciously when we entered his car, and when he deposited us in front of the house of Ero Shan he behaved peculiarly.

But Ero Shan was delighted to see us. He ordered food and drink, and plied us with questions until he had had the whole story from us several times. He congratulated me upon finding Duare, but I could see that his greatest happiness lay in the return of Nalte.

The girls were tired and needed rest, and we were preparing to take them to Nalte's home when the first blow fell that was to put the lives of two of us in jeopardy and plunge us all from the heights of happiness to the depths of despair.

There was a summons at the main entrance, and presently a servant entered the room. Behind him was a file of warriors commanded by an officer.

Ero Shan looked up in surprise. He knew the officer and called him by name, asking him what brought him here with armed men.

"I am sorry, Ero Shan," the man replied, "but I have orders from the Sanjong itself to arrest three suspicious appearing people who were seen to enter your house earlier in the evening."

"But," exclaimed Ero Shan, "no one has entered my house but Carson Napier, whom you know, and these two young women. They are all my friends."

The officer was eyeing our mean apparel and evidently not without suspicion. "These must be those I was sent to arrest if no one else has entered your house this evening," he said.

There was nothing to do but accompany the warriors and this we did. Ero Shan came with us, and a short time later we were before an investigating board of three men. The complaining witness was the driver who had brought us from the house that hid the entrance to the tunnel to Ero Shan's. He said that he lived in the neighbourhood, and having known of the abduction of Nalte he was immediately suspicious when he saw three people, garbed as we were, in the vicinity of the place.

He accused us of being spies from Kormor and insisted that we were but painted corpses like the man I had grappled with at the time of the abduction of Nalte.

The examining board listened to my story; then they examined Nalte and Duare briefly. They questioned Ero Shan concerning us, and without leaving the room they discharged Nalte and myself and ordered Duare back for a further examination by the official examining board the following day.

I thought that they seemed a little suspicious of Duare; and so did Ero Shan, though he only admitted this after we had returned the girls to Nalte's home and were alone.

"Justice sometimes miscarries in Havatoo," he said gravely. "The loathing that we feel for Kormor and everything connected with it colours all our decisions in matters concerning it. Duare admits having been in Kormor for some time. She admits having resided in the palace of Skor, the jong. The examining board knows nothing about her other than what she claims and what you tell them, but they do not know that they can believe either of you. You will recall that the result of your examination was not such as to create considerable confidence in you.

"And you think that Duare may be in danger?" I asked.

"I cannot tell," he replied. "Everything may come out all right; but, on the other hand, if the board has the slightest suspicion concerning Duare it will order her destroyed, for our theory of justice is that it is better to do an injustice to a single individual than to risk the safety and welfare of many. Sometimes that policy is a cruel one, but results have demonstrated that it is better for the race than a policy of weak sentimentalism

I did not sleep well that night. The weight of a great fear for the outcome of tomorrow's trial oppressed me.

## CHAPTER 21

# Flight

I was not permitted to accompany Duare to her examination. She was placed in the charge of the same woman who had guarded Nalte at the time of her examination, Hara Es.

To pass the hours until the result should be made known, I went to the hangar to inspect my plane. It was in perfect condition. The motor hummed almost noiselessly. I could not, under ordinary circumstances, have withstood the urge to have the ship wheeled out onto the plain before the city for a trial flight; but my mind was so distraught with apprehension concerning the fate of Duare that I had no heart for anything.

I spent an hour alone in the hangar. None of my assistants were there, they having all returned to their ordinary duties after the completion of the plane. Then I returned to the house that I shared with Ero Shan.

He was not there. I tried to read, but I could not concentrate long enough to know what I was reading about. My eyes followed the strange Amtorian characters, but my thoughts were with Duare. At last I gave it up and walked in the garden. An unreasoning terror enveloped me like a shroud, numbing my faculties.

How long I walked I do not know, but at last my sad reveries were interrupted by the approach of footsteps through the house. I knew that Ero Shan must be coming to the garden. I stood waiting, looking toward the doorway through which he must come; and the instant that I saw him my heart turned cold. I read the confirmation of my worst fears in the expression on his face.

He came and laid a hand upon my shoulder. "I have bad news for you, my friend," he said.

"I know," I replied; "I read it in your eyes. They have ordered her destroyed?"

"It is a miscarriage of justice," he said, "but there is no appeal. We must accept the decision as the board's honest conviction that they are thus serving the best interests of the city."

"Is there nothing I can do?" I asked.

"Nothing," he replied.

"Won't they let me take her away from Havatoo?"

"No; they are so afraid of the contaminating influence of Skor and his creatures that they will never permit one to live that falls into their hands."

"But she is not one of Skor's creatures!" I insisted.

"I am quite sure that they had their doubts, but the benefit of the doubt is given to the city and not to the accused. There is nothing more to be done."

"Do you think they would let me see her?" I asked.

"It is possible," he replied. "For some reason she is not to be destroyed until tomorrow."

"Will you try to arrange it for me, Ero Shan?"

"Certainly," he replied. "Wait here, and I will see what I can do."

I have never spent such long and bitter hours as those while I was awaiting the return of Ero Shan. Never before had I felt so helpless and hopeless in the face of an emergency. Had these been ordinary men with whom I had to deal, I might have seen somewhere a ray of hope, but there was none here. Their uprightness precluded the possibility that I might influence even a minor guard by bribery; they could not be moved by an appeal to sentiment; the cold, hard logic of their reasoning left their minds impregnable fortresses of conviction that it was useless to assail.

I have said that I was hopeless, but that was not entirely true. Upon what my hope fed I do not know, but it seemed so impossible to believe that Duare was to be destroyed that my mind must in some slight measure have been stunned.

It was dark before Ero Shan returned. I could read neither hope nor despair in his expression as he entered the room where I had finally gone to await him. He appeared very serious and very tired.

"Well?" I demanded. "What is the verdict?"

"I had a hard time of it," he said. "I had to go all the way up to the Sanjong, but at last I got permission for you to visit her."

"Where is she? When may I see her?"

"I will take you to her now," he replied.

After we entered his car I asked him how he had accomplished it.

"I finally took Nalte with me," he replied. "She knew more about you and all that you and Duare have passed through together than any one else in Havatoo. For a while I almost thought that she was going to persuade the Sanjong to reverse the verdict against Duare, and it was solely through her appeal that they at last gave their consent to this last meeting.

"I learned a great deal about you and Duare from Nalte, much more than you have ever told me; and I learned something else."

"What was that?" I asked as he paused.

"I learned that I love Nalte," he replied.

"And did you learn that she loves you?"

"Yes. Were it not for your unhappiness I should be quite the happiest man in Havatoo tonight. But what made you think that Nalte loved me?"

"She told me so."

"And you did not tell me?" he asked reproachfully.

"I could not," I replied, Until after I knew that you loved her."

"I suppose not. She told me that you were planning on taking her back to Andoo; but now that won't be necessary–she seems quite content to remain in Havatoo."

We had been driving along the Korgan Lat toward the stadium, and now Ero Shan turned into a side street and stopped before a small house.

"Here we are," he said. "This is the house of Hara Es, in whose charge Duare has been placed. Hara Es is expecting you. I shall wait out here. You are to be allowed to remain with Duare for five vir."

Five vir are a little over twenty minutes of earth time. It seemed all too short, but it was better than nothing. I went to the door of the house, and in answer to my summons Hara Es admitted me.

"I have been expecting you," she said. "Come with me."

She led me up to the second floor and unlocking a door, pushed it open. "Go in," she directed. "In five vir I shall come for you."

As I entered the room Duare rose from a couch and faced me. Hara Es dosed the door and locked it. I heard her footsteps as she descended the stairs. We were alone, Duare and I, for the first time in what seemed an eternity to me.

"Why did you come here?" asked Duare in a tired voice.

"You ask me that!" I exclaimed. "You know why I came."

She shook her head. "You cannot do anything for me; no one can. I supposed you would come if you could help me, but as you can't I do not know why you came."

"If for no other reason, because I love you. Is not that reason enough?"

"Do not speak to me of love," she said, looking at me queerly.

I determined not to make her last moments more unhappy by pressing unwelcome attention upon her. I sought to cheer her, but she said that she was not unhappy."

"I am not afraid to die, Carson Napier," she said. "As it seems impossible that, living, I should ever return to Vepaja, I prefer to die. I am not happy. I can never be happy.

"Why could you never be happy?" I demanded.

"That is my secret; I shall take it to the grave with me. Let us not speak of it any more."

"I don't wish you to die, Duare. You must not die!" I exclaimed .

"I know that you feel that way, Carson, but what are we to do about it?"

"There must be something we can do. How many are there in this house besides Hara Es and yourself?"

"There is no one."

Suddenly a mad hope possessed me. I searched the room with my eyes. It was bare of all except absolute necessities. I saw nothing with which I might carry out my plan. Time was flying. Hara Es would soon return. My eyes fell upon the sarong like scarf that Duare wore, the common outer garment of Amtorian women.

"Let me take this," I said, stepping to her side.

"What for?" she demanded.

"Never mind. Do as I say! We have no time to argue! Duare had long since learned to submerge her pride when my tone told her that an emergency confronted us and to obey me promptly. She did so now. Quickly she unwound the scarf from about her and handed it to me.

"Here it is," she said. What are you going to do with it?"

"Wait and see. Stand over there on the right side of the room. Here comes Hara Es now; I hear her on the stairs."

I stepped quickly to one side of the door so that I should be behind it and hidden from Hara Es as she entered. Then I waited. More than my own life lay in the balance, yet I was not nervous. My heart beat as quietly as though I were contemplating nothing more exciting than a pleasant social visit.

I heard Hara Es stop before the door. I heard the key turn in the lock. Then the door swung open and Hara Es stepped into the room. As she did so I seized her by the throat from behind and pushed the door shut with my foot.

"Don't make a sound," I warned, "or I shall have to kill you."

She did not lose her poise for an instant. "You are very foolish," she said. "This will not save Duare, and it will mean your death. You cannot escape from Havatoo."

I made no reply, but worked quickly and in silence. I bound her securely with the scarf and then gagged her. When I had finished I raised her from the floor and placed her on the couch.

"I am sorry, Hara Es, for what I was compelled to do. I am going now to get rid of Ero Shan. He will know nothing of what I have done. Please be sure to inform the Sanjong that Ero Shan is in no way responsible for what has happened–or what is going to happen. I shall leave you here until I can get away from Ero Shan without arousing his suspicions.

"In the meantime, Duare, watch Hara Es closely until I return. See that she does not loosen her bonds."

I stooped and picked the key from the floor where Hara Es had dropped it; then I quit the room, locking the door after me. A moment later I was in the car with Ero Shan.

"Let's get home as quickly as possible," I said; then I lapsed into silence, a silence which Ero Shan, respecting what he thought to be my sorrow, did not break.

He drove rapidly, but it seemed an eternity before he steered the car into the garage at the house. There being no thieves in Havatoo, locks are unnecessary; so our garage doors stood wide open as they always were except in inclement weather. My car, facing toward the street, stood there.

"You have eaten scarcely anything all day," said Ero Shan as we entered the house; "suppose we have something now."

"No, thanks," I replied. "I am going to my room. I could not eat now."

He laid a hand upon my arm and pressed it gently, but he did not say anything; then he turned and left me. A wonderful friend was Ero Shan. I hated to deceive him, but I would have deceived anyone to save Duare.

I went to my room, but only long enough to procure weapons; then I returned to the garage. As I stepped into my car I offered a prayer of thanks that the motors of Havatoo are silent. Like a wraith the car slipped out of the garage into the night, and as I passed the house I whispered a silent goodbye to Ero Shan.

Approaching the house of Hara Es I felt the first qualm of nervousness that had assailed me during this adventure, but the house seemed quite deserted as I entered it and ran up the stairs to the second floor.

Unlocking the door of the room in which I had left Duare and Hara Es I breathed a sigh of relief as I saw them both there. I crossed quickly to the couch and examined Hara Es's bonds. They appeared quite secure.

"Come!" I said to Duare. "We have no time to waste."

She followed me out of the room. I locked the door on Hara Es, found another sarong for Duare in a room on the first floor, and a moment later Duare and I were in my car.

"Where are we going?" she asked. "We cannot hide in Havatoo. They will find us."

"We are going to leave Havatoo forever," I replied, and just then I saw a car pass us and draw up in front of the house we had just left. Two men were in it; one of them jumped out and ran to the door; then I opened the throttle. I had seen enough to turn me cold with apprehension.

Duare had seen, too. "Now they will discover everything," she said, "and you will be killed. I knew that it would end in disaster. Oh, why didn't you let me die alone? I want to die."

"But I won't let you!"

She said nothing more, and we sped through the now almost deserted streets of Havatoo toward the Kantum Lat and the Gate of the Physicists.

We had gone about two miles of the three that we must cover before we reached our destination when I heard an ominous sound such as I had never before heard in Havatoo. It sounded like the wailing of sirens such as are used on police cars in the large cities of America. Instantly I knew that it was an alarm, and I guessed that the man who had entered the house of Hara Es had discovered her and that our escape was known.

Closer and closer came the sounds of the wailing sirens as I drew up before the hangar where my plane stood; they seemed to be converging upon us from all directions. I was not surprised that they should have guessed where they would find us, for it would have been obvious to even duller minds than those of Havatoo that here lay my only chance to escape.

Fairly dragging Duare with me, I leaped from the car and ran into the hangar. The great doors, operated by mechanical means, rolled open at the touch of a button. I lifted Duare into the cockpit. She asked no questions; there was no time for questions.

Then I took my place at her side. I had designed the plane for training purposes; and it had two seats, each accommodating two people. I started the motor—and such a motor! Silent, vibrationless, and it required no warming up.

I taxied out into the Kantum Lat. The sirens were very close now. I saw the lights of cars bearing down upon us. As I started toward the Gate of the Physicists I heard the staccato hum of Amtorian rifles behind us. They were firing at us!

I nosed up; the wheels left the ground; the great gate loomed directly ahead. Up! Faster! Faster! I held my breath. Would we make it? Responding perfectly, the light ship climbed almost vertically in the last few seconds; she sped over the top of the lofty gate with only inches to spare.

We were safe!

Far below, the lights of Havatoo lay behind us as I turned the ship's nose toward the shimmering ribbon that was the River of Death—the River of Life to us—that was to guide us down to that unknown sea where, I was confident, we would find Vepaja.

Duare had not spoken. I felt her arm against mine trembling. I reached over and laid a hand upon it. Why are you trembling?" I asked. "You are quite safe now."

"What is this thing we are in?" she asked. "Why does it not fall to the ground and kill us? What keeps it up?"

I explained as best I could, telling her that there was no danger that it would fall; and then she drew a deep, long sigh of relief.

"If you say that we are safe; then I am afraid no longer," she said. "But tell me, why are you making this sacrifice for me?"

What sacrifice?" I asked.

You can never return to Havatoo now; they would kill you.

"I do not want to return to Havatoo if you cannot live there in safety," I replied.

"But what of Nalte?" she asked. "You love one another, and now you can never see her again."

"I do not love Nalte, nor does she love me. I love only you, Duare; and Nalte and Ero Shan love one another. We are on our way to Vepaja; I would rather take my chances of winning you there than live a Sanjong in Havatoo without you."

She sat in silence for a long time; then, presently, she turned and looked up into my face. "Carson!" she said in a low voice.

Yes, Duare, what is it?"

"I love you!"

I could not believe that I had heard right. "But, Duare, you are the daughter of a jong of Vepaja!" I exclaimed.

"That I have known always," she said, "but I have just learned that above all things else I am a woman."

I took her in my arms then. I could have held her thus forever, as our marvellous plane raced onwards toward Vepaja and home.

Printed in the United States
90669LV00002B/255/A